PRAISE FOR CLARISSA KAE

A hauntingly romantic debut

— ESTHER HATCH

Eerie. Inspiring. Masterful.

— ADAM BERG

Clarissa Kae entraps readers with her exquisite writing and master storytelling. I couldn't stop reading.

— JESS HEILEMAN

PIECES TO MEND

CLARISSA KAE

CARPE VITAM
PRESS LLC

For those without a voice
For those without clear memories
For those who doubt their worth

You are not alone.

ACKNOWLEDGMENTS

When my little family rescues horses, they come to us neglected, abused and horribly broken. Day by day, through gentle care, these discarded animals begin to hope...and then to trust—and then to thrive.

This book is a love letter to rescuers of a different sort. Bit by bit, when I had little trust and more than my fair share of shame, I was given a soft place to land. Alan Hansen, Edmond Mortensen and Michael Kirk gently led this lost soul to a safe harbor. I would, quite literally, not be here without their kindness.

And Damon, his unflappable belief in me is a safety net I frequently need. Kaela, Ava and Isla Belle—your inherent goodness brings a light into our home.

Kathleen & Brian for allowing me to be your One And Only (with a wink and a nudge).

Josi Kilpack—without your warm confidence, I wouldn't have the courage to release this book. Thank you for your friendship, for your encouragement—and for saying the right thing at the right time (it's a gift I'm incredibly grateful for).

To my writing family, Esther Hatch, Jess Heileman, Adam Berg, Connie Williams, Loretta Porter and my ARC readers, Sarah Reynolds, Jill Warner, Chantell Farley, Shelley Strong and Evelyn Hornbarger—because of your willingness to listen, proof read and generally babysit my writing, I am able to do what I love.

—Clarissa

SCARLETT ASHLEY

PRESENT DAY

T he assisted care facility no longer felt warm or inviting. The walls were drenched with despair. And grief.

Marjorie, the woman I loved most in the world, closed her tired eyes with a smirk, completely aware of her impending death. The muffled conversations from the nurses' station outside her room grew louder, marking the end of the day shift—and my time alone with her. The facility was stuffed with chipper staff and cheerful paintings—all the things that once gave me hope. Scooting my chair closer to Marjorie's bed, I clasped her hand between mine and wished for the millionth time that she was my grandmother by birth, not marriage. In a way, she'd raised my husband as well as me.

Releasing Marjorie's hand with a squeeze, I slipped my phone back in my lap. Everett had taken the video call despite London's time being two in the morning. The uneasiness between us had softened in the last few weeks. Grief had a way of shutting out other concerns. It'd been just over a year since he'd taken the assignment abroad; the so-called emergency lasted longer than the projected three months. Everett had packed just weeks after Marjorie broke her hip. Video calls and letters were thoughtful, but technology couldn't drive Marjorie to her appointments. Or tuck a blanket around her shivering frame. Most of all, technology didn't soften the sting of abandonment.

As if on cue, Marjorie's hand twitched. She would never admit it but she could always sense my feelings regarding Everett. Or any man.

Gently, even though I knew she wouldn't wake, I smoothed her arthritic fingers flat against the bed. When my own grandmother had passed, her hands twisted into tight fists. It was the only thing I remembered from the viewing, aside from my mother's haunted eyes.

Dabbing the moisturizing cream with my finger, I coated Marjorie's lips. Her last words to Everett were in teasing, a rare lucid moment. With a gleam in her eye, she lied, saying she wouldn't wait for him to return before joining her late husband. It was all a game; no grandmother had ever loved a grandson more.

A soft knock on the door chased peace from the room. I'd no longer be alone with the one and only Marjorie Ashley. Our afternoons together filled the void since Everett left.

Twisting Marjorie's wedding band on my middle finger, I settled against the back of the chair. When Everett flew to London, Marjorie had offered, more like *commanded,* that I wear the ring. We'd been married—sort of—for years but I'd never worn a wedding band. It wasn't the only thing missing in our marriage. Marjorie was taking more than my secrets to the grave. Her death would bury the only family I really had, however tenuous the link. Marjorie had a gift. She would uncover the skeletons in our closets. The act would be gentle, the patient rarely recognizing the extraction. Except me. I always knew.

The door creaked open and Marjorie's daughter stepped inside. Missy cleared her throat, and I braced myself for her nervous ramblings. Her eyes flitted about like a startled deer. She stumbled like a giant in a china shop to the other side of Marjorie's bed. Missy's large frame was an Ashley trait, but today, her lankiness felt strangely out of place.

Missy gave a half-hearted smile. "Hey, Scarlett ..." She rocked on her heels. "So ... how is she?"

Glancing at the medical pump, I answered, "Same."

Missy nodded and gingerly sat down. She was close to six feet tall, her legs too long for the simple, average chair provided. Her dark eyes took in the room like she'd just discovered the severity of the situation. She would do the same tomorrow.

"She's not in any pain." It was the only thing I could think of.

"Good. That's really good. Really good." She folded her hands in her lap, only to unfold them. Her fingers were stained with charcoal. The sight pulled at my heart, reminding me of Everett. He, like his aunt Missy, sought comfort in sketching, creating beauty from the mundane. Other than their shared height, art was the end of their similarities. Everett was never timid. Or nervous.

Missy looked at her mother and then back at her hands. She blinked but said nothing.

"Are *you* okay?"

"Yes, why?" Her eyes widened. She twisted a finger around the hem of her shirt. "Do I look okay?"

Motioning to Marjorie, I said, "Your mother is dying."

She blinked again, swallowing hard. "It's as much your loss as it is mine."

"Not quite." This time I blinked. Marjorie was the mother, the grandmother, the glue to all my broken parts. She was everything. "I'm not technically related."

"Everett would beg to differ." A whisper of a smile appeared on her lips.

"Everett would never beg."

Missy smiled, her face transforming to a younger version of Marjorie. "He's an Ashley, through and through."

"That he is." *Proud and perfect*, I almost added.

"Did you call him?" Missy's brow furrowed, the playfulness gone.

"He'll be on the next flight."

"But did you—"

"Yes," I said a little too loud. She'd just finished her third divorce but constantly worried about Everett and me. "He said he'll think about coming home."

Missy frowned—the sad, puppy dog kind of frown—and for some reason it irritated me. This woman was beautiful and talented beyond reason. She could hold court with a number of curators and critics alike but could not understand sarcasm if it hit her in the face. Clenching my fist, I wondered how it'd feel to punch something. Maybe I was slowly becoming an Ashley after all.

"Don't worry." Twisting Marjorie's ring again, I wished again that Everett was here. "She teased him back and said she wouldn't wait."

"But she was teasing, right?" Missy wasn't asking. She was begging. Pleading.

Guilt crept in. Missy was grieving the impending loss of her mother. She needed comfort, not criticism.

I offered what I hoped was an easy smile. "She'll wait. Especially for Everett." He was her pride and joy. She'd do anything for him. As would I.

"And he's coming." Missy swallowed hard. She was twice my age, but at times seemed more like my youngest sister, a decade my junior. "Scarlett?"

"He's getting on the next flight." When Missy raised her eyebrows as if to question, I added, "I promise, he's coming. We talked after Marjorie fell asleep. He got off the phone to book the flight."

Missy's shoulders relaxed. Even thousands of miles away, Everett provided relief to his family—at least the women.

"Have you called Richard?" I had to ask. He had more right to hold Marjorie's hand than I did. Richard Ashley was the last man I wanted to see, but he was Marjorie's son. And Everett's father.

"No." Missy shook her head, her salt and pepper hair falling in front of her shoulders. If she ever dyed it, she'd look closer to my age instead of my mother's. "Have you?"

She didn't bother looking me in the eye. We both knew the answer to that question.

"Has Everett?"

I shook my head. "Not that I know of." Everett's father wasn't someone we talked about, not in years. We'd focused on my family for the past decade.

"Is he going to?" She picked at her stained fingers. Something was off. "Call, I mean. Is Everett going to call his father?"

Missy had flown back and forth from New York since Marjorie's first fall. I'd spent the last year trying to interview her for a local article and never, not once did she ask—or even answer personal questions. She'd become hesitant, evasive. But this, the complete lack of eye contact and fiddling with her clothes—something was most definitely off.

The machines beeped softly, punctuated by the sounds of visitors in the hallway. An elephant had stalked into the room—or rather a lion —and it didn't have to do with Marjorie's impending death.

"What's going on?" Part of me didn't want to know. The room felt smaller. I shifted in the chair. "I mean, really. You're being weird."

She stiffened. "It's nothing."

"Right." I should be grateful not suspicious. It was wrong but I was too tired to coax anything out of her tonight. Leaning over, I brushed an errant hair off Marjorie's forehead, whispering, "See you tomorrow."

"You're leaving?" Missy asked, like she had every night.

"I'm just down the road." When Marjorie broke her hip, Everett and I tried moving her into our house. She'd flat out refused, believing she was a burden. Marjorie had barely let us move her into a nearby independent care facility a few blocks from us. Her pride took another hit when she was transferred to the intensive care unit.

"I know ..."

"Is it the drive?"

"No." Missy always stayed in Marjorie's home an hour north in Tule, our hometown.

"Because you can stay with me." The invitation would be rejected —again. Everett was family, but Gainesfield would never be Missy's home.

"I know." Missy reached for her mother's hand. "I've been cleaning out Mom's house and found some things."

Tension filled the room, and I didn't know why. Marjorie's home had been a sanctuary for Everett and me. The mere thought of her house should bring warmth. Not unease.

"Mom kept a lot." Missy's gaze turned apologetic.

"Not really. We emptied everything upstairs." Before Everett and I purchased our money pit of a house, we spent weekends helping Marjorie sift through her belongings. Everything she could need or want was left on the main level. "There's not much to go through."

"She kept records." Missy nibbled on her lip, anticipation in her eyes. "A lot of records."

"And?" My phone pinged.

Everett texted, *Flight leaves tomorrow at noon. Be home soon.*

Home. Everett was coming home.

I texted back, *When do you get in?*

It was probably a lost cause, but I hoped he'd arrive Saturday. My cousin was getting married, and I'd either be able to skip it or bring Everett—meaning, my family would be on their best behavior.

Sunday, I think. I'll forward itinerary.

I tried not to sigh. Last minute tickets were never stellar, and I couldn't remember if I'd told him about the wedding. Our conversations typically stuck to Marjorie or work, his oil contracts and my op-ed articles.

"Scarlett?"

My cheeks burned. Even thousands of miles away, Everett could make me blush. "It was Everett. His flight leaves tomorrow."

"He'll want to see them too." Missy stood and pulled keys from her pocket.

"See what?"

"The files." She stared a little too intently at the keys in her hand.

"Is there a reason you're acting like this?" I stood, my back complaining from the hours of sitting bedside on top of the day's desk work. "What files?"

"Yours." Missy didn't meet my gaze. "Your files."

"I don't have any files."

"I know I'm not supposed to know—"

"Know what, Missy?" I hated that she flinched, but there weren't any files. There wasn't anything to know.

Silence stretched between us. She finally blinked and said, "There's a whole box."

"Of what?" I shook my head. "Don't say files."

She gave a half-shrug as if to say, *Then what should I say?*

The air stilled. My lungs went heavy.

"I didn't open it," Missy whispered. Struggling for a moment, she squeezed the keys in her hand. "I brought it. Just in case."

Softer, I asked, "Just in case, what?"

"In case your mom—"

"What does my mother have to do with this box?" And then it hit me. Mom had talked to Missy. "How does she know you're in town? It's a good ten minute drive from her side of Tule."

"I saw her at the grocery store. Now she comes by in the morning." Missy appeared to shrink in front of me. Her timid voice poured guilt on my shoulders. "I didn't tell her anything."

"You shouldn't have to lie for me." But the thought calmed me.

"She doesn't know, does she?" Missy's eyes lit with mischief, a stark contrast from a moment ago.

"I could build a house with what she doesn't know." It didn't make sense but the less my family knew, the safer I felt. It wasn't them, it was me. I was broken long before the Ashley family kept my secrets.

"That she's Everett's mother-in-law." Missy's face brightened. "She'd die."

I smiled, this time genuinely. The room felt light again. And warm.

"I parked by you." Missy opened the door, the warmth disappearing in an instant.

I could only nod and follow her outside. She pulled the box from her trunk and shoved it into my backseat. Missy patted my shoulder, the touch both awkward and endearing.

Without another word, we parted. Alone in my garage, I debated on what to do with her impromptu gift. Missy was wrong. She had to be. There weren't any files. In high school, Marjorie was Everett's guardian, not mine. Pulling the box from my sedan, I froze. Across the lid, in a faded black marker, read *Scarlett Delfin*.

❧ 2 ❧

EVERETT ASHLEY

FIFTEEN YEARS AGO

Tule was unlike any other California town—Everett should know. He'd moved more than a dozen times in his seventeen years. Only in Tule would a Confederate flag be as popular as a Mexican flag, both displayed with pride on cars and in front of houses. Country music and Mariachi bands competed for radio air time. Tule was the red-headed stepchild of one of the bluest states in the nation. California both needed and ignored the agricultural valley. The small towns—Gainesfield, Tule, and Visalia—stuck out like flies in milk. Or like Everett, a six-foot, four-inch behemoth of a teenager.

Unable to look him in the eye, or in the general direction of his head, Everett's grandmother patted his hand. His jaw and head throbbed with every breath, every swallow—every move. Everett had insisted he was well enough to attend school. Anything was better than suffocating in his grandmother's pity. Kind and attentive, Marjorie Ashley loved Everett, the one fact he clung to. And the very reason he needed to hurry and graduate. Everett didn't deserve her tender care. He was an Ashley man, just like his father. They deserved the pain they inflicted.

The high school counselor nodded along, scribbling notes. He simultaneously listened to Marjorie and scanned the thick folder from the social worker. Everett glanced at the clock on the wall. It had been exactly seven days and ten hours since he last fought with his father. The pain snapped alive at the memory, the line of surgical staples on his head pulsing once more.

Both father and son had landed in the hospital. The elder returned to prison shortly after the fight while the younger was unceremoniously dumped at Marjorie's house. Everett's mother, the source of the struggle, was nowhere to be found. Again.

"No." Marjorie shook her head, the gray chignon coming loose. "I'm not comfortable with that."

His grandmother's distress pulled a distracted Everett into the conversation.

"I'm sorry, Mrs. Ashley, but the social worker believes he's missed roughly two years of school. I've added it up as well. There's an incredible number of absences." The counselor looked from Everett to the grandmother, concern etched in his narrow face. Pity. That's what Everett saw. "We could place him with the sophomore—"

"He'll be eighteen—"

Everett leaned over to his grandmother and whispered, "It doesn't matter. I'll be fine."

Marjorie briefly closed her eyes and inhaled a shaky breath. "This boy has been through enough."

Everett didn't understand her warmth or her continual kindness. He only knew he needed her to be happy. He gave a pleading look to the counselor, who answered with a nod.

"Mrs. Ashley, I'll place him in the sophomore honors class and at that, only temporarily until I can figure out a better option."

"You can do that?" Hope filled her steel blue eyes. The deep lines of her face were courtesy of a mercurial son, and now a broken grandson.

"I just did." The counselor wrote a note before standing. He offered a hand to Everett.

Everett instinctively flinched and then groaned at his reaction. The counselor's face fell. Just as Everett feared, the familiar elephant settled nicely in the room. Like every school before, the counselor had just discovered how deep the hurt, how long the pain.

Everett nodded with a scowl and left the office, opting instead to wait for his school schedule by the receptionist. This was how it always worked; different school and different city but the rules and procedures never changed. The only difference was the parent, or in this case, the lack of. Marjorie had already proven to be twice the guardian his father was.

In a few minutes, Everett's schedule was handed over and Marjorie was at his side. She wrapped her arms around his waist, his frame seeming to swallow her once tall figure. Ever so quickly, he gave her a hug before stepping back from her embrace.

The entry door opened and closed behind him, most likely from his student guide. Each school went to extremes, offering up either the most popular or the most rejected students to befriend the new kid. Everett didn't turn around. He grabbed the schedule and tried to think of an escape. He didn't need his grandmother to witness the awkward conversation, the lack of eye contact and unasked questions. With strangers or neighbors, the massive cut down his face did the talking.

"Mr. Fink sent for me?" Despite the question, the voice was confident. And female.

"Yeah." The receptionist nodded toward Everett.

He'd now be forced to face the girl. Every known curse word, creative and otherwise, crossed his mind; halted only by the hope in his grandmother's smile. He turned to the right, keeping the injured part of his face hidden.

The girl stepped forward and slid a piece of paper across the receptionist's counter. "I'm supposed to get a signature for this too."

The office phone rang as a couple walked through the entry door, circling Everett and the girl. The receptionist quickly signed the light blue paper and greeted the couple. A whisper of a smirk appeared on the girl's face before a mask of innocence slid back down. With the paper hidden, Everett assumed in her back pocket, she reached for his schedule.

She hadn't looked at him yet, allowing him to study her. Her hair, thick and dark, was streaked with auburn highlights. She'd pulled it up into a messy ponytail, obviously caring little for her appearance. From her profile, she seemed ordinary, normal nose, chin, and lips. She would be easy to draw. And easy to forget.

"Sophomore ..." She held out his schedule but instead of facing Everett, she smiled at Marjorie.

The expression lifted her cheekbones, highlighting her near perfect face. Her eyes, large and brown, glinted with something more, something deep. Her brows and lashes, thick and black as ebony. A delicate strand of hair fell from the tie and in an instant, she was extraordinary.

Her hands, petite and fragile, still held Everett's schedule. He hadn't taken it, nor had he spoken. It wasn't until she rolled her eyes in teasing did he realize he was staring.

With a playful laugh, she told his grandmother, "Scarlett. Scarlett Delfin."

"You're too tiny to be a Scarlett. Letty sounds more like it." Beaming at Scarlett, Marjorie patted Everett's elbow. It was the highest Marjorie could reach with her curved back. Without another word, she left Everett in the girl's care.

Scarlett held open the door, waiting for Everett. She hadn't flinched at his scar or flirted. She hadn't given a clue about herself. Everett needed hints, needed something to help navigate the awkwardness. Everett groaned but finally followed, hitching his backpack to his shoulder.

"I like her," Scarlett murmured. Her face had already dimmed to the stoic nature of nothing, like before.

Everett wondered if she did it on purpose, come alive one moment and disappear the next. His fingers itched to draw her, both of her.

"This is where you say something." The statement was just that. She'd not infused judgment or condemnation in the words. It hung there, waiting.

"Like what?" It came out as a growl. He waited for her to snap back.

Scarlett said nothing. She looked down and started walking.

Guilt slammed into Everett. "Wait," he called.

She didn't stop. She didn't speed up, but she didn't stop. He jogged a step—and inhaled sharply from the pain. He sank to his knees, his vision blurry. She yelled something he couldn't hear over the pounding in his head. The doctors had warned him, said it would be weeks, maybe even months, before he would fully recover.

Scarlett touched his forehead with the back of her hand. "I'm so sorry."

"Not your fault." Everett winced at his tone.

"Pretty sure it was. I wouldn't slow down. It's not like you know where to go." She arched an eyebrow, the spark back in her eyes. She pursed her lips, the same lips that were no longer ordinary. Up close, they were fuller, more pronounced. "You're not even supposed to be walking yet, are you? Let alone running."

"I—"

She cupped his jaw with both of her small hands. His mind went blank. Her brow furrowed; she gently twisted and turned his head, inspecting the injury. Everett held his breath. He'd never been touched like this, whatever *this* was.

"I don't know if Vitamin E will help the scarring. Not that you could put it on yet. The wound needs more time." Scarlett stepped closer, emotions swirling in her dark, chocolate eyes. She seemed oblivious to the intimacy while Everett drank in every inch of her. The light whisper of freckles on her olive skin. The lack of makeup and raw curiosity spoke of quiet confidence but there, when her focus stayed on him, Everett saw something more.

Shame.

He knew regret, shame, and guilt. They were old friends. It saddened him, and he didn't understand why. Scarlett was a stranger. She was nothing and nobody to him.

And yet, his hand drifted to her face, tucking the delicate strand of hair behind her ear. She flinched and jumped back, the moment broken by a simple touch. Her eyes widened. She'd gone from intimate to terrified in a snap.

"I'm sorry." Everett held out his hands in surrender. He'd crossed a boundary, for him and her. "I don't know why I did that."

Her chest rose and fell. Panic settled in her eyes, and there they were again, Everett's longtime companions. She'd been hurt, down to the marrow of her soul. Wounds like that never healed; Everett knew that much.

"I swear, I've never touched a girl." It wasn't a complete lie but he needed her trust—even if he didn't understand why.

Something about his voice appeared to calm her. The smirk appeared. "I wouldn't admit that out loud."

"It's true." He rolled his eyes when it came out as a growl again.

"I believe you." She turned, this time waiting for him to join her. "I wasn't kidding though. It won't win you any friends. At least, not from the right crowd."

"Friends are the least of my worries."

"But enemies should be."

An unfamiliar surge of protectiveness came over him. "You have enemies?"

"Whoa, easy boy." She scanned him, sweeping over his face until he felt naked. And vulnerable. "Why would you care?"

"I don't know."

Scarlett shrugged, giving the impression of not caring. Her darkened countenance suggested otherwise. "That makes two of us."

She switched gears and prattled on about the school and the layout. He didn't hear a word of it. His thumb and index finger twitched, his mind already on the impending strokes of his pencil.

Everett followed her to the classroom. With his arm, twice the length of hers, he leaned forward and opened the door for her. Scarlett gave an unfiltered smile, warming him long after they entered.

❧ 3 ❧

SCARLETT ASHLEY
PRESENT DAY

T ule wedding receptions came in two varieties, ultra conservative with the white dress and elevator music or Hispanic with bold colors and brassy music. To my mother's horror, my cousin's bride had done the unthinkable. She'd chosen a cream dress and upbeat pop music.

Tucked in the corner of the dance hall, I hid in the shadows of the wedding reception and checked my phone for the hundredth time. Everett hadn't answered my last text or sent me his flight itinerary.

My feet ached, having spent the day—and now evening—in heels. Helping the caterer, the usher, and whoever else I could flag down made for an easier way to pass the time. With Missy in town, I couldn't use Marjorie's health as an excuse to get out of family events. Or Everett. There was a mutual dislike that kept my parents in-check with Everett around.

I peeked at my phone again. Part of me was excited he'd be home, the other part didn't want him to return. Like the old adage, *out of sight, out of mind,* it was easier to pretend everything was fine when we weren't tripping over our problems.

With a reverent hush from the surrounding guests, the bride and her father danced under the dangling lights of the hall. The entire town of Tule had come, much to my dismay. Glory days were awkward at best. High school moments were better left to yearbooks and faded memories.

The mock cathedral ceiling and stained-glass windows offered a false sense of freedom. Twice, my mother caught my gaze drifting to the side exit, her eyebrow arched with a mother's threat. Nearing my thirtieth birthday meant nothing to her. A child I would always be.

My brother sat in one of the wicker chairs on the periphery, his thumb scrolling through his social media feed, oblivious to the daggers his wife sent from across the hall. She was somewhere between nine and twenty months pregnant with their third child. Each gestation became infinitely longer, for all involved. At the moment, she was losing a battle of wills with her son, his tantrum muted by the music.

Across the hall, my youngest sister, Elaine, sat next to her beaming fiancé. His hand twisted Elaine's, conveniently showing off the ring. He'd proposed weeks before, but Dad must have finally given him the ring from the family store.

My father sat on the other side of Elaine and wrapped an arm around her shoulders, his crooked, half-smile more amused than proud. He scratched his forehead. Dad's olive skin was the only similarity I inherited from him. My four adopted siblings looked more like my biological brother and father than me. Everett once joked that *I* was the adopted one, not them. I didn't know what was more surprising, the fact that he joked or that he knew I didn't belong.

Catching my cousin's eye, I mouthed, *congratulations*. He nodded with a smile. I slipped from the hall, feeling infinitely lighter.

"Where are you off to?" David, my brother's closest friend, appeared at my side. Rubbing his jaw, he gave me a conspiratorial grin. "Count me in."

Giving him a wide berth, I shook my head. "Home, David."

"I'll join you." He ran his hands through his blond hair, his skin perpetually tan regardless of the season. Tule was in the middle of absolute nowhere. Even in a suit, David looked every inch the surfer instead of a small town preacher's son. His position as Tule's mayor was cemented long ago with his easy smile and charm, much to his father's chagrin and mother's pride.

"No." It came out too quickly. My phone pinged, and I hurried toward the side door. "Sorry, I have to take this."

David reached for my hand. "No, you don't."

"Sorry—"

"I'm not." He stepped closer, his cologne tickling my throat. He'd never been this forward, this aggressive. Either he had hit a dry spell or I looked as desperate as I felt. "C'mon, Scarlett. For old times' sake."

One of the caterers stopped abruptly in front of me. We had worked side by side in the kitchen earlier. Her eyes flitted between us, settling on me. "Can I talk to you for a sec?"

"Sure, what do you need?" David gave her a winning smile, one that should make her weak in the knees.

The poor girl didn't stand a chance. She blinked, an internal debate written in her furrowed brow.

"David, stop." Pulling her along, I returned to the dance hall. Ironic that a crowded room offered more privacy than the quiet hallway.

David followed us, his eyes sliding between the caterer and me. "Can I help?"

"No." She gave a look of panic and quickly hid something behind her back.

"Can you give us a minute, David?" I waited, hoping a moment of awkward silence would move him along.

David slid a finger down my forearm. "I'm just trying to help."

"That's not helping." I caught my sister's pleading gaze a few feet behind the caterer.

With eyes wide, Elaine mouthed, *help me,* as my mother dragged her across the room. They headed straight for us, breaking up a circle of dancers in their wake.

I sighed, wishing I'd already escaped. The caterer looked at my mother and sister, then back at the floor, her shoulders slumping. The room became infinitely smaller.

"Scarlett, you're not going to believe it." My mother squealed and grabbed both of my hands. "Done. Already booked."

"What's booked?" One look at my sister's flushed face and I knew. "Oh, the wedding."

"New Year's." Mom's expression took a wistful turn. She'd rushed ahead to make plans. She had tried, and failed, to do the same with my brother's wedding.

I tried to listen to her ramble while keeping an eye on the fidgeting caterer. The long day had suddenly turned into a marathon of a night. What I'd give to have the tension Everett brought. At least David wouldn't be near me, and Mom would be too busy throwing badly veiled insults at Everett instead of planning her children's lives.

Mom placed a dramatic hand on her chest, her gaze far off. "Well, sort of. January second is close enough."

The words hit me harder than they should. Taking two steps back, I swallowed the hurt. She was my mother and maybe, just once, she'd remember.

Elaine glanced up, her voice timid. "That's her birthday, Mom."

This was ridiculous. It shouldn't matter. I was a grown woman. Maybe I was tired or maybe it was late—either way, my heart was a little too close to the surface.

My mother gave an airy wave. "Well, she can learn to share."

"You forgot," I said softly. She was my mother. She knew the feeling of being forgotten by her parents, a fact my grandmother confessed in her final days.

"Oh, honestly, I did not." My mother lifted her chin, her eyebrow arched. The music changed to something loud and obnoxious, igniting squeals from several tweens. Mom sent a condemning glare at the DJ. Her definition of appropriate music was limited to hymns. With a quick shake of her head, she returned her attention to me. "Scarlett, not now. Just don't."

"She didn't forget you." David wrapped an unwanted arm around my waist.

My mother softened at his words. He was born to a preacher and had grown into a self-professed *man of the people,* both of which gave him unlimited pardons.

I pulled from his grasp and stepped back. The caterer slid forward, angling herself between David and me. She held out a note, whispering, "Hurry. Read this."

"Who—" The answer was in the elegant and ever exquisite calligraphy. *Scarlett* was written across the top. Only Everett could write like this. Opening the note, I felt a storm begin inside me, growing with each beautifully drawn letter.

I'm home.

Home.

The image of our half-remodeled house entered my mind. *Home.* Of all the words Everett chose, it had to be the one I'd never really felt. The note shook in my hands. *I'm home.* Everett Ashley was home. My heart leapt—and then sank. He had the power to elevate me. And completely destroy me.

The caterer gave me a puzzled look and went back to work.

"Scarlett?" David reached for the note.

I stepped back. Everett. Everett was home. I should be happy or confused—but all I could feel was the familiar hum, the pull that had always been there. I had no idea how long he would stay, but all I could feel was the warmth of hope.

"What is going on?" Mom's shrill voice pierced my thoughts.

"Nothing." Folding my arms to hide the tremor in my hands, I scanned the room.

Everett wrote the words in the note, but the idea of him physically coming here and handing over a note seemed too far-fetched. Romantic whims weren't us.

"I didn't forget you, Scarlett," Mom warned. "Do not make a scene."

"Wouldn't dream of it." Frustrated, I turned around—and froze.

In a tailored black suit, Everett Ashley filled the doorframe of the side exit. I knew him, and yet I didn't. It felt longer than the months since I'd seen him. To me, he seemed to have grown another inch or two, leaving him closer to seven than six feet tall. The scar, once a puckered line from his temple, down and along his jaw, seemed almost invisible. In the dimmed dance hall, I could see the darkened countenance, his pride and temper forever at the ready.

I was all too aware of how close David stood. Everett walked toward me, his stride graceful. I didn't know if I should retreat or advance. For roughly half my life, he was both my greatest secret and the absolute center of my everything, both good and bad. And here he was, in the flesh.

In a rare show of strength, Elaine tugged my reluctant mother away. Glowering at David, Everett reached my side.

"Aren't you a handsome devil?" David clapped Everett on the back, sounding as clichéd and hollow as his mother. "What brings you here?"

Everett towered over him and in a low voice said, "You may leave."

David's eyes widened. He recovered quickly, but not fast enough. With deceptive gentleness, Everett grasped my elbow and guided me outside to the chilly night. His touch heated me in a way it shouldn't. Silently, he slipped out of his jacket and wrapped it around my shoulders. He waited for my hand to grab the lapels before letting go. Warmth radiated from him, igniting affection and a burst of nervous energy all at the same time.

Everett took in the sight of me, just as I had done to him a moment ago. "Plum. It looks good on you."

"Only you would say plum instead of purple."

"Only you would deter a compliment with a segue." His voice rumbled deep. He looked at me like he always had, tearing through the hidden layers. "What happened?"

"Where should I start?" I hadn't seen him in months—an eternity with Marjorie's decline. "You'll have to be a bit more specific."

Everett smirked and folded his arms, settling in for our own battle of wills. "Why are you sad?"

"Again, you'll have to be more—"

"Tonight." He rubbed the scruff on his jaw. When I didn't answer, he reached out and pulled the ends of his jacket, bringing me closer. "What made you sad *tonight?*"

"I don't know." It wasn't a lie. But it wasn't the truth.

"Yes, you do." He nodded in the direction of the dance hall. "Your mom? Marjorie? The wedding?"

Fighting to keep the stupid emotions in check, I looked away. Marjorie's gift of knowing my thoughts wasn't as strong as Everett's. He'd inherited some from her and the little he did have was more than enough. It wasn't fair, the power he held. "You can't just show up and think I'm going to vomit everything."

"Me." He sighed. "I made you sad."

"I didn't say that." It came across silly and stupid, like a pout. He arched an infuriating eyebrow, looking more like my mother than my— I swallowed the thought. He wasn't really mine.

Everett tucked two fingers under my chin, raising my gaze to meet his and ever so softly whispered, "I'm home, Scarlett."

❧ 4 ❧

EVERETT ASHLEY
FIFTEEN YEARS AGO

In California's agricultural belly, November through February blanketed the towns with thick, deadly fog. The weather pushed school schedules back to mid-morning, allowing the sun to burn through the layers. Students and businesses could delay, but teachers were never allowed to skip—fog delay or not. In those bitter winter months, teachers woke hours early, allowing ample time to crawl through the curtain of fog—coffee cups clutched in their hands. Schools became tense with tired teachers and bored students.

But it wouldn't have mattered for Everett. He was dealing with a different fog. The teacher droned on, his name already lost and forgotten in Everett's hazy brain. He glanced at the clock and wondered if the doctors were right about the length of his recovery. His first class, on his first day, was just before lunch. The meeting with the counselor had taken most of the morning. His eyes kept drifting to Scarlett's chair. Cruel or ironic, she was across the room, second seat to the front in his direct line of sight.

Everett couldn't shake this feeling, this pull to her. The intensity frightened him. Girls his age and women his father's age would tease and flirt with him. They were his for the taking, but he'd barely toler-

21

ated each and every one. He didn't trust them, nor did he trust himself around them. But Scarlett, her touch had left its mark.

His fingers twitched. He looked down, discovering he'd sketched Scarlett's profile four times in the margins of the textbook. He slammed the book shut, wincing as the class collectively turned in his direction.

The students looked at him, then at each other, their expressions ranging from pity to curiosity. Except Scarlett. She kept her head down, her focus on the textbook.

The slight rejection bothered him. Stung, if he were being honest.

The bell rang, interrupting Everett's thoughts and the attention of the class. He purposely took his time packing his bag, keeping Scarlett in his peripheral vision. The teacher approached her desk. An irrational surge of jealousy came over Everett. He'd watched what a man could do to women, his father the worst offender. Everett paused, the feeling unfamiliar. His father was just as irrational—maybe this was the beginning. His father wasn't born angry, at least not according to Marjorie. Everett sighed. He wasn't his father. And Scarlett was still a stranger to him. The teacher was just doing his job. Everett shoved the last of his books into his backpack and silently blamed her for his mood.

He swung his bag onto his back and left the class, turning when the door clicked open behind him. Scarlett's hand was on the handle with her head still turned toward the teacher, nodding in response to something he must have said. She kept moving and barely missed walking into Everett. Scarlett mumbled an apology but didn't look up.

Everett steadied her, his forearms under hers. "You okay?"

"Oh, yeah, sorry." Her face lit with recognition, a genuine smile appearing. "How are you holding up?"

Everett shrugged, not sure what to say.

"Are you sure you're cleared to be here?" Scarlett hesitated a moment. Her face brightened, morphing the plain, forgettable features into a striking muse. "Do you want to go to the office?"

"No." He must've growled because the surrounding students rushing from other classes scattered like cockroaches. He knew how menacing he could look. He'd spent enough time in hospitals bored out of his mind with only pen and paper to entertain himself. Sketch after sketch, he'd drawn his face and the nurses' reactions.

Scarlett held up his hand, inspecting the charcoal stains on his thumb and index finger. Another smile. Everett waited for the flirtation, the pleas to be sketched or see his work.

Scarlett did neither.

"What do you see?" She looped an arm through his and gave a little wave, indicating the school.

Her touch burned through the sleeve of his hoodie. Colors. Colors and textures were what he saw, but with her arm in his, the world had shrunk to only the two of them. "Nothing."

Scarlett dropped her arm, slipping from his in an instant. Her mask slammed down hard, hiding her thoughts and feelings. "I'll see you around."

She picked up her pace, her cheeks flushed with embarrassment. The world around Everett turned gray, the colors evaporating.

"Scarlett, wait." Everett was an idiot. An absolute idiot.

A lanky boy, tan with sandy blond hair approached her. Scarlett flashed him a neutral smile, nothing like the honest one she'd given Everett earlier. The boy carried himself with the sureness of a junior, possibly senior. His laugh came easily, like most teenagers. At nearly eighteen, Everett had attended a dozen schools and had never, not once, been as carefree as this kid. It didn't matter. Everett was here until graduation and then he'd be gone forever.

Everett reached Scarlett and slowed his steps.

"Sorry, David." She adjusted her ponytail. "Maybe next time."

"You said that last week." David gave a ridiculous pout. A group of seniors wearing *King of the Year* hoodies gathered in the small courtyard ahead, calling for David to hurry up. "Just come. We could hang out afterwards. Besides, Andy'll be there."

"You're about to be left behind." Scarlett motioned to his friends. They'd begun whistling and making kissing faces.

"I'll call you later," David said before turning and joining the rowdy teenagers.

Scarlett's face fell as he walked away. She spun around, straight into

Everett. Her elbow smacked into his bruised hipbone—Everett inhaled sharply at the pain.

"Seriously?" she snapped, her eyes lit with frustration. "That's the second time today."

"I'm aware." Everett focused on breathing, instead of his hip. The pain radiated down his leg. He squinted, every color and every sound heightened.

"Sorry. I'm sorry." She held up her hands; her apology rushed.

"It's fine."

"You're a terrible liar." Amusement tugged at her lips.

David's group of friends shouted something indecipherable her way. David shook his head, laughing.

"What are they saying?" It was obvious they were making fun of her, but Everett didn't know why. Scarlett was pretty, beautiful at moments, but not scandalously so. Her figure wasn't outrageous, although her sweatshirt didn't reveal much, and she was too composed to be an easy target.

"Nothing," she said too quickly.

Another boy joined the group and tackled David to the grass, humping him. The boy's tongue wagged like a panting dog. The rest of the seniors roared with laughter. They turned in Scarlett's direction, anticipation in their faces. A spark of fear lit her eyes—a look Everett knew well—and her color paled for a moment before returning to the glow of olive skin. Her throat visibly tightened. An unspoken threat had been sent.

Everett was lost, not understanding how she was involved. He draped a possessive arm over Scarlett's shoulder, turning from the group. The laughter died immediately. His frame alone deterred teasing, but Everett, like his father, had a murderous stare. It was as practiced as his fighting.

Scarlett eyed him, her back stiff. "That's not the way to make friends."

"Making friends was never the plan." He fought the urge to pull her close, to tuck her into his side.

"You had a plan?"

"Pretend all you want." He knew a caged animal when he saw it.

"Pretend what?" She checked her watch and led him between the art buildings to a smaller, hidden parking lot at the end of the fence. The outdoor high school was built like a college with each building connected only by sidewalk and sunshine. An old table sat under an enormous oak tree on the perimeter of the school, concealed between the cars and the building.

"You have a plan. You know exactly how this whole thing works." Everett twirled his index finger in a circle. "You're counting the years 'til you're gone."

"Years?" Scarlett arched an eyebrow.

"Fine, months."

"You realize they're just going to replace teasing David with you, right?" She circled out from under his arm. "What you did back there doesn't change anything."

"You should probably just accept it then." Everett lifted his chin. He'd helped her even if she wouldn't admit it. Maybe he was more like his grandmother than he cared to admit.

"I already did."

"How's that working for you?"

"Perfectly." She clenched her hands into tight fists and shoved them in her pockets. "Look, Superman, high school isn't the same for people like me. You doing whatever that was doesn't help. You can't save me. Which, by the way, I don't need saving."

"Tell that to your face." He shouldn't care but he'd watched this before. His father was skilled in brutality, from minor digs to all-out mental warfare. Richard Ashley could confuse the pope into submission. "You were scared."

A breeze blew between them, twisting her hair. Her eyes lit, her jaw set and her hair wildly untamed. Everett was done for, wishing he could capture her like this, alive with fire. He could only stare.

"That was nothing. *That* I could handle." She rocked on her heels, sounding more like a toddler wanting to stamp her foot. "Thanks to your little performance, Andy's going to grill me about you."

"Who's Andy?" The jealousy in his voice was unmistakable, the fact written on her widened eyes.

"He's my brother." Her expression softened.

"Oh." Everett rubbed the back of his head. He'd forgotten about that detail, Scarlett having family, having someone else caring about her.

"They're close." Her voice caught, and she broke her gaze. "David and Andy."

"Your brother's okay with it?"

She shrugged. "You tell me. He was there."

Everett spun around, as if he could see them through the buildings he had walked by. "He was there? And did nothing?"

"They're just teasing. It's not like they mean it."

"Mean what?" Everett watched the transformation, the slight hunch in her shoulders, the resignation in her stance. "Did they hurt you?"

"No." Scarlett fidgeted and then said too quickly, "I have to go."

"Where?"

"To eat lunch."

"Me too." He wasn't letting her out of his sight. He blamed it on his head injury, this obsession with Scarlett Delfin, a stranger. He'd been warned by the doctors about possible behavior and memory lapses. But the sight of her, determined to be strong and yet wholly vulnerable, wouldn't shake him.

"That wasn't an invitation."

"Duly noted." Everett wouldn't eat with her, but he wouldn't leave her alone either. He frowned. The idea didn't make sense. Nothing with this girl did. He felt bound to her, an intense connection that defied all reason.

"Who are you?" Scarlett looked around as if someone could help answer her. "And they call me a mystery."

"Who says you're a mystery?"

Scarlett rubbed the bridge of her nose. "It's called a rhetorical question for a reason, Everett."

She said his name, her voice echoing in his head. He grabbed the memory, wanting to hold it a moment longer. He shook his head—and immediately regretted it. Dizzy, he brought a palm to his head. In an instant, her hands guided him to the wooden table a few decades past its prime. She situated Everett, his legs long enough to sit on top of the table with his feet flat on the ground.

She scrambled next to him on the table and held up two fingers. "How many finger—"

"Two." He groaned, although it sounded more like an angry lion than a pained high school student. "I told you I'm fine."

"You mentioned that." She smiled wryly and added, "How's that working for you?"

"Those were my words."

"We're breathing the same air, want to whine about that too?" Scarlett's hands fell to her lap, her tone now somber. "I get that you're fine, but really, should you be here?"

"I will go insane if I spend one more day staring at a wall." It'd taken a considerable amount of begging his grandmother to get here. If he went home now, Marjorie would never let him go.

"How, exactly, are you supposed to be Superman if you're hurt?" Sitting on the table, Scarlett wrapped her arms around her knees and rocked back, her head cocked to the side.

"Oh, *now*, you want to be saved?"

"Are you always this moody?" She rolled her eyes. "I was kidding, you know."

"The sarcasm gave it away."

Scarlett winced again.

Everett wanted to kick himself. His tone was curt and his words were sharp. He reached for her. "I'm an idiot."

Her head snapped up, her eyes unsure.

"I don't know how to do this." He stared at his hand, realizing he'd placed it on hers. His thumb instinctively drew small circles on the back of hers. "I'm sorry. I already said that. I don't know what to say that would mean more than *sorry*."

Nothing. Scarlett said nothing, her expression wary.

"You're making me nervous. Please say something." His tongue felt dry and his throat shriveled.

"For never touching a girl, you sure touch a lot."

His hand froze and his arm went stiff. "I'm s—"

"Stop saying that," she said softly.

He pulled his hand back, his face hot. "What do you want me to say?"

Scarlett didn't meet his gaze. Her eyes lingered on his hand, back on his thigh. Everett didn't know what that meant, what was okay and what wasn't. Scarlett seemed to dance along the fence, a moment with contact and then without.

Risking, Everett shuffled sideways on the table, making room for her. He held out his arm. "Come here."

She hesitated and then leaned forward, only to pause. The quiet debate appeared on her face.

Everett became instantly aware of his stature compared to her tiny frame. "You don't have to. Just if you want."

His voice seemed to pull the unease from her mind. She brightened and curled into his side, sending Everett into a mixed state of relief and confusion. She tucked her knees under her arms and leaned in.

"You *are* a mystery, just so you know." He didn't know how long she'd welcome the embrace but he'd take it.

"You're no picnic either."

"Scarlett?" Everett debated on asking, wondering again why he cared. "Did they hurt you?"

"No, not really." She sat up but allowed Everett to coax her back, nestling her close. "They're just boys being boys."

He tipped her chin, forcing her to look at him. Her large, dark eyes searched his. Oh, he was in deep. "That doesn't make it right."

"Yeah, well, Superman can't be everywhere." A flicker of a smile appeared.

"I'm here now."

5

SCARLETT ASHLEY

PRESENT DAY

The fog was rolling in, the night air chilly and damp. Tule took on a magical quality in the late fall. The church's parking lot lamps twinkled with the added moisture.

The music pulsed from inside the church, the brick wall barely containing the bass. From where Everett and I stood, the event sounded more like a night club than a family wedding. My mother had to be losing her mind listening to pop songs.

Everett kept his finger on the bottom of my chin. He leaned closer. A rush of warmth filled me, prickling my skin. After months of no contact, I was starved for affection. David must have seen it. He was more bold than usual. The thought of David chilled me.

I lifted my chin from Everett's touch and tried to ignore the disappointment in his eyes. Shaking my head, I backed into the brick wall. "I don't know, Everett."

"About what?"

"This." I sucked in a quick breath. "Us."

"Hey ..." He ducked down to try and meet my gaze. "It's okay."

"It's not," I snapped and then winced. It was harsh. And biting. "Sorry. I just don't know."

"What's wrong?" His brow furrowed, concern etched in every line of his beautiful face. "Talk to me."

"Don't do that." I cleared my throat, sounding more like Missy than myself. "Don't pretend to be patient and understanding. Just don't." My voice cracked at *don't*. I shut my mouth to keep the emotion in check. Hands shaking, I folded my arms.

This was ridiculous. Everett hadn't been home an hour and I was already picking at him.

Everett straightened. I'd forgotten just how tall he truly was. He filled my entire view, except for the periphery cut off by the brick wall.

"I'm—" *sorry*. I covered my mouth before I could finish. In a rush, he'd flown home for his grandmother, not me. He'd left to help save a failing oil contract, but if you asked my mother, it was just an excuse to be rid of me. I was a parasite that took without asking—without giving back. "I should go."

"Which part scares you the most?" He frowned, the movement pulling the scar into a once frightening expression. It never scared me, but it didn't exactly invite tender feelings in others. "The part where I'm home, or the part where we tackle Marjorie's health?"

We. A lump formed in my throat. *Marjorie.*

Everett eyed me a moment before adding, "Maybe it's time for us to get help."

He should've said *you,* not *us.* I'd already tried the whole counseling thing. If a professional couldn't fix me, Everett didn't stand a chance.

"I promised you." Everett leaned his shoulder into the wall, keeping our distance the same. He was careful, always careful.

"You don't have to do this." He owed me nothing. Gripping the lapels of his jacket on my shoulders, I braced myself for the reaction. This conversation was a decade overdue.

"Of course I do," he said firmly.

"Just stop, Everett."

The door swung open with several teenagers bursting through. At second glance, I realized they were my sister's friends and in their early twenties. A tall blonde took in Everett's frame with unabashed admiration. Even with a scar, he was painfully beautiful. The tuxedo outlined his fit physique, but the black hair, defined jaw, and steel-blue eyes made for an alluring combination.

Drunk with lust, the blonde sidled up next to Everett, ignoring both the whine of her male peers and my annoyance. She appeared oblivious to the fact I was wearing his jacket. A breeze played with her hair and ruffled her modest, knee-length dress.

Everett's jaw tightened and my guilt crept in. He could have the beautiful blonde. He could have any number of women, but he clung to me out of moral obligation. He could have been happily married to someone else. Maybe it was time. What's the saying? *If you love someone, set them free.*

"You must be cold." I offered Everett's jacket to the blonde.

He scowled and snatched the jacket before she could take it. He pierced the blonde with a glare before turning it on me.

"Put it away," I said, referring to his glower.

"Then tell me what to do." He clenched the jacket in his fist and sighed. "Except leave. That's not happening."

"Scarlett?" Mom's shrill voice pierced the air.

Everett straightened again, his mood darkening further. I wondered if he'd give me up, tell her the truth like he'd wanted to for years. Keeping his gaze on me, he nodded a stiff greeting to my mother. "Jennifer."

"I didn't know you were coming home." Mom's words were laced with suspicion. Jennifer Delfin was a veteran high school teacher. She could demean and encourage at the same time.

"It happens from time to time," he replied evenly.

Even in the dimly-lit night, I could see Mom's rising anger. Everett brought out the worst in her. And in my family. At least, that was the lie they sold themselves.

"Why, is the question." She brushed phantom dirt from the skirt of her emerald green dress. It matched her eyes and the enormous earrings dangling from her ears. "Your grandmother—"

"Mom," I snapped. There was a line between being right and being cruel. This wasn't the time or place to pick at old wounds.

"Is dying." Everett's voice came low and void of emotion. "Kind of you to remember."

A chill swept across my neck. The stoic tone pulled me back to the tug-of-war between him and my parents—or worse yet, he and I.

Mom rolled her eyes. "Kind of you to remember Scarlett. A girlfriend might forgive your little abandonment, but a mother—"

"Enough." My voice cracked, breaking the word in two. I was the one who'd nursed Marjorie. I was the one who'd cried at night after Everett left. Not my mother. I'd never spoken a word to her about how I felt. Everett and Mom hadn't earned the right to bicker about Marjorie or me.

They both refused to look at the other, the tension snapping between them. Mom threw back her shoulders. "Excuse me if I seemed insensitive. I tend to worry about the vulnerable. As a mother, I tend to worry about my—"

Spinning around, I turned and climbed over the brick planter lining the walkway. Azalea plants, long past their prime, raked at my dress.

"Scarlett," Mom called, her tone bitter.

I kept marching.

"This is ridiculous," Mom shouted, each word louder than the last, "Don't make this about you."

With my key stuffed in my bra and my purse in the trunk, I didn't have to navigate the dance hall and risk seeing David, or worse, the rest of my family.

"You should probably scream, Jennifer. That might make her turn around." Like a drum, Everett's sarcasm carried, following me as I searched for my car. "Nothing says *come here* like an insult."

The side exit where we had stood faced north, or maybe west. Pulling out my key, I clicked the lock icon and listened for the beep of my car. Nothing. I kept to the walkway lit by overhead lamps and kept pushing the button. Small or not, downtown Tule wasn't exactly safe.

The sound of quick, heavy steps on the sidewalk meant Everett was following. Embarrassed and angry, I didn't want to talk to him. And yet, there was relief knowing he was near. A normal person would have been excited to see their husband. There'd be a hug or a kiss. *Something.*

Everett came to my side, his jacket instantly around me again. He kept an arm around my shoulders, securing the jacket in place, and guided me under the nearest parking lot lamp.

He leaned his back against the lamppost, admitting, "That's not how I thought it'd go."

"She's never going to change." I felt a tug, a pull toward him, and blamed it on the wedding—and the fact that he was here, in the flesh. Or maybe, just maybe, he was danger and safety wrapped into a neat little package that I just couldn't quit.

Closing my eyes, I stepped forward and placed my head against his chest. His arms encircled me, and all the world felt right.

"Everett, I shouldn't—"

"Shhh," he cooed, his head against mine. "Scarlett?"

"No."

He chuckled and tightened his grip. "I love you."

The hair on my neck stood on end, a chill wrapping around my heart. It was too much, too loud a declaration to be genuine. Pretty words didn't erase the past. Today's affection didn't heal the abandonment. He'd left when I needed him the most. I stiffened and then realized he'd anticipated my reaction.

"Everett, we can't." There were too many reasons to count. It was easy to blame the distance between us on his London assignment but in reality, I was the reason.

"And I know you love me." He inhaled, as if vulnerable.

He leaned in. I held my breath, on the cusp of fear and need. This was wrong, *we* were wrong. Everett came closer, so near if I moved, our lips would touch. An ache clawed its way in. He must have seen the struggle because he smiled, victory on his lips.

Under the jacket, Everett slipped an arm around my waist, keeping his distance exactly the same. "I won't kiss you."

"Good." I was a terrible liar. This, whatever *this* was, had always been us, Everett and Scarlett. Awkward, unsure, and intense.

His other hand brushed my cheek and then traced the outline of my jaw. Briefly, I closed my eyes and leaned into the touch, pretending all was right with us. I wrapped my arms around him and leaned against him. He'd promised he wouldn't kiss me, and part of me wanted to test that. My hands ran along his arms, feeling the taut muscles he'd worked for; every day the same regimen he'd kept since he was a boy. He didn't move closer. The familiar feeling of safety came rushing back—but this time, something else mixed in. He smirked, reading me like he'd done for years.

"I won't hurt you," he whispered.

"I know," I lied.

The yearning grew, this need to be close. Danger had that affect, the staring into a raging fire, gawking at an accident or even leaning over a precipice. Everett—he was the sheer cliff I'd fallen from. And would fall again.

"I love you," he repeated, his breath tickling my skin.

My heart, already fragile, broke a little. I shook my head; I wanted to believe him but I couldn't. He cared for me—and always had. But no, he loved being the hero more than he ever loved being mine.

"Don't," Everett growled. He'd seen my face. Groaning, he gently placed his hands on my shoulders and stepped back.

"I'm sorry." And I was. He'd always been kind and gentle but deserved so much more than I could give him.

Everett released my shoulders and cupped my face in his hands, an ache sinking low in my chest. He touched his forehead against my temple, his chest rising and falling in rhythm with mine. I froze, completely confused. A moment ago he'd stepped back and now he leaned in. For a moment, just a brief moment, I wondered if he was retaliating for all the ups and downs, the hot and cold I'd given him.

Everett shifted and ran his hand down my left arm, leaving goose-bumps in its wake. Turning my hand, he placed a sharp piece of cold metal in my palm. "Marry me. For real this time."

"What?" I froze. He'd put an engagement ring in my hand. My mind raced. We were growing apart, not closer. With Marjorie dying, our last connection would be gone. "Everett—"

"Don't overthink this." He held my hand up to the lamp, the light shining on an enormous center diamond. Dozens of tiny diamonds glittered on the tiny sliver of a band. It was too cliché for my father's store, a two-carat gemstone perched on a micro pave band. And yet, it was the exact ring I'd dreamed of—I'd never told a soul. Hope burst in. Everett knew me. He'd always known me.

I slipped the ring on my finger, so different than what I'd grown up with. No creativity or custom accents that showcased my father's talent. And then it hit me. Everett hadn't asked my father. Everything was still a secret. Nothing had changed. Nothing would ever change.

This wasn't real. This was just another Band-Aid, a dream at best.

I stepped back. Instead of following me, Everett bent on one knee. "Let me give you the wedding, the ring. Everything."

"My family is right here, Everett." They were in the church celebrating my cousin's wedding. Soon, we'd be celebrating my sister Elaine's as well.

"You deserve your time in the spotlight."

"Would you stop?" I snapped, hating myself for how I was acting. "We are not this. You are not the *get on one knee* kind of guy. I'm not the blushing bride."

"Actually—"

"Everett," I warned but couldn't stop the smile. I was very much the poster child for blushing bride. It wasn't something to be proud of —not when I'd been married for this long. We'd never crossed that line, and it was all my fault. "We are not okay. We have years of being *not okay*."

"We'll figure it out."

"Get up, Everett." It bothered me, his giant frame on bended knee.

He shook his head, his scowl on full display. "I don't care, Scarlett. Do you understand?"

"You're a ..." *man.* And men had needs.

"A man who loves you." He stood and in one step, held my hand. A goofy grin that should've been on a boy instead of a grown man appeared. "I promised I would take care of you."

"And you have. You were never the problem." One night, over a decade ago, had left its mark; though the memory was foggy and the details fragmented. The box of old files in my garage held more secrets, more obstacles that kept me at arm's length. "But really, come on, Everett, if I had kept my mouth shut."

I couldn't look at him. It'd hurt too much. The words kept coming. "I shouldn't have told you. You wouldn't feel this need to protect me."

"You still think I'm here because I have to be? After everything, you *still* think that?"

"You flew halfway around the world because your grandmother is dying. Moral obligation is kind of your thing."

Everett blanched, his mouth hung open. His back straightened, an argument forming in his eyes. He was no longer the outcast child. He was Everett Ashley, an international bulldog of an attorney, but this was a debate he would not win.

My lip trembled and I prayed I wouldn't cry. He'd never believe me if he saw tears. He would stay, console ... and hold me. It was my fault that Everett saw me as an orphan, someone in need of shelter and love instead of a living, breathing adult woman.

Avoiding his gaze, I sank to the ground, my back against the church's brick building. He sat next to me on the cement, tension radiating from him. Only Everett would sit beside me on a dirty sidewalk in an expensive suit. He folded his knees and groaned, his head in his hands.

"I'm sorry, Everett."

"Would you stop saying that?" he growled, and in some odd, dysfunctional way, the sound offered comfort. "And don't tell me I don't love you."

"Everett—"

He lifted his head and glared at me. "I've done enough thinking for the both of us."

"And ... what did you decide?"

He scoffed and pointed to the diamond. "Thought it'd be obvious."

"I don't need a ring." I needed a cure to an insatiable, irrational fear. Not a diamond. But the fact that he'd given me one, endeared him all the more.

"Yeah, you do." He sighed, his big, irritated sigh, and pulled me into his lap before I could protest. Cradling my head against his chest, he said, "You need a wedding too. And you need to be touched."

His chest was too comfortable. Too warm and inviting. I heard his heartbeat and wished it didn't affect me.

"Scarlett, I need you to listen to me." He waited a beat before starting again. "You're all I ever wanted. Whether you believe it or not,

I staked my claim long before that night. I told you once, I wasn't giving up without a fight. I don't care if you're ninety and we're still figuring this out. It's you and me, Scarlett." He squeezed me against him. "You and me."

Unsure, I curled into him. Intimacy wasn't something he could just brush off, no man could. No man would. "I can't promise—"

"I know." Everett threaded his fingers through mine. "And I don't care."

❧ 6 ❧

EVERETT ASHLEY
FIFTEEN YEARS AGO

For three days in a row, Everett stared at the empty desk, his thought only on Scarlett and her absences in his English class. *Her* English class, he corrected himself; *she* was the sophomore, not him.

The rest of his schedule consisted of classes with other seniors, including Scarlett's brother Andy and his blond friend, David. Everett had been tempted to ask her brother where Scarlett was but doubted Andy would say a word about his sister. Every time Everett tried, he felt David's blue-eyed stare, confirmed whenever Everett risked a glance. The less Everett said to Andy, the less Everett would give away to the ever-observant David. Everett had not yet figured out the school's hierarchy—nor had he ever cared at previous schools—but one thing was certain, David kept watch on both Scarlett and her brother.

Mr. Munoz dialed the front row of lights down and turned the overhead projector back on. It sputtered for a moment before quickly dying again. He had spent the better part of class fiddling with the machine. His face kept flushing, and from the whispers, Everett gathered that Mr. Munoz was the technology advisor for the fledging tech club. A boon to a teacher's pride, Mr. Munoz had yet to give up on the projector's reincarnation.

Everett's fingers moved swiftly across his notebook, shading the cartoon version of Mr. Munoz and the projector flying through the classroom window. The thought bubble above the cartoon teacher held several keyboard symbols in place of swear words. Everett would send the drawing to the local newspaper tonight, along with the other sketches he'd saved from math class. Tule's archaic paper had barely begun publishing Everett's reprints; *LA Times* had bought the originals when he was still in middle school. Sarcasm was ageless.

Mr. Munoz turned his back to the class and mumbled to himself, a hand on his belt, the other massaging his neck. Everett should have felt pity for the teacher instead of capitalizing on his frustration. But drawing was Everett's only ticket to freedom.

He had saved every penny, socking his money away. Only once did his father find the stash. Richard stole the money and attacked Everett with hours of questions. Everett let his father think it came from selling stolen drugs. It would have been easy; his father was both addict and dealer. Richard Ashley, eager for a scapegoat, labeled Everett a user and a thief, shipping him off to Grandma Marjorie's house for a week as punishment, complete with a peppering of bruises.

Late that night, Marjorie stumbled upon Everett's habit, his search for postage stamps proving too loud for sleep. He waited, fear in his throat, and addressed envelopes in his hand. With a sigh of relief, she opened a bank account the next morning in both their names. She had a knack for knowing exactly what Everett had thought, as if she had a direct line to his memories. Once a notary, Marjorie had an old friend witness all the necessary forms; the money and rights would never slip to his father's hands. With her sweet voice and gentle smile, it was the first time Everett realized his grandmother's strength and savvy foresight.

The bell rang. Everett signed the bottom right corner with his initials, *EA,* so close they appeared to be on top of each other. He waited until the last student cleared the room. Every jostle, no matter how small, still hurt. He gave one more glance at Scarlett's empty desk before following the other students out.

"Where's your girlfriend, Ashley?" David stood directly across from Mr. Munoz's door, leaning into the building's wall. David wasn't the first idiot to emphasize Everett's girly last name. The teasing never lasted, and Everett rarely cared, not about high school and not about little boys pretending to be men.

"Hiding from you." Everett didn't have to straighten his stance to intimidate. His six-foot, four-inch frame cast a long enough shadow. He would know. His father still held two inches on Everett.

David smirked and folded his arms, no doubt thinking it made him look serious. His soft blue eyes and easy smile resembled a Ken doll, not a tough guy. His smooth, uncalloused hands said more about him than the overeager posture. His bleached hair had Everett pinning him a lazy mama's boy, naïve of work and want. The manufactured highlights meant David didn't actually go outside often, but cared enough to look like it—the very opposite of Scarlett.

"Are we going or what?" Andy jogged to David's side, elbowing him. Andy's black hair and dark features contrasted his friend's. Andy followed David's gaze and met Everett's frown.

Descending the steps from Mr. Munoz's class toward them, Everett rolled his eyes while David narrowed his. David waited a moment before breaking his gaze.

"Yeah, let's go." David tried scowling but looked more like a pouting toddler than a jilted teenage boy.

Several other seniors gathered in Andy and David's wake while Everett waited on the step, wondering if he should break through the crowd of idiots and ask about Scarlett. It would force Andy to answer, but high school tended to twist things. Good intentions became cruel in an instant.

Everett felt Scarlett before he heard her voice.

"Something on your mind, or can I get through?" Shielding her eyes, Scarlett looked up at him. Her color was off and dark circles underlined her chocolate eyes. Even in the shadow of her hand, Everett recognized despair. And utter exhaustion.

"Where've you been?" The judgment was all too clear.

Scarlett didn't need condemnation, she needed a friend. A fact he could read within moments of meeting her. She looked away, her back stiff with pride.

"I don't care that you ditched. I just wondered if you were okay."

Scarlett turned back, her mouth open in disbelief. The surprise of a stranger caring clenched Everett's heart.

"I'm okay." She was anything but. The neutral mask that made her nearly invisible slid into place.

"Right." Everett went up two steps and opened the door for her.

Scarlett hesitated before climbing up. When she reached him, he noticed the half sheet in her hand, the same light blue paper the receptionist signed the day he arrived. The details fell in line. His first day, she had asked the receptionist to sign a hall pass. He'd watched the deception unfold without realizing it. Scarlett had covered her tracks before she disappeared with the pre-signed hall pass.

This wasn't her first time skipping class, not with this much foresight. There was no way her brother knew. Everett had almost given her up. Scarlett pasted an innocent smile before greeting Mr. Munoz. Everett should leave. His father was the king of deceit, but Everett couldn't let Scarlett go.

He shut the opposite door softly and took up the same position David had earlier, leaning against the classroom wall. Everett wasn't going to let her out of his sight. She wasn't *okay*, and it bothered him. The fact that Scarlett bothered him, bothered him—he shook his head. He was losing his mind.

A moment later, Scarlett studied him on the steps, appearing sometime during Everett's internal struggle. Her lips tugged, a whisper of a smirk on her face. The smallest of movements transformed her features, a spark in her eye, the upward tilt of her cheek. The very picture of her, the contrast of beauty and vulnerability, dark circles under bold, thick lashes —it sunk into Everett. This—*this* was the reason he couldn't shake her.

"Did you hang up your cape?" She took a step and pretended to think, one finger tapping her chin. "Why else would Superman wait outside? He didn't rat me out, so he can't be waiting for the teacher ... hmm, if only I knew why."

"Are you done?"

"Not even close." Scarlett leaned over the rail, her arms folded. Without thinking, he came to her. Even with two steps left before she touched the ground, he towered over her. Her eyes widened and she swallowed. Her nervousness made him pause.

"Where were you?" he whispered, inches from her.

Scarlett's brow furrowed for a split second. If he'd not been so close, he would have missed it. She was hatching a lie—the tightening of the lips, the drum of her fingers. She opened her mouth, and he straightened, backing up.

"Don't lie to me." Everett didn't care about his tone. Richard Ashley spoke only with lie-soaked words. Everett had been played, deceived enough for one lifetime.

"I didn't say anything." But—*how did you know?*—came across.

"I know a lie when I see it." He turned from her, not knowing where to go or what to do. If she was like his father then—no, he wouldn't be a part of it. Lies were dangerous thoughts that soon turned to action. Lie, hurt, and deny, that was the order of people like Richard. A cycle Everett had lived since infancy.

"You wouldn't believe me if I told you."

"Try me."

"I don't know you." Her voice was closer, but Everett didn't turn around. He would be tempted to stare or worse, ask to draw her.

"Your point?"

She stood next to him. "I won't lie to you, but I won't tell you where ... yet."

He made the mistake of looking at her, the hope in her eyes. Her hands flexed and relaxed only to flex again. She reminded him of a frightened cat he had once rescued. The little guy meowed for food and attention but danced in a circle, too skittish to trust. Everett nodded, and she relaxed slightly.

"Did you bring a lunch?" It came across as a challenge, forcing Everett to sigh. Nothing came out right.

Scarlett chuckled beside him, the accusation and tension gone in an instant. She reached for him, her delicate hand on the sleeve of his hoodie. "You are awful, truly awful."

"Thanks, I think."

She beamed, humor in her eyes. She squeezed his arm before dropping it. Everett pulled it back, returning her hand to his forearm. When she looked at him, he dropped both hands, embarrassed. He hadn't thought about it, he just felt the loss when she moved. He wanted her near. It gave him comfort, a warmth that he didn't realize he needed. She studied him, not with the curiosity of his peers but with the intensity of prey, like a deer on the plains.

"I won't hurt you," he said stupidly. "I'm not an idiot. I only talk like one."

Her lips quirked to a half smile. She looped an arm through his and started walking. Everett breathed in relief, Scarlett on his arm melting something inside him—until he heard her stomach growl and a familiar voice.

"Scarlett!" David called from across the courtyard, a bag from the corner burger joint in his hand. "I brought you lunch."

Her hand tightened on Everett's arm while she gave David a deceptive smile, bright and sure. David jogged to her, ignoring Everett completely. Except for the slight tremor in her hands, she would seem calm, flirtatious even. The smaller and lithe Andy followed behind David, his attention solely on Everett.

"We already made lunch plans," Everett barked.

With tanned skin and bleached hair, David flinched at the statement. Everett almost laughed at the reaction. David was the epitome of Pretty Boy, a facade of manhood.

"What are you doing?" Andy asked, suddenly concerned with his sister's welfare. They didn't look alike, not in the eyes or frame. He was gangly and proud, his chin jutted. His olive skin was a shade lighter than Scarlett's, but his hair was dark—his face Hispanic.

"What do most people do at lunch?" she asked sweetly, too bright to be real.

Everett felt the venom in her words and cheeky smile.

"What are you doing *with him?*" Andy nodded toward Everett while David grinned like an idiot, his teeth as bleached as his hair.

"I'm sorry, who's *him?*" Scarlett leaned forward on her tiptoes, whispering loudly to Everett, "Do you know who my brother's talking about?"

"Think about what you're doing, Scarlett. Think long and hard." Andy looked her up and down, condemnation in his dark eyes. He was trying to be the older brother but sounded more like a parent.

"Think about what?" Everett asked, loving the boom of his voice for once.

Andy's dark gaze snapped to Everett's with a flicker of fear. He jutted his chin and pulled a hat from his back pocket.

When Andy still didn't answer, Everett added, "Tell me. What is she doing that she needs to think *so long* and *so hard* over?"

Scarlett shrugged, her eyes feigning innocence. "Lunch. I need to think long and hard about lunch. I could choke you know. Eating can be pretty dangerous."

"You're playing with fire." Andy placed the hat on his head, his hand curving the bill. The more irritated he became, the less Scarlett's hand trembled. He clenched his jaw—so unlike his sister at Everett's side. Even angry, she held a flicker of concern while he held none. Andy was proud. Proud men were volatile.

"I don't think she's the one in danger," Everett said evenly.

"Is that a threat?" David rushed to his friend's aid, a touch too eager. His blue eyes danced. He cracked his knuckles but couldn't hide the wince.

"Does it need to be?" Everett took a step forward, stopped only by the pressure of Scarlett's hand. A quick glance at her panicked eyes set him back. She would pay for his behavior just like Everett paid for his mother's, courtesy of his father.

"Have a nice lunch." Everett lifted his arm and pulled her next to him. With Scarlett cradled to his side, they walked to the old coupe, a gift from his late grandfather. Everett opened the door for her and silently cursed. He folded himself into the driver's seat, debating on how to apologize for whatever pain would await her at home. If Andy was anything like Richard, Scarlett had good reason to escape. The dark circles under her eyes weighed on Everett's shoulders.

She covered his hand with hers but said nothing.

He squeezed her fingers. "It won't always hurt this much, I promise."

"I never said I was hurt."

"You didn't. You don't have to. You can keep your secrets, Scarlett." Everett started the car, the engine roaring to life. "But—"

"Don't lie to you."

He killed the engine and pulled her hand to his chest, forcing her to look at him. "That's not what I was going to say."

Scarlett arched an eyebrow as if to say, *Then what?*

"But I'm here if you ever *do* want to share." Everett wished he'd said the same thing to his mother.

She rolled her eyes. "Of course you'd say that, Superman."

"If you'd find me a horse, I'd be your knight in shining armor, too." He shrugged with a dramatic sigh. "Until then, this is all I've got to work with."

"You can *joke?* You actually made a joke?" She threw back her head and laughed, the sound rich and glorious. If Everett could draw sounds, her laughter would be deep in color and wide in strokes.

"What in our relationship makes you think I'd joke around?" Everett deadpanned.

"Everett Ashley, I am impressed." She pulled the tie from her hair, running her fingers through the ends. "And a little surprised."

"Yeah, well, Superman has secrets too."

SCARLETT ASHLEY
PRESENT DAY

My hands shook as I gripped the steering wheel. My mother had offered her house, wanting me to stay the night instead of driving home in the foggy weather. But Everett's sudden appearance changed the dialogue—not that I had shared a roof with my family in years. There were reasons I stayed to my side of the valley. All of them had to do with my childhood.

I turned up my car's radio, ignoring the buzz of an incoming text. It was my mother again, and her anger could wait. She wanted to know the details of Everett, why he was in town and when was he leaving. She would continue to call until I answered, each time more frantic. I knew this, and yet it didn't stop me from sending her to voicemail. Or leaving her texts unanswered.

Everett had tucked me into my car, waiting in the parking lot for me to drive away so my family wouldn't try to stop me. They'd begin their pleas out of concern. The fog *was* thick, but the argument always turned to protecting me from Everett. It didn't help that Mom thought I was *shacking up* with Everett or *living in sin*. She used both terms interchangeably, but I doubted she'd feel any relief when she knew the truth of our marriage. Secrets were easier to keep when one of them lived abroad. Soon Everett would be back in London.

I took the downtown exit toward the house I shared with Everett. Alone for the first time, I questioned Everett's proposal. The timing. The ring. Everything.

Before he'd left to London, my first big break as a journalist was crumbling. A salacious exposé on predatory producers manipulating their assistants, all female, was more than just a project. It had stirred something inside me. At first, I thought it was because Everett's aunt Missy was a former assistant in the center of the story. But the feelings didn't die when the story imploded.

The fear and weight on my chest had grown since Missy had given me the box. It sat untouched in my garage. I couldn't bring myself to haul it into the house. It was something I'd hoped to face with Everett. Monsters weren't as scary with Superman around.

Turning on the last street into my neighborhood offered comfort. Everett wouldn't be home yet; he'd opted to visit Marjorie before coming home. *Home.* The thought settled around my shoulders like an old blanket. This was us, sharing a house and bank accounts like family —I swallowed the thought. Roommates seemed more appropriate, mostly because I'd kept him at bay.

The hands-free set kicked on, signaling a phone number I didn't recognize. It was close to one in the morning. Nothing good ever came this late. I pushed the button to reject the call, but my finger slid, hitting the answer icon.

"Where'd you run off to?" David's voice crackled through. He must've been driving as well. Two Bluetooth devices connecting made for a crappy call.

"Headed home, David." *Why are you calling me,* I almost added, but with David I never knew if I'd get the truth. Or if I really wanted it.

"Can we meet?" There was a hint of a question, so unlike the David I knew. He normally assumed the sale; it's how he solidified his political career.

"I'm tired, David."

"No, I mean, I know. I know ..." He sighed into the phone. It was hard to picture him sighing. Everett's default setting was irritated while David's was smiling. "It's just I was hoping we could talk."

"About what?" It fell out before I could stop myself. I'd let the door open for David to kick in.

"Some things should be said in person." There was a seriousness to his tone that didn't sit well. David was charm and charisma, dancing himself out of trouble time and time again.

"Not tonight."

"When did you leave?" The sound of a car blinker came across the speaker. He wasn't on the freeway, a comforting thought. Even if he left Tule right now he wouldn't be here for another hour. By that time, Everett would be home. "I could be there in Gainesfield in no time."

"David, I really should go." I couldn't remember a time I'd heard his voice on the phone. There was a flicker of memory tucked in the back of my mind. "How did you get my phone number?"

"Oh, come on, Scarlett," he whined, pulling the memory to the front.

His voice—my car, he wanted to help me with Marjorie. He was with my brother and used his phone. Marjorie was having corrective surgery to fix her hip. She was weak with pain and worry—women who broke their hip after turning sixty had a shockingly high mortality rate.

Just getting Marjorie in the car was an exhausting task, each angle and shift of her body hurt. David was begging to accompany us to the doctor's while my brother snapped at his kids in the background. The knot in my stomach had grown, but I didn't know if I was being stubborn. I needed his help. Marjorie was in so much pain. Resentment had threatened to come alive. The fact that David was offering and Everett was half a world away had grated on my nerves. Marjorie's pleading frown and curt shake of the head gave me courage. Like every time before, she knew exactly how I felt. She never reprimanded me for irrational fears, just silently encouraged me. And loved me.

It wasn't until David appeared outside the doctor's office that I knew Mom was involved, the only other person who knew Marjorie's schedule. It was an accidental slip, a mistake I never repeated. Mom had confessed but stopped short of apologizing, swearing it was her concern for both Marjorie—the grandmother of her sworn enemy—and me that prompted her to enlist David.

Help was the reason for my mother's and David's intrusion. *Help* meant I couldn't take a stand against them, because *help* was kind and caring. And yet, it never felt that way. David's presence always felt gray, not dark enough to be black and not light enough to be white.

"You don't have to say anything. Just listen." David's voice pulled me back to the present just as a train honked from a few streets over. Living without Everett had made all the little sounds seem big, the midnight horn now would wake me with a start. It'd take hours to fall back asleep.

A second later, I heard a similar train echo on the Bluetooth coming from David's phone, sounding eerily similar. "It won't take long."

"No, David." Leaning back against the headrest, I tried to remember if he'd ever been to my house. Anything connected to my childhood, including my family, I gave a wide berth, dancing around emotions and feelings, never letting them get too close. Distance kept things in neat little boxes. My feelings and thoughts jumbled together whenever I was around my family. Everett blamed my childhood, but I was responsible somehow, in some way. Other people, especially parents, couldn't be at fault for my fears. I was the problem. Not them.

"I'm just worried." The speakers quieted like he'd parked. "I get that you and Everett have history and whatever, but I'm just ... just worried."

"I'm fine." My voice caught and I silently swore. He didn't need to know about Everett's proposal. No one needed to know. Although the one person I wanted to share it with wouldn't remember. Marjorie kept forgetting things, her mind muddled by the drugs in her IV.

"You didn't look fine tonight." He chuckled. "I mean, after Everett showed up. You looked plenty fine before then."

Slowing the car, I shifted in my seat. I'd never been comfortable with his flattery. He was the preacher's son and captured Tule's trust for the last five years as the mayor. But a few dark moments I couldn't quite remember involved him. The stain had yet to lift.

This was the problem—me assigning others guilt without evidence. I didn't trust my parents, my brother ... or David. "Look, I promise, it's fine. I mean, I'm fine."

"Listen, Scarlett ..." David waited a beat. "You don't want me and all ..."

The sentence hung there. Part of me felt obligated to reassure him, the other part just couldn't.

"...but I still care about you. Always have." David sighed again, the sound just as foreign now as it was a moment ago. "But have you ever wondered why bad things only happen when he's around?"

"David—"

"How many times have you cried because of him?" David gained strength in his own conviction, his voice taking on the same fervor his father used. "And how many times have I made you cry?"

"That's not a fair question." The black sports car parked in front of my neighbor's house looked suspiciously similar to David's. "You were my brother's friend—"

"I never left you." He scoffed and made a tapping noise. "I stuck around."

"With my brother." My stomach tightened. "And your fiancé."

It was a cheap shot, bringing her up. She'd left him at the altar the year after I graduated college. David had just been elected to city council. She hadn't bothered to tell him why. She fled the chapel in the limousine and never looked back. A broken heart looked good on David, securing him the sympathy vote every year since.

"Seems we have more in common than not."

I braked a little too hard while pulling into my driveway, his words hitting their mark. Everett had left. The sting was very much alive. But David didn't know there was more to the story. He didn't know the cavern that stood in my marriage—David didn't even know about the marriage.

Parking in the driveway, I got out of the car and switched the call from Bluetooth. "David—"

"I'm sorry, I shouldn't have said that." The interior light flickered on in the black sports car. The driver was a man.

"Are you in Gainesfield?" My feet were rooted to the spot, and my throat went dry.

Under the street lamp, David exited the car, the phone to his ear. "Can we talk? Please?"

"No."

Even in the poorly lit street, David's megawatt smile flashed. He was perma camera-ready.

My hand gripped my phone, not sure what to do. I should've driven to see Marjorie with Everett, not home. He hadn't seen or talked to her yet. And now I was alone. "What are you doing?"

"You look scared." David sounded slightly offended.

My heart raced. It was stupid, this odd dance with David. There was nothing, no evidence for my hesitation. But it was as real as the car I drove. Solid. Unwavering.

Pretending, I looked at my phone for a second and lied, "Everett just texted me. I have to go."

He ended the call and called out, "I'll go with you."

David took two steps forward. A sliver of panic crept in. With one glance at my phone, David would know I'd lied.

"I'll drive." He stopped walking and nodded toward his car.

And then a thought hit me. "How did you know?"

He paused and cocked his head to the side. He was still two cars away but close enough to read his features. "Know what?"

"Where I live?" Folding my arms to still the shaking, I focused on breathing slowly. I hadn't shut my car door yet. I could jump back in and drive away.

"You're making me sound like a stalker." David gave a light-hearted chuckle. He took another step, his hand outstretched. "Come on, Scarlett."

"I need to—"

"Be at Everett's beck and call." David waited a beat before adding, "This is why I'm worried. He isolates you from your family and friends. There, I said it."

"That's not true." But it wasn't a lie, either.

"He has all the characteristics of a psycho, Scarlett. I'm sorry to be the bearer of bad news, but your family's worried." David tapped the hood of his car. "And now he's back."

"I appreciate your concern but I'm fine." My voice betrayed me, catching in all the wrong places. I rubbed my bare arms and wished for the second time I'd gone to Marjorie's facility. "Really, I am."

"I'm not giving up, Scarlett." His bravado made me squirm. It didn't ring true. He wasn't the savior he thought he was. "He doesn't want you, just the idea of you. He won't even marry you, just keeps stringing you along. If he loved you, he'd make an honest woman out of you."

"You have it backwards, completely backwards," I whispered, wishing I hadn't said anything at all. The less David knew, the less my family would know. The conversation chilled me more than the December air.

"What do you mean?" David neared, his voice softening. "Talk to me."

"Nothing, David." Fumbling with the car door, I hurried to say, "I need to go."

"He wants to marry you?" He didn't bother hiding the suspicion, his eyebrows raised. "Everett Ashley wants to get married?"

"Good bye, David." I opened the door and sank to the seat. A smart woman would have parked in the garage and shut the door before getting out—or better yet, gone with Everett to visit Marjorie. David wouldn't have risked a visit if Everett was around.

David caught the door, leaning in. "But you don't want to marry him."

"I didn't say that."

"You said much more than that." David reached for me, his hand caressing my cheek. I recoiled. "Oh, that's right. Only Everett's allowed to touch." I froze—a memory, vague and out of reach, began to stretch and come alive. He burst the image by saying, "There's so much we need to talk about, Scarlett. You might not be ready to hear it yet, but I'm willing to wait."

"I'm not trying to be a jerk, David, but really, there's no *we*," I said as firm as I could. "There was never a *we*. The only *we* I've ever known was with Everett."

"Was," David said too brightly. "You said *was*."

❧ 8 ❧

EVERETT ASHLEY
FIFTEEN YEARS AGO

Busy chaos filled the school's administration office. The harried receptionist juggled notes from students and counselors while alternating her shoulders for the two separate phones attached at either end of the high counter. Dizzy from all the movement, Everett searched his pockets and backpack for the note excusing his tardiness but came up empty. Marjorie had left the note on his backpack this morning. Like an idiot, Everett told the doctor's office he didn't need a written excuse because his grandmother had already given one. The school's receptionist held up a finger for him to wait and answered the ringing phone. Everett had never cared about being in trouble before Tule, but he couldn't give Marjorie one more thing to worry about.

"Mr. Ashley, how are you today?" His school counselor extended a hand, but Everett couldn't remember his name. He could barely remember to breathe after the doctor poked and prodded his injured head. "You okay?"

"Yeah, yeah." Everett searched the memory of his first day, trying to remember the counselor's name.

The man let his hand fall and leaned into the receptionist's counter.

He cocked his head to the side, his brow furrowing with what looked like concern. Everett took a step back. He didn't need anyone's pity.

"Let me know if I can do anything for you." The counselor straightened his stance, his attention still focused on Everett. "How's your head?"

Absently, Everett touched it and winced. "Doctor says it's healing. Wish he could figure that out without touching it."

A soft chuckle followed a lazy smile. "Did you just come from the doctor's?"

Everett nodded slowly, still unsure of moving his head too quickly.

"I'm still shocked you're here. Most kids would milk it for as long as they could." He stopped and with a conspiratorial grin added, "No shame in using it to gain sympathy with the ladies."

Despite himself, Everett smiled, picturing a younger, lankier version of the geeky man before him. "I'll think about it."

"Mr. Fink, I need to transfer a *parent* to your line." The reception- ist's voice dropped at *parent*. Whoever it was stole the humor from the counselor's expression.

"Thanks. Hey, Mr. Ashley needs a hall pass. He was at a doctor's appointment." Mr. Fink clapped Everett on the shoulder. Everett swal- lowed the groan. "Oh, tell Mr. Munoz it's a go on the work credit for you."

Before Everett could ask what a work credit was, Mr. Fink disap- peared behind his closed office door. The receptionist slid the hall pass across the counter and reached for the phone. Despite having three desks behind the counter, she seemed to be the sole occupant. Everett grabbed the blue paper and shoved it into his pocket, still confused by the term *work credit*.

He opened the door and squinted. Even with the overcast clouds, the hidden sun was too bright. The bell rang, too loud and too clear. The sound echoed in his head. He felt every inch of it.

Everett checked his watch. He'd missed all his morning classes. At this rate, he wouldn't graduate. Navigating his father's fists and moth- er's moods had taken up most of his thoughts for the past seventeen years. Graduating high school was never in the picture. He paused on the sidewalk, accidentally creating a barrier for the other students rushing to their classes. Everett patted his shoulder where Mr. Fink had touched him a moment ago. The gesture had seemed sincere, as if someone other than Marjorie cared. The thought darkened. Mr. Fink was quite literally paid to guide and help him. Everett was still just another kid, another troubled student needing a counselor. He scowled, ignoring the sudden distance between him and his fellow students. By some miracle he stayed upright, slowly making his way to English.

"What color is your sky today, Superman?" Scarlett held out a brown paper bag.

Everett shook his head and swore under his breath.

"That's not what they're called." She opened the bag and pulled out a chocolate chip cookie. "Say it with me, coo-kie."

"Cookie."

"That bad, huh?" Her face softened.

"I didn't say anything."

"Say that to your face." Her smile grew, lighting her eyes and unveiling the startling structure of her cheeks, jaw—of everything.

Everett stepped closer, his body like an umbrella, shadowing her entire frame. A faint blush touched her cheeks. Her eyes widened, the ink of her irises swallowing the deep brown of her eyes. Desire. He'd sketched it a million times and recognized it dozens of others. He shivered—a cold sweat of panic. He hadn't a clue what to do with it. Scarlett blinked, and faster than he could move, left the cookie in his hand and raced up the steps to class.

He stared dumbly at the cookie. His stomach twisted and his mind reeled, too much confusion for one day. He followed the other students into the classroom, groaning when Mr. Munoz called him to his desk.

Scarlett tucked her chin when Everett passed her desk. He wanted to grab her by the shoulders and force her to look at him, force her to say what she actually wanted. He'd give it to her, anything—

"You sure you're okay?" Mr. Munoz appeared to be examining Everett's face.

"Why does everyone keep asking me that?" Everett snapped and then rubbed his temples. "Sorry. Didn't mean it to come out like that."

"You didn't hear a word I said. That's why I asked." Mr. Munoz didn't soften his tone nor did he back down. He just stood there, not leaning on his desk for support or glancing nervously around the room for help. He didn't snap back. He didn't react. At all.

In fact, no one did. The rest of the class was busy writing their daily prompt from the board. Mr. Munoz had spoken in a voice so low, the rest of the students hadn't heard.

Straightening, Everett pulled out the note from his pocket and handed it over. "Not sure if I give this to you or take it to the other classes I missed."

The teacher glanced at the note, then back Everett. "I'll take care of it."

"Thanks."

"I saw your work this weekend." Mr. Munoz grabbed a folder off his desk and flipped it open, showing a stack of stapled newspaper clippings. Each contained two, sometimes three, of Everett's drawings.

"E.A. does nice work." Everett bit back a grin.

Mr. Munoz lifted last month's test on Greek and Roman Mythology, revealing stapled sketches from newspapers. He tapped the bottom corner of the test where Everett had drawn the rough sketch of a cartoon. Mr. Munoz then tapped the newspaper clipping on top, the finished cartoon sketch sent to the *LA Times*. "Look familiar?"

"Maybe." Everett tried to remember when the sketch of Mr. Munoz throwing the projector out the window would run.

"Your counselor says you're roughly a year, possibly two years behind schedule to graduate."

"I'll take your word for it." Everett honestly had no idea. He only knew of Marjorie's constant worry—of his future and his past. Sometimes, when she was in the room and Everett would remember a rough day with his dad, Marjorie would flinch—like she was experiencing his memory first hand. "My counselor mentioned work credit this morning, but I don't know what that is."

Mr. Munoz closed the folder and tossed it onto the desk. His gaze flicked to Scarlett and then back to Everett. "I had another student a few years ago who uncovered a loophole in our education system."

Everett had followed Mr. Munoz's gaze.

"Not Scarlett, Everett. Her cousin, if you must know." Mr. Munoz didn't sound annoyed but he didn't sound pleased. His voice remained neutral, painfully neutral. His facial features moved subtly, making it difficult for Everett to read him.

For years, Everett had relied on little details, the slight wrinkling of the nose or the exhale of breath. It wasn't just a hobby; it was survival.

Mr. Munoz cleared his throat, gathering Everett's attention. "I teach two English classes at the junior college. If you pass those classes, they simultaneously count toward both college and high school. If you sign up for an internship program, you can get even more credits."

"Internship for what?"

Mr. Munoz scratched his head, appearing to think, but Everett doubted it all. He suspected Mr. Munoz already had a plan ready and waiting.

"You've accomplished something that most people twice your age will never do." Mr. Munoz waited a beat. "You're published."

"As an artist. Not a writer."

Mr. Munoz pulled out the stapled clippings and tapped on a dialogue bubble. "Those are words, Everett."

"Okay, yeah—"

"In my class, if you are published at any point during the semester, it's an automatic A." Grinning, Mr. Munoz let the arrogance show for a split second. "You'd have two college level English classes with A's."

"What's the catch?"

Mr. Munoz sighed, returning to the neutral teacher. "Get someone else to do the same thing."

Everett felt the hairs on his neck stand on end. Mr. Munoz was more observant than Everett had given him credit for. The teacher had noticed something between Scarlett and him.

"Why?" Everett couldn't help it, he needed to know—and then he saw it, the stack of sticky notes, one on top of the other, documenting the phone calls to the Delfin family.

Graded papers were turned over, the desk calendar marked in abbreviations only Mr. Munoz could understand, and everything was covered by or in folders. Everett guessed that Mr. Munoz wouldn't have left a stack of sticky notes, not unless he wanted Everett to see it. He could make out *Delfin*, *mother*, and *reported* but nothing else.

"Why?" Everett repeated.

"Because someone gave a crap about me when they didn't have to." Stoic—not even a whisper of a grin on Mr. Munoz's lips. He had an uncanny way of looking straight at Everett despite his smaller stature. "Do we have a deal?"

"I ..." It felt wrong, too good to be true, and if Everett was being honest, it felt like betrayal.

"It'll be an uphill battle." This time Mr. Munoz sat down and dug a sealed envelope from a drawer. "Her family will fight it, if they find out."

"Fight what?"

"Connect the dots, Everett." Mr. Munoz tapped the envelope on the desk, the beginnings of a frown appearing. "If she gets double the credits, high school and college, she's as good as gone. Out of the house."

"Yeah, my point. No parent wants their kid at home." No one. That's what grandparents were for; that's what Marjorie was for.

"Not every parent, Everett."

9

SCARLETT ASHLEY

PRESENT DAY

Touching my cheek, I still felt David's hand. I'd left David standing in my driveway and drove laps around the neighborhood, not returning until I knew Everett was on his way home.

My phone beeped with a text, again. Mom had sent a dozen texts when I left the wedding reception. Whether she knew David had followed me from the wedding, I didn't know. And thankfully, he hadn't camped out. Both he and Mom still believed I lived with Everett as a girlfriend, not as a wife. The one small technicality leveled me with guilt and relief. Relief that I had one solid, legal link to Everett and his family but guilt that I'd shackled him to me. And lied to my parents.

My stomach twisted and shame crept in. David's words echoed in my mind, *Oh, that's right. Only Everett can touch you.* David's observation was spot-on and I couldn't explain the phenomenon. Everett was safety —he was home. Even now, turning into the driveway of the home we shared, I felt the familiar flutter of excitement and comfort. No other man's touch had ever soothed me.

Everett had purchased the fixer-upper, but of late, it had felt more *his* in my mind than *ours*. The feeling made zero sense, especially when I was the sole occupant for the last year. Palming my phone in one hand and my heels in the other, I walked to the front of the house, lit with newly installed lights. The renovation had slowed to a screeching halt when Everett left. It took a few months for me to start a new normal, scheduling time for the house and Marjorie. I could install a few lights here or paint the baseboards there, but standing in front of the house, I was massively underwhelmed.

The cool Bermuda grass chilled my bare feet, the front yard small and unassuming. Like every home on this side of the street, the back-yard held two-to-three acres while our front yards were quaint and tidy. The small side yards added to the illusion, providing the desired privacy of farm-zoned lots in the middle of Gainesfield, the seventh largest city in California. Behind our street, a meandering equestrian easement sewed the ends of our lots together, a livestock tunnel at the far end. Our neighbors rode their horses under the four busiest streets in the city with no one the wiser, popping out the other side to miles of hiking and horse trails.

An oil baron built the two-story mansion as a country cottage, staking his claim in the late 19th century oil rush. The mansion's plot of land, once isolated by decorated lawns and stables, had shrunk. The city's growth had nibbled away the forty-acre estate. Its sister mansion, the abandoned Astor house, stood abandoned in Tule, still surrounded by its original acreage. In high school I would ditch and visit the Astor house. It was one of only two places I'd ever felt peace in Tule.

Everett's rental car slowed to a crawl, pulling into the driveway. Like a kid waiting for approval, I worried about his opinion. Unfolding himself from the sedan, Everett rested his arms on the top of the car door. The home wasn't finished, and at the rate I was going, it never would be.

His silence heightened my critique. He wouldn't be able to see the iris or azalea blooms for several months, December the gloomiest for flowers. The exterior still needed paint, although the structural repairs were finished and windows now took the place of boards.

"It's hard to believe it's the same house." Everett's timbre carried over the grass. He shut the door and came to my side. Sliding an arm around my waist, he whispered, "It's incredible."

He had touched me at least a dozen times in the few hours since returning. Desire had always bubbled under the surface, the tension palpable, but this was new. Something had changed, or rather, someone.

"I didn't get a lot done." Twisting the diamond ring with my thumb, I felt my face flush.

He pulled me closer. "You've done enough. More than enough."

Everett scratched behind his ear, the light catching on his wedding band. He'd purchased it years ago. Publicly, Everett had treated our arrangement as a legitimate marriage. My face grew hotter still.

He turned to me, his scarred side now shadowed, and my breath caught. He was beautiful, long, dark eyelashes and defined features, his jaw and cheekbones. A scowl formed, and I couldn't help but smile.

Everett Ashley could intimidate a terrorist with a look. The outward beast was part habit, and part performance. "You okay?"

Not trusting my voice, I nodded.

"Hey." He rubbed his hands up and down my cold arms. "What's going on?"

My waist had chilled, more from the loss of his touch than the night. And then suspicion crept in. It was an ugly thought, but for someone who professed to never touch women, he'd always been more than comfortable holding me. Everett would have had complete autonomy, freedom to touch anyone in another country. A chill crept up my spine. He was a man—and a deprived one at that.

"Scarlett?" His voice was covered with worry.

I swallowed the rising jealousy. I had no right to be angry. This was all my fault. "How long are you staying?"

"Forever." He smirked and went to his car.

"You know what I meant." The garage door was still open. Between my car and Everett's old coupe sat the box of files Missy had given me. With some luck, Everett wouldn't see it.

He pulled his luggage out of the back seat with one hand, the other guiding me forward at the small of my back. Another touch. "I've taken a leave of absence. Sort of."

"You what?" The sound of the garage door swallowed my question.

Everett patted the unfinished doorframe connecting the garage with the washroom. Before he'd left, the connection was still being built.

Following him, I asked, "Everett, what did you do?"

To my annoyance, he didn't answer. He was opening and closing cabinets, inspecting the craftsmanship. He ran a hand down the granite counter, turning the laundry sink faucet on and off. He gave a slight hesitation. Something must have snagged or didn't stand up to his level of perfection. Frowning, he turned the faucet back on and bent over, listening.

"Everett."

He snapped to a stand, a question on his face.

"Can you play plumber tomorrow?"

"Yes, ma'am." He smiled sheepishly and rubbed his eyes. "I think I've been up for twenty-four hours straight."

"You came straight to the wedding?" Suspicion again. There was a reason he'd hurried, risking my family's ire. "Why?"

"I had an epiphany." Everett set the luggage on the counter. "How's the bed situation?"

My face flushed even more, and if his smirk was any indicator, the blush was deep, deep red. "Um, the same."

"Lead the way." When I didn't move, he sighed. "I can talk and walk at the same time."

"Then by all means, lead the way."

Everett held out his hand to touch the framework marking the end of what used to be the servant's entrance a century ago.

"Focus."

His hand snapped back. "I'm just admiring—"

"Talk and walk."

"I was going about it the wrong way. Spending time in L.A., then New York, and finally London." He kept his arms at his sides, the index and thumb on his drawing hand twitching. The hours he spent, recreating the original splendor of the house on paper. "I just had an epiphany that it wasn't working."

"What wasn't working?"

He glanced back at me. "Us."

I froze, my heart in my throat. He *had* changed. There was someone else. Women had admired him for as long as I could remember. *Men have needs* was a mantra my father had repeated since I was small, too little to understand. Everett was human—and beautiful. How long could someone turn their back on invitations, on ever-present temptation?

I felt instantly hot. It wasn't just my face. It was my neck, my hands —all of me. This wasn't the first time I assumed there was another woman. The thought, the suspicion, crept in because the facts remained—I was broken and he was a man.

The memory of my mother standing next to Marjorie's hospital bed, a hand on her hip. She'd arched her eyebrow and said, without a trace of warmth, *He's not coming back. If Marjorie couldn't save him, what makes you think you can? He's been after one thing and one thing only.*

Everett kept walking down the hall, standing at the base of the entrance stairs. His critical eye collected the exposed flaws and neglect not yet tackled. Without a sound, I turned into one of the few rooms Everett had remodeled before moving in. The dresser, the nightstand, and even the bed, he'd refurbished from an estate sale. This was him, turning disaster into art.

His footsteps faded. He would be distracted for who knew how long.

Neatly folded in the closet were the sheets, blankets, and oversized air mattress he normally used. They waited in the comfort of the home, like I had, for him to return. Just as before, I set it in the space between the door and the bed, an arrangement he insisted on when we moved in together. He would sleep, his arms and legs hanging off the queen-sized mattress. No matter how hard I would protest, he'd refuse to take the bed.

I clicked the inflate button, waiting until the inner machine couldn't cram anymore air into the plastic rectangle. Leaving the hallway light on for him, I got ready for bed and lay under the covers, my mind cluttered and racing. The hurried sounds of him brushing his teeth and washing his face came sooner than I thought. Everett turned off the lights. The bed shifted when he sat, his shoes falling from his feet with a muted thud.

He didn't stand or move to the air mattress. Instead, Everett slid under the covers—the same covers that I lay under—and whispered, "What's your schedule tomorrow?"

I counted to keep my breathing steady ... *one* ... *two* ...

"Scarlett, I won't ..."

My heart leapt in my throat, my pulse beating wildly.

"I know." But I didn't. Flexing my sweaty hands, I swallowed hard. He hadn't moved to the air mattress yet. He always moved. At least, before—I squeezed my eyes shut. *Before* was a year ago. My chest tightened, feeling both heavy and shallow.

"Talk to me—"

I shook my head.

"Hey, Scarlett. It's okay. Talk to me—"

"I can't," I blurted out. Frustrated, I bit my lip. He didn't need to know I hadn't changed. That nothing would ever change. "Nothing. I'm just confused."

"With what?" He was a foot and a half taller than me and at least twice as wide. When he moved, the mattress became a boat lost at sea.

My eyes adjusted to the darkness, allowing me to see the outline of his head. I exhaled slowly, pretending that fear was leaving my body instead of air. This was Everett. *He is safe ... he is safe ... he is safe.*

"Scarlett?"

I was safe but not yet ready for the talk he'd come for. Not tonight. Tomorrow was a procrastinator's paradise, a place I needed. I couldn't handle answers tonight. I could barely handle him next to me.

"Scarlett—"

"I have a deadline next week," I blurted out. "I'm not behind, but I'd like to stay on top of things."

"For yourself or someone else?" There was an underlining question. He had encouraged me to break out, stop my weekly op-ed article for the newspaper and resurrect the producer project, a piece on predatory producers taking advantage of female interns.

"Both, I guess." Another half-truth. Between Marjorie and the house, I'd barely been able to keep up with my one measly article.

I waited for him to press the issue, but his breathing slowed. He'd fallen asleep—on the bed. The same bed. We were sharing a bed. The thought repeated, pounding and echoing in my mind.

Everett shifted in the dark, still very much awake. "I didn't see any plans."

Before we moved in, he'd kept a detailed list of what he was capable of doing and what he'd have to hire out.

"They're around." Rubbing my fingers along the seam of the pillow, I confessed, "I put them away somewhere. It was kind of depressing, seeing everything that still needed to be done."

His hand found mine. "We should have been working on it together."

"Did you really take a leave of absence?"

"I never should have left."

Everett must have adjusted to the dark because his hand moved to my face. We'd always been familiar with each other, from the beginning. But the way he now reached for me, as if he were ... I couldn't think the word.

"It would have been stupid to pass up," I repeated the lie I'd told him the year before. To be fair, I thought he would never return. His contract was an easy out. He could have started over. Maybe that was still a possibility. I swallowed hard and whispered, "Good night."

With that, I turned over, out of reach. He leaned over and hooked an arm around my waist, dragging me back. My body went rigid, every muscle taut.

He curled around me. "I'm not giving up. Leaving London was easy. I'd do it again if it meant I get to hold you at night."

"Everett—"

"Don't." His voice caught, silencing me. "I love you. Let that thought play and replay in that head of yours. Spin it again and again. Just know that I'm going to be here." His arm tightened. "Right here."

I wanted to tease him or crack a joke. It was too much to be genuine. The hard fact still lay unsaid; we'd never been married, truly married. The connection between husband and wife had never happened. And then he'd taken the so-called work emergency when his own grandmother broke her hip.

He'd left when everything was falling apart. All thoughts ceased when he threaded his fingers through mine, his breath on my neck.

Everett surrounded me. "Scarlett, I'm here. I won't cross the line, but I'm here."

My heart slowed, matching his calmer, steady pace. He was going to break my heart. And I was going to let him.

❧ 10 ❧

EVERETT ASHLEY

FIFTEEN YEARS AGO

The classroom became cramped, Everett's head spinning from both the earlier doctor's visit and now, the conversation with Mr. Munoz. Everett felt Scarlett's gaze in every step back to his desk. Mr. Munoz had given him an unbelievable offer, graduate high school *and* have college credits, so long as Everett dragged Scarlett along. Suspicion consumed him. Trusting wasn't Everett's strong suit. It felt wrong, a betrayal of his only friend. Everett stifled a groan. It *was* wrong. He would be using her. The little voice in his head tried to soften the accusation, suggesting Everett was just *killing two birds with one stone* and *college credits were just an added bonus of helping Scarlett*. The voice sounded more like his father than himself.

Everett sank into the desk. *Killing two birds* was a phrase his father had repeated in the darkest moments of Everett's childhood. He gripped his pencil and felt it bend in his clenched fist. He tried to think of anything, any*one* else.

Mr. Munoz's plan had to be a sham, and Everett wouldn't touch it without more information. Why would an English teacher care so much about him or Scarlett? Everett was a brand-new kid and Scarlett was as visible as she allowed herself to be. There was more to Mr. Munoz's offer than Everett was told. There had to be.

Mr. Munoz erased the daily writing prompt from the dry-erase board. Everett scanned every inch of the teacher, searching for clues, trying—and failing—to read him.

"What, no projector today?" A kid behind Everett called out.

The class snickered, hushing instantly when Mr. Munoz turned around. "Scarlett, read for the people too busy to learn."

Her head snapped up, the words coming out in a measured cadence like a newswoman. "How do words influence culture?"

"Or history." Mr. Munoz added *history* underneath *culture*. "Spoken or written, how do words affect people? Countries?"

The students eyed each other, the teasing dissipating. Mr. Munoz was giving a new section a week before Winter Break. They'd barely finished a round of Greek and Roman mythology. Introducing new material meant Mr. Munoz would be expecting schoolwork done during the break. A quick scan around the classroom and not a single student protested—other than an eye-roll or an elbow jab. They had expected it. This was the path for the college-bound overachievers. Until a few weeks ago, high school graduation wasn't even a thought for Everett, and now with Mr. Munoz's prodding, college was a possibility. A tempting possibility.

"Don't all speak up at once." Mr. Munoz folded his arms and leaned his back against the dry-erase board. He appeared to be settling in. "Come on, what did we just talk about? How did mythology shape Greek and Roman culture?"

"The plagiarism or the gods?" The same kid behind Everett started up again.

Mr. Munoz shrugged. "We're all plagiarists in some degree or another. Give me something more."

"Culture can unite a country?" A brunette to the side of Scarlett spoke up, changing the statement into a question with an uncertain lilt.

"And?" Mr. Munoz urged her with a nod.

"Well, if you can't communicate, then you can't be united, I guess." The brunette's face fell. Scarlett whispered something to the brunette. She perked up and added, "Myths were like the religion, and if they couldn't share their religion, then they couldn't unite and be one, like one culture. So without the words, they couldn't communicate their beliefs."

Mr. Munoz turned his gaze toward Everett, holding it a moment.

"And you can't build roads without instructions, spoken or written. Those kinds of things unify a culture too." The brunette beamed, her eyes flickering between her teacher and Scarlett, as if it wasn't obvious enough.

"Thank you, Scarlett." Mr. Munoz didn't turn around and face either girl. He kept his gaze on Everett, appearing to drive a point home. Everett was at a complete loss. He wasn't used to being surprised by people. First Scarlett, now his teacher.

"Her name's Lisa." Scarlett had finally found her voice. "I would have said something different."

The brunette balked at her, her cheeks flushing.

"Perfect, I look forward to hearing it." Mr. Munoz turned his gaze from Everett to the class. "You can use a play. A sonnet. A story passed down verbally. Find an example of words that influenced a culture, modern or ancient. Because we're dealing with words spoken *and* written, both a presentation and a report will be done."

Hands shot up along with a growing chorus of teenage groans.

"You'll be working in pairs." Mr. Munoz tapped the front desk, startling the half-asleep swimmer. "Derek will be with Lisa, if he can stay awake long enough."

Everett froze, half eager and half terrified that Mr. Munoz would pair him with Scarlett. He felt her gaze, as if she knew what was about to happen, but kept his eyes straight ahead. He was drawn to her, and it frightened him. He knew his pedigree and the hurt that existed in his genes. Maybe that was why Mr. Munoz sought him out, knowing Everett would use Scarlett to better his own life. Everett was no different than his father. If he was being honest, there was another reason altogether for his fear. The pencil snapped in his fist, cutting off his thoughts.

"Everett and Scarlett. Jimmy and ..."

Everett's eyes shifted to Scarlett's, her face wiped clean of emotion and thought. She ducked her head and began writing in her notebook. Mr. Munoz droned on, announcing partners and then specifics of the project, but Everett heard nothing. Scarlett's blank look had taken center stage and refused to surrender. Paranoia started to seep in. What if she knew about Mr. Munoz's offer?

Students stood in a rush as Everett realized the bell had rung. He awkwardly stuffed his notebooks into his backpack, the cookie Scarlett had given him just before class still on the desk. Gently, he gathered the cookie and the crumbs into his hand, ignoring the growing warmth in his chest. He gave a nod to Mr. Munoz and left, following the drowsy swimmer struggling to walk outside.

"Not a fan?" Scarlett leaned on the railing, her chin perched on top of her folded arms. She mirrored a puppy waiting to play. The thought brought a smile to Everett. Her eyes flicked to the cookie. "Is that a yes?"

Everett broke off a piece and shoved it in his mouth. The chocolate chips were hard from the cold December day, but a homemade cookie, regardless of what kind, was his favorite. His grandmother had taken it to another level of late, making sure everything in the house was from scratch. Marjorie instinctively knew his memories of missed meals. Cooking was her way of making up for lost time. Everett wasn't supposed to know. Marjorie would mumble so low he could barely hear her, but Marjorie's devotion was loud and clear.

"They're good." He bit off another chunk and held out the remainder to Scarlett.

She smiled, cradling her stomach. "I already ate half a dozen when they were warm."

"When were they warm?" *You ditched again, didn't you?* was the real question.

Scarlett narrowed her eyes for half a second before returning to the vacant expression.

Everett held up his hands, one still holding the last of the cookie. "That came out wrong."

The facade lifted. Scarlett shoved her hands in her pocket pouch of her hoodie. "I didn't ditch this morning."

"Great."

She lifted an eyebrow, and his hands came down.

"I mean, it's fine if you did and fine if you didn't," Everett stammered like a nervous idiot. "Never mind."

Scarlett's lips quirked, revealing the glint in her eyes. "You're going to need to be a little better at speaking if we're doing a presentation."

"Or you can speak and I can just stand there."

"Like an ogre?" She looped an arm through his and stole the last of the cookie.

"I'm a talented ogre."

Scarlett laughed, the sound bright and warm. "That you are, Superman. That you are."

"Are you okay with it?" He didn't miss the slight catch in his voice. "The whole being partners with me?"

"What did Mr. Munoz say to you?"

Everett stiffened, and Scarlett withdrew her arm. He grabbed her hand, surprised at how cold she was. She kept her head down, her eyes on his hand. He should release her. He shouldn't have touched her—but he couldn't stop. He brought his other hand on top to warm hers.

"Are you going to answer me?" Scarlett whispered, still not looking up. "I know it's about me."

Everett flinched. She met his gaze. Sadness lined her eyes and mouth. And something else, something deep and dark lay just beneath the hurt. A surge of protectiveness made him want to scoop her up and run away, far from here and from anything that would bring her this much despair. Would she come if he asked?

Scarlett shifted as if to step back—clearing Everett's mind.

"He offered a deal, sort of." Everett released Scarlett's hand and shoved his hands in his pockets to keep the temptation at bay. "I didn't say yes, just so you know."

"You must not have said no, either." Scarlett returned her hands to her hoodie's pouch. "It's Mr. Munoz. He's known for pretending to be a superhero too. What did he offer?"

Everett squinted at the sky; despite the clouds, the foggy day was still bright. In a way, the weather was like Scarlett, not even the gray of hurt could stop her from being Scarlett, alive and bright. "I stay in the class, despite being a senior, and take his classes at the junior college. I guess it'll count for both high school and college. I'd graduate. A freaking miracle at this rate."

"What else?" The words came soft, and had Everett not studied her for an hour every day, he would have believed they were devoid of emotion, but Scarlett was never numb. She was feeling personified, emotions all at once and all together.

"I take you with me."

"You what?" A nervous laugh escaped. She covered her mouth for a quick second before collecting herself. "You take me where?"

Everett shifted his weight. "He's, uh, worried about you, I guess. He wants you to be able to leave."

Scarlett's face drained of color. "He what?"

"Scarlett?" Everett cupped her elbow, steadying her.

"I can't."

"He said it would be an uphill battle. That your family—"

Scarlett stepped away, her eyes wide. "My family doesn't even want me in his class, but he's the only honors teacher for English. They have no choice. They're not going to let me do anything, not even remotely, that has to do with him."

"What—why?"

She cradled her forehead, the other hand on her hip. "My family blames him for my cousin's breakdown. And other stuff."

"Do you?"

She shrugged. "They say she was always crazy, that people that smart have a glitch in their brain."

"I didn't tell him yes." Everett stepped toward her, shadowing her face.

"But you want to." Scarlett tilted her head to the side, understanding in her eyes. "You won't graduate without his help, will you?"

Everett scowled, recoiling. "Don't do it for me."

She rolled her eyes. "That's right, I forgot. Only Superman can be the hero, no one else can. Can't ever be the other way around, can it?"

"I didn't say that," he snapped back, immediately regretting the tone.

"Everett?" Scarlett kicked absently at the grass.

"I swear Scarlett, I didn't mean it like that."

She smiled sadly and whispered, "You can't save me, Superman."

SCARLETT ASHLEY

PRESENT DAY

The morning light bathed our bedroom, softening the image of Everett on the bed. It'd been an hour since I curled my hair and finished getting ready. There was nothing keeping me in the house, yet I stood in the hallway, staring at Everett's sleeping frame on the bed. The left part of his face, the scarred side, was down and his mouth open. His right leg and arm dangled over the bed, along with half the bedding. The man could sleep like the dead.

My stomach did a little flip. He'd slept on the bed, not on the air mattress. I tossed and turned all night, aware of him next to me. The only contact was his arm draped on my waist. At midnight, I placed his arm on the mattress—only to pull it back over me an hour later. I was just as confused and on the fence this morning as I was last night.

Back in high school, my mother once said Everett was like a police dog, only safe on a leash. Funnily enough, no one would ever be dumb enough to put a collar on him, let alone restrain him. I had hidden behind his intimidation. My family's tempers were silenced when Everett was around. He never complained. He would take it, misguided prejudices and misaligned opinions, all of it.

Checking the time, I silenced my phone and gave into one more moment of watching. Missy and I alternated Sundays when she was in town, even after I volunteered to do all the Sundays. Marjorie was an easy excuse to tell my parents I wasn't driving the hour to attend church with them. Everett would be wasted today and possibly tomorrow with jetlag. He probably wouldn't even know I'd left.

He wiped his face sleepily and flipped onto his back. The bedding twisted more. This was my favorite side. The scar was the reason he was sent to Tule, the finale of continued parental abuse, according to the assigned social worker. The puckered skin, now thin and only visible in between shavings, reminded me of two uncertain teenagers in need of each other.

With my laptop in tow, I slipped from the house and drove to Marjorie's care facility. I parked in the farthest stall from the front entrance, loving the feel of the sun on my face as I walked. It'd been foggy and cloudy for months but I'd felt somehow connected to Everett, assuming he was experiencing the same dreary weather in London.

A little girl in a blue gingham dress twirled in front of the entrance, the hem muddy. The automatic doors began closing only to hesitate and open again. The girl giggled and the doors tried again, only to stop once more.

"You never did that."

I jumped. My mother stood next to me. "You scared me."

"Apparently." She didn't look at me, her focus still on the young girl.

"What are you doing here?" It fell out before I could stop myself.

Mom arched an eyebrow, her gaze now on me. "Missy wasn't at church last week."

"She was here with Marjorie."

My mother waited a beat and then asked the question I knew was coming, "So you could have come to church with us?"

"Marjorie needs—"

"Has Missy." Her words had lost their normal vigor.

"Mom—"

"I didn't come to argue." She waved her hand in the air. The skin around her eyes tightened, aging her by a decade. Mom looked more like her father every day, a tall, skinny man with a severe frown. Even when he gave a rare laugh, he looked unhappy. Both her parents had died—her father a few years ago and her mother last April. "Is Everett here?"

"No, he's at church." The lie came easy.

Her eyes snapped to mine. "It's about time."

"You realize the irony of that statement, right?" When her brow furrowed, I added, "You aren't at church, Mom."

She rolled her eyes and repeated the little hand wave from earlier. "I go every Sunday."

"Not this Sunday."

"Don't be difficult." Mom straightened her back and looked around the parking lot.

"He's not here."

She began walking toward the entrance.

I didn't move. "What are you doing?"

"Visiting Marjorie."

"She isn't accepting visitors." Her doctor limited the amount of visitors, and I doubted my mother was on that short list. Marjorie's lucid moments were becoming less and less frequent. She seemed to save them for Everett. The doctor said it would be easier on all involved if the visits were kept to immediate family. I smirked, remembering Missy's gleam. She was right, my mother would die if she knew Everett was her son-in-law.

"Why is that funny?"

I wiped the smile off my face. "Sorry, I was remembering something Missy said."

"If I can't visit her, then at least I'll leave some flowers." Mom waited a moment, her profile to me, suggesting she was waiting for me to join her. The inner toddler in me kept my feet planted where they were. With Everett back, I suddenly felt bolder. Or maybe just more immature. "Scarlett Delfin, would you stop playing games?"

Her shrill voice ran up my spine. I obeyed before I could stop myself. Mom didn't go to the refrigerated flowers. Instead she held a teddy bear with *It's a Boy!* printed on its chest. She eyed my stomach and then pursed her lips.

"Pretty sure Marjorie won't need that one."

Mom dropped the bear like it'd burned her. She wiped her palm on her pants, something she would have chastised her children for. "You spend more time with your boyfriend's grandmother than you do your own family. The family that never abandoned—"

"What's going on, Mom?"

She arched her eyebrow. She was either irritated because I had interrupted her or because I was at the facility instead of church. Or both.

Ignoring me, Mom stood on the tips of her shoes, and in her teacher voice said, "Ah, there they are. Flowers are always in the back."

This was a woman who taught for years at the juvenile detention center and now ran all three facilities in the county. Nothing scared her, yet something was off and it frightened me. Following her, I slid between her and the glass case.

She frowned and motioned for me to move. "What are you doing?"

"That's a great question. Mind answering it?"

"I already told you."

"Right." I leaned back, keeping the case closed. "You drove down— on a Sunday of all days—to visit Marjorie, the grandmother of your sworn enemy."

"Don't be so dramatic, Scarlett. You're being—"

"Honest." With a shrug, I moved out of the way. "Must be big if you're driving all the way down here. Today, no less." I had to add the last bit. It was a cheap shot, but she had begged me to attend church with her every week. Every. Single. Week. Driving an hour one way to sit between David and my mother didn't make me want to be a better person. It made me want to disappear.

"Why does there have to always be some sort of hidden agenda? Some weird accusation?" Mom grabbed the nearest arrangement. The lift of her chin and the tightening around her eyes—she was definitely hiding something. Being with Everett had taught me a few things. He'd always had a fascination with reading people. "I've known Marjorie longer than you've been alive."

Folding my arms, I leaned against the counter and ignored the surprised look of the employee behind the register. "Does it have to do with you or Dad?"

Mom offered an apologetic smile to the employee. I'd embarrassed her, which meant my question was a little too close to home.

"Both?" I wasn't giving up. She'd come for a reason, and I'd rather get it over with.

Mom's lips went taut, pushing her smile closer to a sneer. She nodded to the employee after sliding her card in the register. "Thank you for your help."

With a quick scoop of my arm, I cradled the flowers to my elbow and walked out. Mom wasn't allowed in Marjorie's room which meant I'd be the deliverer. Whether my mother had figured that out yet, I didn't care. She was stalling, and I was running out of time. Marjorie would soon be wondering why I wasn't there. She became confused easily of late, and I didn't want her to feel abandoned. Not now, not ever.

"That was uncalled for, Scarlett."

"Are you going to tell me?" I should have apologized but I couldn't, not with Marjorie waiting.

Mom's eyes widened in shock. Her lips went taut, her gaze downcast. She began to pay far too much attention to her purse.

"Really, Mom. Whatever it is, just spill it."

"I thought he was at church." She adjusted her purse strap and motioned past me.

I glanced over my shoulders and caught Everett's profile. Unaware of an audience, he ran his hands down his tired face. He massaged his neck with one hand only to hurry and check his pockets, pulling out the fob from his rental car. Squinting, he looked through the entrance glass and clicked the fob a few times—I assumed he was checking to see if the car was locked. He slipped the keys back in the pocket and went back to massaging his neck. The dark circles under his eyes should've made him more menacing, but to me, it'd softened his typical scowl.

"He looks terrible." Mom cleared her throat—why, I didn't know. Reading her mind was becoming harder and harder to do.

Ignoring her, I went to him. Everett saw me within a few steps. It only took his signature smirk, and the pull was there. It wrapped around me and guided me to him. There should be awkwardness, a sort of reconnecting. It'd been *months* since we lived together. And yet, I closed my eyes and wrapped both arms around his chest—his arms around me. I breathed in the smell, the feeling of home. No matter how many times I wanted to disappear or how many times I'd given him more problems than solutions, he'd never pushed me away. Or rejected a hug. If it was all out of obligation, I didn't care. Not now.

Mom cleared her throat again. This time I knew why.

I pulled back. Everett hesitated before releasing me.

"Jennifer." He kept a hand on the small of my back. The simple touch steadied me.

"Everett." Mom pursed her lips, more frown than smile. "I wanted to bring Marjorie flowers."

Glancing down, I'd accidentally crushed the small bouquet in my impromptu hug with Everett. He broke out in a grin and said to me, not my mother, "That was nice of you."

"It really was her." I gave a little wave to my mom.

"I didn't know you had it in you," Everett said, genuine surprise in his voice. "I'm not sure they're allowing visitors."

"No—I mean, I know," Mom said a little too hastily.

"Just family." Everett's eyebrow was raised. He would know she was hiding something as well. "Is there something I can help you with?"

"Yes," Mom blurted out. She quickly covered her mouth and looked around.

My stomach dropped. She'd not come to give Marjorie flowers—a fact I already accused her of, but the truth tasted bitter. Everett had just returned, and for some reason I knew my mother would take full advantage of that. I didn't know how or why. I just knew she was always two steps ahead of me. Or rather, us.

"What can I do for you?" Everett was a wash of calm—and it shook me. He'd spent the better part of our lives hating her and my family. Yet he stood there, collected and kind.

Mom's eyes flitted about, not looking at him or me. She shifted her feet and nibbled her lip. Standing next to Everett, she appeared small. Almost fragile. And then I looked again. She *was* small—she'd lost weight. She wrapped both hands around her purse strap, and I realized she'd done it to keep from trembling. My mother was in trouble, and all I'd done was accuse her of the worst.

Her normal Sunday routine consisted of firing invitations—or thinly veiled commands—for me to join her for church, not standing in front of Everett. Or buying flowers for his grandmother.

Everett massaged his neck again and patiently asked, "Jennifer, something appears to be wrong. Bad enough that you'd accept help from me. It's easier to rip the Band Aid off."

Mom's brow furrowed in confusion. She gripped her purse straps tighter, her finger nails digging into her palms.

"He means spill it, Mom." The plastic wrap cradling the flowers crinkled again when I took a step toward her. "The sooner you say it, the faster he can help."

A phone beeped and all three of us searched our phones. Fishing her chirping phone from her purse, papers fell to the floor. Before I could grab them, Mom folded and slid them back in. I caught just a glimpse, my heart sinking. They looked like litigation paperwork—Mom and Dad were filing for bankruptcy again. Dad was an artistic genius but an absolute idiot with finances, not that my mother was a saint in that regard either.

"Sorry, I have to go." Mom fiddled with her phone before rushing toward the door. She held the phone to her ear, saying, "I'll call you when I'm on the road."

Everett turned to follow. I put a hand on his arm, freezing him in place. Only the slightest touch halted him.

"She's hiding something." There was a hint of suspicion in his voice and in the ticking of the vein on his neck.

"I'm fairly certain they're filing bankruptcy again."

Everett's gaze snapped to mine. "Again?"

"It won't be the last." This time it would be different—that's the story they'd tell themselves. They'd blamed my uncle the first time they filed, labeling him a criminal for screwing them over in some new *get-rich-quick* scheme. The second time was the president's fault; he was personally out to get every small businessman. They would cling to the lie like the drowning child to the lifesaver. Digging themselves out of their financial disaster would keep their tenuous marriage afloat until the next event.

"How many times have they—don't answer that." Everett wiped his face with his hands and sighed.

"You should go lay down."

Everett flinched. "I told Marjorie I was coming this morning."

"She was awake last night?" I shouldn't have asked.

He shrugged. "For a minute."

"Were her eyes open or closed?" She had a tendency to talk with her eyes half closed but then start snoring with both eyes wide open. It was becoming harder to tell when Marjorie was really there.

"I'm not completely sure. I kept the lights dim." The doubt in his voice squeezed my heart.

This wasn't what Everett needed to hear right now. His grandmother, the only guardian he really had, was slipping away down the hall. For nearly thirty years, I'd done nothing but exist and take from those surrounding me. Marjorie, Everett, and now my parents—every one needed something I couldn't provide.

12

EVERETT ASHLEY

FIFTEEN YEARS AGO

The Delfin family lived on the eastern border of Tule, just below the foothills of the Sequoia National Park. The small farming community had become cramped with many Los Angeles transplants snatching the cheap housing and relaxed lifestyle. The Delfins were no different, both parents just one generation from the big city life. Everett missed the anonymity of a city. Scars and broken homes were overlooked in big cities. But L.A. didn't have Scarlett. The power—the pull—she held on Everett was stronger than anything a city could provide. He opened her door, wondering how he'd come from avoiding his peers to seeking her out.

Fumbling with the keys, Everett turned on the car and made a U-turn in front of Scarlett's house. He ignored the temptation to look at her in the passenger seat, her legs folded. He hadn't a clue what she'd told her parents, but her mother hadn't given him a second glance when Scarlett rushed out the door saying, "It's for a school project."

Telling parents where he would or wouldn't be wasn't part of Everett's life. Avoiding home and parents was his talent, along with making sure the rent was paid and food was in the fridge. The amount of food in his grandmother's home had tripled since his arrival. Marjorie was bound and determined to undo his father's influence. It didn't matter. The end of each month sent his mind racing. The memories of frantically searching his father's pants and mattress for rent had yet to fade. Marjorie would blink tears back—as if she could see his memories. He'd shove the feelings down, not wanting to hurt her.

"You're scowling." Scarlett picked at her nails.

"You're not even looking at me."

She rolled her eyes. "I can feel you scowling."

"That's not a thing." In the rearview mirror, several kids came bursting into the street from what looked like her house. "How many siblings do you have?"

Scarlett hesitated. "Five."

"Are you being serious or are you kidding?" He couldn't look at her yet. He was still trying to not scowl but his brow kept furrowing up and his lips downturned.

"One older, four younger." She pulled the ends of her ponytail over her shoulder, inspecting the ends.

Not being at school somehow made Everett nervous. Their contact had been limited to the high school campus. He wondered if their fragile connection would be broken once she stepped into his grandmother's home. Relationships soured when entering an Ashley home—familial or friendly. The eager women his father had brought over and the daughters dragged along were nothing like Scarlett. Her motivations were veiled, the hurt in her past even more so. Unlike the other girls from his past, Scarlett wasn't asking or begging for attention, she was actively hiding.

"You want to talk about the weather next?" she asked, giving up on her hair and tossing it back over her shoulder. "What do you really want to know?"

Everett shook his head, eyebrows raised. "It was just a question, Scarlett."

"Tell that to your face."

"I'm not scowling!" Everett smacked the steering wheel and flinched.

Scarlett giggled, her face turned to the window. Her reflection showed a wide smile instead of fear. Maybe that was part of Everett's fascination. With a barely contained grin, she spun around, her eyes lit with mischief. "I couldn't help it."

"If you were going for *I'm sorry*, you're failing."

"I'm sorry?" She threw back her head and laughed. "Okay, I *am* sorry, but you have this perma-scowl thing that for some reason makes me, no—*begs* me to tease you."

"I don't—"

Scarlett leaned over and touched the furrow on his forehead. "That, right there."

With her one touch, the nerves disappeared. Everett settled in, a grin on his face and the oddly comfortable girl to his right.

"Do you have any sisters, brothers?" She tucked her hands inside the sleeves of her hoodie. "If you do have a sister, I have to see a picture. I'd kill to have your family's height."

"Nope, just me."

Scarlett closed her eyes for a brief second. "What I would give ..."

"I don't know." Everett shrugged, turning off the main road to the pebbled drive. Most farm homes were set deep into the farmer's land, an island among fields—or orchards, depending on the farm. "It might have been nice to have someone to talk to."

"Siblings aren't allies."

"Neither are parents." Hundreds of knocked down almond trees surrounded the road. The land sold a few years earlier to developers. Everett's grandparents sold most of the acreage when his grandfather fell ill with another round of intestinal cancer, giving Marjorie a tidy sum to live in comfort for years to come.

Scarlett nodded at the trees. "You're an Ashley."

"Uh, yeah." Everett slowed, the two-story house coming into view. In roughly five years, the city planned to turn the pebbled drive into a main artery for traffic—if Tule continued to grow at its current rate. Marjorie still claimed five acres of buffer, but the years of relative silence were ending.

"As in Ashley Almonds."

"The very same." It didn't mean much to Everett. That was long before his time. It was his father's legacy, son of a wealthy farmer, spoiled by a kind and honest man. He'd read the yellowed newspaper clippings Marjorie kept in the closet, tucked away in his father's child-hood room.

"Where'd they get the name Everett? Your parents, I mean." Scar-lett unbuckled her seat before Everett had stopped the car.

"Marjorie named me after her first child, a stillborn. My parents debated between Jack Daniels and Mistake."

Scarlett didn't respond. Her focus was on the two-story house complete with a wraparound porch. Despite Marjorie's age, she refused to let the house crumble and hired out what she couldn't accomplish on her own. Everett took in the house, trying to see it through a stranger's eyes. It'd always meant home to him, even when he was only passing through with his parents. But the crisp white paint and steel-blue accents gave more than a farmer's life feeling. It gave respect, safety. It was a home that had been cared for, a roof where babies were raised, even if not all of them made it to adulthood.

Several ancient oak trees shaded the front of the house with an enormous white Pyrenees dog yawning on the grass next to the porch steps. His tail, the size of a large cat, swished against the porch flooring.

"How could you ever leave?" Scarlett whispered, her fingers tracing the outlines of the house on the car window. She wrote *Letty*, the name his grandmother had given her. "How could you want to be anywhere else?"

"I don't."

In unison, they both left the car. The dog barked a greeting but didn't move toward them.

"What's his name?" Scarlett hitched her backpack on her shoulder.

"Not a clue. My grandma said he—or maybe it's a she—just showed up one day. He roams the farm and comes back once, sometimes twice a day." Everett had several sketches of him, or her. Everett wasn't curious enough to check. The furry thing could look awkward one minute and regal, almost terrifying the next. That Dog, as Marjorie called it, had a soft spot for the woman but for the most part, ignored Everett.

Scarlett stepped to the porch and kneeled a few feet from the dog, her hand outstretched. "Hey, big guy."

That Dog swatted his enormous tail and barked a loud, deep greeting. Scarlett's smile grew. She kept her position low but edged closer. Her new friend got up and met her half way, cementing their relationship with two sniffs of her face, followed by a lick from a ridiculously long tongue. Scarlett laughed, wrapping her arms around his neck. Everett wished he could capture the moment. The beauty in her eyes, the upturned tilt of her lip, and the dog eager to keep her near. Everett felt a pang of jealousy. He joined the new friends only to have the dog lay back down with a sigh.

"I like him." Scarlett brushed at the dog hair on her jeans, her grin light and innocent. The dog pawed at her leg, groaning until the paw landed on her ankle.

"You have an admirer."

She swatted Everett's elbow. "Yeah, well, there's a lot to admire."

"Is that a fact?" He'd not seen her this relaxed. Or this happy.

Scarlett held out her arms. "That's how long the list is."

"So sad." Everett held out his arms. Her sudden confidence emboldened him. "That's how long my list is."

"Ah, so sweet." She clasped her hands to her chest and batted her eyes. "I had no idea you had a list for me."

"For me. Not you."

"Yep." She wrapped an arm around his, beaming with mischief. "The list that *you* keep about *me*."

"I give."

Scarlett's face fell a little, as if she'd not wanted to win so easily. Everett wanted to rewind, hold her joy a little longer. Her furry friend sat up and sniffed at her.

"Let's go inside before you start adding to your list." Everett saw the glint reappear. He opened the door and watched her duck under his arm, the nerves reappearing. He was off his game, his ability to read the little quirks and tells of people. She was an ever-moving target. That, or he was the target and her aim was dead on.

Scarlett had taken the backpack off her shoulder but not yet let go. It hung suspended in her hands, her eyes on the canvas painting taking up the entirety of the living room wall, a recreation of a place that only existed in Everett's mind. In the center of the oil painting was this same house, but instead of orchards it stood in the center of a meadow island.

Everett blushed at his grandmother's pride. There wasn't a wall in the house that didn't display an Everett creation.

Scarlett turned to him, her hand reaching for his. "You did this?"

He scratched his neck and felt instantly small. He wanted to ask how she knew, but her hand dropped. She stepped to the bottom right corner where he'd etched his signature *EA*.

"So, the uh, office is behind the kitchen. I'll grab some water and meet you in there." He couldn't stand there and watch her look. Her appreciation felt almost intrusive, making him feel naked and vulnerable. Every piece framed in this house was painted here, where he was free. And safe.

He breathed in relief when he heard movement down the hall. It'd been several years since Marjorie had framed the large painting. Oil on canvas was supposed to have been an experiment. It was the first time Everett convalesced at her home after a fight with his dad, the first of many stitches. Hours after his father left, Marjorie disappeared "to town" as she liked to call the ten minute drive to Tule's main shopping center. She'd come back with bags of art supplies and moisture in her eyes. The shopping bags were warm and her face was stained with lines of dried tears. She'd sat in the car and cried.

Holding a cup with ice and water, Everett braced himself for Scarlett's questions about the painting, questions he wouldn't have answers for. He took a step inside his grandfather's old study. A brand-new computer sat on the desk, a desperate attempt from Marjorie to "stay modern" for her grandson. Scarlett's back was to him. She appeared to be holding something and completely entranced. Her backpack lay on the floor next to her shoes.

"I brought you some water."

Scarlett didn't move nor did she look up when Everett reached her. With shaking hands, she held out a sketch—of her. In the drawing, she was the girl that visited Everett in his sleep. Her hair loose and billowing around her shoulders, the hair tie on her delicate wrist, and her eyes wide, bright and unveiled. The slightly crooked smile. There, in that drawing, she was perfect.

A tear slid, almost hesitantly, down her cheek. Everett's heart dropped. He hadn't meant to hurt her.

"Scarlett, I'm sorry." He reached for the paper, but she didn't move. "I should have asked you if it was okay, I've just never actually done that before. Most people ask me to draw them, not the other way around. I just draw. I didn't mean anything by it—"

"It means something to me," she whispered.

"Scar—"

"This ..." Her lip trembled. "She's pretty."

Everett looked around, not understanding—then cursed himself for thinking that searching an otherwise empty office might help.

Scarlett stiffened and quickly wiped the one tear from her cheek. She feigned a smile, handing over the picture. "It's beautiful."

"You do know that it's you, right?" Everett didn't take the paper.

Scarlett's teetering smile faltered. "I gathered that."

"And it makes you sad?"

She blinked at the gathering moisture. Groaning, she pushed the paper to his chest. "I don't know why. I just saw it and stared at it. I—I mean, that girl in the picture isn't me. That girl looks so, so I don't know ..."

"So you?" He was completely lost.

Her eyes flicked back to the sketch still shoved against his chest. "Just not me. She looks beautiful and captivating and just *something*."

"Yeah, that's kind of how you are sometimes."

"What do you mean?" Her gaze snapped up.

Everett backed away. He wasn't the brightest kid in school, but he knew what that sounded like. "Not what I meant."

Scarlett rolled her eyes. "I wasn't accusing you of anything. I'm genuinely asking, what do you mean by *sometimes*?"

Everett tilted his head toward the sketch. "That's what you look like when it's just us. Or when you've let down the wall thing that you do."

She looked at the drawing again. "The wall thing?"

"You have this thing that shuts out emotion or thought." Everett shook his head. He sounded like an idiot. "I mean to other people.

Everyone has ticks or tells. But when you do this wall thing, you stop it all. Like you don't want anyone to read you."

Her mouth opened to an *O*.

"But when it's gone or when nobody's around, this is what you look like." Everett tugged at the collar on his hoodie. "At least, to me."

With a crooked grin tugged on her lips, Scarlett Delfin was back. "Like I said, you have a list."

13

SCARLETT ASHLEY
PRESENT DAY

After tossing and turning on the bed, I gave up. Everett's ability to fall asleep next to me gave me a twinge of envy. His mind didn't race with all the worries, nor did he seem to be bothered by the year separation.

Sliding out from under Everett's arm, I squinted at my phone's screen, the light too bright. Thankfully, it was five in the morning. I'd been staring at the dark ceiling for who knew how long.

For hours last night, Everett and I sat on opposite sides of Marjorie's bed, each holding one of her hands. She had drifted in and out for weeks, but whenever I'd video chat with Everett, her mind would wake and the banter would begin. But not last night.

Everett had focused on Marjorie's face with sheer determination, willing her to wake. I'd felt like an intruder, sitting there with him, a witness to her decline and his despair. He would work his jaw and blink rapidly, reality crashing down with all the venom grief could wield.

He'd said nothing to Missy when she arrived for her shift, giving only a brief nod and a grunt. The silence stayed through dinner. Only when we lay in bed did he reach out and pull me close, my heart still racing at the touch. It was impossible to sleep with Marjorie's death lurking around the corner, but now with Everett home, he'd added an entirely different level to the insomnia.

There was another unasked question, a second elephant that had tip toed into our half-finished house. With Marjorie passing away, Everett would have no reason to stay in Gainesfield, no root to keep him coming back. Marjorie had always been the glue that cemented us together—without her, was there any hope for us?

I locked the bathroom door, then unlocked it. And then locked it again. Every night I had to check and recheck the locks to the house, especially when Everett was in London. But with him in the house, I'd never broken the habit of locking the bathroom door. He was—technically—my husband. He'd never complained and always knocked, staying on the other side of the door. It was stupid and ridiculous, this weird fascination with feeling unsafe. I twisted the knob, unlocking it once more. My hands went sweaty. Risking a glance at the mirror, I froze. The look of terror, wide eyes and pale face, stared back at me. There was absolutely no threat of danger, but the girl in the reflection was running from the darkest of monsters.

With my thumb, I pressed the lock button again. I stepped away from the door, my back against the wall. I was nearly thirty years old—nothing had changed. Nothing would ever change. A tear fell down my cheek, adding insult to injury. There wasn't anything to cry about.

Frustrated, I refused to look at the mirror, even after taking a shower and getting dressed. My reflection had never done me any favors.

With Everett still asleep, his face taking on the haggard look of exhaustion, I silently slipped from the house and drove to Gaines-Print's downtown office, a three story, silver building surrounded by historical homes. Three times a week, my op-ed article was featured on the front page of the local newspaper—an old teacher had given me a killer reference.

The job provided the flexibility, allowing me to still care for Marjorie, but according to my family—and even David—it didn't count as a *real* job. And in a way, I secretly agreed. Everett was the only one who thought writing was an actual career, but as a lawyer, hours spent were billable whether it was research or an empty page.

Juggling folders and both my workbag and purse, I closed my car door with a swing of my hip. It wasn't two steps before my phone vibrated. Shuffling the paperwork, I rummaged through my purse finding nothing. The phone vibrated again, this time on my hip, where my workbag lay *under* my purse. It'd take more finagling to reach my phone than I dared.

The familiar quiver of panic—*Marjorie.* The care unit could be calling. I was listed as the primary contact.

My phone kept vibrating during the short walk to the entry doors and a relatively empty reception area. A quick nod to the receptionist and straight into the conference room I went. I couldn't risk talking, not with the phone ringing. Dumping my purse on the table, I found my phone and with trembling hands looked at the screen. No number showed. Not the care unit. They were careful to always use the same line. This was just another telemarketer.

I folded my arms to keep the shaking under control and sat back in the chair. My pulse raced, the rhythm jittery like I'd had fatal doses of caffeine. Slowly, I gathered my things back into my purse.

If I could trust my legs, I should walk to Will's office, the senior editor, but I had promised myself I'd quit meeting in the conference room. He preferred to meet in his stuffy office with his guests sitting in the awful bucket seat. The horrible furniture sucked me in with a vengeance, bringing my elbows and knees together in awkward angles, and reduced my already pitiful stature to nothing. Will would peer over the desk at me, and with a sigh, claim he was too busy for whatever meeting he had requested. Short for a man, only a few inches taller than me, he wore custom shoes, giving his pride more height than it should. Sympathy won out. The poor man wasn't always this way. He'd not cared about his stature until his wife's miscarriages and the subsequent fertility tests.

Windows lined the corner conference room, half showcasing downtown and the other half displaying the foyer and receptionist. Four rolling chairs and a thin, long table made up the sorry room, but with the recent merger, GainesPrint would finally get its overdue facelift. The journalists, or as my family called them, the *real employees,* seemed excited with the merger, hoping for a pay raise.

My phone vibrated again. Even with the sound muted by my purse, it still made me pause. Any moment it could be The Call. It was the real reason Everett had rushed home. And the reason he could very well leave.

I debated on looking, the caller could just be another solicitor or it could be the doctor. Any second Will could—with my luck—walk in and launch into his diatribe of *cell phones at work* etiquette. The awkward gait of his custom-heeled shoes echoed behind me. Whomever, or whatever, needed me could wait.

"Scarlett." Will skipped his usual monologue and silently took the seat closest to me, not at the head with the largest office chair affectionately nicknamed *The Throne*.

"Good morning?" Cracking my laptop open, I slid everything but the folders aside.

"So ..." He leaned back in the chair and folded his hands in his lap. He'd pursed his lips, never looking me in the eye.

"Something wrong?" I'd have to tread carefully, extracting both his mood and his decision on next week's columns. With Marjorie, I always tried to be a week ahead, allowing for a quick submission for a breaking story—but this was Gainesfield. Salacious stories were echoed from other cities.

He frowned, not with his dramatic scowl and drum of his fingers. No, he simply frowned. Gloomy. And sad.

I felt a twinge of worry. The last time I saw him in this state, his wife had miscarried two months shy of delivering. It wasn't their first time.

"How's Carol, Will?"

"Fine, fine." He gave a little wave; she wasn't the reason for his mood. "Listen. I, uh, need to talk to you."

"Oh." Payment. They were filing for bankruptcy. It had to be that. The merger was supposed to save them, but—

"It's not about your fee." He finally glanced up, and for the first time, looked almost childlike.

I'd never realized how petite his frame truly was; all the years sitting above me or in a larger chair had padded his stature, but here, close to me, I probably outweighed him by twenty pounds.

"It's actually good news. For you." Will gave a halfhearted smile. "The merger was a domino effect. Which is when a bigger fish comes and picks us up and then an even bigger fish takes both the bigger fish and us. So we're all one fish. If you understand the metaphor."

The return of his condescending explanations lightened the mood. The irony was not lost on me. For a man who made his living by words, he'd certainly never mastered their power or learned to wield them.

"Domino effect. Big fish. I think I got it."

"You might want to sit down, Scarlett."

"This doesn't sound like good news." I sat, not remembering when I'd stood. Twisting my hands, I kept them in my lap instead of folding my arms. Taking a defensive posture wouldn't help if I needed to negotiate whatever he was offering.

"With the merger, well *mergers*, some positions are now redundant, which means—"

"I know what redundant means, Will." It fell out before I could stop it.

"Right, right." His face didn't flush red in frustration, he sounded almost distracted. "Local journalists will stay, but everyone else will be cut loose or shipped to the New York headquarters."

"Oh ..."

Will and Carol Nations had spent a fortune trying to conceive and were now in adoption limbo with their two foster babies. Adoptions through private agencies were quick and relatively easy, but the Nations family was still paying off failed fertility bills. They found their children through the county's child services, starting as foster applicants. If they left to New York, they would lose their children. If they stayed, they would commit financial suicide.

"It's a promotion, I suppose." He wiped his face with both hands, lingering on his mouth. They fell back to his lap as he finally turned the chair and looked me in the eye. "They would like to offer you an inhouse position. No more lowly opinion pieces for you."

"Thank you but—"

Will arched an eyebrow. "I told them you'd say that."

"Technically, I haven't said anything. You cut me—"

"You'd be the senior editor of journalism, the entire division." Will leaned forward to make his point. "You would go from a columnist to just under the director."

There was only one person I knew in New York that had that kind of pull. I was a local girl that published a small column three times a week. What I wasn't, was a journalist. That ship sailed when my project imploded years earlier. I had zero credibility. But I knew who did.

Lincoln Davenport, son of my hometown's most senior detective. He was behind this, he had to be. I was in no way qualified to be the head honcho. Lincoln was the only one who was competitive enough to stretch this far out on a limb. He had misread me once again; a title and salary weren't enough temptation to be under his thumb. And yet, I needed him. Or rather, my new project needed him.

It was a gamble either way. The tipping point was an enormous man asleep at home whose grandmother was on the brink of death. "The answer is still no."

Will's mouth fell open, and I wished for the millionth time Everett could draw him. "You don't even know who bought us."

"Global Piers."

He held out his hand, emphasizing each word. "Global. Piers."

"Same company, even if you split the name."

Will waved away my sarcasm. "Listen to me, Scarlett."

He reached for my hand, an odd gesture for both of us. Every muscle in my body froze. This was Will, a longtime colleague. My heart pounded. My back went straight as a rod. There was nothing to fear. My throat went dry. This was ridiculous. I swallowed hard and focused on the worn table in front of me.

"Take the job." He hadn't noticed. His ignorance was oddly comforting. "There's nothing for you here."

His words sent me back. *There's nothing for you here.* There was Marjorie, that's why I'd stayed. Once upon a time, I believed I was a journalist. "I don't know, Will."

"You know, you could just write. Take the job and start working with publishing houses."

"I'm not a writer." There wasn't a creative bone in my body.

"Keep telling yourself that." He let go of my hand and stood. "My other columnists are worthless. They've always been. You've rewritten their stories every week for years now."

I tucked my chin, my hands wringing in my lap. Taking over a writer's article was the biggest faux pas in my industry, but I'd taken pity on the new columnists. My check had tripled, but so had the subscription income.

"Think about it." Will turned to leave.

"Do you want these?" I motioned to the proposals I'd brought for review.

He glanced over his shoulder. "No, we're flying reruns for now."

"Will?"

He kept his back to me, his profile showing.

"I'm here. If you need anything."

He nodded and without another word left, his custom heels clicking across the cheap linoleum floor.

❧ 14 ❧

EVERETT ASHLEY
FIFTEEN YEARS AGO

E verett was mesmerized by Scarlett's every move, even in the relatively demure room, his late grandfather's study. Captivated, Everett watched her, harboring the growing embarrassment. Scarlett kept her grin firmly in place. The simple expression unveiled her stunning features and effectively tucked Everett's heart in her back pocket. She gently laid the sketch he'd drawn of her on the *L* part of the well-worn desk, the center piece of the home office.

"This was a library, wasn't it?" She turned on her heels and scanned the floor-to-ceiling bookshelves, the opposite wall paneled with large windows and a cushioned bench along the bottom. Thin skylights cut into the vaulted ceilings added to the natural light in a room darkened by rich, walnut bookshelves, desk, and flooring. The light gray curtains —so light they looked almost white—and the matching area rug in the center of the office gave breath to an overly earthy room.

"Yeah, when my grandpa took the company back from my dad, he didn't want to drive to the processing plant in town." Everett fired up the computer and checked the modem.

The office had two separate lines, one for the home line and one for a dedicated office line. The office line was now permanently connected to the temperamental modem. Everett had covered it with towels when he logged on. The screeching of the modem connecting to the internet triggered a massive migraine, his head not yet healed.

"You don't find it ironic?" Scarlett ran a hand along one of the shelves. "The Ashley Almond family?"

"Almonds are ironic?" Everett waited. She was entirely too pleased with herself, and he'd yet to catch up.

"The wood." She twirled a finger in the air, indicating the room. "It's walnut. Stained darker than its natural color, but still, this is for sure walnut."

"How would you even know that?"

She turned her gaze back to the shelves. "In our old house, Dad redid the floors. We tore everything up and laid hardwood flooring." She paused, her eyes crinkling. "Beautiful hardwood floor. He combined different woods in the piano room, which actually became the office as well when my parents finally broke down and bought a computer."

"You miss it." Everett knew houses were more than four walls. His was a living breathing reminder that cloaked him with comfort the moment he stepped inside. Laughs and tears stained the walls. Emotions weren't easily forgotten.

Scarlett shrugged, the moment gone. "You're an only child."

"Is that a question or a statement?" He grabbed the folded chair from the corner, setting it next to his grandfather's rolling chair.

"You tell me."

"One and only kid from Richard and Cara Ashley." He clicked on the internet icon and nodded at his grandfather's chair. "Have a seat."

"Did both your parents grow up here?" Scarlett folded one leg under her as she sat.

Everett sat on the edge of the desktop facing her. "My mom's family moved to Tule when she was in high school. She was the new kid in town. Pretty. Blonde. Naturally, my dad had to have her. And here I am, the result of the senior's spring formal or dance thing. Whatever they called it."

He studied her, watching him. He should have shrugged off her question but he hadn't. The slight dilation of her pupils and drum of her fingers on the armrest meant she was digesting the information.

The social worker had done much the same thing. So had the therapist, but he felt none of those effects with Scarlett. His hands didn't
start sweating. His heart didn't pound nor did his head throb with
deafening—repetitive—thoughts. Thoughts that scared him. And kept
him up at night.

But there was nothing. Just the twitch of fingers yearning to sketch
the light sprinkle of freckles along her nose and below her eyes. When
she cocked her head to the side, they disappeared, the color faint
against her olive skin.

Scarlett raised her eyebrows. "I should tell you to stop staring."

"You don't want me to."

Scarlett balked and then rolled her eyes. "Where'd you get that
little bit of info? Wrong info, I might add."

"Your breathing slowed." Everett found himself smirking. He'd
never articulated the little details he noticed on people, but the blush
creeping up her neck was entirely too tempting. "The pulse on your
neck too. And your hands relax."

Scarlett's hands instinctively flexed under her awareness. "They do
not."

"Right."

The blush deepened. She leaned forward, her gaze intense. "Two
can play at this game."

"A staring contest?"

The modem behind him squawked; the internet connection was
complete.

"Oh, no you don't." She hopped to a stand and folded her arms.
"Give me one minute. Two, if you think you can last that long."

With Everett perched on the desktop, her head met Everett's chin.
The intensity of her stare was more adorable than powerful. Everett
swallowed hard. She was mere inches from him. Scarlett hadn't been
this close to him since the first day of school when she touched his
scar. An urge, a need he'd never felt before, burned in his chest. He
hooked an arm around her waist. His other hand cradled her neck. She
inhaled sharply but didn't pull away.

Her back stiffened.

"I-I-I'm scared," she whispered, her breath tickling his lips.

His heart sank. He wrapped her into his arms against his chest. He tucked her head under his and held her, his heart cracking. He'd scared her. Frustration bloomed to anger. He—an Ashley man—had scared her. The same blood that ran in his father's veins, pumped in his own.

She pulled back, mumbling an apology.

"For what?" Everett flinched when it came out as a bark. "I scared you."

Her head snapped up, confusion in her eyes. "What?"

"I wanted to kiss you. I scared you." He dropped his hands but couldn't retreat, the desk was behind him and she still stood in front of him.

"You didn't scare me." She bit her lip and looked down at her feet. "I just got scared, but you don't frighten me. Despite being ginormous and all."

"I didn't scare you?" He studied her, watching for signs of lying.

"It's hard to explain." Her voice caught. "But, no, you don't scare me."

Everett didn't know what to do. The brown-eyed girl with moisture welling in her blinking eyes tempted him.

"You make me feel safe." Her gaze flicked to his lips.

"I make you feel safe?"

"You're repeating everything I say." Scarlett grinned, wiping the sadness from her face.

"Because I'm lost."

She cocked her head to the side, the end of her ponytail following suit. "I am not scared of you."

"Just of kissing?"

"I'm not totally sure. And I have no idea why I told you I was scared, or really why I tell you anything. It just kind of comes out." She straightened. The realization on her face meant she'd not thought of those facts until that moment.

"Yeah, I know the feeling." Everett pulled on her hand, missing the warmth she brought. "I tell you crap I've never told anyone."

A blush touched her cheeks and she stepped closer, returning to the same place, inches from Everett. She framed his face with her soft, cold hands. He wrapped an arm around her waist. "So this doesn't scare you?"

She shook her head. A few loose strands of her hair fell.

The innocence in her eyes nearly undid him. He had been kissed by eager girls but this kiss, his first true kiss, would be initiated by him, not her. Scarlett would be different—Scarlett *was* different.

Everett lifted her chin with a finger and whispered, "I promise to keep you safe."

He kissed her nose. She inhaled sharply. He grinned and kissed her lips gently, a delicate whisper of a kiss. He wrapped a hand in her hair, his other arm on her waist tightening and bringing her closer.

"Well isn't that sweet." The sarcastic voice of his father, Richard, froze Everett to the spot.

Scarlett jumped back, a hand covering her mouth. She stifled a giggle before paling, losing all color when she looked past Everett to the doorway. She cleared her throat, the color back in an instant, and her facade slid carefully in place.

"Good morning ...?" Scarlett furrowed her brow, pretending to not know who the older version of Everett was.

"You're a plucky one, aren't you?" Richard taunted, his voice flooding Everett with conflicting emotions.

Everett closed his eyes for a brief second and wished like hell he had a way to shut down thoughts and feelings like Scarlett. She stepped forward and squeezed Everett's hand, the exchange hidden to his father. Everett's stomach filled with dread, his heart heavy. He couldn't squeeze her hand back. His throat went dry. Words failed him. He was afraid of no one. No one except his father.

"And you're Dick, right—oh, excuse me, Richard. You're Richard." Her voice caught.

Everett's mouth fell open and then snapped close. He'd not seen her this bold. She hadn't a clue who she was baiting. Richard inflicted pain at will, regardless of who it was.

"Claws and everything." Richard's tone was eerily similar to Everett's maturing voice.

Everett stood and faced his father who filled the door frame of the office. Richard had gained weight, and like most of the Ashley family, not an ounce of it was fat. He was a specimen of the male form, at least if Everett believed the descriptions of his father's many admirers.

Richard stared a bit too long at Scarlett's face. "Son, it's time to take out the trash. We need to talk."

"Too late, Everett. The trash is almost in the office," she said dryly, not missing a beat. Her hands trembled at her side. Her bravery was just another mask.

Richard smirked, to Everett's relief. "My, oh my, you're quick."

Everett hooked a finger in the belt loop of Scarlett's jeans. "Hey, will you give us a minute?"

"No." She didn't turn to him. Before Everett could rush her from the room, she said too loud, too forceful, "We need to work on our school project. Oh, but you know, your little daddy dearest can help us. I mean, we're studying Greek mythology." She pasted a snide smile on her lips. "I'm sure he knows the stories, especially the ones where the son kills the crappy father."

Richard threw back his head and laughed. "You've got a winner there, Everett."

"Please, Scarlett," Everett whispered. He lowered his voice even more and said, "This is me, keeping you safe."

She turned, her eyes bright with fury, her hands still trembling. "And this is me doing the same."

15

SCARLETT ASHLEY

PRESENT DAY

A slow nod to the GainesPrint's receptionist and I was back in my car. Will, in all his prickly tenderness, had still offered the job to me. He should have asked for my offered position instead of taking a lateral move, if he'd actually accept the transfer. Carol had quit her teaching position when the foster babies came. They'd dreamed of a family, and she hadn't wanted to miss a second of it. Her decision left Will as the sole source of income.

Driving home, Lincoln Davenport reappeared in my mind. He was the son of a Tule detective and believed he was the lone savior and social warrior of our time. We'd worked side by side on an investigative journalism branch of Global Piers when I was still in college. He knew of the producer project—and had never forgiven me for burying it. There was another rejection that I wondered if he'd ever forget as well. Not that he'd ever tell me. He prided himself on his social and political awareness.

There had to be a way to help Will. If Lincoln's character was still what he professed to be, maybe, just maybe he could help.

Exiting the freeway, I remembered the unknown number and with one hand, slid my phone out of my purse. Doubt had crept in. Marjorie's care unit had never called from a blocked number. A few blocks away from my neighborhood, I pulled into a grocery store parking lot. If for some reason the call had to do with Marjorie, I needed to brace myself. For once, Superman would be in need of me.

I parked and looked at my phone. Seventeen voicemails. *Seventeen.* I could have sworn I only heard the phone vibrate once, maybe twice at most.

My throat tightened. This could mean only one thing. Marjorie.

Holding my breath, I pressed the messages icon.

"Hey—" David's chipper voice came alive. I deleted it without listening and went ahead and deleted the other five voicemails he left before moving on.

"Scarlett ..." Dad hesitated. And then hung up.

The next three voicemails were just a half second of nothing before the call ended.

And then Will's secretary left a harried message about canceling the columnist positions indefinitely, followed by a series of *so sorry*'s. She must have just been told.

"Scarlett, I uh ..." Dad again. This time his voice wavered. "Mom said you still, uh, keep in contact with Everett ..."

Great. Dealing with my family's aversion to Everett would be a fantastic addition to an already heavy Monday.

"...can you, uh, ask him to call me?"

My father, Lucas Delfin, was asking for help. From Everett. My pulsed raced. He wasn't asking for Everett. He was asking for a lawyer. Mom had papers in her purse. They could just be asking for advice. The idea didn't sit well, but that was all I could handle at the moment.

The next message played before I could call my father.

"Why is your phone going straight to voicemail?" Mom wasn't accusing, there was a hint of panic in the tone, not anger. She must have called at the same time Dad was, or maybe my phone was glitching. "Just call me."

My mother's voicemail put me in an awkward position, placing me smack in the middle of my parents' continual tug-of-war. Both called, signaling crisis mode. The order in which parent I called back first could either trigger or dampen their tempers. The phone rang. Everett was calling, and for the millionth time, he unwittingly created a buffer between my parents and me.

"Hey, your phone's back on." After all this time, the timbre of his voice still brought a grin to my face.

"I didn't know it was off." I must've clicked the *Do Not Disturb* icon instead of vibrate.

The house was only a few blocks away, once built in the middle of nowhere as a dainty little cottage—only the uber wealthy would deem a nearly three-thousand-square-foot home a *cottage*. In the early 1900s anything around two thousand square feet was a mansion. Thankfully what history called scattered was now centrally located.

"I take it you heard from your parents."

"They called you?" A knot formed in my stomach. "I didn't know you'd given them your number."

"I didn't." His scowl was loud enough. I was fairly certain my parents could feel it up in Tule. "Maybe Missy or Marjorie gave it to them?"

"Oh." It hung in the air, the memory of the woman who bound us together. Her ability to feel what I felt and see the hidden childhood memories—the same moments my brain kept from me—made Marjorie more than a grandparent. She was a lifeline. Her crinkly smile and kind eyes were deceptively warm, covering the solid steel interior, an Ashley trait.

"I'm headed up there in a few." He didn't have to say it, but the invitation was clear. From the sound of his footsteps, he was in the renovated hallway by the bedroom. The old wood floors were damaged beyond repair. We had ripped them out—*we*, meaning Everett—and stored them for another project.

"I'm here." Pulling into the garage, I noticed the rental car was gone and the lawn freshly mowed. Everett was never idle. Even when sitting, his hands were busy sketching. Getting out of my car, I noticed the box was gone and his old coupe from high school wasn't dusty. Everett must have pushed it out to wash it. The knot in my stomach tightened. Everett sold his truck when he left for London, joking that as long as the coupe was in the garage, he'd be forever tied to the house. It was his way of saying, *I'm coming back.* As I circled the coupe, I saw a *For Sale* sign taped to the inside of the driver's window.

"What do you think?"

Surprised, I spun around, my heart in my throat. "Everett!"

He arched an eyebrow. "What?"

"You can't just sneak up on me like that."

"You're right, I should let you stand here and assume the worst." His eyes darkened. I didn't know if it was from the lack of sleep or the fate of his grandmother, but his mood was stormy. He ran his hands through his damp hair and narrowed his gaze. "Well, what is it?"

"Nothing." I started to sidle past him but with one step, he cut me off. "Move."

"I'm selling the coupe." Everett shrugged but his enormous frame in the tight space between the garage wall and the twenty-year-old car made him look ridiculous.

"Congratulations."

"It doesn't run." His nostrils flared. And he thought *I* was assuming the worst. "It hasn't run in years. If I sell it, what does it matter?"

"You're asking me?" Sighing, I rubbed my temples. "You're the one upset."

"You had the look, Scarlett." Everett threw both hands in his pockets and leaned forward, his scar pulsing with the vein on his neck. "You had it last night—"

"What's really going on?"

He pulled out the ring from his pocket and held it up, inches from my face. "You tell me."

I opened my mouth to explain but nothing came out. There wasn't a reason. I'd been too preoccupied with everything else, Marjorie for one.

"What do I have to do to make this real?" His voice wavered. "I meant what I said."

"I know." I reached for the ring but he retreated.

"Do you?" His face softened, his scar dimming back to almost nothing. "I'm serious, what do I have to do? I'm headed to talk with your parents. Shouldn't that count for something?"

"Oh—I never called them." Spinning around Everett, I fumbled to my car.

Everett was right behind me. "Hey, I'll drive."

"I'm looking for my phone, not my keys."

"You'll need both." The slight downturn in his voice put me on edge.

"Why?"

He made a face, hesitating—and in that moment, I didn't want to know. Not yet. I climbed over to the passenger seat and waited until we were on the road to look at him. His eyes flicked to the ring in the cup holder between us, piercing me with guilt.

"I'm sorry, Everett."

"I wasn't going to bring it up. I kept promising myself I wouldn't." He clucked his tongue to a hotheaded teenager passing us in a crappy little speedster. "I guess I just thought, which is dumb, I know, but I just thought if I proposed you'd get it. You'd know and we could start over. Especially with ...everything else going on."

"I'd get what?"

He shot me a look, the hurt etched in his eyes. "That I need you."

That I need you. The words settled on my shoulders. He'd said he cared for me over the years, not just with words but with the little things he insisted on doing, the house, the bank account ...the working side by side in the kitchen or in his office. His affection, I knew. It was just the depth, I was never quite certain. *I need you.*

The ring sat in the cup holder. He didn't need me; he had it backwards. I needed him. I had always needed him—even before I met him. His sudden appearance in high school was a balm to a wound I didn't know I had. He was the reason I left Tule. He'd paved the way. He had held my hand through it all, the way family would—the way family *should*. The way mine never had.

"Your silence doesn't give me much hope." Everett adjusted in the seat. His long legs and broad shoulders needed more room than my little sedan offered.

"I just don't know what to say."

"That's a bunch of crap." He kept his profile to me. "You have plenty to say. You just don't trust me enough to say it."

"You're in a mood." Turning away from him, I folded my arms.

"That's a start."

"Fine. Have it your way. I think you're wrong. You don't need me. You never did. You were the big bad, Everett. No one ever screwed with you. You weren't in need of help. You were never afraid. I was. I needed you. People were different when you were there and you know it. How did I get out of Tule? Oh, that would be with you. How did I get into college? Again, that was because of you. So how exactly do you need me?" My hands shook. I rubbed the bridge of my nose. "How did this even start? How did we go from talking about my parents to this?"

"It's not much of a stretch. Your parents called, which by the way, why do they bother living together? They have the most dysfunctional marr—"

"Really?" Swatting his shoulder, I asked again, "Really? *They* have the most dysf—"

"You know what I mean." He bit his bottom lip but the smile still came. "I talked to them both. Then called you. *Then* I saw the ring on the dresser. There, that's how I got from your parents to the ring. And no, you're wrong. I need you."

The edge had lifted with the argument, the tension melting away.

"I didn't mean to leave the ring." I hadn't thought about it because the fact remained, he'd barely returned. He'd left. That was the elephant I couldn't admit yet.

"Because you didn't think about it. At all." He rubbed his left eye with the palm of his hand. Jet lag was a beast. "It's not fair for me to show up and expect everything to change, I get that. But do me a favor and quit jumping to conclusions."

"I didn't—"

"What were you thinking when you saw the coupe?" He glanced over, eyebrow arched.

"Fine." I refolded my arms and felt like a toddler. "You said as long as your car was in the garage, you'd come back."

"I did not."

"Not in those exact words, but yes, you did."

"Am I on trial here?" He smirked. "Quit finding proof where there is none."

"Says the lawyer."

"Scarlett?" His voice dropped—as did my heart. "Answer me. Do you want to be my wife?"

"Always." It fell out before I could stop myself.

He reached for the ring and held it out. "Then promise me you'll never take it off."

Taking the ring, I cradled his hand in both of mine. He was promising forever when he'd left—his actions promised an end, not a beginning. "Are you sure, Everett—I mean, really, really sure that you want to do this?"

"You are all I ever wanted."

❧ 16 ❧

EVERETT ASHLEY
FIFTEEN YEARS AGO

"Y ou're looking good, son." Everett's father possessed whatever room he walked into, filling the space like water, seeping into every nook and cranny. Richard Ashley smirked and came farther into the office. Tapping the side of his face, he said, "Scar adds a bit of character."

"Not sure you know what *character* is," Scarlett snapped, shocking Everett. This wasn't the fragile girl he knew. The only evidence of fear was in her trembling hands at her side. "We're studying, if you must know."

Everett dropped his hand from the belt loop of Scarlett's jeans. Her mind could be set and her heels dug in but she didn't know the apathy Richard held. He didn't care who was hurt, so long as his wants were met.

"Studying, huh?" Richard ran a hand through his dark hair. "So, that's what they're calling it these days."

"No, jail is what they're calling it." Scarlett picked at her nails, pretending not to care. This was a whole different girl than the sometimes invisible teenager from school.

"Is that right?" Richard set his hands on his hips and rocked on his heels. "Then how come I'm here? And not in your little jail?"

"Funny, I was wondering the same thing." Scarlett sat in the chair and propped both knees against the armrest. A slight quiver in her voice was the only hint of unease. Her bravery appeared to be growing. Her sitting dwarfed her already tiny frame.

The sight of her, small and delicate, jolted Everett from his muted shock. "Where's Marjorie?"

Scarlett arched an eyebrow. She'd not heard Everett call his grand-mother by her first name. She'd also never met his father—someone Everett hid affection from at all costs.

"She's still downtown meeting with your social worker." Richard clucked his tongue. "She's been a naughty girl, that one."

"That's rich, coming from you," Scarlett murmured.

"Both judge and jury, now are you?" Richard took three long strides and sat on the cushioned bench under the windows. Everett felt a sense of pride in his father's uneven steps. At least Everett wasn't the only one still recovering from their fight. Richard's regal presence transformed the worn seat to a throne, his arms and legs outstretched. "She's the one disobeying the court order, not me."

"Visitation." Scarlett frowned. Her ease and comfort with this topic didn't feel right. "Your parental rights haven't been terminated yet."

Everett's stomach threatened mutiny. It twisted painfully, his mind dizzying. "Why is she in trouble?"

"Because she's refused your father's visits." Scarlett pivoted the chair toward his father.

"How do you know?" Everett hated the accusation he'd thrown at Scarlett, but he couldn't help it. She knew far too much.

"I've watched it," she said evenly. "Four times."

Richard shrugged. "Looks like I'm not the only rule breaker in the family."

"What do you get out of the deal?" Scarlett asked, her hands flexing in her lap. "People like you find an advantage in someone else's mistake."

Everett looked from his father to Scarlett, completely lost. She knew too much and was gambling more than she could afford. His father was not a man to bait.

Richard smiled, revealing straight, white teeth. He rubbed the scruff on his jaw, looking every inch the bad boy he was in high school. "Get that girl a muzzle, Everett, or a leash at the very least."

Everett reached for Scarlett's hand but she pulled away, asking, "Marjorie paid the fine, didn't she?"

"There wasn't a fine, Scarlett. Let's go." Everett tried again, placing a hand over hers.

She stood, effectively brushing him off. "Five grand or six?"

Richard ignored her, his focus on Everett. An amused smile appeared on his lips. "This one's as bad as that cat you had."

Scarlett stopped. Distracted, she turned around to Everett, her face softening. "You had a cat?"

"Yeah, whatever happened to that cat, Everett?" Richard bent a leg over the other at the knee. "Just kind of disappeared, didn't it?"

Scarlett tried to pivot back to his father. Everett's hand on her shoulder kept her from fully turning. The sound of the front door opening and closing echoed into the otherwise quiet house. The door reopened once more and the murmur of women speaking carried down the hall.

"Everett?" Marjorie called out, her tone shaky and unsure.

"We're in the office." Everett didn't need to shout. Even in elementary school, his rumbling voice was heard above his classmates.

Everett's dark haired social worker entered first, tugging on the end of her suit jacket, a few sizes too small. Her heels didn't add much height to her stocky frame. She offered Richard a nervous smile before finding Everett and Scarlett. Her eyes widened slightly at his friend.

Marjorie appeared a moment later, her posture more bent than it was this morning. She wrung her hands and shook her head. Beside her, the social worker gripped a folder to her chest, her purse balancing on the edge of her shoulder.

"Good morning, Mrs. Ashley," Scarlett said gently, warmth radiating from her. "It's good to see you."

"Oh, Letty?" Marjorie smiled, her eyes crinkling—her son forgotten for a moment. Everett was instantly more nervous. Marjorie had a knack for knowing exactly what had happened—down to the details, as if she witnessed everything. "That's right, the school project was today."

"Marjorie. Richard. Let's talk in the kitchen." The social worker spoke with a slight Mexican accent. Richard smirked—he'd found a weakness. Everett cringed, knowing his father could use any detail to manipulate a woman.

Scarlett stepped toward Marjorie, pulling a laugh from his father. He yawned loudly and started toward the door. Passing Scarlett, he gave her a playful nudge on her shoulder. "Have fun babysitting while the adults talk."

The social worker warned, "Mr. Ashley—"

"Lead the way." Richard held out a hand, winking at the woman who—in her own way—looked down her nose at him.

The woman waited for an annoyed Richard and a sighing Marjorie to leave before taking a step toward Scarlett. "It's good to see you."

"And you." Scarlett fidgeted under the woman's attention.

"How are you?"

Scarlett nodded instead of answering. Her accusations and questions against his father swirled in Everett's head. She'd conveniently thrown out facts about visitation and parental rights. Without a sound, she called to Everett, an intangible pull to her side. A surge of protectiveness brought him to her, his pinky hooking hers. Scarlett wrapped her hand around his small finger and squeezed.

"How are your parents?" The woman adjusted the folder in her arms, not because it was slipping, but because she seemed to need something to do with her hands.

"They're good," Everett answered for Scarlett, despite never really meeting them.

"It's been a long time, Scarlett. A long time." Regret filled the woman's face. "He's not here, if you're wondering. He's in Oklahoma with his sister."

"Who?" Everett said, noticing the slight flinch of the social worker.

"A foster kid." Scarlett dropped his hand, shoving both of hers in her back pockets, her head down. "My parents fostered kids for a while."

"Kids?" The woman's mouth fell open. She collected herself and asked, "They continued to foster—after everything?"

Scarlett's shoulders slumped. Everett didn't know if he should push his own social worker out of the room or curl Scarlett into his arms.

The woman lifted her chin. "If you ever need anything, anything at all—"

"I'm fine." Scarlett's facade slammed down, her tone flat.

"I'm sorry I couldn't—"

"I'm fine," Scarlett repeated. "Thank you, but I'm good."

The woman nodded and opened her mouth, only to close it again. She offered her hand. "It *is* good to see you."

Scarlett hesitated but stepped forward and shook her hand. "Thanks."

The social worker added, "I hope your foster siblings are good to you."

Scarlett swallowed hard, her face paling. "They're actually adopted now."

"Oh." The woman raised her eyebrows in surprise.

"Four of them. Two brothers and two sisters." Scarlett looked over her shoulder at Everett, her face unreadable.

"B-b-brothers?" The woman stammered. "They adopted *boys?*"

"Younger. Much younger." With a look of guilt, Scarlett's lips went taut and her back hunched further.

"Tell them congratulations, then." Worry lined the woman's forehead and framed her eyes and mouth. "And take care of yourself."

She nodded at both Everett and Scarlett before leaving the room, her heels echoing down the hall. Keeping her back to him, Scarlett sat behind the desk.

"You okay?" Everett mirrored his earlier stance on the desktop.

"I could ask you the same thing." She typed *Greek mythology* into the search engine.

"We're really going to pretend nothing happened?" He crossed his ankles.

She flicked at her thigh. "I said I was fine."

"I'm sorry." Everett kneeled in front of her, covering her hand.

She rolled her eyes. "Would you stop saying that?"

"Like you do what other people say."

That brought a smile to Scarlett's lips. "I'm the poster child for obedience."

"Yeah, right. You wouldn't leave my dad alone for anything." He shouldn't have brought it up. He should have focused on her pain, but Richard would never forget her taunts.

"Sorry, I know he's your dad. And to be honest, he's a little intimidating." She bit her trembling lip and gave a slight shake. "It's different when it's your own family. I should have respected that."

"Whoa, that's not what I was talking about." Everett didn't feel the normal tie to his father, an oddity according to the therapist he'd been forced to see. "He's dangerous, Scarlett."

She gave a one shoulder shrug, dismissing his warning. "Men typically are."

"I'm serious."

"So am I." Scarlett turned her head, her focus on the windows. "I haven't seen her in forever."

"I didn't know your siblings were adopted." *What happened* was what he wanted to ask, but her wariness kept the words in check.

"Most people don't." The conversation was closed. "And it doesn't matter how big and bad your dad is. I don't care."

"I gathered that." He heard her voice in his head. *I've watched it, four times.* She knew about visitation because she'd lived it with her siblings.

"Terminating parental rights is hard. A long, crappy process." She kept her profile to him. "Your grandmother has to obey the court or he'll win."

"It's all for show." He squeezed her hand. "He wants something."

"He could move you across the country, Everett." Scarlett faced him and snapped her fingers. "Just like that, you'd be gone."

"I'll be eighteen before he can do anything."

"You're missing the point."

"Three weeks, Scarlett." Everett held up three fingers.

She pushed his hand away. "I can count."

"I'm not going anywhere." When she didn't answer, he squeezed just above her knee.

She squirmed and laughed. "I heard you."

"Hey." Everett waited for her to look at him. "I meant what I said. I'll keep you safe, including your secrets."

"Oh my gosh. I said I'm fine." She gave a nervous laugh and motioned toward the computer. "We should probably do what I came for."

Everett leaned over and kissed her forehead. "Pretend all you want, Scarlett. You love that I'm not going anywhere."

Her cheeks flushed. "Whatever. You're the one with the list."

❦ 17 ❦

SCARLETT ASHLEY
PRESENT DAY

E verett scoffed and changed lanes. He'd guessed—accurately, as always—that I'd read into the selling of his beloved coupe. The blame, I still believed, lay with him. He'd told me, joke or not, that the coupe tied him to the house. But his voice, just a moment before, still echoed in my head. *You are all I ever wanted.*

The diamond ring, the perfect, beautiful ring that I never asked for and always coveted, was in the palm of my hand—much like the man in the driver seat. Why—*why*—did he want me? Not the trite answer a hero or the hopeless romantic would give. I needed to know the real reason. He was protective and loyal to a fault. He would take care of me and lie to my face if he thought it would keep me safe, unhurt. But the question, the deep divide that kept my heart just out of reach, had never been answered.

I opened my mouth to ask but snapped it shut. The last time I begged for the truth, he disappeared to London.

"Promise?" Everett's voice carried a measure of uncertainty. "Promise me you won't take it off."

Sliding the ring on my finger, I felt the weight of it all, what the ring meant and what the next few hours with my parents could bring with its sudden arrival. "You do realize we're driving to my parent's house, right?"

He smirked and I wished I could see the left side of his face. His scar, once a symbol of all that he'd come from, was the reason he appeared into my life. The puckered skin, now nearly invisible except to Everett, pricked the tenderness in my heart. It brought a warmth only Everett could give. He gave me safety, even when he seemed surly and unrestrained as a teenager. I should have been afraid of his enormous build and constant frustration, but the gentleness in his eyes belied it all. Sometimes I wondered if he'd never been scarred, would he have ever looked my way? If I hadn't been the first person that day in Tule, would he have taken the role of Superman?

Everett shot me a victorious grin. He knew exactly how my parents would react. David's warning rang in my head. *He isolates you from your family.*

"Not sure who they're going to be more pissed at, me for not telling them or you for not asking Dad's permission."

He shrugged. "You could always tell them you're married."

"Are you trying to kill them?"

"It's true." He smiled wide, his eyes sparkling with mischief.

"They're going to kill me. And you." Biting my lip, I failed at hiding a matching smile.

"Eh, that's nothing new." He reached for my hand, his thumb toying with the center diamond. His enormous hand enveloped mine. A twinge of delight shot up my arm. I caught the beginning of a blush in the side mirror and tucked my chin. Everett didn't need any ammunition. "Did you ever call them back?"

"Oh—" *Crap.* Pulling out my phone, I called the store, the car's Bluetooth picking up the call. No answer. Clicking on Dad's picture, I called his cell. It went straight to voicemail. Then Mom's cell. Again, straight to voicemail. Between me and my parents, no one could operate their phone today.

"Try the house."

"Why call me but then not answer?"

"Your dad sounded paranoid. He knows I'm coming, but he was

pretty wound up. He thought someone was listening in on his phone calls."

"What?" Staring at the phone, I should have been surprised, but Dad had begun to buy into a lot of theories that didn't make sense. "Why would anyone care?"

"Yeah, well, he always wanted to be James Bond."

I coughed, nearly choking on a laugh. Everett had never been more right. Dad would have killed to be smothered by beautiful women and conspiracies.

At the first Tule exit, Everett took the awkward curve toward the outskirts of town. We could have stayed on the freeway but he drove the same way to Tule every time. He turned onto the back road, slowing to a crawl as we inched by the old two-story house, the wrap-around porch still white and clean. My breath caught, like it had years ago, the first time I drove past his grandmother's house. Marjorie's old car was in the driveway waiting for Missy to drive it back down to Gainesfield.

Everett stopped the car, letting it idle while we both stared.

"I miss it." Swallowing the grief, I tightened my grip on his hand. "I miss it something fierce."

He squeezed back. "Me too."

Slowly, we faced the windshield and drove the rest of the way to my parents' house, his hand still in mine.

"Are you going to be okay?" Everett made the final turn into my parents' subdivision. They believed their home was on the upper rungs of middle class until starter houses popped up out of nowhere, much to the chagrin of my mother. "I mean, as much as I'd love to see your parents freak out, I want you to be okay."

"You never told me why they called."

"He said he needed help." Everett sighed like a man twice his age, the way he always did. "Figured if he was calling me, it must be an emergency."

"You didn't ask why?"

"Uh, no." He cleared his throat and parked the car. "I said I would talk to you before committing to anything."

"Oh."

"He said he was looking for a lawyer but wouldn't give any details beyond that." Everett pulled his hand from mine and turned off the car. He motioned to me and then back to him. "Us. Us being here does not mean we're agreeing to anything. In fact, we should agree to *not agree* to anything that goes on in that house."

Shifting in the seat, I felt the loss of his touch. "Why did we come then?"

"He said he needed help." Everett scratched his neck, clearly uncomfortable.

"Right." This was who he was, always saving the day.

He growled and unbuckled his seatbelt. "Oh, just say it already."

"Superman."

"Like you would do anything different." He shot me a glare, his eyes burning, but instead of igniting fear, it sparked something else altogether. He must have noticed because he stopped, a whisper of a smile on his lips. He leaned over, his hand cradling my jaw.

I covered his hand in mine and leaned into his touch. "I should have been afraid of you."

He arched an eyebrow. "Me?"

Smiling into his hand, I said, "Right, like you don't purposely intimidate people."

He placed his forehead against mine. "You intimidated me."

The low rumble of my father's motorcycle sent me back, shrinking from Everett's touch. For a moment, he didn't move, his eyes staring into mine with unanswered questions. He retreated after a weighted silence.

I grabbed his shoulder. "No, sorry. I don't know why I ..."

The garage door on the left opened and Dad pulled in, the rumbling of his motorcycle now almost deafening. Everett grabbed my hand and kissed my wrist, shivers dancing up my spine. He opened the door and unfolded his long legs with a grace I envied. Mom's garage door—on the right—opened, and her white SUV pulled into the driveway.

"Full court press, huh." Everett's brow furrowed as I climbed out of the car. "Is that even allowed?"

I playfully swatted his arm. "People miss work all the time."

"Not Jennifer Delfin."

Shrugging, I stepped forward. "Like you said, he needed help."

"She's a teacher not a lawyer." He took one step, equaling two of mine.

"Who owns half the business, which let's be honest, that's got to be what he's calling about." That would be the *only* reason Dad would call Everett. Or any attorney.

Standing on the sidewalk, I didn't know if I should wait at the front door or walk through the garage. Having Everett with me changed everything, even if they didn't know about the ring yet.

The slamming of a car door and then the murmur of a restrained argument made the decision for me. Tugging on Everett's sleeve, I led him to the front door. Mom and Dad must've seen us because both garage doors squawked to a close.

"This is oddly familiar." He smirked and chuckled like he had fifteen years ago, unrepentant and proud. "I'm driving you home and your parents are pissed. Some things never change."

"Oh, come on. You miss this." Elbowing his side, I was rewarded with his full smile. My breath caught. He was truly beautiful. Straight teeth. High cheekbones. Dark features. He was quite literally the romantic hero—tall, dark, and handsome. Well, aside from the permanent scowl.

"Yeah, no." He wrapped an arm around his side, pretending to be more wounded than he was. "Being a kid again? No thank you."

"Whatever. You got to see me every day." I tried elbowing him again.

He enveloped me into a hug, warming me to the core. "Yeah, and so I put a ring on it."

Gripping his shirt, I leaned into him, his arms tightening. I closed my eyes and wished for the millionth time we could run away.

"Say the word." Everett's chin was on the top of my head. "Say the word and we'll be gone."

"I didn't say anything."

"You say a lot, even with your mouth shut."

The murmur of my parents' argument grew, their distorted figures appearing behind the muted glass of the door. Sighing, I tried to pull away but Everett's arm held me fast.

"It's you and me, Scarlett."

"I know."

He relaxed his grip but kept a hand on the small of my back. "We don't agree to anything here."

Nodding, I said, "Got it."

The door swung open, revealing the panicked eyes of my father and the stone-cold stare of my mother.

"Scarlett." Mom swallowed what looked like her pride and added, "Everett."

"Come in, guys." Dad waved us forward, his eyes flicking to Everett's hand on my back. "Thanks for, uh, coming."

Dad puffed out his chest, his eyes narrowing. If Everett wasn't here, he'd pull me into a deep hug or guide me to the couch and put me on his lap. The worst was when I'd try to make excuses. He'd pout or ridicule until I'd give in.

Everett guided me forward, steadying me once more. Dad worked his jaw and sat on the couch in the living room. Mom closed the door and followed behind us. Mom and Dad had kept the same lowercase *n* shape with the furniture as they had when all six kids lived at home. The two couches made up the legs and the two recliners made up the bottom of the *n*. With Dad on the far couch, it left Everett and I to either sit separately in the recliners or sit together on the nearest couch—uncomfortably far for an emergency meeting.

Everett gave a subtle tug on my back, guiding me to the nearest couch. I bit back a grin. He wasn't going to play games. Dad sat the farthest from the one person who could help him.

Mom grumbled something indiscernible and sat on the recliner closest to us. She grabbed the clanking keys for her school on the lanyard around her neck as she sat. Leaning forward, she clasped her hands together. "I'm sure you've heard by now what's going on."

"Not a word." Glancing back at Everett, he mirrored my confusion.

Mom sat up. "The paper? The news? It's everywhere."

"We live in Gainesfield, Mom. Not Tule." My stomach began twisting. News. The paper.

Everett pulled out his phone, frowning at the screen.

"Your father ..." Mom crossed her legs and straightened her back. She was a fighter to the very end, and this was the posture she took when the odds were bleak. "...he is being accused of something—"

"I didn't do it." Dad sounded more like a toddler than a fifty-something-year-old man. He puffed out his chest in the same way his dad and brothers used to. We—when Dad and I were on the same team—would poke fun at their little professor personas. It tugged at my heart watching him now.

"I'm not a criminal attorney." Everett didn't look up from his phone. "Before you go into detail, be aware that my help is limited."

"Crimin—" I stopped myself with one look at Mom's pale face. "What is going on?"

"What I *can* say is you need a lawyer." Everett glanced up, his gaze drifting from Dad to Mom.

I reached for Everett's phone, but he moved it, giving me a subtle shake of the head.

He slipped the phone back in his pocket. "It's time for full disclosure."

Dad visibly bristled while Mom clenched her jaw. At Everett or Dad, I couldn't tell.

"Your father received a letter today," Mom started, sending a pointed look to her husband. "And apparently that letter was also sent to the paper and the news station."

"From the beginning." Everett rubbed his temple. His patience was being tested. If he detected a lie, my parents were on their own. No one could read people like Everett, a skill my parents were about to see firsthand. "And don't leave anything out."

Glaring at my dad, Mom ticked her head in our direction, motioning for Dad to take over. He shrugged and huffed.

Everett stood, dwarfing us further. "Listen, why don't you two put your heads together and let us know when you're ready to talk."

Dad's mouth fell open in shock. He came from a long line of Hispanic pride—and no one, *no one*, could tell him what to do or when to do it. He mirrored Everett and stood, folding his arms. "Excuse me?"

Maybe, and possibly only in Dad's version of reality, this looked like a good idea. He was at best, five-feet, five-inches tall but would lie and say five-eight. He was outmatched in both stance and knowledge. And worst of all, Lucas Delfin needed Everett. Not the other way around.

❧ 18 ❧

EVERETT ASHLEY
FIFTEEN YEARS AGO

Everett waited for the harried mother of four to cross the parking lot before easing into a space by the Delfin's jewelry store. The strip mall was relatively new by local standards. As far as Tule was concerned, anything younger than twenty was labeled *new* and anything older than fifty was *classic*. The term *old* was met with a firm *tsk* and a shake of the head.

Scarlett's phone line was busy the last two nights, and their school lunches were spent on campus, under the watchful gaze of her brother, Andy. Her demeanor had changed, and Everett couldn't get her alone to ask why. She wouldn't slip from her newly appointed chaperone at lunch or return a note passed just before class. They had made plans last week to go over their project today, and he prayed she remembered. Doubt snaked in. It wouldn't be the first time he was forgotten.

They'd not yet spoken of Everett's father at the house, other than her apology for tearing into him. A fearless Scarlett was an unusual sight, and if Everett were being honest, her recklessness shook sleep from him at night. His mother was once bold, vibrant even, before succumbing to the moody, selfish imp after years with Richard Ashley.

Everett tried to ignore the same harried mother wrestling her kids into her minivan, the shopping cart drifting back into the street.

Another woman, two teenage daughters at her side, grabbed the shopping cart and exchanged a nod with the tired, younger mother. Everett wondered if his own mother ever experienced a kindred moment. He'd forgotten the sound of her voice, the smell of her clothes. She'd been in and out of his life for years until one day, she never came back.

He swallowed the rising emotion, shoving it down before he could feel sad or something worse. Everett slipped behind a group of suit-clad men funneling into a sushi restaurant. Despite the faux bell towers and pseudo mission décor, the strip mall didn't have a Mexican or Spanish restaurant, only sushi and sandwiches. Tucked in the back far corner, sat the small jewelry store of Scarlett's family.

The artist in Everett hated the location. The lack of visibility and the shadows cast from the roof dimmed the front displays of the store. He hadn't realized he was staring until a female customer grinned with appreciation.

Everett cursed under his breath. People were either afraid of him or in awe. Except Scarlett. She'd been neither. He'd watched the same reaction from those surrounding his father. Men wanted to be Richard; women wanted to be with him.

A mechanical bell chimed as Everett opened the door. A woman gathered paperwork from the glass counter, her smile tentative. She continued talking to an older version of Scarlett's brother Andy—Mr. Delfin. Both had the same dark features and tendency to jut the chin. The woman's focus drifted to Everett before returning to Mr. Delfin, who hadn't acknowledged him yet.

The glass counters were arranged in a half-circle, allowing customers to browse with ease. The wall behind Mr. Delfin was littered with swords and movie memorabilia from *Lord of the Rings*. Everett stifled a scoff. Mr. Delfin was one of *those* people, the geeky people obsessed with weird fantasy movies. But then, Everett felt a wave of relief. He had worried about her hesitancy with her family. If her reluctance was only from embarrassment, Everett would gladly join them. He'd seen his fair share of other family issues.

At the arch of the circle, a man nodded and gestured with his hands. Everett heard Scarlett's voice and pretended to look at jewelry, realizing she was on the other side of the man. Everett felt the pull, the drowning of everything but Scarlett. Noises were muted and colors faded—except her. He took another step to the side and saw a wide smile and eyes lit with mischief. She was winning whatever game she'd decided to play.

Scarlett lowered her voice and then raised it a few words later, wrapping around Everett's mind like a snare. He snuck a quick glance to the man, now leaning over the glass counter. The man looked maybe twenty or possibly mid-twenties. He nodded along to what she was saying, offering a smile and laugh at all the appropriate places.

Everett felt the prick of jealousy. He'd never talked with an easy cadence, except with her. Scarlett slid a piece of paper across the counter to the man and then a pen next to it without breaking the conversation. The man signed without looking. Subtle—so soft Everett almost missed it—Scarlett's face flickered from confident to relieved and then back to a false confidence.

She offered her hand and again—so quick that Everett doubted he saw it at all—a flash of fear before a flirtatious grin and tilt of the head. Still beaming, the man tipped his head toward Mr. Delfin on his way out. The mechanical bell chimed, and Scarlett's stature dropped in an instant. The smile, the joy, all of it disappeared, her lips tight as she appeared to be watching the man leave from view.

"Tough crowd?" Everett whispered, edging closer.

Scarlett's lips parted but she said nothing. The momentary tightening of her mouth was the only indication she was surprised. He fought the rising defeat and silently cursed himself for showing up.

"I forgot ..." Scarlett mumbled the rest of the sentence, her fingers fumbling with a display cushion on the counter.

"It's okay, I tried to remind you—"

"We could always look it up at your house anyway." She'd cut him off, her attention now on her father.

"Look what up?" Everett kept his tone neutral.

Without turning from her father, Scarlett said, "The project. I forgot my notes at home."

Everett smiled, only to dip his head when she finally looked at him, an eyebrow arched. "I thought you meant you forgot about us working. Today. On the project, I mean."

Her lips quirked, revealing a genuine smile—the look she gave when he made a mess out of words.

Everett rolled his eyes. "Don't start."

"I didn't say a word."

He pulled his keys from his pocket, his mood brightened by the fact she'd not forgotten him. "We can stop by your house—"

"No." The facade slid back in place, and her focus shifted to her fingernails. "Let's just go."

"What happened—Scar?" Mr. Delfin scratched his head.

Everett tucked his chin, the left side of his face, the scarred side, was exposed to her father. He shouldn't be surprised that her father commented.

"Nothing, it's handled." There was a tremor in Scarlett's voice.

Everett's head snapped up, and with one look at Mr. Delfin, Everett realized his mistake. Her father wasn't referring to Everett's scar. The man hadn't even looked at him yet.

"He seemed more than handled when he left." Mr. Delfin drummed his fingers on the glass counter. "Did he give a deadline?"

Scarlett shook her head, her eyes flicking to Everett's with a silent plea to leave. "No, he was grateful for all you were doing to make it right."

"Yeah, I guess. He still misunderstood." Mr. Delfin frowned, drawing Everett's full attention. The man's face was youthful and his skin olive, although more like Andy's than Scarlett's. Her features were a tangled weave of both exotic and plain. Mr. Delfin's eyes were black, not just from color but from something Everett knew well, a dark past. The older man nodded at Everett, as if seeing him for the first time. "Have you been helped?"

Everett held out his hand like he'd watched his father do and tried to smile. Scarlett's words echoed in his head. *You're scowling.* Mr. Delfin didn't bother hiding his scrutiny.

"He's my research partner for English, Dad." Scarlett scribbled Everett's phone number on a piece of paper and left it on the counter. "Mom said she couldn't drop me off, so Everett offered to pick me up."

"So you're not staying?" Her father rubbed the beginnings of a goatee.

Everett waited for Scarlett to make fun of his blatant whimpering, but her face remained neutral.

"We could clear the work counter in the back. We'd just have to borrow the computer, move it to the back and of course the printer." She tilted her head as if thinking. "That would work. Oh, and the modem."

"I was teasing." Mr. Delfin gave a halfhearted chuckle, his eyes on Everett. The man wasn't teasing, and his gaze wasn't kind.

Scarlett tapped the counter. "If you get lonely, I have no problem taking over the back of the store. Maybe even the front."

"And making a disaster again." Mr. Delfin must not have noticed the dust blanketing every counter or the complete lack of organization in merchandise in the counters and on the walls. It was a smorgasbord of jewels, figurines, and random movie paraphernalia all crammed into the small rectangle of a jewelry store.

Scarlett nodded and walked around the half-circle, slipping through the narrow space between the front two counters. With her father's stocky frame, she would be the only one able to get through, leaving Everett to wonder how Mr. Delfin navigated his own store.

"Have fun, Scar," her father called.

Scarlett folded her arms in front of her, her walk slow and her shoulders hunched. "I should have warned you about my nickname."

"It's fine." Everett unlocked the passenger door and held it open for her. He wished he'd parked farther from the store, not trusting they weren't being watched. He wanted to wrap his arms around her. Seeing her wasn't enough, he needed the comfort of her touch.

"Liar." She peered up at him before sitting. "I saw your face when he said Scar."

"I wouldn't blame him if he'd meant my face. It's hard to miss." Shutting her door, he risked a glance and caught her father watching, leaning against one of the front counters. He wasn't smiling nor was he frowning, his face blank. Everett's stomach turned to stone, and he didn't quite know why.

19

SCARLETT ASHLEY
PRESENT DAY

Everett and Dad were standing, Mom and I were sitting, and no one appeared to be backing down. My loyalties were strained with guilt, my parents on one side, Everett on the other. What they didn't know was that Everett was technically and legally—although in name only—my husband. I felt the weight of the secret on my left hand. The ring present but unnoticed.

The guilt grew, multiplying in waves. They were my parents, my blood, and they should tip the scale, but Everett—I couldn't, I *wouldn't,* go against Everett. Years ago, Mom accused me of being brainwashed by him. And David added his concern the other night. The accusation had sent me reeling in high school but now, it stung for another reason all together. David believed Everett had all the marks of a psychopath, but I was the one who'd lied. I was the one hiding. Everett had done what he thought was right, protecting and caring for me, but what if it was all a lie? What if the threat I had always felt wasn't real—the question echoed in my mind like it had for roughly fifteen years.

Facing my parents, Everett held out his hand to me, his jaw set and hands flexed until his gaze settled on me. His eyes instantly softened. "We'll be back, Scarlett."

"Oh, sit down." Mom rolled her eyes. When no one moved, she huffed. "Scarlett, tell Everett to sit down. We can discuss this like adults."

The anger, the resentment, radiated from Everett. The temperature of the room tripled.

Giving a little wave to Dad, I asked, "Can we?"

The tension coming from Everett waned. I fought the temptation to glance up at him, knowing he must be smirking, the expression my mother hated most. Teaching juvenile delinquents did not endear her to sarcasm.

"Lucas, if there's a shred of intelligence left in that head of yours, get over here." Mom was smiling, barely. The thinly veiled anger had reached its peak.

Instead of tucking his tail between his legs, Dad puffed out his chest and sat in the recliner next to her. "I'm not the one trying to leave me high and dry."

"Neither am I." Everett's voice rumbled. To Dad's credit, he didn't flinch. Although I doubt he missed Everett's tone. "I just need to know the truth. All of it."

Dad met his gaze and waited, I assumed, for Everett to sit. Mom narrowed her sights on me. Like *I* was going to tell Everett to sit. That was not who we were. Mom and Dad dug at each other for the better part of their lives. That was their marriage. Not mine.

Then again, my marriage wasn't exactly real.

"Fine." Dad leaned back in the chair and picked at the bits of jewelry polish under his nails. "A kid came in—"

"Kid?" Everett pulled out his phone and opened the *Notes* app. "Under eighteen or over?"

"College age. Twenty-ish." Dad cleared his throat—in the same way he hated other people doing—and added, "He claimed his grandma died and left him a bunch of costume jewelry."

"Are you a licensed pawn shop?"

"No." All three of us answered, Dad the most emphatic of all.

Everett gave me a sidelong look. He would have questions for me later. "Are you in anyway considered a pawn shop?"

"No," Dad said in his *obviously* tone.

"You will be asked this very question by law enforcement, your attorney, and more importantly, *their* attorney." Everett typed something on his phone, making my dad visibly nervous. "Kid came in, and what happened?"

"I did what I always do."

Mom and I exchanged an annoyed look. Ironic, since a couple decades before, I would have skewered her for not showing him enough warmth.

"And what do you always do, Lucas?" With one name, Everett warned my father. The middle-aged man had been reduced from a Mr. Delfin to a Lucas because of his arrogance.

Dad bristled. And then I saw it, the brief flicker of panic. He wasn't trying to be difficult. He was scared. My stomach twisted tighter.

"He has them fill out a form." Scooting to the edge of the couch, closer to my parents, I offered, "They fill out a form declaring the jewelry not stolen, and Dad makes a copy of their driver's license."

Everett shot me a scowl. He wanted to hear it from Dad, not me. He turned back to him. "And you did this?"

"Yeah, I set aside the costume jewelry, because I can't get anything from that."

"Meaning?" Everett arched an eyebrow when Dad sighed.

"He can't melt it down and make something new." Ignoring the glare from both Mom and Everett, I folded my hands in my lap. "The form explains the value of recycled gold and that the store isn't a pawn shop and won't resell the jewelry."

"You'd think it'd be simple like that, wouldn't it?" Mom lifted her chin and sniffed. "Funny how we aren't a pawn shop, but it certainly looks that way, doesn't it?"

"I'm not a filthy pawn shop, Jennifer. You're not there, you don't know—"

Everett cut off my dad with a wave of his hand and turned to Mom. "How does the store act like a pawn shop?"

"He stopped melting jewelry when Scarlett left. He rarely does custom work or really anything that resembles work." Mom pulled the lanyard from off her neck and wrapped the nylon around the attached bundle of keys. "Bottom line is this. A kid sold stolen jewelry to Lucas. He knew it was a killer price, for the real stuff, not the costume crap. Lucas knew something was off but did it anyway to make a quick buck. He didn't melt it down, he didn't even polish the wedding ring set, but dipped it in the ultrasonic machine for a half-assed cleaning job before putting it out in the case. How is that not a pawn shop?"

"They didn't even check for the wedding set. They're looking for the sapphire." Dad threw his hands in the air, as if Mom was the unreasonable one.

"They?" I asked, my voice quiet. "Stolen?"

Mom and Dad turned their focus from each other to me, both appearing surprised that I was still there.

"Supposedly," my dad answered just as softly.

"That kid confessed," Everett added dryly.

"Confessed?" Gripping the edge of the couch, I felt reality crashing down. "You can't confess unless there's been an investigation. You've known. For a while. Why ask for help now?"

"I didn't want to worry you." Dad leaned forward, elbows on his knees.

"Didn't want to worry or didn't want to tarnish your Daddy Dearest image?" Mom inhaled slightly, realizing how it sounded. She looked to Everett. "They're close, Scarlett and Lucas. That's all I meant."

A long time ago, yes, but not in forever, I almost added.

"I need the play by play." Everett sat next to me, too close by the tense smile my mother wore. "The kid came in, sold the jewelry, and filled out the form. Then what?"

"I tore apart some of the pieces—"

"One." Mom held up a finger.

"Tore apart one, and?" Everett gave a nod to Mom.

"Fine." Dad folded his arms and frowned. The store had been his domain, the one area he held court, and Mom didn't intrude. The back of the store was very much a hoarder's paradise, and at the moment, Dad could've easily been the star of a hoarder's reality show, with his panicked guilt and sidelong glances. "I cleaned the wedding set and a couple necklaces. They went in the center cases. Then a while ago, some detectives came in with a stack of pictures. I didn't recognize the pieces until I was halfway through the stack."

"What did they say?" Everett was typing again on his phone. "The detectives."

"They were looking for some stolen jewelry. It's not uncommon for detectives to come in."

"To a jewelry store, yes it is. For a pawn shop, no it's not uncommon at all." Mom sighed to herself. "He has a reputation for buying jewelry."

"That's not true." Dad growled. He actually growled, but instead of inciting fear or respect when Everett did it, the expression made Dad's stature shrink. The recliner seemed to swallow him, or maybe it was his pride that evaporated. Either way, he appeared more like a frightened dog than a criminal.

Everett held up his phone. The store front said in gold letters, *We Buy Gold*. "If that doesn't announce your pawn shop status, I don't know what does."

"People aren't borrowing against their jewelry. I'm not holding it for them." Dad scoffed. "You're a lawyer, you should know this."

Dad's tone was arrogant, his hand motions over the top, but his eyes belied his worry, his desperation.

"Does it state anywhere on the form that the seller can buy back their jewelry?" Everett flipped the phone back around and began typing again. "I'll take your silence as a yes."

"That doesn't make me a pawn shop."

"Tell that to a judge." Mom shifted so that her back was toward Dad. "Show them the letter."

Scowling again, Dad stood and fished out a letter from his cargo pants. This was a man who peddled high-dollar jewelry but dressed himself and decorated the store closer to the socioeconomic clientele of a back-alley discount store. Being an *artist* or *creative genius* was his favorite defense whenever I, or Mom, tried to explain why the sales no longer came.

"Here." Dad handed the letter to Everett. "It says they're going to charge me with larceny."

"And conspiracy to commit grand larceny." Everett wiped his face and stood, the letter still in his hand. "They sent you a letter instead of arresting you. That's a first."

"Do I need a lawyer?" Dad asked.

"You can hire one or have one appointed." Everett offered the letter back to my father. "Either way, you need to get ahead of this."

"That's it?" Mom balked. "That's all the advice you have?"

"Mom—"

"I have given *no* advice." Everett folded his arms and braced himself in front of them. "But I can tell you what I would do if this letter found its way to my firm." He wiped his face with both hands. "First, I'd get a lawyer, and I'd make sure it was a damn good one. I would not discount my chances of prison for anything. Second, write everything down but do not put names on it. There will be a warrant signed—"

"They already came to the store."

"What?" Everett's hands dropped, along with his mouth. "They already issued a warrant? That's a detail I should have already been told."

Dad rolled his eyes. "I can't read your mind."

Mom gripped the armrest of the recliner and said slowly, "They confiscated the jewelry, but Lucas was there earlier that day and—"

"Jennifer," Dad snapped.

"You hid something." Everett rubbed both his temples, his patience long dead. "You are an idiot."

Seething, Mom rushed to a stand. "How dare—"

Jumping to her side, I reached for her, trying to put an arm around her shoulders.

She waved me away but then gasped. Mom snatched my hand, the ring sparkling, front and center. "What is *this*?"

20

EVERETT ASHLEY

FIFTEEN YEARS AGO

Everett stared at Scarlett, her face drawn as she sat on the bench in his late grandfather's home office. The computer was complaining but still working. The printed paper in Everett's hand bothered him almost as much as the girl staring blankly out the window. She'd been quiet and *off* since he'd picked her up from her father's store.

He reread the paper arguing the feminist's perspective on the mythical Medusa. He'd hoped the answer to Scarlett's mood could be found in the black and white words. Scarlett had printed the article but waited on the bench instead of at the desk. The soft light coming in from the window gave an otherworldly quality to her face. The temptation to draw her doused by the pain in her features.

"Okay, I'm lost." He came to her, hoping she'd look at him. "Why Medusa?"

"We don't have to do Medusa." She traced something on the window. Everett assumed it was a tree or possibly the big white dog returning. Shrugging, she said in a haunted voice, "We can do whatever myth you want."

"I wasn't arguing, just wondering why her."

Scarlett closed her eyes, her palm against the window. "I'm going to winter formal with David."

Everett focused on breathing, his blood pulsing. He clenched his teeth to keep the growing anger at bay. They—whatever *they* were—was never truly defined, but he'd thought his claim, his interest, obvious. They were connected—an intense, unexplainable bond. At least, he thought they were.

He balled his fists, the paper falling to the wood floor. Scarlett flinched. Everett froze. She couldn't have heard the paper hit the floor, the sound too soft. Nor could she hear the screaming in his head. Yet she flinched all the same.

Scarlett squeezed her eyes, shutting them even tighter. "I don't want to go."

Her plea melted Everett's frustration. He sat beside her and forced his hands to relax from their clenched position. "What can I do?"

She shook her head but didn't open her eyes. "He made a big deal, had flower petals in the front yard and in my bedroom. Mom saw it and said I have to say yes. That she raised me to be a good girl. She stood there until I called and told him I'd go."

Everett had to strain to hear the words, her voice barely above a whisper.

"She said I was rude. Ungrateful. But she doesn't know ..." Scarlett turned to him, her eyes hollow. "I shouldn't feel this way, but I do. I can't do it. I can't go with him. I don't even have any proof."

Everett felt a pit in the middle of his stomach. He'd interrupted his father one too many times to be naïve. Against his judgement, he asked, "Proof of what?"

She folded her arms over her knees and stared straight ahead. "Nothing."

"Why not go with me?" He already knew the answer.

"You didn't ask."

"I didn't know." It was the only excuse he had. Everett never paid attention to dances or parties.

"And even if you did, there's no way she'd let me back out now." Her arms tightened, drawing her knees tighter. "I don't like to be alone with boys."

Everett straightened. He was very much a boy. And they were very much alone. He cleared his throat and offered weakly, "Can I go with you? Find a date and go double or something"

"You want to?" Her head snapped up, her cheeks flushing. "I mean, you'd go on a date with someone else?"

He held out his hands in surrender. "I'm trying to comfort you and not kill David. If that means I have to find someone to double with, I will."

"You'd come?" Hope filled her chocolate eyes. "You'd be there?"

"I can't promise that I'll be nice to him." Everett was rewarded with a half-smile. "I swear, if he touches you—"

Her eyes widened, and her head pivoted back, staring ahead again. "He'll touch me."

"What?" Everett didn't fight the growl this time. "What do you mean by that?"

"He thinks it's funny to corner me at the house." She swallowed hard. "He doesn't go too far, just kisses and sometimes ...touches. My mom likes having the preacher's son around."

"What's too far? Too far for him, or too far for you?" Everett was standing now, his voice echoing back to him. With a hand on his fore-head, Everett paced. "It's a game, Scarlett. Like a cat and its toy. First, people like him push the kissing, then it's another boundary."

"Until they're bored."

"Scarlett, look at me." He stood in front of her, a tremor of panic in his heart. "They don't always get bored. Sometimes they get tired of waiting and decide to take what they want."

She didn't move, nor did she meet his gaze. "I know."

"You can't go with him."

"I can't *not* go."

Everett kneeled before her, angling his head so she had to look at him. "Tell your mom. Tell someone. *Please*."

"She knows." Scarlett scooted back on the bench, avoiding him.

"Don't, don't, don't shut me out." He followed her. "You don't understand, Scarlett. If he's alone with you—"

"My brother will be there."

Dread filled the air. Everett didn't trust the brother any more than he trusted David, and Everett wasn't stupid enough to ignore the fact that he'd started a turf war. Everett had laid his arm around Scarlett. "It's my fault."

Her eyes flicked to his, confusion written in the furrowed brow and open eyes. "How is this your fault?"

"It's a pissing contest. I thought I was helping by intimidating David at school. He's trying to one-up me." Doubt crept in when he said it out loud.

"David's been a problem long before you showed up." Her lips quirked, and the beginnings of a smile formed. "But thanks for trying to take one for the team."

"Don't go." Everett sat next to her, his hand on top of hers. "I've seen what happens to women who ..." He searched for the words. "Something happens inside them, something breaks."

She threaded her arm through his, laying her head on his shoulder. They stayed like that, the humming of both their pulses in sync.

After a pregnant pause, she said, "Did you know that Medusa was pretty once? Some stories say she was powerful as well."

Everett tried not to scowl. He hated that she was changing the subject. "Your scholar said as much."

"But then Athena, a goddess, another woman, someone who should've been in her corner, punished her." Her hand gripped his bicep. "Poseidon desecrated Medusa in Athena's temple. And so Athena punished her, like it was Medusa's fault." Scarlett winced at Athena.

The hair on Everett's neck stood on end. He had a distinct feeling that Athena could have been a version of Scarlett's mother. "What happened next?"

"She became angry. And hated."

Everett covered Scarlett's hand on his arm. He didn't know if David was Poseidon in her story, but Everett knew enough to not ask. As long as Scarlett risked speaking, he would listen.

"Her death was celebrated. Her killer—Perseus—became a hero. Her children from the rape helped Perseus—befriended him. Loved him. How is that fair?"

Everett squeezed her hand. "It's not."

"She's never restored. Everything is taken. And she goes down in history as a monster." Scarlett's voice cracked, swallowing the last of *monster*.

"I'll be there," Everett promised. "I'm not sure how I'm going to do it, but I'll be there."

She nodded and he gently guided her back to the desk. The room was heavy, despair and worry in the air.

With sheer determination, they spent the next four hours searching the internet, an unspoken agreement to switch from Medusa to Persephone or Artemis. It wasn't until Everett stood on her dimly-lit doorstep, that uneasiness crept in between them again.

"It's going to be okay." It was all he could think of.

"Mom said she can either whip up a dress or take me shopping on Monday." She shoved her hands in her back pockets and swayed.

"An earthy color." Everett pretended to tuck a strand of hair behind her ear. "Forest green or plum would complement your skin and eyes. Bring out the red in your hair."

Scarlett bit back a grin. "That was kind of unexpected."

"I try." He'd surprised himself by saying it.

"Might as well look good if I'm going to feel bad?" She tried to laugh but it fell flat.

Headlights turned down the street. The car slowed and pulled into the Delfin's driveway. Everett felt, more than saw, Scarlett stiffen. Her brother and David spilled out of the car, laughing and teasing each other. They quieted as they neared Scarlett and Everett, David wearing a smirk.

"Did you hear the news, Ashley?" David sidled up to Scarlett, lifting an arm over her shoulder. "Scarlett and I have a date."

"You stink." She stepped closer to Everett, her hand raking his side. He sandwiched hers in both of his.

"It's the smell of a man." David elbowed her brother.

"Basketball," Andy explained looking suddenly self-conscious. He looked at their clasped hands and for a brief moment looked ashamed. "You should play some time."

David pivoted, almost smashing into Andy. "What did you say?"

Andy shrugged. "He's twice our height."

"I don't play basketball." Everett's voice rumbled and he worried if her family could hear him.

"Of course you don't." David rolled his eyes, or at least appeared to. In the darkening sky, it was hard to see.

"I box and fight." Everett didn't mind the silence following his confession, except from Scarlett. Her face was shadowed by his body.

"By yourself?" Andy asked.

Everett wished he could see more of his face and gauge his sincerity or figure out the sudden diplomacy. "Yes and no. I have a punching bag and other gear."

"Your parents are okay with that?" Andy folded his arms, a hand on his jaw. "How'd you pull that off?"

David grunted. "Let's go, I'm hungry."

Andy followed David into the house but not before giving a nod to Everett.

"I think my brother has a man crush on you," Scarlett deadpanned. "Not sure why though."

"Maybe he'll go to the dance with me."

"Unless you go blond, I doubt that." She snickered. "Maybe that's why he loves David so much."

"We could switch. I take you, Andy takes David."

The front door swung open.

"Scarlett Rose Delfin, what are you doing?" Mrs. Delfin appeared with a flood of light from inside.

Scarlett spun around to face her mother. "I was coming inside."

"You say yes to David and then stand out here with another boy? Why? To play games with the preacher's son?" Mrs. Delfin pursed her lips and offered a polite hand to Everett. "I'm so sorry to bring you into this. I'm sure you're a nice boy, but my daughter needs to learn some manners. We do not encourage this type of behavior. She was taught better."

Scarlett tucked her head and slipped past her mother. Behind Mrs. Delfin, Everett caught David's victorious grin at the dinner table at the far end of the living room. Next to him sat Andy, frowning at his plate.

"I'm sorry if I caused any problems, Mrs. Delfin." He turned, flinching at her small gasp. He'd forgotten to circle the other way and hide the puckered skin. With the front door open, Mrs. Delfin's shadow touched Everett on his long walk to the coupe.

21

SCARLETT ASHLEY
PRESENT DAY

In the living room of my childhood, tension rolled in. I was surrounded by family portraits and handmade decorations, but I didn't feel at home. I felt more foreign here than anywhere else in the world.

"We're engaged, Jennifer." Everett wrapped an arm around me, ignoring the glares from my mother.

Mom pulled my hand toward Dad. "Did you know about this?"

"No." He gave nothing away, his focus only on the ring. The second piece of jewelry I'd worn that he hadn't made.

Deftly, Everett guided my ringed hand from my mother's grasp. He tucked it against his chest and beamed at me. Whether it was for show, or not, my heart didn't care. It warmed under his bright smile.

"And just *when* were you planning on telling us?" Mom's voice turned shrill.

Everett scoffed. "You'd rather discuss nuptials instead of prison time?"

"Did you even bother to ask for her father's blessing?" Her head swiveled between Dad's stoic face and Everett's profile—his gaze still on me. "How could you let this happen?"

"How could you let this happen?" Everett repeated slowly. He squeezed my hand and released it. "Meaning what?"

Mom waved away his comment. "You know what I mean."

"No, I really don't." Everett rubbed his jaw and motioned for her to continue. "Please, enlighten me."

"Don't bait me, Everett Ashley," she warned.

"Let me get this straight." Everett's tone held an edge. Mom professed to own a sharp tongue, but Everett was a master. The man's entire career was built on words. "I am worthy when it comes to bailing out Lucas, but not quite up to snuff when it comes to your daughter. Did I miss anything?"

Mom pointed a finger at him, shaking her head. "It's your job. We were looking at hiring an attorney—"

"You didn't put too much thought into it. I practice business law, Jennifer. Not criminal defense."

Mom shrugged. "Does it really matter?"

She hadn't a clue how ignorant she sounded. I stifled the sarcasm, saying more gently than I wanted, "Yeah, Mom, it does."

"And it's Mrs. Delfin, Everett," Mom snapped, completely unaffected by my comment. "We wouldn't oppose if you had the decency to show us respect. Something you've lacked from the beginning."

"Showing respect? Yeah, instead of *respect,* I drove to your house at a moment's notice because Lucas did something stupid." Everett jutted a thumb in Dad's direction. "Respect is something you earn. Isn't that one of your little *do as I say, not as I do* sayings?"

Mom pointed to the door. "Get out."

"Mom—"

"Get him out of here, Scarlett, or so help me." She spat the words.

"Let's go, Everett."

"Not you, him." Mom held up her hand to Dad, who moved next to her.

"Forcing someone to choose never goes well," warned Everett, his thumb making small circles on my back.

The temptation to turn into his chest and hide was all too real. He would wrap his arms around me and shield me from them—it's what he did. He became my voice when guilt tied my tongue.

"Dividing a family isn't wise either," Dad added softly, his gaze on me.

"I couldn't agree more." Everett turned his back to them and waited for me to make the first move.

With his hand no longer touching, I reached for him—my heart pumping and my throat closing—I needed to feel him. In an instant, his hand was back and we stepped toward the door.

"Scarlett Rose Delfin," my mother barked. "If you walk out that door—"

"Choose your words carefully, Jennifer." Everett's tone was sharp, and heavy. "They could be the last you ever say to her."

"How dare you threaten me?"

"'*If you walk out that door*' sounds like a threat to me," I said, turning around to their shocked faces. Everett's touch steadied me, infusing a bravery I had with everyone but my family. "We came to help. *He* came to help, knowing how you'd treat him. Dad faces felony charges, and all you can think about are your petty differences."

Mom opened her mouth, but Everett shook his head once to cut her off.

"There's going to be a wedding, Mom, but right now, you and Dad are going to find an attorney while Everett and I are going to research a few things." Taking a shaky breath, I braced myself. "We're going to get through this. All of it."

Everett cupped my elbow. "We will."

"I can't deal with this." Mom shook her head, her voice catching. "This is just, I can't—say something, Lucas."

Dad held out his hand and cried, "And just what am I supposed to say?"

"Congratulations," Everett said dryly.

"You didn't even ask permission." Dad placed a hand on his belt. Inside, a knife was hidden behind the buckle. For being a paranoid prepper, he'd given no forethought to the crisis he was in. No amount of guns, ammo, or food would solve this. "I'm her father."

"I believe I did."

"When?" My head snapped up, catching the realization on my father's face. "Everett asked you?"

Dad shook his head in disbelief. "That doesn't count."

Everett's phone rang in his pocket. Fishing it out, he answered, "What'd you find out?"

"Did you really put me on speaker?" the man asked. "Let me guess, your hypothetical story is listening?"

"Hypothetically, yes." Everett smirked and my parents each took a step toward the phone, the focus back on my father's fate instead of mine.

"Conspiracy is hard to prove, but the larceny, that's easier."

Mom covered her mouth and turned from the phone, her back bent.

"What about the pawn shop thing? Aren't they held to a higher standard than jewelry stores?" Everett asked, tilting the phone while he spoke, then back when he was done.

"Not sure that matters." Dad opened his mouth but Everett's friend kept going. "Here's the thing, the detectives discovered the jewelry in his possession. Whether he knew it or not, he was in possession of stolen property."

Mom gripped the armrest of the recliner and gingerly lowered herself down.

"That can't be it," Dad begged, motioning to the phone. "There has to be more."

Everett's friend sighed. "But again, this isn't legal advice. This is only a strangely specific hypothetical situation."

"Exactly." Everett eyed my mother. "Why send a letter of intent? Why not just arrest him?"

"Yeah, that part is weird." The guy sounded like he was either yawning or stretching. "But maybe it's because the Fresno detectives are trying to be respectful to the Tule community? Does your hypothetical man have good relations with Tule police?"

Dad nodded with misguided hope. His old neighbor at the strip mall had been an animal groomer who cared for Tule's canine unit. But the neighbor relocated and the police never once spoke to my father. When I helped out from time to time at the groomers, they'd joke with me, but kept their distance from Dad. Jewelry stores were magnets for trouble, and canine teams didn't want to get stuck doing favors for needy businesses.

Everett saw my slight shake of the head and answered, "What's the next step?"

"They'll charge him. The whole process. They'll book him. Pray that it's a slow day, or he'll be there forever."

Dad paled and sat without blinking.

"Got it. Can you send me that list of attorneys when you get a chance?" Everett split his attention between my parents, neither holding their color. "They don't have to be in Tule. Gainesfield or Fresno is fine."

"Sure, but warn them not to go cheap."

"Right." Everett gave a forced laugh. "Like you even know what that word means."

The man chuckled and said, "You sure you want to stay in California, Everett? We'd take you back in a second. Say the word, man."

Everett stroked my cheek with the back of his hand. "Yeah, I'm sure."

"She's a lucky woman." The friend sounded a little deflated. "Let me know how your hypothetical situation goes."

Everett smiled, his hand still on my cheek. "Will do."

"What does that mean, the whole process?" Dad asked, his voice small.

"To be honest, I'm not a hundred percent sure." Everett frowned. "I'm not familiar with criminal proceedings, but I want to say they'll do fingerprints and figure out bail."

"*Bail?*" Mom cried out. "We don't have money for bail."

"Or an attorney." Dad hung his head between his hands.

Before I could comfort my father, Everett squatted, balancing on the balls of his feet. He was infinitely less intimidating at this height. "If they sent a letter, I'm sure your attorney can secure a release on your own recognizance."

Both my parents glanced up.

"Meaning no bail." Everett held up a finger. An emotion I hadn't seen before slid over his face, almost calculating, but not quite. "But first, you have to get an attorney, and trust me when I say this, whoever you involve at this point could be liable. Meaning, if Scarlett gives you a dime, she could be added to a civil suit."

"What, why?" Mom's head swiveled from me to Everett, his statement dashing the last of her hope.

"That's one area I'm slightly more familiar with. The burden of proof in the civil court isn't as rigid. Scarlett could get wrapped up in the suit—"

Mom and Dad exchanged a look of guilt. Dread filled me. I rubbed my temples.

"What aren't you telling me?" Everett's tone changed from sympathetic to accusatory with their fidgeting. "What did you do?"

Running my hands through my hair, I cursed under my breath. "You lied to me."

"We didn't lie to you." Mom's hands gripped her knees. "We said we were changing the will and that it'd be easier to put you on the house's title now as opposed to later. It's not like money was exchanged."

"When?" Everett placed a hand on each of my shoulders and ducked down, his face the same level as mine.

"Six, seven weeks ago?" Roughly the same time the detectives probably came to the store. My parents had known, but instead of getting help or coming clean, they thought of their home and their own lives—ensnaring me in the process.

"Great." His hands fell away, one rubbing his jaw. He stood and motioned to the door. "Lucas, Jennifer, find an attorney."

"Where are you going?" Mom shot to her feet.

"Doing the same for your daughter," Everett tossed back.

22

EVERETT ASHLEY
FIFTEEN YEARS AGO

verett had never attended a school dance before, and if tonight was an indication of future dances, this would be his last. He'd searched for his dad in back alleys and seedy bars —a futile attempt to get the rent paid. But tonight he was full of terror, not rage.

Searching the school's gym, Everett wrestled with his panic. Despite being several inches taller than everyone else, he'd not been able to find Scarlett. He'd come early and combed through the campus, finding and destroying hidden contraband, from condoms to alcohol. His father was a master at surviving police raids, as talented—almost— as Everett's gift of finding hidden treasures.

Scarlett had called Everett's home, giving the little information she could siphon from her brother and David. They were headed to a restaurant—although no one would tell her the name, not even her mother, who correctly suspected that Everett would show up—and were to be arriving at the dance by nine.

It was past eleven, and Everett had wiped the nervous sweat from his forehead and neck more times than he could count. He tossed his jacket and tie to the nearest metal chair. He'd bought a pager a few days ago, checking it for the thousandth time. He weaved in between couples and circled groups of laughing friends. Still no sign of Scarlett, David, or her brother.

Down a shadowed hall to the payphone, Everett slipped past the couples forced from their cars by the teachers policing the parking lot.

Marjorie answered on the first ring, her voice shaky. "Any word?"

"No, you?" He wrapped the cord around his wrist, unwrapped it, and then began again.

"It doesn't work like that, Everett." Marjorie wasn't chastising him but her words stung all the same. "I can't see her mind without being near her."

Everett struggled to hear above the pounding of his pulse. Marjorie normally shied away from talking about her ability, but her love for Everett trumped all else. She had always been the only person Everett could count on. "Nothing on the pager either."

As if on cue, Everett's pocket vibrated. "Wait, it's going off."

The line ended, his grandmother hanging up before saying good-bye. Everett swallowed the guilt. Marjorie deserved a quiet, tranquil life and so far, Everett had given her more chaos and heartbreak. He dialed the number on the pager and waited for what felt like eternity.

"Hello?" A gruff male voice answered.

"I got a page from this number."

"I didn't page anyone." The man sounded annoyed but a muffled woman's voice stopped the man.

"Hello?" The woman held a slight shake in her voice, not as much as Marjorie but definitely closer in age to his grandmother than his mother. "Ah, yes, your sister helped me in the restroom. They need to fix those locks, but she was sweet and held the door. Tell your parents she's a good girl. She was worried she'd be in trouble, but she was headed there now."

"Wh-where? Where is she headed?" Everett gripped the receiver so hard it groaned, threatening to break under the pressure.

"To the church. They were headed to the church. Such a nice—"

Everett dropped the phone and sprinted to the car. Jamming the key into the ignition, he threw the car in reverse. His tires squealed, and he gunned for the exit. The head PE teacher chased his car, yelling for other staff members. Everett knew the general direction of the church, having dropped his grandmother off when her car was in the shop. His lungs burned—he'd not realized he was holding his breath.

Scarlett was smart, enlisting the help of a woman and calling herself Everett's sister. It was nearing midnight, and the Tule police took the city's juvenile curfew seriously, a running joke from the residents. An elderly mother would've been eager to assist.

He cursed himself, realizing the church was the perfect place to get Scarlett alone. A restaurant or the school would be filled with people, but a church on a Saturday night? It'd be free of holiness and help.

To his relief, a dozen cars and trucks were parked. People. Witnesses.

He slowed the car and turned toward the darkened church. The street lights were off, as were the parking lot's. And then his stomach hardened. Each vehicle had a buffer of empty parking spots. The muffled music and foggy windows gave even greater privacy. He racked his brain, trying to remember the car David drove. He needed to find her, *now*.

Music blared by the dumpster in the far corner, coming from a late 80s sports car with its doors open. In his mind, he kept hearing her voice. *I don't like to be alone with boys.*

He turned off his car and shoved the keys in his pocket, threading his finger through the keyring. He'd learned over the years to use anything as a weapon. Anything.

Everett circled the car, listening for her. The driver and passenger seats were empty. His hand on the driver's seat, he peered in the cramped back seat. Empty.

The familiar bark of David's laugh carried in the cool night air. Holding his breath, Everett cocked his head to the side and listened. The laugh sounded closer to the church. He kept to the shadows and made his way to the back door.

A whimper. He froze, his body rigid. And then nothing.

Every muscle taut and every sound amplified. He waited a beat before starting again. Everett reached the back door. A rustle. He spun around. No one.

He pictured David leaping out from behind a bush or tree, an arrogant laugh or snide remark for Everett's paranoia. He'd take it. He'd do anything to know Scarlett was okay.

And then he felt her. She was here—she was near.

Flower plants lined the building with an occasional bush or tree, but both were too young for someone to hide, the bushes low and the trees thin. The image of Scarlett sitting in his car the first day they met, so small, so fragile, appeared in his head.

Everett took a step closer, his ears tuned to the faintest whispers of sound. Another step. He looked again at the bushes butting up against the wall. They were no more than half a foot tall. Not even a small child could crouch behind one.

Someone laughed, this time behind him in a vehicle. It didn't sound like David or Scarlett. He took another step and braced himself against the brick wall. Peering into the darkness, he saw nothing.

His heart sank. Any minute, the city's curfew would be enforced. Three cars roared to life, headlights following suit—and then a faint rustle. Keeping his hand on the wall for balance, he squatted and saw the outline of a bare foot on its side.

"Scarlett?" he whispered, the panic rising. Whoever this was, he or she was lying down.

No answer.

"Scarlett," he said louder.

Nothing.

Several other cars turned on. Headlights flooded the parking lot, filling the wall and bushes with light. Scarlett lay on her side. In the fetal position.

"Scarlett," Everett whimpered and sprang into action.

Her dress was ripped up to her hip. Her knees tucked under her arms. She stared straight ahead at the bushes, the side of her face against the dirt.

"Scarlett, talk to me." He touched her neck for a pulse. His own pounding heart made it impossible to tell. There were stains along her dress, but he couldn't tell in shadows if it was blood or something else. He placed a hand on her back. She was breathing. He scooped her up, her body cold.

Clutching Scarlett to his chest, Everett raced to his car and deposited her in the passenger seat. He pointed the vents toward her, pushing the heater on high. He sped toward safety, toward Marjorie. He eyed Scarlett, not knowing if she needed silence or conversation. Her body swayed with his jerky driving, slowly relaxing in the warmth.

Everett needed his grandmother, his mind unable to think. With the house in view, he felt exhaustion flood his limbs. Relief filled him. He parked as close to the house as he could, the bottom of the car door scraping against the first step.

Scarlett shook her head, her bare feet on the floor mat, her hands in her lap. "Take me home."

The front door creaked open. "Everett?" Marjorie called, worry etched in each syllable. In seconds, her body stooped lower, her eyes filled with horror. Everett's heart sank.

Scarlett hung her head in her hands. Everett stood numb, a hand on the door, the other outstretched to help Scarlett to her feet.

Marjorie's hand, soft from time and wrinkles, lay on his forearm. She shuffled past Everett and placed a hand on Scarlett's shoulders. "Come inside, my dear."

Without a word, Scarlett obeyed, following his grandmother to the living room. Marjorie guided her to the old leather sofa and placed a heavy quilt around Scarlett's shivering frame. The kind woman brushed the dirt off Scarlett's cheek, murmuring under her breath. Everett watched the scene as if he were someone else, a stranger living his life. Part of him wanted to see what Marjorie discovered, part of him couldn't stomach the thought. Everett debated on the next move, if he should whisk Scarlett to her house or call an ambulance for evidence. He swallowed hard. Evidence of what, he didn't know yet.

"Close the door, Everett," Marjorie said, keeping her profile to her grandson.

Grateful for a task, he shut the door, surprised at the relief he felt when the lock clicked. The simple movement that he'd made dozens of times before shook him from his stupor. He sat on the other side of Scarlett. She scooted from him, closer to his grandmother.

Everett clenched his teeth and stood, anger coursing through his veins. Scarlett was safe, but David wouldn't be—not if Everett had anything to do with it.

"Sit down," Marjorie ordered.

Everett, like Scarlett, obeyed.

Marjorie squeezed Scarlett's shoulder. "I'm going to call your parents, Letty."

Scarlett's head snapped up, her eyes filling with life. "Letty?"

The woman gave a sad smile. She blinked, the grief apparent.

"Letty." Scarlett's face transformed, color touching her lips and cheeks again.

"Sit tight, Everett."

"No." He balked. "We have to do something."

They looked at him, Scarlett with wide-eyed surprise, and Marjorie with a stern warning.

Everett held up his hands, jumping to his feet again. "We need to call the police. David's still out there. This has to be reported. He can't get away with it."

"There's nothing to get away with." Scarlett dropped her head, her voice barely audible. "I don't remember ... don't remember anything."

"They need to test you or something." He dropped to his knees, his hands covering hers. He flinched when she pulled them away. "Scarlett, we have to. It's the right thing to do."

"That's for her to decide, Everett," Marjorie said firmly. "She needs to call the shots, not you."

"What does that mean?" The pounding in his head tightened his stomach, threatening mutiny.

Marjorie shifted in front of them, an internal struggle displaying on her face. "If we call the police, they need evidence of an assault." Marjorie bit her lip, her face settling from frustration to sadness. "They'll have to examine her, *all* of her. She'd have to take off her clothes. Doctors, nurses, and police will have to collect samples. They'll take pictures—"

"He can't get away with this." Everett wouldn't contain the growl.

Scarlett curled into herself, squeezing her eyes shut.

"It's nearly impossible to convict someone, even with evidence." Marjorie sent her grandson a pointed look. "Even if he gets convicted, he won't serve jail time."

"You don't know that."

"Yes. I do," Marjorie said softly.

Everett punched the floor, groaning with the pain. This wasn't the grandmother he'd known. She'd fought for him. She'd protected him. Everett would do the same. "We have to try."

"*We* have to support, not push." Marjorie motioned to Scarlett.

"This *is* supporting."

"Everett Ashley, you do not know the difficulty that lies ahead." Her tone, Everett had heard it before and it meant she was immovable. "If she reports, we support her, every step of the way. If she does not report, we support her. We do whatever she needs, because this is a road she cannot—she will not—walk alone."

"You can't possibly—"

"You have a choice. You can choose to be right, or you can choose to be hers." His grandmother, soft and wrinkly, had drawn the line. "There is no more black and white, Everett. Not with this. There are no easy roads from here."

She sent one last piercing look at her dumbfounded grandson before shuffling to the kitchen.

23

SCARLETT ASHLEY

PRESENT DAY

Everett gave a curt nod to my parents, their mouths still hung open. They hadn't recovered from my father's grim future. Everett's silence on the drive back made me question my own accidental involvement. My mind searched the past few months, wondering how my parents could have me on the title and what I had agreed to. One thing I knew for sure, I never signed any paperwork. If Everett knew, the bulldog within would take over and he'd deliver them to the opposing council with fervor—but they were my parents. It felt wrong. The bone-deep kind of wrong that made my lungs freeze and heart skip.

Vaguely, I remembered Mom creating a living trust for her and Dad. Granted, I only half listened because she'd started the conversation bragging about how little it cost for the online program, comparing her price tag to the thousands her twin sister had spent in attorney fees. Mom had ignored my comment about the internet not always being the best resource.

"We need to pull the title." Everett's low growl squashed my thoughts. "We need to find out exactly what or who is listed."

His tone was neutral which usually meant he was beyond angry, well into furious.

"I should have warned, I mean warned her about—"

"Don't." Everett held up one finger. The animosity between my parents and him ran deeper than pride, the anger and hurt stronger than blood. I was their only common ground—and the spark to their argument. "There's only one person to blame here, and it's not you. Scratch that, there's probably two people. I doubt your dad lifted a finger with the title. You're not the one at fault. How can a mother— how can she screw you over like that? Again and again?" He flinched. He'd said the same thing about his mother abandoning him.

"I should have told—"

"Don't," he snapped. The word came hard, slamming into my chest. His voice was sharp, biting. He clenched his jaw and stared straight ahead. He'd never spoken like that before, at least, not to me.

My throat tightened. I was an idiot. He'd said *don't*. He hadn't yelled at me; it wasn't something terrible. He hadn't tried to change my mind or rewrite history. It was just a word, one stupid, little word. If Everett knew I'd never signed anything, there'd be more than a weak word. *Forgery* was anything but weak. Nothing would make Everett happier than my parents receiving a punishment.

Blinking, I turned to the window, wishing for the first time the distance was shorter between my home and my parents'. The fear, the real nugget that sat in the back of my mind, stood up and gave a little wave. It'd been silent long enough. Everett had been gone for years and people changed, good or bad, up or down. One thing always stayed the same—change. Fear nodded in my head and sat back down.

The truth was, I didn't trust *us*. Everett was safe but were we? He cared for me, that I knew. But were we—battled and bruised souls— were we good for each other?

A lump formed in my throat. What if everything had shifted between Everett and me? I couldn't even tell him about the title. Our connection, although never fully defined, had always been intense. But could it reach across the Atlantic and survive? Was it still what we needed, nearly fifteen years later?

David's face crept in my mind. In his own way, he'd been as constant as Everett, although without the warmth and comfort.

And the tears.

"It's not you," Everett spoke, an apology in his tone.

The lump in my throat thickened. Not trusting my voice, I said nothing.

"If I were a nice guy, I would keep my mouth shut. I'd smile and nod, but I can't do it, Scarlett. Not with them."

The unsteadiness in his words made it hard to breathe. *You are a nice guy*, I wanted to say.

"This isn't your mess to clean up." Tapping the steering wheel, Everett opened and closed his mouth. "But somehow they convince you that you're at fault."

I felt his gaze but didn't turn to meet it. He was just as guilty of leaving me with a mess that wasn't mine.

"By your mom looping you in on the title, she's forced you to be involved. On one hand, I want to congratulate her for her quick thinking. On the other hand, I want to scream at her. It's like her one mission in life is to complicate yours. If I had a third hand, I'd dismiss both ideas, saying she's not smart enough to know it would all work out in her favor."

"None of this is in her favor," I managed to say. A good daughter would defend her mother. My silence was my confession.

"She knows I'd defend you, no matter the cost."

Turning to face him, I shook my head. "She doesn't know about us." No one but Marjorie knew we were married.

"Scarlett, everyone knows about us." His steel blue eyes bore into mine. They were lit, sparkling with a rage I thought he reserved for his father. Not me.

My heart broke a little at the sight.

He searched my face, and I lowered my eyes. "Do not, do not, even for a moment, think the worst."

"You've said my name twice in that tone, that I-hate-everything tone." Folding my arms, I underlined my point by saying, "You only speak like that when you're done—"

"Scar—"

"With an argument." Rubbing my temples, I cradled my head in my hands. "And you say *I* jump to conclusions."

"If the shoe fits." The bark in his voice should have hurt, but for some reason, it felt less angry and more like the familiar, temperamental Everett.

"I'm sorry—"

"I hate it. I hate all of it." Everett's eyes turned murderous, his vein ticking on his neck.

"What I meant was I'm sorry you got dragged into this."

"What about you?" His face looked like he was going to explode. "You're not even angry? Come *on*. What do they have on you? When is enough, enough?"

"I didn't say I wasn't angry." The reality was, I couldn't. There was too much weight, too much shame for me to blame them. I'd not been exactly honest with my parents in over a decade. "Quit spinning it back on me. You're always having to come to my rescue. Superman should be able to retire. Or at least take a break."

He softened at his old nickname. For having the stature of an ogre, his heart was never really cold. Or hard. "Superman is lost without someone to rescue."

"There are plenty of willing volunteers." *Even in London,* I almost added. Jealousy never looked good, but try as I might, it wouldn't abandon me. That was Everett's job.

"But only one Louise."

"Lois. Her name was Lois Lane."

Everett bit back a grin and in the exact same pronunciation, he said, "Tomato, tomato."

"Heaven help me."

"Heaven?" He gave a dramatic shutter. "After everything—heaven?"

"Fine, *Superman,* help me." Warmth spread through my chest. This, this was us.

"Done." Everett placed a hand over my headrest and glanced backwards.

"Done, what?"

He guided the car across the two lanes and exited to the Automall, a small oasis of a town. It consisted of a dozen dealerships and two gas stations, nothing else. Sitting halfway between Tule and Gainesfield, the Automall should have died the month it was built but surprising everyone, it'd grown every year since its inception.

"I'm helping you." He pulled into the nearest dealership and turned off the car. "A certain someone just said, '*Superman, help me.*'"

"And this saves me how?"

He leaned over the middle console. My pulse quickened. Time stopped. My lungs refused to work. He closed the gap, his lips inches from mine. "I want you to remember this moment."

I could only stare.

"Call me Superman or whatever, but remember this moment, remember me saying this." His eyes flicked to my lips before returning my gaze. "I will protect you from your parents. From yourself. And there's not a damn thing you can do about it."

I opened my mouth to speak, but a foreign look crossed his face and he pulled away. His words were pretty but his retreat stung. The mercurial nature of who we were pierced me. Nothing had changed between us. I was both saddened and reassured—and ultimately frustrated with myself. Insanity was doing the same thing over and over, expecting a different result. Maybe I was crazy to my core.

Everett frowned, sadness etched in his eyes. "You're helping them out because they've twisted you into thinking it's your fault and it's your job to fix their stupidity." He furrowed his brow, withdrawing more. "They're full of so much—"

"They don't think it's my job."

"But you think it's your fault." He sat back, the distance feeling miles away instead of mere feet.

"No, I don't."

Mimicking my voice and giving air quotes, he said, "'*It's my fault.*' Five seconds ago, you said that, not me."

"It's my fault you're being dragged into this."

"It's my job to be in the middle of it." His eyes narrowed, glowing with anger. And pain.

My face went hot, but I didn't know what was happening, what we were truly arguing about. "Are you pissed at my parents or me?"

"All of it!" he shouted, his eyes wide and hands clenched.

I stared at him, my mind both blank and racing.

Everett deflated in front of me, shrinking to half his size. He wiped his face with both hands.

"Please, just take me home," I whispered.

"I'm sorry." The words came muffled. He let his hands fall to his lap, revealing a worn face that didn't belong to him. "I don't know ... I don't know what's going on."

He observed *everything* and remembered every detail that could piece together a person. He could discover hints of someone's past and character within minutes. It was the reason he was the only person allowed to criticize my parents. Even when it hurt. "What *don't you know?*"

"Why I'm mad. I knew nothing would change. It's my own stupidity, I guess." He unbuckled his seatbelt.

Reaching over, I grabbed the clip part of the seatbelt. "Would you just stop for a minute?"

He looked at my hand, his lips quirking. A touch, even the simplest gesture, had always softened him. He wasn't smiling, but it was in the right direction.

"What hasn't changed?"

"Jennifer and Lucas Delfin." The edge was back. "Nothing's changed. Not that I expected it would, but you will never be *you* while they behave like, well *them.*"

I held up three fingers. "One, what does Jennifer and Lucas Delfin have to do with you?"

Everett scoffed and rolled his eyes at the same time, looking more like a stroke victim than a frustrated man.

"Two, what does their behavior have to do with *me being me?*"

He held out his hands as if to say, *everything.*

With both my hands, I lowered his right arm. "Three, what is this really about?"

Everett raised his right knee, laying it on the center console. He picked at the seam of his jeans and confessed, "I saw a therapist when I was in England."

"And you talked about me." It wasn't a question. I didn't know if I should be frightened or flattered.

"You're surprised?" He arched an eyebrow but gave up when I had no reaction. "She had a theory about the relationship you have with your father. And your mother."

"And?"

He didn't answer. Tension rolled in, growing with each silent moment.

"Everett?"

"She had a theory about high school, about that night."

Darkness filled me. *That* night. The air became heavy, stifling. The temperature rose. My hands were sweaty. The car too small.

"And that maybe there's more to the story." He gave up on the pant seams and tapped his knee. "At least more about Lincoln Davenport. Why you reacted the way you did."

Lincoln. I latched onto the name Lincoln Davenport. Discussing him was better than *that night*.

"And about Kelly."

"No." My heart leapt to my throat, my vision blurry. Kelly. The first foster kid from my forgotten childhood. His dirty blond hair and blood shot eyes. No, not him. I couldn't go there. His touch. Tears. My father. No.

Scrambling, I opened the door and ran blindly. My flats slipped. I gulped air, coughing. My pulse went wild. Pricks, electric little pricks up and down my arms. My skin felt hot, on fire.

"Scarlett." Everett was beside me in an instant. "I'm going to touch your shoulder."

I shook my head.

A stupid tear fell down my cheek. With the back of my sleeve, I wiped it—rough and angry—off my face. There shouldn't be tears. This wasn't something to cry about.

A hush from a small group of salesmen stopped me in my tracks. A woman running from a scowling man would not bode well for Everett. He circled me, hiding me from their view and the afternoon sun. His eyes gentled, filling with pity. Horrible, horrible pity.

"Why? Why would you bring him into this?" Hugging myself, I gripped my elbows, squeezing them as hard as I could. "How do you even know his name?"

Everett took a step closer and said softly, "I wasn't trying to hurt you."

"There's nothing to hurt." It wasn't a lie. There were gaps in my memory, Kelly being the biggest, disjointed blank space.

"Scarlett?"

To his chest—I couldn't look at him—I pointed a shaky finger. "Those records were sealed. She told me they were as good as gone."

"Who's *she?* Do you mean the social—"

"Why?" It came out as a strangled cry. Another tear. "Why would you dig it up?"

He came closer and held out his palms. "I'm sorry."

"No," I said to his arms. My hands trembled, the shaking creeping up my arms. Panic squeezed my chest. My hands shook. Wouldn't stop. Hard to breathe.

"Scarlett, look at me. Please, breathe. Look at me."

Anger snapped me back. "You don't get to do this. This is my life, *my* life. Skeletons are meant to be hid."

"It wasn't your skeleton to hide." His hand was on my shoulder, his eyes worried, confused.

"You don't get to decide what is and isn't mine." The anger boiled to fury, triggered by his gentle touch. Everything he'd ever done for, or to me, was kind and perfect. But not this. And he wouldn't convince me otherwise. He didn't get to magically appear like Superman. He didn't get to show up for the final act and be the hero.

And then the realization came crashing down. The thought pummeled my stomach. My hands slid to my knees, my mind coming to a screeching halt. Everett's increased anger toward my parents. He'd never liked them but his new level of intolerance—if he knew about Kelly, that meant he knew everything. *Everything.*

Bile crept up my throat. The world became darker. I felt dirty. Naked. Ashamed. Everett knew. Everything had changed.

"Scarlett, please—"

"You say you love me." I met his gaze, daring him to prove me wrong. "You say you want to protect me."

He flinched. His arms went rigid. There was no coming back from this. Not this.

Brushing his hand off my shoulder, I tucked my heart away. "This isn't love, Everett."

A week or two, maybe three—soon, I would be gone. Superman would never truly love a victim, only an equal.

❧ 24 ❧

EVERETT ASHLEY

FIFTEEN YEARS AGO

T he night had felt like a dream—a horrid nightmare he couldn't shake. Everett had failed. He never protected his mother, and now, he'd allowed Scarlett to be hurt. Everett paced the kitchen, the promised cup of water in his hand. He'd put ice in it, only to wonder if Scarlett was too cold for ice, then dumped it for hot water, then worried she wouldn't want anything hot. He slammed the cup on the counter, bracing himself on the cool granite, the last remodel his grandfather had done, finishing weeks before his death. It'd started as a father-son project, a last-ditch effort to bring Richard Ashley home—and the skinny, steel-eyed grandson, Everett. Neither grandparent gave up on getting Everett the childhood he deserved. And yet, no one seemed to care about Scarlett's.

Twice, one right after the other, he pounded the counter with his fist, the water rippling in the cup. With a long swipe of his arm, he shoved the cup into the deep sink and stared at the black phone hung low on the above cabinet. His grandfather had put three phones in the kitchen, one above the sink, one near the hallway, and one at the end of the long granite countertop. He'd vowed to give Marjorie not only an enviable kitchen but one easier on her arthritic spine. Reaching and bending were kept to a minimum. All necessities, like a phone, were tripled and installed in the most convenient places.

Everett gripped the phone and dialed *911*, ignoring the howl of Marjorie's big white dog just outside the house.

"What's your emergency?" The dispatcher crackled through the static line, perks of living on the outskirts of a small town.

He hesitated, caught between his conscious and his grandmother's warning.

"Hello?" the woman asked.

"You're female ..." Everett held out the phone. This could be the end of Scarlett. The dog barked—over and over again.

"Sir?" The sound of a keyboard came through. "Sir? What's your emergency?"

He shook his head, his grip tightening.

"Are you able to speak?" The voice became urgent. "If you can't speak can you make a sound ... sir?"

Everett cursed himself. He couldn't do it—but he couldn't hang up.

"Sir—"

"Everett?" Marjorie called from the living room.

He hung up the phone with a slam and bent over the sink. His stomach tightened, his lungs seized. He gasped for air. Memories of his father burst into his head, one by one they ran through his mind. Richard's hands at Everett's neck. The smell of his own skin burning. The feeling of helplessness rose in Everett's throat, mixing with bile. His lungs convulsed. He coughed. Gagged. The images running wild.

Two loud knocks on the front door echoed down the hall, ripping Everett from his internal prison. The sound of the dog's bark growing and shrinking with the opening and closing of the front door. Everett turned on the faucet and rinsed his face. His hands shook in the water. He clenched both hands under the running water, fear in his veins. He'd never felt this out of control. Not with his father, not with the therapist—never.

The murmur of a man and woman filtered in. A protective rush surged in Everett. He ran to the living room, his hands still wet. The dark, stout back of Mr. Delfin kneeled in front of Scarlett, his hand on the couch and his wife shaking Marjorie's hand.

"Ready to go?" Everett announced to the living room.

Marjorie frowned and gave her grandson a subtle shake of her head. She knew what Everett was thinking.

Mr. Delfin stood with a turn. He scanned Everett from head to toe, his fingers flicking at his side, a tell of nervousness. Everett tucked the information inside and took in the room. Scarlett hadn't moved, nor did she look particularly relieved with her parents' arrival. Marjorie's back was painfully straighter—she wasn't sure about something. Mrs. Delfin's thin lips pursed, a calculating glint in her eye. Everett could almost taste the tension, the colors—if he could paint the feeling— were bold. Black and red.

"Ready for what, son?" Mr. Delfin asked, a slight scoff on his lips.

"To take her to the hospital."

Marjorie dropped Mrs. Delfin's hand. "Everett—"

"It's the right thing to do." It came too strong, too forceful.

Mr. Delfin puffed out his chest. "There's no need for that."

"That's a doctor's call isn't it?" Everett took a step inside the living room, every muscle taut and ready to spring. His pulse ran, adrenaline pumping in his blood.

"I'm her father. I know what's best." Mr. Delfin folded his arms across his chest, his eyes narrowed. He was short and thick, at one point probably scrappy, but Everett had already summed up his strength. The older man's biceps and torso were marbled with fat. The deception would give an untrained fighter hesitation, but confidence for someone like Everett. Marbled fat was from lack of cardio. Mr. Delfin's reach would be too short, endurance would be lackluster, and his puffed up chest meant he'd overestimate his abilities. He'd last less than a minute.

"No offense, but being a father doesn't mean much around here." Everett traced his scar, ignoring the dramatic repeat of Mrs. Delfin's gasp. She'd seen it before and if she were truly affected, Mrs. Delfin would have reacted the second Everett entered the room. "If not the hospital, the police."

"Let's not rush to any conclusions." Mrs. Delfin put a hand on her husband's forearm, her knuckles turning white as she gripped Mr. Delfin. Her face remained impassive. "We don't know what happened."

"You're here, you obviously know something." Everett's blood hummed beneath the surface. He was too eager but couldn't pull back. He mirrored Mr. Delfin's posture, folded arms and glaring eyes. It didn't take a genius to figure out who'd lose. A middle-aged, out of shape father or a six-foot-four teenager who maintained his fighting shape by practicing—daily?

"Let's get you home, Scarlett." Her mother stepped to the couch and held out her hand. "Andy's home, worried sick."

"It's about time," Everett growled.

Mrs. Delfin gasped with a melodramatic jump.

"Show some respect, son," Mr. Delfin snapped, looking more like a rabid dog than a concerned father.

Everett rolled his eyes. "Your son—"

"Everett," Marjorie warned. She sat on the couch, an arm wrapping around Scarlett's shoulders. "How are you feeling?"

The simple question pierced Everett to the core. He rushed forward. Mr. Delfin cut him off, stepping in front of him. Mrs. Delfin sat on the other side of Scarlett—the focus now on the pale girl.

"It's time to go home, honey." Scarlett's mother gave a little pat on her shoulder.

Scarlett looked at her, confusion written on her face. "Mom?"

"Uh, yeah." Mrs. Delfin eyed Marjorie before squeezing Scarlett's shoulder—none too subtly. "It's time to go. It's late. Your brother's worried about you."

"He came home?" Scarlett furrowed her brow. She cocked her head to the side as if trying to remember something. "He wouldn't come. I tried to find—"

"We'll talk about it later." Mrs. Delfin slammed the topic shut. Whatever her son did or didn't do would be kept for their ears only.

Another loud, long bark, this time sounding just outside the front door. Scarlett stood, Marjorie's and her mother's hands falling to the side. Against his judgment, Everett opened the door. The Great Pyrenees nosed the door open farther, shouldering its way toward Scarlett. She sunk to her knees while the white horse of a dog raced to her. Wrapping her arms around the dog, Scarlett buried her face in its neck.

Mr. Delfin took a step—the dog growled a warning. He retreated with a huff. "Stupid dog wouldn't quit barking."

The dog growled again, this time turning toward the open door. Two quick knocks on the doorframe announced the pair of police officers.

"Mrs. Ashley?" The older of the two stepped forward. "Mind if we come in?"

"It looks like you already did," Marjorie said dryly.

Wearing a guilty expression, the policeman shrugged and motioned the younger officer inside. "We hate to see you again like this, Mrs. Ashley."

Everett's head spun around to face his grandmother—both Delfin parents doing the same. He searched his brain for a memory, a reason the officers would be familiar with Marjorie. She had a tendency to keep secrets, hers and those surrounding her.

"Joseph Davenport, spit it out." The hunched back and achy joints hadn't diminished Marjorie's soul, hardened like steel with the tears of a faithful matriarch.

The older detective smiled weakly. "We received a call—"

"We'll leave you to your family matters." Mrs. Delfin motioned for her husband and then hesitated over her daughter. "Scarlett?"

Scarlett's hand gripped the fur of the dog, her eyes slowly returning to normal and the facade appearing once more. She swallowed hard and caught Everett's gaze. The moment wasn't lost on her parents, both visibly frustrated by the unspoken connection.

Davenport cleared his throat. "A young woman was hurt tonight, Mrs. Ashley, and we need your help."

"We've made no report." Mr. Delfin returned to his folded stance, sending a look of disgust to Everett. "As her father, I won't allow this."

The younger, lanky officer scratched his chin, a knowing smile appearing. "We weren't talking about your daughter, but I'm sure we can make time for another report."

Scarlett stepped forward, her simple black dress helping her invisibility, boring sleeves and shapeless, baggy cut, aside from the jagged rip exposing her entire right leg. The messy curls and no makeup announced her disinterest in the date. Everett vowed, one day, he'd give her a reason to care. A reason to dress up and celebrate.

Mrs. Delfin tried her hand. "Officers, my son was with my daughter. How they got separated, we don't know—"

"We've spoken to Andy." Davenport clasped his hands in front of him. "And David."

The younger stepped forward, he couldn't be much older than Everett. "We haven't spoken to your daughter—"

"What about him?" Mr. Delfin pointed a condemning finger toward Everett.

"Both boys had the same question. But it's been solved." The younger man pulled out a thin notebook, flipping a few pages to get to his notes. "He was seen at the high school until nearly midnight."

An awkward silence rolled in. The policemen hadn't said who the woman was, but Scarlett's fidgeting hands told Everett she already knew. Marjorie briefly squeezed her eyes shut—she knew as well. Scarlett wasn't the only victim tonight. The Delfins wouldn't admit there was a crime, but the idea was confirmed by the officer's statement and Marjorie's reaction. Richard accused Everett of selling drugs when the opposite was true—Andy or David was guilty of terrorizing the other girl. They had most likely divided, and conquered, the girls. And Everett would prove it. Somehow, someway.

"Look, we need to get our child home." Mrs. Delfin voice came warm, inviting. "I'm a teacher and these kids need their rest."

"We just need to ask Scarlett a few questions, that's all." The younger police officer appeared to be more eager than his superior, Davenport, who kept eyeing Marjorie.

"High school is filled with stupid teenage boys. We talk to our kids about this kind of thing. Scarlett knows how to avoid certain situations." Her father looped his thumb in his front pant pocket. He'd deftly undermined Scarlett's perspective before she opened her mouth. If she *had* been in a predicament, it would have been her fault, according to her father. Everett felt his temper blurring his mind. Mr. Delfin didn't notice. "She's been taught and probably doesn't want to get this other girl in trouble."

"Tell them, Scarlett." Everett couldn't touch her, not with her parents here, but he would help in any way he could.

Scarlett shook her head and whispered, "Kelly."

Both her mother and father exchanged a worried look. A silent argument took place.

"Who's Kelly?" Joseph Davenport was now engaged, taking a step forward.

Marjorie appeared at Scarlett's side, an arm around the young lady's waist. Marjorie's lip trembled, her eyes pained.

"Scarlett used to have an imaginary friend named Kelly." Mrs. Delfin's voice came too bright, too hopeful. She was lying, and with a dark look to her daughter, silenced her.

Everett kept his face neutral and lied, "That's not what I heard."

❦ 25 ❦

SCARLETT ASHLEY

PRESENT DAY

E verett said nothing more on the rest of our drive home to Gainesfield. He pulled in the garage and without a word, slammed the door. My words echoed in my head. *This isn't love.* They were equal parts truth and lie. Digging into someone's past wasn't love—but neither was shackling Everett to me. He deserved so much more.

He marched to the coupe where a pile of work clothes sat on the hood. He pulled his collared shirt over his head. Scars littered his muscled back and arms. He tossed the shirt on the top of the coupe and grabbed his faded, threadbare *Ashley Almonds* shirt. He must've changed in a hurry when my parents had called. And now, instead of talking, he was probably headed into the kitchen to do his version of yelling.

Pulling the once navy shirt over his head, he stopped and turned around just as I reached him. His facial scar was visible along with the ticking vein on his neck. He was past anger, past frustration, and for a moment, I didn't know what to do. If we stayed distant, it'd be easier to leave. I'd tried before when he was in London. Twice, actually. But before I could finish packing, the doorbell would ring and flowers would be delivered. He had a knack for knowing when I was pulling away—no, he had a knack for knowing *me*.

Everett clenched his jaw and spoke slowly, barely containing his temper, "There are samples inside for the counter and backsplash."

"You didn't have to go to Tule." *Thank you* was what I should have said.

Everett swallowed, the internal struggle obvious. He pulled the hem of his shirt down. "You don't like being alone with them."

He grabbed an old Tule hat from the top of the coupe and ran his hands through his hair before tugging it on.

"Or my brother." I covered my mouth. It'd just come out.

Slowly, as if any sudden movement would scare me off, he lowered his hands. He'd heard me. He always heard me.

"I shouldn't have said that."

"Especially your dad." Everett kept his profile to me. "You stiffen when he touches you."

All I could do was nod. Of course Everett would notice, but it didn't comfort me. Everett knowing made me feel worse. Made me feel weak. And worthless.

Some things, no matter how wildly unfair, changed a person forever. Richard Ashley tormented his son, the evidence covering Everett's torso with cigarette burns and jagged scars. A dozen healed fractures made up the man before me. He was acted upon and could have forever been the wounded boy. But Everett eventually overpowered his father, changing the game from victim to victor.

That was a luxury I would never have. The feeling of being powerless, of being the prey, wasn't even what hurt the most. It was the humiliation of not knowing. The confusion and feeling insane. I had nothing concrete, not a shred of solid evidence for how or why I felt this way, of why I felt panic around David or any other man aside from Everett.

"Will you please, just please, come inside?" Everett closed his eyes for a moment before entering the house, leaving the door open.

I couldn't follow. Not yet. Opening the passenger door of his coupe, I inhaled the smell of leather cleaner, the same brand Everett's grandfather had used. Everett kept the tradition as tribute. The smell brought a memory of us cleaning his car. We'd vacuumed and conditioned the seats before washing the outside. His grandmother drove up with an old friend, and both Everett and I were soaked, the big white dog tattling on us with his deep bark. The old woman offered a mischievous grin and told Everett he should be teaching me to drive not forcing me to clean. Twisting the thin gold band on my right thumb, I remembered her pained face when she'd fallen the first time.

Quietly, I left the car for the torn apart kitchen. Everett stood in the middle. Cabinets pulled from the walls were shoved aside. His back was to me, his neck sheen with sweat and his hands on his hips.

I flexed my thumb, feeling the ring so thin it was hard to remember I wore it. The memory of Marjorie's chuckle pierced my thoughts. It gave a pain of homesickness that I hadn't felt in years. Silently, I wrapped my arms around Everett, my head against his back. He covered my arms with his, threading his fingers through mine.

He turned and picked me up by the waist, setting me on a displaced countertop. "We can't keep doing this, Scarlett."

"I know."

He set a hand on either side of me, bracing himself. "You have to talk to me."

"Not about Kelly." The name sent a shiver down my back.

"It's time ..." He swallowed hard and added, "Letty."

"Letty?" Everett was fighting dirty. And it worked. The last of my resolve crumbled at his grandmother's nickname for me. He'd never used it before. "I miss her. She's not even gone and I miss her."

"I used to be her favorite." He smirked his very Everett smirk, a crooked grin with a hint of scowl. "You kind of stole her from me."

"She knew." Wringing my hands on the old tile countertop, I took a solidifying breath. "At least, I think she did. The way she'd look at me sometimes."

Everett puffed out his cheeks and held up a finger. "Don't move."

He took a moment before disappearing, returning with the box from Missy. He held it with both hands as if deliberating. "This might change things."

"I don't want it." Covering my head in my hands, I asked, "When did Missy tell you about it?"

"She didn't have to." He pulled my hands down from my face. "I made the box. I collected it all. Child welfare checks and police reports. All of it."

I froze. The room felt small. The walls seemed to bulge. *I collected it all.*

"Breathe, Scarlett."

I shook my head. Everett had collected files on my life. There was no turning back from this. The betrayal—he'd chosen his own idea of healing over me. The cut ran too deep.

He ducked, cutting a few feet off his height. "Marjorie looked the other way when I gathered the few things she did have."

"Stop."

"If I could do this for you, I would." Everett reached in the box and grabbed a folder. "You're not alone. But you do have to do this."

My hands shook and turned cold. A lump formed in my throat. My head went hot, blazing. On fire. "Don't."

Everett set the folder next to me, a hand over mine, the other on the folder.

I ripped my hands from underneath his.

"Scarlett."

"I said *don't*," I snapped at him, then paused at the grief on his face.

He blinked and I felt his desperation. It held me fast. He replaced his hand over mine and opened the folder. I pulled away. This wasn't a game or a problem to solve and toss aside. This was my history, my life. It was *me*, Scarlett Delfin, or rather, Scarlett—I swallowed the rest of my name.

Squeezing my eyes shut, I turned my head. My stomach twisted, tighter and tighter. The air, too stale. I coughed. Bile crept up my throat.

"Scarlett." Everett's arms circled me.

Startled, I shoved off the embrace and scurried backward, scrambling off the counter. "I said *don't*."

His mouth hung open, hurt in his eyes. "Scarlett, please."

"You can't save me." It came out hoarse instead of the scream I'd wished for. The dirty, dust-covered counter held the folder, the filth of my past forever between Everett and me.

"Would you stop?" He pounded a fist on the counter, papers spilling from the folder. "You're not broken and I'm not Superman."

"Then quit trying to fix me!" I cried, the last part choked by a strangled cough.

"Damn it, Scarlett, I'm not giving up." He braced himself against the counter, his eyes wild.

"You can't have it both ways, Everett. You can't give up if I'm not broken. Which is it—"

"I'm not him!" he snapped, his vein ticking. Shaking his head, he blew air into his cheeks. Exhaling, he said evenly, "You need help."

"That's not for you to decide."

"I promised—"

"We were kids, Everett. *Kids.*" Our story began and ended before we were ever old enough to know better.

"You were never a kid." He blinked, moisture gathering in his angry eyes. "Answer me and I'll drop it forever, I promise."

Before I could cut him off, he scooped up the papers and read, "'Andrew Delfin, biological oldest son. He does not appear to be afraid but confused, asking: *Why would my dad care what Kelly did?*'"

The smell of cheap wallpaper—Kelly's ashen face—his high pitched voice. Images flickered in my head. Dizzy. I felt dizzy. "Everett—"

"'Interviewed both parents. Dad anxious to get interview over with, stating: *I don't know, ask my wife. She wanted the kid. That's all this is, kids being kids. Touching isn't a big deal.* Mother denies incident, notes Scarlett's vivid imagination.'"

"Enough." My limbs became lead. Heavy. Too heavy.

Everett looked up from the paper, pausing for only a brief moment before reading again. "'Kelly shows remorse. He states he wanted to be like Andy. Male dominance present in the home. Scarlett shows signs of emotional trauma, from Mom or Dad unknown. Cannot determine if sexual or physical abuse occurred. Parents reject offer of therapy sessions for Scarlett.'"

"You said *answer me.*" I wiped something wet off my cheek—it's not tears. It couldn't be. Tears came from joy or sadness. I felt nothing, not then. Not now. "What's the question?"

"Why would a parent ignore evidence? 'Scarlett blanks, unable to speak when asked questions. Her teachers say she was a curious, articulate child until Kelly joined the family. Keeps to herself now. Unexplained school absences. Wary of peers.'"

Out. I needed out. The door to the garage was just a few steps forward.

Everett pulled a second paper from the folder. "'Marjorie Ashley—'"

"What?" It was scarcely a whisper but enough to halt Everett's onslaught.

His lip trembled, his eyes searching the paper. Hope appeared; maybe, just maybe, he'd stop. He leaned against the counter, his countenance darkening. "'Marjorie Ashley petitioned to be Scarlett Delfin's legal guardian.'"

"Legal guardian?" She had tried. The room began to spin.

"'Mrs. Ashley gives detailed testimony of multiple incidents involving Kelley and father. Possibly brother, Andy. Asked Mrs. Ashley for signed affidavit stating how she was given info. She declined. Informed Mrs. Ashley without proof of assault or negligence ...'"

Another step and my hand was on the wall. Gone. I needed to leave, *now*.

Everett dropped the paper, and with his long legs, he gracefully crossed to me, his eyes filling with anger. "Answer this. If it was me, if I was the one in need—what would you do?"

"I'd let you go," I lied, not able to meet his glower.

"I tried that." He shifted his feet, as if deciding on something. "It didn't work."

"Stop, Everett, please," I begged. An idea crept inside my head. Lincoln Davenport. He wasn't the savior I was looking for, but I'd take anything over reliving this past, reliving what my brain had locked away. Some things were supposed to be forgotten.

"I saw it." He worked his jaw and then swallowed hard. "The first day I met you, there was pain. There was hurt. But there was also color. You had both. The light and the dark. I can't walk away. Try as I

—" He clenched his jaw and flexed his hands at his sides. "I can't walk away."

"Ev—"

"I'm sorry," he growled, the sound raw and animal-like. "I don't know how to do this."

"Me neither." The air turned lighter.

He tipped his head toward the folder on the counter. "It's hard to stomach."

"I don't have an appetite."

"Marjorie was better at this."

My head cleared a little. "She was instinctive."

"It wasn't instinct." He arched an eyebrow. "She knew things because she saw them."

"She can't see inside my head, Everett. That's not possible." I once thought the same thing until I saw a therapist. I echoed the doctor's thoughts, "Some people are born with a heightened awareness. She was an empath."

"You and I both know she knew things. It was more than just empathy."

Everett reached for my hand, sliding his finger under mine. Instinct, from years of trusting him, trumped fear. My fingers wrapped around his index finger.

"I'm sorry this happened, Scarlett. I'm sorry that it hurts you."

I squeezed his finger but let go. His face fell. Marjorie wasn't magical, and we weren't a fairytale.

Taking a step back, I finally asked, "What if I never get better? What if I never read whatever else is in that box? What if this, if *this* version of me is all you get?"

"Scarlett—"

"Could you stand by and watch me be this?" I motioned to all of me. "Could you do it? Sit on your hands and let me be?"

"I won't let you."

"So, that's a no." Folding my arms, my throat thickened. This had to be said. Now or never. "You are everything I needed."

His face paled, reading me like he'd done for over a decade. "Don't you dare—"

"A part of you knows I'm right." A part of me knew I was wrong. "Marjorie knew it too."

Everett pointed to my thumb where her ring sat. "That we were family. That's what she knew."

With a twist, the ring was in my palm. An ache opened in my chest. "Maybe our family dies with her."

He backed away from my outstretched palm, his eyes wide. "She gave that to you, not me."

"It's not mine, Everett." With another twist, I pulled the engagement ring off. The ache grew to a chasm, my heart breaking inside. "Neither is this."

"It's easy for you, isn't it?" The words dripped in sarcasm. It was the resentment he always denied, no matter how many times I asked. He finally let it take center stage. "After everything we've been through, you're just going to walk away?"

"Just walk away?" My thumb pushed the rings around on my palm. "Because this is so easy."

"Sure seems like it."

"We were never easy, Everett." Gripping the rings, I clenched my hand into a tight fist, the prongs of my engagement ring digging into my skin. "I wanted it. I wanted it all. I fantasized about it—the picket fence, the two dogs, the loving husband. All of it."

"You and me both."

"But there's a disconnect. Something's broken." Tapping my temple with my right hand, I kept my left hand tightly closed. There was a comfort in feeling the rings. "I tried."

"Not enough."

"I went to her, the social worker."

Everett paused, arching an eyebrow.

"I asked her for a therapist." Opening my fingers one at a time, I exposed the rings again. The secrets starting coming, the way I'd spent my time after he left to London. "I went. Twice a week at first. Then several different medications and diagnoses later, I quit."

The counseling was supposed to be my little skeleton kept neatly in the closet. If I could mend, fix myself, then it'd be like nothing ever happened.

"Why didn't you tell—"

"And went to another therapist." Reaching for him, I grabbed his hand and hesitated. "He helped, a little. But I haven't been back in weeks."

"Weeks?" His eyes widened as the realization caught up to him. "You've been seeing a therapist recently?"

I gave him the rings but didn't let go, not yet. "What if this—me, right now—is as good as it gets?"

✤ 26 ✤

EVERETT ASHLEY
FIFTEEN YEARS AGO

In the high school parking lot, Detective Davenport leaned against Everett's coupe, crossing and uncrossing his ankles. His salt-and-pepper hair softened the severe frown and clenched jaw. He'd just been turned down by Everett's counselor. Mr. Fink refused to grant permission, citing the fact that Everett needed every second in class, not with a detective.

Marjorie had sent him packing as well, twice in the last week. Two days ago Everett overheard a little of their history when Joseph Davenport asked about Missy, Everett's aunt. Nearly eight years older than Everett's father, Missy had left her senior year and never came home. Every Sunday she'd call Marjorie, and since Everett had begun living here, Missy started sending cards written in calligraphy, some including a small sketch or picture of a painting—one of her paintings. He'd studied both the letters and the paintings, her slight hesitation over anything masculine and her affinity for animals.

And here, looking at the older policeman leaning against his grandfather's car in the school parking lot, Everett wondered what role Davenport had played in his aunt's history. Joseph had either dated Missy or was once her confidante before she left.

"Missy's doing well, if you're wondering." Everett smirked, catching the older man by surprise.

"She was a good girl." Davenport had recovered quickly and greeted Everett with a handshake. "So's your grandmother."

"Mr. Fink said I don't have to talk to you." Everett's tone was light but the slight tension behind Davenport's eyes confirmed Everett's suspicion. The policeman wasn't giving up anytime soon.

"How is she doing?" Davenport kicked at a phantom rock on the asphalt. "Scarlett, I mean. How's she holding up?"

Instinctively, Everett's hands clenched into fists. He shoved them in his pockets to hide the emotion. He didn't need the detective to know how he felt. He'd not been able to speak with Scarlett alone, not since her parents ripped her from his house. He should have kept his mouth shut but he couldn't. He had to act—do *something.* "I wouldn't know."

Joseph Davenport rubbed his neck, sighing. "I can't do my job if no one's willing to talk."

"The other girl won't say anything?"

He shrugged. "Half the football team has been with her. Nobody cares about someone who gives it away."

"What?" Everett snapped. He took one long step and towered over the officer. "She doesn't count because she's not—"

Davenport held up his hands. "I don't agree, son. I don't agree at all."

"I'm not your son."

"It's not right." Davenport wiped his face. Sadness and regret fell in the lined eyes and mouth. "It's a tough case is all I'm saying. And without Scarlett, it won't go to trial."

"Why?" This was madness. Pure, unadulterated insanity. He'd lived with crazy, his parents were the very definition, but *this,* not being able to get justice because the victim was human; this wasn't possible. It couldn't be. The world wouldn't be this cruel.

"Scarlett is a credible witness, especially since she didn't report her own—"

"She's credible because she *didn't* report?" Everett growled. "Are you saying that because she didn't report the same crime, she's a better witness?"

"I'm not saying it's right—"

"You're serious?" Everett balked and looked around to make sure this was real, that he was awake, standing face-to-face with a police officer in the school parking lot. "So, you're telling me that Scarlett is screwed no matter what? She reports it, that means she's not credible. She doesn't report it, she's credible? That makes absolutely no sense. Isn't her testimony going to basically say, *I got attacked?* Isn't that reporting it?" Everett had to stop. He was on the verge of giving details he shouldn't have. Marjorie had let a few things slip out. Scarlett was attacked, even if she didn't remember.

Davenport's frown deepened, aging him a decade in less than a second. "Listen—"

"No." Everett pointed a finger at his chest, his blood pulsing. He hadn't slept. His worry over Scarlett stole his nights. The image of her face on the dirt and ripped dress haunted him. "Answer me. How is this possible? What do I have to do to keep her safe? It's obviously *not* calling the police."

"Everett—"

"No!" he shouted and threw shaking hands in the air. "Don't give me some stupid line. Tell me the truth."

Davenport sighed. Raising his eyebrows, he motioned to Everett as if to say, *are you done?* "If you'll let me speak, I'll answer."

Everett groaned but held his tongue.

"I've been an officer for longer than you've been alive." The man rubbed his neck and kept his voice low. "I'm only telling you the reality of things. I joined the force because of the injustice of it all, only to realize some things never change."

"What more would the court want?" Everett folded his arms and gripped the backpack straps, clenching them with tight fists. He'd grown up looking at kids like Scarlett, born with two parents and stability. Until moving to Tule, Everett watched girls like her with a twinge of jealousy, thinking they were able to con their way out of mischief and skip off into the sunset. But now, according to Marjorie and Davenport, girls weren't allowed to defend themselves. She was guilty of the highest crime, being born a female.

"I'm not saying it makes sense. I'm not saying it will ever make sense." Davenport shook his head once and then gave a far off look. "I wish I could say it's because we're a small town, but it's not. Anytime a girl or a woman accuses a man, there is always doubt. Is she telling the truth? Is she overreacting? And there's always concern for the *poor man* and his *poor family*. No one cares about the girl or the reoccurring trauma that happens during the depositions."

"Why did you come?" Everett clenched his fists tighter. "Please tell me there's a reason you came. Other than to spread rainbows and sunshine."

Davenport gave a slight smile at Everett's sarcasm. "They're not bad people, the Delfins. They're parents. They have to know the risks of filing a report. Any report. If she were to apply to a college or a job, she'd be marginalized, dismissed. All because she accused someone."

"I'm not buying it. I think you're all full of it." He'd not meant to shout, but the several students leaving for lunch froze, their eyes wary. Quieter, Everett repeated, "You don't know that. Nobody does."

"Your aunt does." The officer folded his arms, his hands gripping the sleeves of his jacket. "So does Marjorie. They know it all too well."

"What's that supposed to mean?"

"Missy." Davenport gave a curt shake of his head, his eyes full of pain. "Her high school boyfriend took things too far. Even got him convicted—divided the town like a modern day civil war. The guy spent four months on probation and was able to have his record wiped clean."

The missing details fell in place. Marjorie's concern for Scarlett reporting and her warning to Everett. His grandmother had walked this all-too-familiar path. Dread filled him. "But things have changed since then."

"Yes and no." The detective squinted at something far off as if gathering his thoughts. "Missy had to relive the trauma over and over again. Before it even went to trial, she had to recount her experience over and over again. It was months of torture. All for a measly probation sentence."

"But—"

"She fled, not just the city but the state as well. I don't blame her one bit."

The world seemed to shift in front of Everett. He didn't know what to do or where to go. Right seemed wrong and wrong seemed right. He couldn't lose Scarlett. He needed her. She was the only one who saw him—not the scars, not the father—but him. She'd touched his face and looked into his eyes that first day. She heard his growl and didn't back down. Since long before he could remember, he was either in his father's way or invisible to either parent. Marjorie took him in, but she was filled to the brim with pity. To the world, Everett was a broken boy, but to Scarlett, Everett was Superman.

"What happens now?" It was all Everett could say.

"I don't know, Ashley. I really don't know." Davenport cleared his throat and tugged on his collar. "I'm just glad I don't have any daughters."

SCARLETT ASHLEY
PRESENT DAY

The box with my name sat on the displaced kitchen countertop. Everett and I stood facing each other, the tension thick and heavy. It'd been countless hours of counseling and I was no better today than I was when Everett left. And now, I'd finally admitted it to him.

Inhaling sharply, I reached for his hand and gave him the rings.

Everett dropped the rings, his hand immediately cupping my face. The rings rolled, crashing into each other next to the floorboard. Everett gathered me against his chest and lowered us both to the dirty, dusty kitchen floor. I stiffened. His arms tightened in response. He turned my body across, putting me in his lap, my feet against the humming refrigerator.

"I'm a jerk." His lips grazed my forehead as he spoke. "I didn't realize. I didn't know."

"Knowing doesn't change anything."

"It changes everything." He breathed in—like he used to, as if he relished the scent of me. "It means you cared enough to try."

It means you cared enough to try. For weeks after he left for London, I stared at the ceiling in our room at night, hearing every creak and every rustle. Even though he was thousands of miles away, I'd still set up the air mattress, placing it between the bed and the door. It wasn't just the habit of blowing it up for Everett, it was the comfort—as if the air mattress, even unused, made his absence a lie. That he was still here, so long as his bed was made and ready.

Like the house, the air mattress was his idea. Roughly seven years before, at two in the morning, I called him, too scared to speak. He knew it was me and rushed to Lincoln's office. My keys were in Lincoln's car. So was my purse. I'd kept my phone hidden in my bra and called. Leaning against the car door, I was barefoot and silent. Pulling into the parking lot, his tires squealed. Everett didn't turn off the car but opened his door and ran to me. He picked me up and pulled out an old air mattress, placing it between his bed and the door. It was the first time in years I'd slept through the night, no doors opening in the late hours like my childhood home—and no separate room like we'd always done. Just Everett. Just me.

I never told him what happened with Lincoln. The rambling voice-mails Lincoln left did the job for me. Everett bought this house and moved me in. Marjorie had told him I loved its sister mansion in Tule. I'd never told her, she just knew things like that. Until London, Everett had slept on the air mattress like a watchdog.

He was safety and danger rolled into a beautiful package. He was everything I wanted, and in a way, everything I feared. Everything that came together as Everett Ashley was my greatest fear. Not the scowl or the temper—those were never frightening to me—he was too gentle, too tender of person to fear in that way. It was his insistence, his continual drive to be Superman, that kept my heart under lock and key. Because whether he'd admit it or not, he was more in love with being a hero than being in love with me.

For as long as I can remember, Everett was bent on saving me without really looking at me. He could read my moods and thoughts, but never, not once, has he looked at me as anything other than broken, a damsel in eternal distress. He cared for me, that was a truth I knew in my soul, in the very center of my being. But that was the beginning and end of his affection, even if he refused to think it. He'd protected—and hurt me—for the better part of fifteen years. Try as I might, I couldn't end it. Dysfunctional as we were, he was still my one and only love. And he deserved so much more than this. He deserved more than me.

"I'm sorry, Scarlett. For digging things up. I'm sorry you have anything to dig up."

Worry crept in, his arms becoming less comforting and more stifling. I shouldn't be held. I shouldn't want this. If I were kind, I'd leave and let him move on. But the core, the inner part of me, couldn't leave. I was every bit as selfish as my mother accused me of. There wasn't an argument that didn't end with her saying *don't make this about you.*

"It's not right. And it's not fair, this hand that you've been dealt." Everett's voice lulled my thoughts to a quiet slumber.

I squeezed my eyes shut and counted to ten, needing a clear head.

Opening my eyes, my thumb and forefinger betrayed me, rubbing the neckline of his faded shirt. Words tumbled out. "When you left ...I felt ...lost." Lost was safer than what I really felt. What I still felt.

"Every step closer, every time I tried to be better, the harder you pushed. I shouldn't have left. It was the coward's way out." He stiffened, his breathing shallow. "But nothing was working. For you or Marjorie." He cleared his throat. "I can't be the only one trying. I mean I couldn't keep being the only one."

"You say you're the only one trying, but you're the one that left." He'd already admitted he shouldn't have left, but I still had to say it. And yet, the anger wasn't coming. "Everett, nothing's changed."

"And maybe nothing ever will." He sighed and I wasn't quite sure if it was in defeat or in acceptance. "But I sure as hell am not giving up."

"Would you stop?" Pushing against him, I looked him square in the eye. "You did give up. Professing love doesn't change the fact that you left." It didn't change my history—including the parts I couldn't remember. Our reality was very much the same as it was fifteen years ago.

"I was wrong. And maybe I still am wrong." His confession silenced me. He was too quick to apologize, too perfect to be human. "What can I do?"

"I don't know." My words were whiny, but I was frustrated that he was apologizing and taking responsibility for it. I wanted to be angry. "You're not perfect."

He raised his eyebrows and looked infuriatingly amused.

"I know I'm not perfect. I'm not even okay." My voice caught. "I will never be okay. Do you understand? I can't be fixed. They can say I have depression or anxiety or that I'm just crazy. And maybe that's really what my problem is. I'm insane. But you *not giving up* doesn't change anything. What happened, it just happened. And there's nothing Superman can do to fix that."

The threat of a smile appeared. I scowled in return.

"You can't say Superman and expect a straight face." He rolled his eyes. "I mean, come *on*."

I gripped his shirt and whispered, "I'm serious, Everett."

"What do we do?" He was no longer smiling. "What happens now?"

And there it was, the moment I feared. Everett Ashley was thinking about an alternative. With or without me, I didn't know. My throat went dry. I stared at him, not able to speak. Not able to move. He was everything to me. He was the friend, the brother, the first love —the only love I'd ever had, in every aspect.

A rush of sadness—no, something deeper, something darker—came rolling inside. I clamped my mouth shut, both hands covering my lips. And then a tear. I wiped it, fear in my throat.

"It's okay ...it's okay ..." Everett cooed.

"No." This wasn't okay. I was losing control. An overwhelming wave of helplessness pushed up and out of me. Tears fell. My shoulders shook, then my hands. The trembling grew. I gasped for air—and then, a sob. Of all the times to lose control, it had to be in front of him.

"Stop," I whimpered to myself and shook my head. *Stop*, I willed myself. Panic seized my chest. I had to stop. Crying wouldn't solve anything. Tears wouldn't let me be intimate; they wouldn't fix whatever was wrong with me.

Everett wrapped his arms around me, cradling me. He murmured in my ear, repeating, "Shhh, I'm here."

Memories flickered, not fully appearing before fading again. Kelly and his shrill voice. Lincoln Davenport and his dismissive jabs. My father filling the bathtub. My brother shaking his head. The paralyzing fear.

My sides ached. And then nothing. As quick as it'd come, the fear, the sobs—evaporated, leaving me weak, exhausted. But more than anything, humiliated.

Everett guided my head to lay against him, his hand cupping my jaw and his voice now hoarse. I wanted to say *I'm sorry for what just happened—for everything*, but the words wouldn't come.

"It's okay. *We're* okay, Scarlett." He wiped my hair off his chin. "We're just a bit busted, but we're going to be okay."

"But what if it's all in my head?" The tears kept coming. "What if I *am* crazy? What if nothing actually happened—"

"You have all the signs, Scarlett. If it helps, I know something happened and so did Marjorie. I don't know if she had some sixth sense but she knew." Everett motioned to the box. "Besides, there's a host of evidence."

"There's no evidence!" I screamed then quickly covered my mouth.

He cradled me once more to him. "When you look at your father, what do you feel?"

I winced.

"When you look at your brother—"

I flinched again.

"When you look at me ..." Everett gently lifted my chin with his finger, his eyes gentle and searching. My mind cleared but my pulse didn't slow down. He wiped the tears from my face, whispering, "Trust that feeling."

"But without evidence or memories, how can I?"

Frowning, he said, "I know it's hard, but you have to trust that feeling."

His phone buzzed in his pocket, vibrating my hamstring. My hands felt numb, unable to move as well as the rest of my body. He nervously chuckled, trying to fish out his phone, and then stiffened. He tilted the screen for me. My father's store.

Everett clicked on the speaker. My father's voice, shrill with panic, burst through, "They're arresting me."

❧ 28 ❧

EVERETT ASHLEY
FIFTEEN YEARS AGO

O fficer Davenport cleared his throat and tugged on his collar. He appeared to be immune to the hundreds of high school students swarming the parking lot.

"I don't think it's a daughter problem. It's a male problem." Everett didn't care how it sounded, even if the words were too loud and dripped with contempt. He hated his father and what that he stole from women. Everett hated himself for all of it. He knew what the male mind consisted of—he also knew men were strong enough to take it at will. And now, with the bitter truth, the unfairness of it all, Everett knew there wasn't a damn thing a woman could do about it. His stomach soured at the thought.

"I do not disagree." The older man held out his hand. "Either way, I'm glad I'm done raising kids. The youngest left for college in September, and hopefully, after years of hearing me moan about the injustice in all of this, my son Lincoln will do his part."

The tension left Everett's shoulders, and he gave the officer a firm handshake. At least one person in Tule was trying to figure out what happened. "They won't even let me talk to her."

"Give it time."

"No." Everett didn't miss the look of surprise on the detective's face, followed by a smile.

"What did you mean, the other night at Marjorie's?" Davenport squinted up at Everett. "You said you'd heard it different. About another incident."

Everett took a step back and scratched his head. "I lied."

"About what?"

"I don't know the details. I'm sure my grandmother knows more." He threw his hands in his pockets, feeling self-conscious. "I just wanted her parents to panic a little, I guess."

"Oh, they panicked." The officer gave a chuckle, confusing Everett. "They swore up and down the next day that nothing happened."

"What did Scarlett say?" He felt Davenport's gaze.

"They wouldn't leave the room long enough for me to ask."

Everett let his head fall back and sighed, breathing in the cool December air. "Something happened."

"I don't doubt it."

Meeting Davenport's gaze, Everett debated on whether he was helping or hurting Scarlett before giving in and saying, "My social worker knows."

"About the Kelly thing?" The officer waited a beat as if making sure they were talking about the same incident.

"Yeah, something about a foster kid." The words felt bitter on Everett's tongue.

Davenport's face brightened. "I'll see what I can find out."

"Tomorrow's the last day before winter break ..." He swallowed hard. "At least at school I can see her and know she's still, you know, okay. But if—"

"I can't promise anything, son, but I'll see what I can do." Davenport gave an uneasy smile. "I know you were trying to help or even protect her, but you were there that night. Trust me. From now on, you'll always be a reminder of that night. To her. To her family."

"What are you saying?" Everett flinched at his own tone.

"That even if the Delfins pretend nothing happened, you'll always remind them. Even if you don't mean to." Davenport sighed, his shoulders hunching. "I'd say cut your losses but it won't help. It never helped me."

Without another word, the officer left Everett to the nearly empty parking lot. There were at least forty minutes left of lunch but no student wanted to spend a second longer at school than required. He searched the parking lot for Andy's yellow Thunderbird, finding it next to David's black sports car. For a preacher's son, David never looked the part. He was heavy on the pride and light on the humility.

Everett found the two friends in the senior quad, near the gym, with four tables shaded by large oak trees. Andy picked at his food, dark circles under his eyes while David joked and teased the fellow seniors. Scarlett was nowhere in sight. Both her brother and David had stood, waiting for her after Mr. Munoz's class, today and every day.

In a last-ditch effort, Everett disappeared from the quad and slipped into Mr. Munoz's classroom. He held his breath and opened the door.

Scarlett sat hunched in her desk, an unopened sack lunch between outstretched arms. She didn't look up. "He's in a meeting."

"I wasn't looking for him."

She winced, then closed her eyes and leaned back in the seat, folding her arms. "What do you want?"

His confidence faltered, Davenport's voice echoing in his head. *From now on, you'll always be a reminder of that night. To her. To her family.*

Scarlett opened her eyes, the silence palpable. "Look …"

"I'm sorry."

She spun in her chair, suspicion in her eyes. Her hair hung loose and untamed around her shoulders, her mouth slightly parted. For a split second, she was Scarlett, raw and wild.

Everett drank in the sight of her. He dropped his backpack at the door and came to her desk, sinking to his knees.

She recoiled and scrambled from the chair. "What are you doing?"

"I don't know." He stayed crouched, wishing it helped him look small. "I don't know what to do. I don't know what to say."

"There's nothing to say." She gave a little shrug, her eyes flitting about the room.

"There's a lot to say. I just don't know what." He rubbed his forehead. "I suck at talking."

Scarlett shot him a genuine smile, her face transformed to an alluring, almost exotic look. "This is true."

"Do you want to talk about it?" The words came before he could stop. Her face fell, and he cursed under his breath. "You don't have to."

"Nothing to tell." She sat on her neighbor's desk, her legs crossed at the ankles. "I don't remember anything. I don't remember leaving the house. It's not like Andy would fill in the gaps. His lips are sealed."

"What *do* you remember?" Everett didn't dare stand or even sit in the chair. This was the most she'd spoken to him in days. He felt the familiar pressure in his chest, the eagerness. He wanted—he *needed*—her to speak. Not just of that night but anything. She didn't pity him, she didn't fear him. She was a rarity that Everett didn't, couldn't, let go.

She picked at her fingernails. "It doesn't make any sense."

"Does it have to?" He sat back and folded his arms over his knees.

"No, like, what I remember doesn't make sense." Scarlett arched an eyebrow and waited. When Everett said nothing, she added, "I remember my bathtub in the old house."

He hoped his face stayed neutral. He must have missed something. An old house and bathtub had nothing to do with that, at least he hoped. "When's the last time you were there?"

Her shoulders relaxed with the question. "I don't know, a year or two. We moved to the new house last year, but before that, in the old house, I'd sneak into my parents' shower. Hated the kids' bathroom. Or maybe just the bathtub."

Her tone took on an eerie quality. A chill crept across Everett's neck. He kept his voice even, asking, "What else do you remember?"

"You mean what other completely crazy thing comes to mind?" She scoffed and rolled her eyes. "Stupid, I know."

"Never said that."

"But you're thinking it." Scarlett shot him a look, daring him to contradict her.

"Not even a little." He met her gaze—held it, needing her to believe him, needing to know what else was hidden behind her dark eyes.

"I hear his voice." Her eyes narrowed, a fire building. "He's crying because he got caught."

Who's he? Everett held his tongue.

"I can see the scar down his stomach. He's picking at it, trying to make it bleed because he was bad." She bit her lip and blinked at the rising fury swirling in the dark brown of her eyes, her voice haunting, hollow.

Everett clenched his hands, not sure what to do. "He was bad?"

"I'm screaming in the hallway."

"Why?"

Ignoring the question, she looked away and held her cheek. "It hurt."

"Were you hit?" Everett saw the invisible scars, his mind filling in the details with the crossing of her legs and folded arms covering her chest. She sank into herself, her face blanking once more. Slowly, to not scare her, he uncurled himself to a stand. "Scarlett, look at me."

She shook her head.

"I don't think you're crazy."

"I wouldn't blame you if you did." Shrugging, Scarlett pulled the ends of her hair forward, the facade in place. "I was a kid. Kids overreact. Boys are just boys, foster or not. Brothers or fathers. They have needs."

Everett's mouth went dry. Her words rang in his ears. He swallowed the rising bile. He needed her out of there—now. "If you could do anything right now, what would you do?"

She gave a caustic laugh. "Superman taking requests now?"

Everett forced himself to remain calm. He clenched his jaw and focused on breathing through his nose. With shaky limbs, he sat on the chair connected to the desk where she sat. "As you wish."

Scarlett elbowed him. "Right."

He laid his head on her shoulder. She didn't stiffen. He tried again. "Tell me. What would you do?"

She laid her head against his. "I'd leave. I'd leave and never look back."

❧ 29 ❧

SCARLETT ASHLEY
PRESENT DAY

L ike the ogre Everett was accused of being, he stood with arms crossed against the back of the couch. Dad's panicked, *They're arresting me,* catapulted us into action. We'd rushed to my parents' house after sending an urgent text to Missy. She would take an early shift at Marjorie's bedside. We'd offered—again—for her to stay at the house with us instead of driving the hour back to Tule.

"You okay?" Everett's low voice carried to where I sat below him. "We do not have to stay here. This isn't our mess."

"I'm okay."

"We can leave at any moment." He squeezed my shoulder.

I placed a hand over his. We both turned to David and my youngest sister sitting on the other couch. He kept patting her knee playfully, appearing determined to not look at us. Elaine nodded her head to whatever David was saying, her lip continuing to be nibbled by her teeth.

David chuckled, his eyes crinkling. In middle school, I had thought he was perfect. Charming and talkative, I'd watch him for hours at my house with my older brother. I'd have given anything for him to acknowledge my existence. He was a freshman while I was a lowly seventh grader. It didn't take long for the uneasy feeling to overcome my infatuation. By high school, I was terrified. A few too many cornered conversations and unwanted kisses left me nervous. And then the touching.

They were just kisses. Innocent. I didn't want to make a big deal over something so little. At least that's what I told myself. It wasn't that much different than the awkward hugs my dad gave—typically from behind or when my hands were full and unable to prevent his embrace. Hugs, kisses—only Scarlett Delfin would be afraid of small tokens of affection.

Everett checked his phone. "They're still not done. But it should work out."

"For Dad?" I glanced up, needing to see his expression. Everett had called in a favor—a friend of a friend of a friend type of favor, and my father suddenly had an attorney.

"It'll be fine." Everett nodded, squeezing my shoulder again. He circled the couch and sat next to me.

"He's coming home. He has to come home," I said more to myself than him.

"Do you want to leave?"

"No." And I meant it.

"What's happening?" Elaine asked, her voice timid.

"They'll head home soon." I hoped my smile was reassuring.

"Everything's going to be alright." David elbowed Elaine in the arm and sat back, as if he were personally responsible for Dad being released.

"Depends on what your definition of *alright* is." Everett threw a dangerous look at David. I felt instantly small. Everett had gone from comforting me to find any reason to tear into David. David didn't know that we'd been consumed in talking about him, my brother, and my father. Everett's already thin patience had evaporated the moment David greeted us at my parents' door, welcoming me into my own childhood home. "He's not in jail for the moment, but prison could still be his future."

Abruptly, I stood and swung my arms at my side, not sure what to do. Everett and I hadn't finished our argument or conversation—whatever it was. We'd rushed to be here for my parents, but I had no desire to witness an old high school turf war. And David's presence bothered me still.

It was just a feeling, something inside that made me squirm and shrink from him. He'd accused me a few nights before of only allowing Everett's touch. David was right. I'd never given him the chance, not since *that night*. The night I still couldn't remember fully. The fear, the panic was all I knew—was all I ever allowed myself to recall. And right now, I questioned everything. "I'm going to the bathroom."

Everett stood next to me. "Let's go."

"I'm fine." With a subtle flick of my hand, I motioned to Elaine, hoping Everett saw it.

He nodded and sat back down, a scowl on his face. There was little doubt that Everett's expression would pin David to the couch. He wasn't dumb enough to follow me, not with Everett sitting in the living room. My parents' bathroom was the closest, their bedroom sharing the living room wall, but I walked to the farther bathroom on the other side of the house. A weird, irrational fear was that my father would walk in while I was in theirs—weirder still, I didn't even have to use it. I just didn't want to be in close quarters with Dad. Or David.

I walked past the laundry room bathroom and the powder room just off the kitchen to the farthest room in the house, my childhood bedroom. There was a small bathroom between my old room and the boys' room, theirs being the largest room in the house. It was able to fit three huge beds and still have space for testosterone-filled wrestling matches.

It'd been years since I lived in this home, but my feet carried me straight to my old room. Several guitars outlined the walls along with four large amplifiers in the corner, each roughly four feet high. My heart sank a little. They had to belong to my father. Some things never changed, his habits, least of all. Dad more than likely had run out of space at the store.

He'd go in phases of collecting things. In a fevered pitch, he'd buy expensive cars or rare movies or, like now, guitars. His problem could be tempered when I worked with him at the store. I'd sell the oldest item out from under him before he noticed, much like my mother would water down her father's whiskey to help stretch the dollar.

The sliding closet door was crooked. Pushing the door open, a mountain of fabric reels crashed down on me, followed by a few VHS movie cases. I stacked the fabric on the bottom of the closet. They'd no longer be organized, but that was Mom's problem at this point. I scooped up the old movies. A familiar, dark red book fell from one of the cases. Picking it up, I felt a rush of warmth. And then fear.

My hand trembled. I looked around, not wanting someone to walk in and catch me. It felt wrong to have the book in my hand, and I didn't know why. I flipped open the cover and read *To Scarlett Delfin, Love Mom.*

With a thud, I jumped back. The room began to spin. I sat on the floor, the journal at my feet. The hot rush of anger washed over me—and then fear popped in again. Cradling my knees, I rocked back and forth.

David's muffled voice carried down the hall, pulling me out of my head. Like a child, I was scared of an old journal. This was what Everett should see; this would change his mind about how badly I was broken. I grabbed the book, but instead of putting it back, I flipped through the first few pages containing rough drawings. I couldn't have been more than six or seven. Slowly, as the pages turned, words began taking over. But then, one picture took up the whole page—a crude drawing of Kelly with a dialogue bubble saying, *I'm sorry.*

Sinking to my knees, I just stared—and felt little bits, tiny pieces of a memory come alive. But just as quickly, my mind shut it out. There was nothing. Not a feeling. Not a memory.

I flipped the page and read about a strange lady coming to the house, asking questions about my body. The woman wouldn't let Mom be in the room when she switched from Kelly to my brother and father. Knowing my mother, she would have thrown an epic tantrum at not being there to control the conversation. The journal trembled in my hand as I read the last line of the entry. *Mom said people like the woman just want be the hero. They don't really like helping me.*

A force outside myself turned the page. I didn't have the strength. The words ran together. I'd had those same thoughts but now wondered if they were my own or placed there by my mother.

Like a bolt of lightning, it hit me. Memories and rumors filled my mind. The whispers of my father at the strip mall. The women at church complaining of my family. The girls in my youth group unsure of my father and brothers. My shoulders tensed. I wanted Everett's arms to hold me, to make the thoughts, the memories, go dormant once more.

The next entry was a few months later. I'd written how sad I was at something my brother Andy had done. I'd compared it to how he treated my foster brother at the time—the entry didn't have the name of the kid, only that I was upset. Andy had stripped the kid down and shoved him in the front yard with a sign saying, *I'm a cry baby*.

The voices down the hall became louder, but I couldn't put the book down. I flipped to another entry and froze. In perfect teacher handwriting, my mother had written a correction, stating that my imagination had run away with me again. She'd addressed it to *Adult Scarlett* and wished that I would be mature enough to know the difference between fact and fiction. I stopped reading at the sentence she underlined. *I knew you were lying when I asked you details on what Andy supposedly did and all you did was cry (it's okay, I still love you)*.

Dropping the journal, I backed away. An image of my mother sitting on the bed with me entered my mind. She reached over and took my hand, shaking her head. She was telling me how sorry she was that she couldn't help me if I wasn't willing to tell the truth.

The journal being at Mom's house made it feel like it was hers, not mine. I felt violated all the same. She'd written in it—no, she'd not just written, she'd *corrected* my thoughts. Everett and David's voices became louder. I should leave the room, return to Everett and Elaine, but all I wanted to do was shake my mother, scream at her for rewriting what I felt in my own journal. And then a thought came in—if she wrote the entry, I'd told her something big, something bad. Naive, I must have told her as a child, confiding in her mother. And she did nothing.

My pulse raced but not with fear. Not with anger. This was something altogether different. I snatched the book and held it against my chest. My heart pounded. I squeezed it tighter, feeling somehow that if I could hold tight enough, I wouldn't lose my grip, my hold on what was going on. I was on the cusp of remembering.

"Scarlett?" Everett whispered.

I jumped and scrambled backward from the door, my breath unsteady.

Everett crouched down in front of me, his eyes wide. He held out his hand. "Hey ...hey ..."

"I found this." The journal was smashed so tightly by my arms, the corners were digging into my skin through the fabric of my hoodie.

"What is it?" His voice was too soft. I wasn't a child. He didn't need to coddle me.

I shook my head.

"Let's go home, Scarlett."

I shook my head again. He shouldn't take me home or anywhere. I was a disaster. This wasn't his mess to clean. Superman couldn't fix this.

"I'm going to help you up." Everett paused a moment before cupping my elbow. Gently, he lifted me to a stand. "Scarlett?"

My face flushed. I was too embarrassed to answer.

"Scarlett, you don't have to answer me, but I need to know." He shifted from my side to directly in front of me. "Is there anything else in here that you might need? Or want?"

My gaze snapped to his, and in an instant, my mind cleared. I nodded toward the closet. "Can you look and see if there's anything else up there?"

Everett leaned his head closer to the door, I assumed to hear if anyone was coming. "Come over here and keep watch."

I nodded and he leapt into action. Keeping my eyes and ears trained on the hallway, my pulse steadied. For a moment, we were Scarlett and Everett again. There was a plan. And a solution.

In what felt like an eternity, Everett came to my side, his hoodie tucked under his arm. "Give me the book."

I handed it over and he slipped it inside with whatever else he'd hid. "Now what?"

"We leave."

"What about my dad?"

"No offense, but you're in no shape to be around him." Everett placed a hand on the small of my back and guided me out of the room. "Don't say anything. You're sick. I'm rushing you home."

Bowing my head, I gave a small nod. The lie wasn't too far off the mark. The shaking had returned as we neared the front door.

"I've got to get Scarlett home."

"They're not back yet." Elaine's voice held a quiver of panic.

I turned toward them, only to have Everett stop me. With my back to them, I felt the rush of guilt again.

"You're really going to take her from her family right now?" David's comment made Everett pause. "This is kind of an emergency situation."

"Stay, Scarlett," Elaine pleaded, doubling the regret I already felt.

"Yes, I'm really going to take her home. It's called taking care of the ones you love," Everett snapped. The silence that followed meant he'd given them his signature glower.

"Ones?" David called out as Everett opened the door. "Last time I checked, you only cared about one person."

"No, David," I said, my voice cracking.

Everett pulled me toward the door. "Scarlett, don't engage. He's—"

"I already told you, David. You have it backwards." Facing both Elaine and David, I reached for Everett, and like I knew he would, Everett wrapped an arm around my back.

"And you told me Everett and you were over." David had walked closer before I'd turned around. There had been a shift in power between him and Everett. David appeared too sure of himself.

"I did not—"

"You've forgotten." Shaking his head, David tsked. "You said *was*, Scarlett."

"Was. Is." Shrugging, I tried to keep my tone neutral. My legs shook. I needed to leave but more than that, I needed David to stop. "Does it matter? It's Everett, David. It's always been Everett."

David's lips stretched to a grin. "And yet, you still don't wear a ring."

30

EVERETT ASHLEY
FIFTEEN YEARS AGO

Mr. Munoz offered only a blank stare to Everett, his poker face worthy of the professional gambling world. "So, you're wanting me to lie?"

"I didn't say lie." Although Everett wouldn't be opposed to lying. Anything to keep Scarlett's parents off the scent.

"Tell me how this is a good idea, again?" Mr. Munoz sat patiently in his chair, his hands folded on his desk. "You think her mom and dad are going to just sign away their parental rights?"

"Do you really want me to answer that?"

"You're insane. Please tell me you know that. Your whole plan is a little extreme." Mr. Munoz leaned back, cradling the back of his head with his hands. "They didn't sign the forms for the community college?"

"No." It hadn't helped that Everett had come, offering to drive her to each class. They'd told her, in no uncertain terms, she would not be graduating high school early to attend the community college, especially if it had anything to do with Everett.

"There isn't a judge in this state that would grant her emancipation." The teacher sighed, as if it bothered him that Everett's idiotic plan wouldn't work. "It's a process that by the time she'd have her independence, she'd already be eighteen."

"What if I had a willing lawyer?" Everett's voice had gone high at the end. Even before puberty his voice had never been that shrill. Desperate times had changed him—and quite frankly, he didn't care.

Mr. Munoz's hands fell back to his lap, his mouth hanging open as wide as his eyes. "You're kidding."

"And ... a judge."

"Do I want to know how this came together?" The teacher stood, a hand on his hip, the other on the back of his neck. "Am I going to get fired for this?"

"Not that I'm aware of."

"That's reassuring." Shaking his head, he folded his arms and nodded at Scarlett's desk. "What does she know?"

"That come June, she's out of that house."

"She'll last that long?"

Everett swallowed the panic. "I honestly don't know."

"This could all go sideways in a second. They are skilled at maneuvering. I know. I've tried to help before." Mr. Munoz tapped his desk with his index finger. "They could charge you with statutory rape. And then it's game over, you're done."

Everett nodded sharply. "I'm aware."

"That's it?" Mr. Munoz scoffed, his finger still on the desk. "You'd go to *jail*, Everett."

"Like I said, I'm aware." He'd faced that threat before, fearing he would be in prison instead of his father. Granted, Everett would be sent for protecting someone, not hitting.

The teacher placed both hands on the desk and held Everett's gaze. "Marry her."

"What?" Everett backed up, hitting the desk behind him. Mr. Munoz had lost his mind. "That's a for sure way to go to jail."

"It's the only way to keep you out of jail."

"And *I'm* insane?" Everett threw both hands in his pockets. "There's no way in hell we can get married."

"You're telling me you can con a judge and a lawyer for emancipation but not for marriage, legally binding her to another adult?"

"My grandmother will be listed as both her sponsor and employer, showing that Scarlett was basically an adult already. If I go in there like a lovesick puppy, the whole thing will implode." Everett needed one hour, just one hour of help from Mr. Munoz. "We'll look like rebellious teenagers that are sneaking behind Mommy and Daddy to go hook up."

"So do it after." Mr. Munoz searched the papers on his desk, for what, Everett didn't know. "Get her emancipated and then walk down the hall and get married in the courthouse. That way, you can't go to jail and they can't keep her in that house."

"If they find out about any of it, they'll lock her away. Marriage or not." Everett's pulse raced. The more he talked the more desperate, the more unstable, the plan appeared—and he hadn't even convinced Scarlett yet. He wanted every detail finished before getting her onboard. If he wasn't careful, she'd shut him out. Not just him but everyone.

"She's not as fragile as you think." Mr. Munoz narrowed his gaze. "She's not some damsel in distress."

"That's not what you said a few weeks ago." Everett couldn't let the panic show. If Mr. Munoz was back pedaling, Everett would have only Marjorie as an ally and that had taken every ounce of trust she held. He wasn't asking a lot, he was asking everything.

"I mean, she's not helpless."

"You wanted me to help her."

Mr. Munoz sighed and gave a firm shake of his head. "Not like this."

"She was—" Everett couldn't say the word. "She was hurt. Badly."

"I gathered that much."

"I'm not talking about the dance." Everett grabbed the straps of his backpack and groaned. He didn't have hard proof but the little things that Scarlett let through. *Boys will be boys. Men have needs.* "I think there's more. And ... that it happened at home."

Mr. Munoz paused for a moment. He pulled out two stapled reports and placed them on the desk between them. "She turned these in. I'm assuming she thought you wouldn't be allowed to work together anymore."

Everett snatched the report on top titled *Medusa's Sin*. "She changed the topic."

"There are some things she's written that, well, I don't know what to make of it." He shrugged with a frown. "She delicately confesses that—if you're right—happened to her. But she never admits it's her. That's not a damsel in distress, Everett. That's a survival mechanism. This is her life."

"You're okay with it?" The paper shook in Everett's hands.

"She's in control of her life, or at least has convinced herself that she is. And you're wanting to take that from her?"

"If she was your daughter, what would you do?" Everett's voice rose.

"I wouldn't hurt my own kid."

"Fine, your friend. What would you do?" Everett couldn't hide the baiting in his tone. He wanted a reaction from the teacher, this man who pretended to care and then when it mattered most, surrendered. "It's okay to help her get to college, but not safety?"

"If—and at this point, it's all speculation—*if* something happened, and *if* it was by a family member, even dismissed by a family member, those wounds are deep." With his palms out, Mr. Munoz took a step toward Everett. "You cannot convince her that her family is evil. Or that you're her one ticket out. That's not how it works."

"Her family *is* evil."

"Oh, I believe you." Mr. Munoz smiled with tired eyes. "They're also people who've done a lot of good. That's not an excuse, it's just a fact. They've spent thousands of hours in the community teaching the discarded kids that they're worth something—both of them. Jennifer in the schools and Lucas in the church youth program."

"That makes me sick." His tongue tasted only bitterness.

"She's not going to believe she's in danger. She'll only believe that she's the danger. The bad part in all of it. She can't believe otherwise, especially coming from you."

"What's that supposed to mean?" Everett already knew but wanted his teacher to say it, say that he was a screw up and that his word wouldn't matter to a girl stuck in a family armed with an image more false and more dangerous than his own drug-dealing, fist-wielding father.

Mr. Munoz handed him the same questionnaire his therapist had. "Adverse Childhood Experience. You've either taken the test or a social worker evaluated you for an ACE score."

"Your point?"

"Scores of four and above signal a horrific childhood existence. Health problems—"

"I know what the score means." Everett tossed the paper on the desk. He'd been down this road.

"Your score is maybe three, possibly four." Mr. Munoz nodded at the paper. "Hers is probably seven. I wouldn't be surprised if it's eight."

Everett took a step back. Then another. He backed into a chair but took another step.

"But from the outside looking in, she's from a caring, loving home." Mr. Munoz rubbed the bridge of his nose. "Her parents fostered several kids and then finally adopted I don't know how many. They're the pinnacle of society, and yet Scarlett shows every indication of deep, emotional scars. Every word she's ever written highlights her emotional upheaval. And how in the hell, are you, Everett Ashley, going to save her?"

"I don't know." The last of Everett's hope evaporated.

"Even if you get her out of that house, her score—if she'd ever take the test—would show her quality of life bleak at best. Her future looks more like a rerun of drug addiction, suicide, sexual and physical abuse—"

"Stop." Everett snapped. "You made your point."

"Look, I've spent years with troubled youth, and for some reason she hasn't tried to self-medicate—that we know of." Mr. Munoz held up a hand. "But you should go in with eyes wide open."

"If anyone knows, if anyone would ever know, what it's like to be alone. To feel like you're just another tool for your parents—" The room dizzied, Everett's pulse racing wild. He would not go down without a fight. "And to have *one* person stand up, *one* person say this isn't right, this isn't your fault—it's me."

Nodding, Mr. Munoz held out his palms again, and Everett saw it for what it was.

"Do not placate me," Everett warned, pacing in front of the white board. "I will *not* give up. You can help me or not, but I swear to you, she will have one person say no. She will have *one* person be there."

"No, Everett. She'll have two."

31

SCARLETT ASHLEY
PRESENT DAY

Gasping for air, I woke with a start, my lungs on fire. I looked around in a panic. I was in my room. Alone. There was nothing to fear. My emotions had been all over the place since finding the journal. Such a little thing had pierced a hole in my head, leaving a gaping wound of greedy feelings.

Patting the mattress, I found my phone with a sticky note from Everett saying he'd gone to see Marjorie and to take it easy. It'd been two days since we'd left my parents' house. On the way home, I'd turned off my phone. Mom would call it a selfish move, but I didn't want to hear from her or Dad. It wasn't the first time I'd cut off contact. Disappear, that's all I wanted to do. Right now, becoming invisible would be my greatest wish, selfish or not.

Turning the phone on, I climbed out of bed, my body stiff from another night of restless sleep. I texted Everett that I was awake, asking what qualified as *taking it easy*.

He responded with a meme, a dog sleeping on his back in front of a rotating fan.

I texted, *Sounds like a great idea in December.*

The bubble image appeared, showing that he was typing. I threw on some clothes while I waited and saw both Marjorie's wedding band

and my engagement ring on top of the dresser. Everett must have collected them. This was who he was, undoing whatever damage I'd caused. He deserved so much more.

My phone pinged. He texted, *Meeting with doctor. Then I'll be home.*

A new wave of emotions came over me. I felt displaced. Taking care of Marjorie had been my job for the last year. Everett had barely returned and was now the contact; he *was* her grandson. But who did I belong to?

A sharp pain pierced my heart. Meeting with the doctor couldn't be a good sign. Marjorie was already declining, that I knew. But somehow, I naïvely believed she was suspended in time. That she'd hold on until life was less complicated with my family and well, with me. Death seemed to have other ideas.

I texted, *I'm coming.*

That's not taking it easy.

If anyone knew what talking to Marjorie's doctor entailed, it was me. It wasn't an easy task, none of it was. I was the one who'd been there for every appointment, every meeting. Everything.

I fired back, *I can handle it.*

My phone rang—Everett was calling. Answering it, he blurted, "Thank you."

"What?" That wasn't at all what I expected him to say.

"Thank you." His voice cracked. "I just wanted you to know that I appreciate everything that you did."

"You're welcome?" The frustration grew—it sounded like he was thanking and firing me all at the same time.

"I don't know how you did it," he whispered. "She looks awful."

"Everett, I'm coming."

"I'll come pick you up."

"I'm not an invalid." I flinched at my tone. It was a sweet gesture.

He sighed into the phone. "I know, I know."

"Thank you, though." With the phone between my head and shoulders, I tied my shoes. "I'm just putting shoes on and then I'll head out."

"Can I—" He cut himself off. "Can I just come get you?"

There was a plea in his tone. It softened me. There was one truth in our mess of a life. I loved him. I might want to kill him, but I'd always loved him. "You okay?"

He waited a beat. "No. I'm not."

"You want to come get me?" It didn't make sense. I should make it easier, not harder on him.

"I just ... I just want to feel like I'm doing something." And then it fell in place. He didn't want to be with Marjorie—or rather, he wanted to run and hide like he'd done when she'd fallen.

I stared at the rings on the dresser. Marjorie's band meant commitment, not just from her husband but from her to me. What Everett meant—truly meant, I didn't know. Everett could face down his father but couldn't stay to fight with Marjorie. He was Everett Ashley, the man most people feared. The man I loved more than any other person—and the man I never really had.

"Please?" Everett begged, a foreign sound.

Nodding, I said, "Yeah. Come and get me."

He mumbled a thanks and hung up. Feeling deflated, I scrolled through my emails, a few from my GainesPrint editor about freelance options and one from Lincoln Davenport. I hovered over Lincoln's email. The fact he'd emailed at all confirmed his involvement with the New York job offer. Glancing back at the rings on the dresser, I swiped Marjorie's wedding band, slipping it back on my finger. If New York was my next stop, at least I could take a piece of Marjorie with me.

The engagement ring lay undisturbed. Everett would be home soon, and I couldn't forget the look of pain when David had said, *you still don't wear a ring.* Everett and I would eventually have to talk about the future, especially with his looming job in London. The sound of his voice, the pleading, made my heart sink. Grabbing the ring, I slid it on, still unsure if it was the right thing to do.

I debated on going upstairs to my makeshift office. Everett had finished the room a couple of years ago, allowing me to work from home and stay closer to Marjorie. He'd placed my journal and everything else he took from my parents' house in the office, safely tucked in the box Missy had given me.

Checking the time, I climbed upstairs. A cheap cardboard table was in the corner of the room, his laptop and briefcase perched near the edge. The sight of it made me pause—was he working from home or gearing up to leave?

A legal pad peaked out from under the laptop. Stealing a couple pages, I walked around the box in the middle of the room and sat at my desk. There had been flashes, brief images of my childhood, since I'd read my journal. There had to be more, my brain couldn't have forgotten everything. A few months back, out of sheer frustration I'd written a timeline and given it to my counselor. It wasn't a true outline, only basic dates like birth, baptism, high school, and college gradua-tion. I'd written *I can't remember* over and over again across the page. Most people recalled their childhood. Mine was a mixture of blank pages and memories too faded to believe.

The doorbell rang. Instinctively, I went to the window and saw the top of a beat up truck. My sister Elaine drove one like it, but she'd never been to my house before. Everett and I still didn't know the fate of my father. Part of me didn't want to know. The doorbell rang again. The last thing I wanted to do was speak to anyone. Mom could have driven Elaine's truck. Or my dad—if it was indeed the same vehicle.

I jogged downstairs, texting Everett, *I think Elaine's here.*

Peering through the peephole, I saw my sister fidgeting on the doorstep, a cap pulled low over her face.

Opening the door, I stepped back to welcome her in. "Hi?"

Elaine didn't move and didn't meet my gaze. Shame surrounded her. The little I could see of her face was red, either from embarrassment or sorrow, I didn't know. She glanced up and down the street. Her truck was parked haphazardly on the street, the back end three feet from curb with the front end covering the sidewalk.

"What's wrong?" My pulse began humming again, not quite racing like it had at my mother's home but close, gearing up for another bombshell. If Elaine was here, something bad had happened.

She took a hesitant step forward, her head down. "Can I come in?"

"Yes," I said dumbly, hoping it didn't come off sarcastic. The relief I'd had from not talking to anyone faded to guilt. Elaine needed me and all I'd thought of was myself.

She stepped around me to the dirty living room. I guided her to the unfinished sunroom, the only room in the house with a couch. Without a word she sat, her head still down.

"Elaine?" I sat next to her, catching a glimpse of her swollen eyes and tear-streaked face. My heart sank. It had to be about my father. Everett had said it could take days to get him processed.

She bit her lip and shook her head.

"Is it Dad?"

"No!" Elaine cried out. Her head still shaking, she curled into the armrest of the couch. Her hat fell from her head, and for a moment she looked like the lost little girl I once knew.

Reaching for her, I stopped before I could touch her, not fully sure it was okay to do. This was foreign territory. The only person I'd ever really comforted was Marjorie.

My phone pinged. David texted, *Lunch. You and Me.*

The image of him next to Elaine at my parents' house made my chest tighten. "Did David do anything?"

Elaine sat up and wiped her eyes. "No, but why?"

"I have no idea, not really." Once more, I reached for her and play-fully pulled on the end of her ponytail. "I don't know what's wrong, and I'm grasping at anything. Or anyone."

My phone pinged again. Another message from David. With a quick swipe, I deleted the conversation.

Elaine covered her face in her hands. "It's me. I can't do it."

"Can't do what?"

She let her hands fall to her lap. "I can't get married."

I opened my mouth—only to close it again. I'd thought she'd come because of Dad. My phone dinged. I was tempted to turn it back off.

Elaine's eyes flicked to the phone in my hand. "If that's Mom, don't tell her I'm here."

I tucked my phone under my leg. "Does Mom know?"

Her lip quivered as she nodded. "She thinks I'm being ridiculous."

"What happened?" My journal was upstairs but it felt like it sat between Elaine and I. Mom had thought I was ridiculous once as well. It'd had to do with Kelly or my brother, the journal was a little vague.

She motioned to my phone. "See if it's her."

I pulled it out. Everett texted, *Does she know about your dad?*

"It's not Mom."

Elaine relaxed, curling against the back cushion. "She won't come here, will she?"

"No, but Everett will be here soon."

"No, no, no, noooooo ..." She groaned into her hands again.

"He won't tell her. They hate each other. His lips are sealed. I promise." That was a fact I could count on. Everett and Marjorie were vaults, keeping secrets was in their genes. "Tell me, what happened?"

She moaned. "I told him something and then he asked Mom and Dad."

"Him?"

Elaine pointed to her engagement ring like I was an idiot. She pursed her lips.

"What did you tell him?"

Her mouth fell open as if the thought of telling me hadn't occurred to her. "Just ... just you know, about babysitting."

"What about babysitting?" And yet somehow I knew. An old memory of my father smacking my younger brother across the face. Elaine was the youngest—the baby. She was a toddler and her pants were down, my brother's face flushed and sweaty. My throat went dry. My brother had been caught again.

"He asked Mom." She cradled her head. "Why? Why would he go ask *her?*"

"What'd she say?" I didn't know what to do—if giving her a hug would make her feel worse or not. Comforting siblings wasn't something I'd ever done. I'd kept to the shadows and left home as a teenager. I was more of an outsider than the spouses my siblings married.

"That sometimes I say things that aren't true and to have my medication checked." She nearly choked on the word *medication*. "She's the one who said I was depressed. She's the one who had me go to the doctor."

Mom had written in my journal, dismissing whatever I'd said about my brother. The entry was right after the social worker had visited. I felt paranoid but I believed my mom tried to rewrite my memories. It was dumb and maybe more like my dad's odd conspiracy theories, but it was a feeling I couldn't shake.

My phone rang and we both flinched. I grabbed it, only to drop it when *Mom* lit the screen. I already knew what she'd say; the same thing she said when my sister Avrie accused my middle brother. This was the same movie, different characters but the same movie I'd seen a dozen times before. Annoyed that my father had to parent, he would give a dismissive wave and pontificate. *Boys are just curious. It's part of growing up.*

Elaine, Avrie, and I had memorized the message since we were little. Boys and men had needs—and girls, we were to be silent and still.

We sat side by side, staring in silence at the phone until Everett came.

32

EVERETT ASHLEY

FIFTEEN YEARS AGO

In the middle of the high school courtyard, David adjusted the baseball cap on his head and wrapped an arm over Scarlett's shoulders. Even from a few feet away, Everett saw the flicker of panic. She straightened and scanned the crowd of students. He stepped forward, marching straight for her. Her eyes locked on him, a plea unspoken on her lips.

He came to her and threw off David's hand, sliding in between the idiot and Scarlett. Her eyes widened in fear. Everett cupped her jaw and kissed her.

She froze—and his heart sank.

He kissed her forehead and whispered, "Sorry."

The apology shook her from whatever stupor had taken over. She wrapped her arms around his waist, warming him. He ignored David's taunts and walked her to her first class.

She stood in front of the classroom door, shifting her weight with an arm still around his waist. "Thank you, for back there."

"I shouldn't have kissed you, at least not on the lips." He leaned in and kissed her temple, more for David's sake than hers. The blond-haired, blue-eyed stalker had followed them to her class.

"I was surprised is all." Her voice felt far away.

Everett leaned in, whispering, "Too soon?"

"Too soon?" she repeated, searching his face.

"It's okay to admit what happened."

She sniffed and looked away. Her arm instinctively tightened when she saw David. Everett wrapped her against his chest, cutting off her view. He glared at David and pointed at him. Students backed away, murmuring about a fight. Everett didn't care. This was one fight he wanted more than anything. He could almost taste the blood in his mouth. He was sure—well, *almost* sure—Marjorie wouldn't mind. She'd asked about Scarlett, even invited the social worker over for a private conversation.

Everett was shooed from the room while the women talked together in private for hours. He'd heard bits and pieces like *broken wing syndrome, overcoming trauma,* and *helping Scarlett heal.* He hated it— like saving Scarlet was a pet project. It wasn't a phase and it wasn't a high school crush. He'd bound himself to Scarlett whether she acknowledged it or not.

He'd written to his aunt about Scarlett and his fears of what could happen to the teenage girl he couldn't quit. Missy had written back, some of her handwriting nearly illegible. She'd admitted the thoughts that kept her shame alive, the idea that she was at fault or at least unable to stop the assault haunted her. His aunt, even decades later, still felt dirty and unworthy. Everett didn't fully understand the reasoning but was nervous to ask more questions. The assault came and went but Missy wrote about the recurring helplessness that kept her heart under lock and key. Everett feared he'd lose Scarlett to those demons—or worse, that he'd already lost a battle he'd not yet fought.

David smirked, laughing at Everett. Andy joined his friend, his face puzzled. His eyes held dark circles and sin. Guilt was painted on Andy's thinning frame. He knew the truth. Andy gave a firm nod to Everett and convinced David to leave.

An hour later, Everett ran to her classroom. He wasn't going to leave Scarlett alone. Not now, not ever again. She shouldn't have to be near her attacker, even if her mind had blanked on the details. All signs pointed to David. That was enough evidence for Everett.

A smile grew on her lips when she spotted him. Scarlett elbowed him and cocked her head to the side. "Business slow for Superman?"

"I've been reduced to long walks on the sidewalk."

"No long walks on the beach, huh?" She playfully hit him with her hip.

Everett drank in the sight of her, loving the return of a smile.

She rolled her eyes. "I'll take that as a no."

"What class do you have now?"

She frowned and her facade fell in place. "P.E."

"I thought you liked running."

She shrugged with a vacant stare.

"What don't you like about P.E.?" Everett clamped down on the fear, his mind running wild with scenarios.

"The showers." She folded her arms across her chest.

He tucked her against him. There had to be a way out.

David jumped in front of them, beaming with an overeager smile. "Aren't you two the cutest couple?"

"Move," Everett growled, towering over him. Scarlett had winced at the sudden movement.

"Gladly." David bowed and backed up. "So, Ashley, what happens when you're not the hero?"

"I'm fine being the villain." He stood between David and her. With a nod, she took advantage and escaped.

David laughed, loud and obnoxious. "You're not the only one who can provide comfort. How long do you think it'll take that little damsel in distress to find a new knight?"

"Is the knight conscious or not?"

"Poor little Ashley, all brawn and no brains." David *tsk*ed. "Always thinking with his fists."

"You can't think if you're dead," Everett spat the words between clenched teeth. Students scattered like cockroaches. He knew he looked menacing.

"So dramatic." David rolled his eyes but not before a flicker of fear surfaced.

It was enough to calm Everett. Whether or not David would admit it, he was still afraid. Ashley men had a monopoly on intimidation.

"Is there anything I should get for her?" David rocked on his heels, apparently unaware that his audience had left. "For dinner. I'll be there tonight. We'll be planning our date this weekend."

Everett lunged for him—David scrambled from reach, eyes drunk with malice. The coward disappeared on wiry legs to their next class, Economics. Everett groaned and followed David, each step taking longer than the next. He'd made it worse for Scarlett, instead of safer. He couldn't help himself.

He wasn't halfway to their class before the bell rang. He'd be tardy, and David would have a snarky comment to add to the teacher's reprimand. A few steps later and a different alarm rang out. It took a moment before Everett realized the loud speaker was announcing emergency procedures. Whispers of a bomb threat followed as students spilled from classes. David's supposed dinner plans ran through his mind. He sprinted to the girls' locker room, the principal's instructions cutting in and out over the speaker.

Everett circled the building and found only two windows, both at least six feet high. He jumped and shoved the latch open. Gripping the sill, he pulled himself up and peered in. The locker room was empty. He ran to the other window, again, empty. Two lines of girls filed out of the building, none of them Scarlett. He pushed through the doors, ignoring the shouts when his backpack clipped the shoulder of a student. He ran past the showers, knowing she wouldn't seek shelter there. The door to one of the coach's offices was left open.

"Scarlett?" No response. He flicked on the light and opened the door, checking under the desk. He blinked twice to make sure his eyes adjusted. No Scarlett.

The next office was locked. He banged on the window and put his ear next to the door.

"Scar-*lett!*" His voice carried a panicked fever.

He ran to the locker room and saw the tip of her shoes peeking out from the corner between the edges of the lockers. He rushed to her, her eyes a vacant stare. He followed her line of vision to the open locker littered with pictures of her and David the night of the dance. Someone had targeted her.

Everett ripped the pictures from the metal, tearing them to pieces.

On the back of each photo was written *tempting the preacher's son* in red marker. Everett swore, tearing the photos from the locker. He kicked the locker and leaned his head against the metal.

Scarlett didn't deserve this. Everett had failed. He couldn't protect her. He'd broken his promise to keep her safe. He'd failed his mother and now he'd failed Scarlett.

With a howl, he punched the metal door. Scarlett whimpered, bringing him back to the school. He sank to her side, his knuckles scraped and bleeding. The loud speaker crackled to life, the principal urging students outside. Everett pulled her to a stand and scooped her in his arms. Cradling her to his chest, he walked outside. A round of clapping greeted him. Scarlett squirmed, tucking her head from view. The taunts began seconds later. The not-so-subtle whispers of her second victim—as if she were the temptress and Everett, the innocent, beguiled boy. With a powerful glare he mowed down the jeers. He carried her to a crooked tree on the periphery of the students. He set her down next to him, worried the teasing would start again if he held her.

She hid behind her hands.

"Hey, talk to me, Scarlett." He pulled on her elbow.

She grabbed his bloody knuckles. "Your hands."

"I'm going to kill him."

"David didn't put the photos in my locker." She dropped his hand.

"Then who did? How'd they get the pictures?" He caught David's scowl just as the preacher's son found a teacher. David pointed at Everett with a look of victory. "David isn't giving up anytime soon."

The teacher nodded and began walking toward them both. A moment later, the lanky teacher stood over Everett. "Can I talk to you for a moment?"

Everett glanced at Scarlett, not ready to leave her alone. "If you can find another teacher to stay with her."

The teacher frowned and scratched his head. "Um ..."

Mr. Munoz walked across the lawn, his glare aimed at the group of freshman wrestling. He stopped mid-step when he saw Everett. With a quick turn, he was beside the other teacher. "Is there a problem?"

"A student said this young man was outside the cafeteria earlier."

The teacher's voice seemed unsure, revealing his inexperience. "That's where they think the bomb was placed."

"What time?" Mr. Munoz appeared anxious but Everett doubted it; Mr. Munoz kept his cards close, his emotions even closer. Everett had spent enough time with Mr. Munoz to know he allowed emotions to show

"Thirty minutes ago."

Mr. Munoz shook his head. "Mr. Ashley's a student of mine. We were discussing a project of his at that time."

The younger teacher's eyes filled with relief. "Oh, okay, then."

Mr. Munoz waited for him to leave before muttering, "So much for not lying."

SCARLETT ASHLEY
PRESENT DAY

E verett left Elaine and me in the upstairs office to talk. I was torn, knowing that Everett and Marjorie needed me as much as Elaine did. He'd called from Marjorie's, a plea in his voice. Yet he'd come and comforted me for a moment before taking out his frustrations on the kitchen remodel.

"I should go." Elaine stood awkwardly in the room, the discomfort displayed with her fidgeting and furrowed brow.

"You don't have to leave, Elaine." Folding my arms, I sat at the desk. The box was between us, although she had no idea what was in it.

Elaine nibbled on her lip. "I don't know."

"You could stay here."

She arched an eyebrow. "Like Everett would be okay with that."

Being a decade younger than me, Elaine had heard the stories my parents told of Everett. But the man who'd shown gentle concern was still a stranger to her. He was supposed to be dangerous and cruel.

Shaking my head, I said, "He's not the ogre you think he is."

When it came to protecting me, Everett couldn't help himself. He lived up to his superhero nickname well.

Elaine's lips quirked. "He's not a saint either."

"Depends on who you talk to."

"I need to go." She didn't move.

Holding out my palms, I mimicked what Everett would do when I'd get nervous. "Not trying to pressure you but you could stay here and go to Cal State Gainesfield."

"You know I can't." She dropped her gaze. "Besides, you know Mom's probably driving around Tule like a crazy person, looking for me."

Mom had called her phone eight times until finally Elaine gave in and told her she was headed home. A loud thud followed by a slew of swearwords carried up to the room.

Elaine's eyes widened. "Not an ogre?"

Chuckling, I opened the door and yelled, "You alive or dead?"

"Me or the pipe?" Everett snapped back, his low voice echoing through the somewhat empty house. The sounds of something being shoved came softer. He must be moving whatever it was to farther inside the house or toward the garage.

Turning back to the room, Elaine had walked to the window, leaning into the frame.

"Elaine?" Steeling myself, I took a deep breath and walked to the box. "There's something you should know."

She straightened but didn't move closer.

"It might be nothing or it might be something. I'm not certain." Lifting the lid, I opened the box, my heart in my throat. "I found my old journal."

"What is all this?" Elaine kneeled on the other side of the box. She picked up a folder labeled *Kelly*. My breath caught. She ran a finger down the worn paper. It had to be at least ten or more years old.

"They're files."

Elaine rolled her eyes. "Thanks, Einstein."

"My files." I waited for her to look at me. "From when I was a kid."

"Why would you have files?" Quickly, she replaced the folder, the wariness returning to her eyes. "You weren't adopted ..." *were you?* was the question left unsaid.

"Before you came to the house, we had a foster kid." Pieces, little nuggets of information, began filling my mind. "His name was Kelly. He was older than me but younger than Andy."

"Okay?" Elaine glanced around as if someone might catch us.

I'd done the same thing at my parents' house—as if finding answers was a nefarious activity, a betrayal of our parents. "I don't know details, and quite honestly, I can't remember."

"Details about what?" She dropped her gaze.

"I think ..." The words wouldn't come. I opened my mouth to speak but my tongue wouldn't work. Grabbing my journal, I flipped to the page Mom had written. I held it out for Elaine to read.

"She wrote in your journal?" Elaine grabbed the journal, her mouth open. "This talks about Andy."

I reached for the journal. "Let me show you where the social worker is trying to talk to me about Kelly, the foster kid."

"She didn't believe you." Elaine dropped the book. "Because you didn't have details."

Silence filled the room, adding more tension with each passing second. My shoulders ached from the heaviness. Kneeling over the box, I put the journal back. There were two files, one labeled *Kelly* and one labeled *Scarlett*.

"I don't have details." Elaine's voice was barely above a whisper. "Mom asked me if I'd told anyone else."

With a hand on a folder, I paused.

"Avrie said the same thing." Elaine sniffed, her eyes on the box. "She answers my calls sometimes. She still won't talk to anyone but Andy."

"Yeah, well he is the golden child."

Elaine's gaze snapped to mine. "How come?"

Shrugging, I ran a finger along the edge of the box. "It's just always been that way."

"But you were Dad's favorite." She bit her lip, looking every bit the sheepish child. "Avrie never was."

"You were Dad's favorite too." More images began falling into place, the relief that I was no longer Dad's favorite when Everett came along. The feeling was odd, a mixture of abandonment and freedom.

Elaine looked away. "Yeah, I know."

In the box, a book was wrapped inside Everett's hoodie. Pulling back the fabric, *Jennifer Delfin* was inscribed on the front. Everett had stolen Mom's journal. Glancing at Elaine, I didn't know what to do. My hands went sweaty. There could be so many answers in there, but most of my siblings eventually spilled everything to my mother, the few times we confided in each other. Mom had a unique way of prying information from us, using each other as competition to get what she wanted. We all knew it; we just didn't know how to stop it.

Sliding the lid over the box, I sat back. "Do you remember anything?"

Elaine clamped her mouth shut and shook her head—which meant she did remember.

"I meant what I said. You could stay, go to college here."

"Who would take care of Dad? Mom?" She shook her head again.

My stomach twisted, and my throat went dry. Being my father's favorite doomed us to the brunt of Mom's temper and the weight of Dad's affection. Elaine attended the community junior college in Tule, barely a half step above high school—which meant she was wholly dependent and easily controlled.

"You can't stay there."

Elaine held up her phone. "I can't stay here either."

Mom texted her. *Almost there.*

"How does she know where you're at?" My voice came hoarse. "I thought she was still in Tule?"

"There's a GPS app or something." Elaine shrugged and put her phone down, the air between us had changed. She was no longer needing consoling; she'd turned suspicious somehow. "I'm on their account, and they can see where I'm at."

"That doesn't bother you?" My family and even David accused Everett of controlling and manipulating me. "You don't think that's an invasion of privacy?"

Elaine stood and faced the window, her arms crossed. "I live with them. What can I say?"

"You can say no."

She rolled her eyes. "Not everyone's like you."

"Meaning?"

"Not everyone gets a ticket out of town." Elaine braced herself. "Everett seems nice and all but didn't you just swap Mom and Dad for him?"

"Not even close."

"He keeps you under lock and key. He even skips town and you're bound to him." Elaine's voice was monotone, almost rehearsed. These were my mother's words.

"Are you trying to justify staying with Mom and Dad? You don't have to—"

Keeping her voice soft, she whispered, "You might have left Tule but it's not like you really escaped. You're still just as stuck as I am."

"I'm not living with my parents."

"You're still living under someone else's roof." The words were firm but her delivery lacked force. "I don't want to jump from my father's house to another man's home."

"Then don't." There was something else going on. "What did he say, your beloved fiancé? What did he say when Mom told him about you being depressed?"

Elaine frowned at *beloved fiancé*. She'd never been fond of sarcasm. "He asked if he could come to the next doctor's appointment."

"Do you want him to go? I mean, you're talking about the psychiatrist right?" I kept my hands in my jean pockets, fighting the urge to shake her shoulders. Not that I really could. She was at least eight inches taller than me.

"I don't know." She hunched over, appearing small and delicate.

"You should do what makes you feel comfortable."

Elaine shot me a look of surprise. "Isn't that a little ironic? You of all people telling me that?"

Taking a step back, I held out my hands. "Name one thing I've done that I don't feel comfortable doing?"

"Anything to do with our parents."

Rolling my eyes, I said, "I meant with Everett."

She scoffed. "Okay, anything to do with Everett."

"Which means you can't name one thing." I shoved my hands in my pockets. "Look, I get that everyone hates him, at least everyone in our family, but that doesn't make him wrong. That doesn't make what

Everett and I have wrong." A feeling of relief filled my belly, turning my bones into steel. It didn't make sense but it felt good—it felt true. "Just because Mom and Dad did or said something doesn't make them right."

Elaine started, her mouth dropping. "Mom's here."

She circled me and scurried downstairs. I followed, hoping Everett was busy with the kitchen. Between Marjorie and my father, neither Everett nor Mom needed a reason to unleash their tempers.

Elaine walked out to the front patio, a false smile on her lips. Following her, I quietly closed the door.

Mom parked her behemoth of a car on the street, her lips stretched into a severe frown. "Elaine, would it kill you to answer the phone?" She turned an arched eyebrow on me, adding a hand on a hip. It was a mother's pose if there ever was one. "And you, Scarlett. What is going on with you? Do you have any idea how hurtful it is to be ignored by your own daughter? Your father was in jail. In *jail*."

"Hi, Mom." Giving a half-hearted wave was all I could do. A mixture of emotions swirled in the pit of my stomach.

Mom groaned and walked up the sidewalk. "Go home, Elaine. I need to speak with Scarlett."

"Goodie." It escaped before I could catch it.

Elaine smirked and gave me a *good luck* smile before getting in her truck and driving away. It would be months, if not years, before I'd be able to really talk to her like this again. Mom would make sure of it.

"My daughter is ridiculous." Mom had caught the smirk, her jaw set. She was teetering between neurotic and irate.

"You have three. You'll have to be a tad more specific." The words took me by surprise. Sarcasm was an old tool in my arsenal but the sudden steel in my bones was new. Strength. I felt strong, and I didn't understand where or how it came.

"Your father's been released. Thanks for asking." She'd ignored my comment completely.

"How did you know Elaine was here?" Two could play at this game.

Mom narrowed her eyes. "How can you be this rude to your own mother?"

A pang of shame set the growing sense of strength free. She was right and didn't deserve to be greeted like this.

"I'm sorry." I took a deep breath and motioned toward the front door. "Would you like to come in?"

Her mouth fell open, her eyes wide. "*Now* you invite me in?"

"You've been here maybe a minute. Is there a specific timeline I'm supposed to adhere to?" I bit the inside of my cheek. This level of snarkiness was something I did as a teenager.

She folded her arms and swallowed hard. "And just how will Everett feel with me being in his home?"

"Our home."

She'd freaked when I moved from the dorms to Marjorie's house, even if she didn't know for nearly a year. But she couldn't undo that decision any more than she could undo this. I repeated it twice in my head but it didn't loosen the knot in my stomach.

"Why do you do this?" Mom closed her eyes for a moment and rubbed the bridge of her nose. "You can't just be honest and answer a question. You have to dance around and make me look like the bad guy."

"Does it matter? I mean really, does it matter?" I motioned toward the front door again and willed myself to be brave. "Where I live is kind of up to me, not you."

She waved a hand in my direction. "Do you feel any guilt for speaking this way? Have I completely failed as a mother?"

Her voice pierced me and I took a step back, feeling the weight of her scrutiny. She was right. There wasn't a reason for my defensiveness. My nerves were on high alert. The journal. Elaine. "I'm sorry. I should have said that differently."

"Apparently, my children never learned how to treat their parents." Mom frowned and returned to her folded arms stance. "Your family needs you, Scarlett."

Dread filled me, and I prayed Everett would come outside.

"And not just with Elaine's issues." Mom shook her head, disgust written on her face. "Heaven knows that child needs help."

"She's almost twenty."

"She should start acting like it." Her hands gripped the sleeves of her cardigan. "She ended her engagement. Threw a tantrum and is walking out on that poor boy."

"It'll work out, Mom. However it's supposed to work out, it'll happen."

She took step closer. "No, it won't work out, Scarlett." Her jaw tightened. Her frustration was barely contained. "She's going to throw away a chance at a good man. Not everyone gets chance after chance."

"What are you wanting me to do?" My heart raced. It was stupid. She was just my mother. I took another step back.

"Nothing. Stay out of it." She made a wide *x* with her hands as if the movement erased Elaine's words. "Let her be."

"She came to me, Mom."

"And what did you tell her?" Mom lifted her chin, daring me to lie.

"I let her talk."

"What did she say?" A flicker of fear appeared in her eyes. She narrowed her gaze, wiping the evidence away.

"She confided in her fiancé, only to have him run to you about it." The image of Elaine's tear-stained face gave me courage. "She was devastated to learn that not only is her future husband more loyal to her mom but that her mom isn't loyal to her at all."

"I've been nothing but devoted, despite—"

"Despite what?" A rush, a force of courage like nothing I'd ever felt before washed over me, willing me to keep going. Fear fell from me, replaced with a foreign anger—calm and collected. It filled me with power. "Despite the fact that your son touched her? That you look the other way when you should be looking at her? Protecting her? That you took her in only to feed her to the wolves in your own home?"

Mom straightened, her cheeks crimson. "How dare you."

"You knew what was happening to her and you did nothing." Each word came louder than the next. The accusation hung between us.

"We don't know what happened, Scarlett. I asked her—asked her a million times for details but could she ever give me any? No. Do you know why? Because it's a lie. Her wild imagination takes over. She doesn't care at all about our family. She cares more about condemning your brother than her own engagement. Have I turned her out for this? No." She inhaled sharply. "Why? Because I'm her mother. I wouldn't turn on her. I'd help her. Just like I help all my children."

"Details don't always come, Mom." The anger subsided, losing ground to a rising fear. I didn't have details, only doubt in its absence. Everett was in the kitchen but I wished he was here now. His presence would make the conversation tenser but there was also safety. And warmth. "Memories can be fuzzy."

"I came here to ask for help, and this is what I get." Mom's lip quivered, fury in her eyes. "I cannot believe this."

"I can't help you with Elaine." *I won't help you* was what I meant and by the look on Mom's face, she heard the intent. Mom's version of helping was maintaining composure for the greater good, the greater good being my family's image.

She picked at the hem of her cardigan. "We plan on paying for your attorney fees."

"What attorney fees?" In the flurry of my father's arrest, I'd forgotten about Mom forging my signature on their home. "Wait, I'm getting sued because of your mistake?"

"It's not that big of a deal." Mom threw back her shoulders. "You were the obvious choice. You weren't married. We wanted to make sure you'd be provided for if Dad and I passed away. If you'd—"

"You forged—*you* did this." She was going to use the attorney fees as leverage. It wouldn't be the first time she'd dangle a carrot in front of me. "Thank you, but I already have an attorney. And I'm married."

"You *what?*" Mom pointed a finger at me, her head shaking. She lifted her chin. "Your father is going to be so depressed over this."

"Over me being married?"

"I can't believe this. I just—I just can't." Mom's pursed her lips. She took a step forward, then back. "First the county screws up the title on our home. Then Elaine has another breakdown and now this. You get yourself married? *Married?* You didn't even invite us? You eloped?"

"Mom—"

Mom held up her hand. "Do you have any idea what your father might do with this? He's been on suicide watch for weeks. How could you be so cruel?" Her lip quivered. "I don't know what I did to deserve this. I'm your mother. I've been worried sick about you. David said you looked awful. Only to come to find out that you've—"

"Mother—"

"No." She shook the pointed finger at me. "You will not talk your way out of this. You're destroying our family. I don't know why I'm surprised. It's just like you. Going off on your own, thinking only about yourself. You don't think your father and I want to be a part of your life? A wedding, Scarlett. It's a wedding. Our daughter got married and we didn't even get to be a part of it."

❧ 34 ❧

EVERETT ASHLEY
FIFTEEN YEARS AGO

Everett cut the engine and gently closed the door of the coupe. In the still of the night, even his breath felt loud. He jogged, as silent as possible, down Scarlett's street and hopped the fence. Her father's worthless mutt whimpered, tucked its tail, and ran to the other side of the house. Everett pulled the sleeves of his sweatshirt over his hands. His pulse pounded in his ears. Without a sound, he pulled the window screen off and slid open her window.

Quick on his feet, he landed softly inside and kneeled at her bedside. "Scarlett."

She recoiled with a start.

"Hey, hey ... It's me, Everett," he cooed, reaching for her. "Get dressed."

"Why?"

"I need you to trust me." His voice shook. He needed her to come and come *now*. "Please."

Wordlessly, she went to her dresser. He turned from her, giving her privacy. A moment later, he helped her from the window, her head tucked in her hoodie. He gave her a leg up to the fence and swallowed the alarm. She'd become lighter, too light. He landed beside her in the front yard. They jogged, hand in hand, to the car.

Everett waited for the questions as they drove away, but she faced the window, arms folded. He turned down his road, and despite inviting Davenport, he flinched at the police car parked in front of his house.

"Everett." Scarlett gripped his arm, her voice cracking.

"It's not what you think."

"Then give me something to think." She tightened her grip. "Now, Everett."

The words wouldn't come. His tongue felt thick, his throat dry. He'd risked everything and now didn't know if he should've. If this didn't work—he swallowed the thought. It had to work. Scarlett needed out of that house. She needed to be safe and free, even if she didn't know it yet.

The front door opened. The living room light spilled out onto the porch and steps. Marjorie stood on the threshold, her hands wringing in front of her.

"I guess she'll tell me, then." Scarlett left the car, slamming the door, and made her way to Marjorie.

The older woman embraced Scarlett with a worried frown. Everett followed behind them, giving a curt nod to a solemn Davenport appearing in the doorframe next to Marjorie.

Scarlett reared back. "What is going on?"

Everett ushered everyone inside and closed the door. He braced himself for the long night. He'd begged and made impossible promises to get everyone here. He'd manipulated the guilt and pity of every adult present. And he'd do it again.

"What is this?" Scarlett's voice pierced the air, tension filling the room.

Marjorie's old friend, Judge Tanner, and Everett's social worker sat on opposite ends of the old leather couch, their backs stiff and lips taut. Detective Davenport paced in front of the fireplace.

A soft knock on the door sent a collective flinch to everyone in the room.

"Aren't we a pretty picture this morning?" Mr. Munoz's voice pierced the heavy room.

With hands clenched, Scarlett whirled around to Everett. "Tell me. Now."

"What, your long-winded boyfriend didn't tell you what's going on?" Mr. Munoz clapped a hand on Everett's shoulder. "I can never get a word in when he's around."

The teacher's comment took Everett back. He didn't want to scare Scarlett off before he knew he could really help. He wanted everything in place before asking her to uproot her life.

Scarlett's shoulders relaxed slightly. "Will somebody do the honors?"

"Your parents wouldn't sign the forms," Everett said dumbly. "For college."

"I'm aware." Her eyes flicked from Everett to the social worker and then back again. "And that has to do with everyone how?"

Marjorie shook her head and clucked to herself, her disapproval evident. She went to the fireplace and hugged herself. Guilt fell on Everett's shoulders. Scarlett's presence poured painful memories into Marjorie's mind. By bringing Scarlett, Everett had added to the poor woman's sorrows.

"You're technically a minor, Scarlett. You need their permission to attend college." Everett shifted his weight. "But if you were emancipated, you would be an adult and could, well, do whatever."

"And how does one become emancipated?" Scarlett's mask was firmly in place, her voice neutral. There was no evidence she'd been woken in the middle of the night or snuck from her room to a house on the outskirts of town.

"I was under the impression the details had already been discussed." Judge Tanner, Marjorie's friend, tapped a finger on his knee.

"She's written extensively on why and how she's independent from her family." Mr. Munoz patted the folder in his arm. "We have a detective and social worker that can also present a similar story."

"And how long have you sat around planning my future?" Scarlett asked evenly. "Without me, I might add."

"You can't stay in that house." Everett reached for her but froze when she glared at him.

Her hands trembled, her lips pinched. "And just where am I supposed to stay?" She held out her arms in surrender. "I'd be homeless."

"Here, Letty," Marjorie said softly. "Stay here."

The judge stood with a groan. "I cannot be a part of this."

"Don't go." Everett felt the panic rising. "Please, it's coming out all wrong, but I don't know what to do. I need her safe. I need to know she's okay, and she's *not* okay in that house." He waved at the social worker. "The evidence is there."

"I'm standing right here, Everett," Scarlett snapped. "Right. Here."

"So am I." Everett's voice rose. He threw back his head and said to the ceiling, "I'm watching it all happen and can't do a damn thing. I want you to be safe and happy. Why is this so hard?"

Scarlett scowled. "I'm not in danger."

The judge gave a nod to Marjorie. "Good night."

"You were in danger, Scarlett." The social worker stood and brushed phantom dirt from her jeans. "But I understand your reluctance to say otherwise."

"You can't expect the poor girl to go against her family, Ashley." Davenport shook his head, his face drawn. "She could have hundreds of reports or investigations into her parents, but she's too old to force the issue. If she were five or six, they'd take the evidence and run with it."

"Again, right here." Scarlett held up her hand.

"Are you?" Mr. Munoz scratched his jaw. "Because I only see the shadow of the girl I knew."

The judge paused, his hand almost at the door. Silence mixed with the tension.

"Everett's not going to give up. He's like a rabid dog." Mr. Munoz tossed the folder to the empty seat on the couch left by the judge. Everett's head snapped to attention. Mr. Munoz sat next to the folder with a sigh. "Pitch your fit or punch him. Do whatever it is that you're going to do to him because he cares. But everyone in this room, well, except the guy leaving, knows you're not okay."

Scarlett tucked her chin while the judge dropped his hand.

"And let's be honest, you're dying. In one way or the other, you're dying. Shriveling away to nothing." Mr. Munoz gave a half-hearted wave as if this conversation was as trivial as the weather. "Only your writing is still strong."

"It's okay, Letty," Marjorie said softly, adding light to a dark room.

Scarlett fidgeted, folding then unfolding her arms. Everett stared at her, willing her to look at him. He needed to see her face, to gauge her reaction.

"If they find out ..." Scarlett whispered.

"What would happen, child?" The judge turned around, his eyes soft. "If they found out you were attending college, what would happen?"

It felt trivial. Unreal. Parents wanted their kids to move on, grow up. Unless they needed to maintain control and keep buried secrets where they belonged.

"I don't ... know." She glanced up at Everett, fear in her eyes. "They're just trying to be parents. And going to the junior college at my age could be dangerous." Her voice lifted at the end into a question. She wasn't buying her own excuses.

"What if we got the forms signed?" Mr. Munoz asked a touch too innocently.

"You mean forging her parents' signatures," Davenport said with a roll of his eyes. "That's not happening. Besides, getting her to the junior college doesn't help her. It'll get her out eventually, but it doesn't solve the problem of today. Of now."

A loud bark came from outside the door. Marjorie smiled an apology and let the horse of a dog inside. Ignoring everyone else, the dog snorted at Everett and padded toward Scarlett, shoving its nose to her middle.

Scarlett cradled the dog's head, her lips cracking to a faint smile. "You don't have to do this. I don't know how Everett convinced you all to be here but I'll be fine. It's not as bad as whatever he's said. I can predict the moods and I know how to avoid certain situations."

"Like what?" the social worker asked. "What can you avoid? Can you predict when taking a shower is safe?"

Scarlett gasped, her hand covering her mouth. Her color drained in an instant. "You don't know what you're talking about."

"Kelly was very observant. He knew what was tolerated, even encouraged." The woman swallowed hard. "He just didn't realize when to stop talking."

The energy of the room shifted. Everyone but Everett exchanged looks. Everett relaxed, knowing the adults' focus was now the same as his.

"If you could have anything, if this were a perfect world, what would you want?" The judge's deep voice carried across the room.

Without looking up, Scarlett answered, "To leave without leaving and escape without escaping. You know, the impossible."

"You mean fallout. Not having them freak out." Davenport glanced at his watch.

Scarlett gave a shrug. "Sure."

"Sure doesn't cut it." Mr. Munoz pulled the folder onto his lap.

Scarlett swept the beginning of her smile away, replacing the look with a stoic expression. The dog nudged Scarlett backward until she sat on the couch. Everett fought the growl threatening to escape. He wanted to shake her by the shoulders and scream. The vacant stares, the shrinking frame, and the hollow tone in her voice created an urgency in Everett. He was surrounded by solid pillars of the community but felt strangely alone.

"I can't go to the junior college." Scarlett's eyes flicked to Everett. It was only a moment but he saw the spark of hope. "It's too close to home."

"Cal State Gainesfield is an hour south." Mr. Munoz turned to the social worker. "They have the same program as the junior college, don't they?"

The woman nodded hesitantly, her eyes wary. "Yes, but there would have to be a paper trail. Scholarships based on need, especially with federal funding and the fact she's not emancipated, will make it trickier."

"What kind of paper trail?" Scarlett lifted her chin with a look of defiance.

"From when you were a kid," Everett whispered so low he wondered if she heard. "Not the night of the dance."

Scarlett's hands instantly shook. She clasped both together and gave a slight nod.

"Tell me what you want, and I'll make it happen." Everett edged closer while Mr. Munoz and the social worker entered their own discussion.

"I don't want the fallout. Doesn't matter how innocent or how trivial, their reaction ... can be extreme." She glanced up, her facade gone. Raw and vulnerable, she finally let Everett in. "I do want to leave. But I'm scared to be alone."

Everett kneeled, his hands on the armrest of the sofa. "You being alone was never part of the plan."

Scarlett gave him a searching look, the hope building. "I can't ask you to leave Marjorie."

"We stay here and commute to Gainesfield." He leaned forward. "We can make this work, Scarlett. I promise."

Her cheeks pinked and she turned away. "It's a lot to ask of you, of everyone."

"Just promise me you'll say yes, and I'll consider us even."

She rolled her eyes. "Right, that's sounds fair."

"I didn't ask the question yet." Everett stared at her, letting the intensity show. Her eyes widened and the blush deepened. He wrapped an arm around the sofa to her hand. The dog's head hid Everett's hand. He squeezed Scarlett's. "But when I do ask, say yes."

❦ 35 ❦

SCARLETT ASHLEY

PRESENT DAY

Tears streamed down my mother's face as she climbed into her suburban, her eyes murderous. She turned on the car and left, but the anger stayed. It steeled something in me, deeper than my bones.

Without a word to Everett, I marched upstairs while he carried on the work. That's who he was, always restoring, always helping. The house was the greatest witness to it all. Before he moved my meager belongings in, he'd renovated the downstairs bathroom and ripped out every upstairs bathtub. To this day, the thought of a bath gave a shiver down my spine. That and 90s wallpaper. The three bathrooms upstairs still hadn't been touched. The holes left by each vacant tub looked more like the gap-toothed smile of a toddler instead of a half-remodeled house.

Opening the box, I pulled out both journals, my mother's journal that Everett stole and mine. Minutes turned to hours as I wrote a timeline, reading between Mom's veiled words. The entries that were particularly happy, except for a line or two about how she's hoping a child will stop acting out lined up with every one of my entries—I'd unwittingly documented every questionable moment, for myself and my sisters.

"You okay?" Everett's voice startled me.

I froze—feeling guilty, both for having my mother's journal and for making the timeline. "Yes, I think. Or maybe no."

He entered the room, filling it with warmth. Even with the dark circles and exhaustion lining his face, he was beautiful. He was mine.

I didn't know if it was the candid moment or the soft afternoon light coming in from the window, but he held me fast. My breath caught; he'd seized a power over me since the day I met him. There was a vulnerability in his eyes that had bound me.

His smile grew—he was reading me. With a confident lift of his chin, he peeled off his construction gloves. "Where's Elaine?"

"She left." Closing both journals, I said, "Mom came and I'm pretty sure I'm disinherited."

"Jokes on them. There's nothing to inherit." He smirked. My heart skipped a beat.

"I've been added to the lawsuit." At this, I couldn't meet his gaze.

"I know." He tossed the gloves on the wood tile in the hallway. "You haven't been served but it's been filed."

"I didn't sign it." There it was, out in the open. "Mom forged my signature."

They'd done so much worse before I ever left home. Mom and Dad could be a united front when it came to their image. Dad's Porsche was given to a friend while my parents conveniently collected insurance money on the supposed theft. It wasn't a day later that my mother taught a Sunday school lesson to the youth on being virtuous, my dad offering his pearls of wisdom throughout the discussion.

"Yeah, I figured that." Everett wiped his forehead with his thumb. "They'll make you feel guilty. So much so, you'd probably commit perjury and say you signed it after all."

"I told her I wouldn't help her."

"Did you now?" He smiled, a rare and genuine moment. His eyes even twinkled, beaming with pride. "Is that a fact?"

"I told her ..." I swallowed hard. "... that I'm married."

In two steps, Everett kneeled at my side.

Shaking my head, I held up a finger to keep him from touching me.

"I don't know what's going to happen. Not with my dad or David or Andy. And I don't know what's going on with us."

He threaded his fingers through my other hand. "Not gonna lie, you drive me crazy." He squeezed it tighter, saying, "But you make me whole. You make everything whole."

"I don't know, Everett." When his face fell, I added, "I try to get everything to stop spinning and when you're here, like right here, everything is okay. I feel safe, I feel like you're home. But when I'm by myself, or when I think about Mom or Dad, everything starts shifting. I start wondering if you're real, we're real. If anything is real. And question why you're still here. I mean, let's be honest, you could be anywhere with anyone."

Leaning forward, he kissed my forehead and tugged my chin upward with a finger. "I can't go anywhere without you. I tried. And failed."

An electric hum snapped between us. I kept my eyes down, wondering if I was the only one that felt it. He brushed a flyaway off my forehead. I breathed in the scent of him.

A burst of memories came alive—and for the first time, they centered on him *and* feeling safe. The memories jockeyed for position. The first was the phone call at two in the morning when my parents were screaming at each other. He drove over, killing the headlights and engine four houses down. He snuck to the window and crawled inside, holding me till I fell asleep. He was gone in the morning, a sketch of me sleeping tucked under my pillow.

Another moment followed; the bomb threat my sophomore year, the alarm ringing on the loud speaker. He'd tucked me to his chest and I knew, just as I knew now, that I was going to be okay. That I was safe.

Another memory, we were in his car. He was teaching me to drive on the dirt roads surrounding his house. My foot slipped off the brake to the gas, shooting us over the cut tree trunk. Shocked, I stared out the windshield. Everett leaned over and said, "Too soon for a Woman Driver joke?"

We burst into laughter and he helped me from the car. It was a whole new level of comfort. He hadn't yelled or guilted me for not knowing how to drive like my parents had. They had me run errands for the store despite being wholly unprepared—and far too young. Legal and illegal were gray areas for my parents, and often viewed as guidelines instead of laws.

But Everett, he was steady. Predictable.

His eyes, both hard and soft, steel and blue, met my gaze. I traced his scar. His hand covered mine. I brought his head to mine.

"You're home to me, Scarlett." Everett squeezed my hand. "And I hope one day you'll feel safe."

"I am safe," I whispered, and maybe, just a little, I started to believe it.

Another memory burst into my head. The dance. His voice screaming my name in the dark and his arms whisking me away. He'd kept me warm and brought me to Marjorie's house. I was safe. *He* was safe.

I brushed my lips against his. He kissed me back, gently. A hunger grew inside me. His lips traveled down my neck. And then fear—I jumped back.

Everett held out his palms. "It's okay, Scarlett."

"How mad are you?"

His muscles went taut. "What?"

Feeling small, I answered, "How mad are you? I know men ... have needs and that—"

He recoiled. "You know that's sick, right? Your father's nuts."

If there was a way to disappear, I'd take it, but he stood between me and the door.

"Men have wants, not needs." He stood and wiped his face. "We're not monsters. We don't just take it. And if we do, that's wrong. On every level, that's wrong. And sick, Scarlett. Just sick."

I said nothing, keeping him in my periphery, unable to look at him.

"I'm not mad, Scarlett." His rough voice said otherwise. "I mean, I'm not mad at you."

Even before Everett arrived in high school, I was surrounded by handsy boys and hormone-crazed girls getting caught up in passion-filled moments. I'd never been caught up in any moment. It wasn't until Everett, with his barely healed face and bruised body, that I'd ever felt an inkling of a desire. It wasn't hormone driven or even lustful. It was a soft, compassionate pull. I'd touched his face within minutes of meeting him—something I'd never done to any boy or man, not before. Nor after. Only Everett could glare with kind eyes, or gently move with clenched fists at his side.

I confessed, "I don't know how to get over this."

"Hey, I'm not mad at you." Everett's face softened but he still didn't look me in the eye. "None of this is your fault."

"I want to be with you, but I'm hurting you."

He scratched his forehead with his thumb. "Isn't that what I'm doing? Every time I touch you, I hurt you or make you freeze?"

"No." I groaned. "Maybe? I don't know. I don't even know for sure why. I don't even know what really happened to make me this way."

"It's not uncommon—"

"It's not just that." I flicked my thighs, needing something to do with my hands. "I want to be with you. I've always wanted to be with you. But I need you to answer me something, and I need an honest answer."

"Okay." He'd broken the word in two.

"If you—if *we* can never, you know—"

"After everything, you're still asking me this?" He took a step back. "What do I have to prove? I'm here aren't I?"

"So much for not being mad." This was the reason I'd kept silent.

As a teenager, I refused to watch one of my father's favorite movies, one about a girl being brutalized. One stupid comment about not wanting to watch it, and for weeks, my family mocked me. If I asked for someone to pass the salt, they'd shake it over my head, laughing as the granules fell down my shirt. Towels disappeared from the bathroom when I showered—my siblings and father picked the lock, stealing the towels and my clothes. I'd cry in the bathroom, determined to not walk through the house naked. I'd wrap myself in the dirty rug and run to my room.

"I wasn't mad at you for freezing up. I get that. Do I want to kill David? Yeah. Do I want to rip your dad's head off? Yeah. Your brother and Kelly? Obviously. Do I want to punch all of them in the skull a few dozen times—yeah, although that might make it a little awkward in court but the temptation is still there." He worked his jaw and swallowed hard. "I'm not mad at you for your reaction to me. That blame lies elsewhere. What ticks me off is you're always one foot out the door. Any slight hesitation on my part and you're bailing. *That's* what hurts. You could freak out every time I touch you, and I would never blame you. But do you know how many times a day I wonder if you're still here?"

"And yet, you're the one that left." The words hung in the air between us. He'd left when our world was falling apart. "You left when Marjorie needed you the most."

"Because ..." He placed both hands on his hips, his bare chest rising and falling. "I was wrong. And I couldn't watch her die. Yes, I felt like you were far away, but that wasn't all of it. I was—the whole thing—it wasn't right. But there it is. It's the truth."

I waited for the anger, the righteous indignation. It didn't come, sorrow filled me instead. He'd left because he couldn't face death. Weakness—or fear—wasn't what I had expected. His vulnerability calmed me, piercing the questions that had plagued me for roughly fifteen years. I reached for his hand, sandwiching his between mine.

"I'm sorry, Letty."

"I know." And I did.

We said nothing, letting the moment be. Mom would call me desperate, eager to buy whatever excuse Everett sold. But this, *us*, felt right.

"What's this?" He nodded at my timeline.

"I don't know if I'm being petty, but I just wanted to make sense of it all." Not that it helped. "I still don't really know what happened."

"What do you want to do?" With his index finger, he slid the paper closer.

"What I've always wanted. Peace. Leave without hearing about how terrible I am for leaving." It came out a little too easily.

"Let's go." He didn't move. Neither did I. "Scarlett?"

"Part of me wants to scream. Tell everyone what I'm thinking. Feeling."

"Do it."

"Part of me wants to hide. Never see the light of day."

"Don't."

"You know what I mean." I shot him a look, receiving a smile as a reward.

"Put this in your column." Everett slid the paper back. "Let the world see it."

"Ha!" Rolling my eyes, I sighed. "I have no proof, and plus, Gaines-field isn't the world."

"People need to see the truth, the real truth." He squeezed my hand. "Most girls don't remember details."

I tried to pull back. He held it firm.

"Most girls blame themselves or worse, doubt anything happened." A look, normally reserved for his father, crossed his face. "But the biggest problem is the ambiguity, the not knowing. That part needs a voice."

"You, the lawyer, would be okay accusing without evidence?"

"I see plenty of evidence." He added when I scoffed, "If I brought both these journals and compelled your sisters—both of them—to testify, I bet it'd sway a jury. Or at least get them to think."

"That would encourage false accusations." I flicked my pen on the desk. "That isn't right either."

"There is nothing black and white about this." Everett blinked and turned his head. "Marjorie told me that, the night of the dance."

Marjorie. The woman had bound us together. She'd loved us both—and was on the verge of leaving us.

"I'm sorry, Everett." Leaning forward, I wrapped my arms around his neck.

He pulled my hands from off his neck, holding them in each of his. "I'm a coward."

A single tear slid down his cheek. In all the years, I'd known him, he'd never cried. Not when he had to battle his father in court, not when Marjorie had fallen, and not when I'd given him the ring back.

Cradling his head between my hands, I asked, "What can I do?"

"Wait with me." He brushed off the tear. "Doctor said it's time."

❧ 36 ❧

EVERETT ASHLEY

FIFTEEN YEARS AGO

E verett stomped his shoes to stay warm, Scarlett's birthday present in his pocket. He'd parked around the corner in the university faculty parking lot and waited.

And waited.

Cal State Gainesfield's campus had few trees and even fewer hiding spots. It'd been at least an hour, and he was beginning to lose feeling in his feet. He debated on jumping back in the car and turning the heat on blast, but he worried he'd miss the Delfins arriving. Frustration turned to anger at the thought. He still couldn't believe what Mr. Munoz had told him. Winter break was in full swing, but Jennifer was eager to get rid of her troublesome daughter. She planned to leave Scarlett alone in the dorms. Scarlett had been granted temporary emancipation to enroll for the semester, and the Delfins were none too pleased.

He hated that his grand plan had backfired. There wasn't another soul around except for the skeleton crew for basic necessities. She was supposed to be given freedom by attending the university, not a remote house arrest. Jennifer was assured by the dean—a personal friend of the judge—that she would be looked after because of Scarlett's underage status, regardless of emancipation. Everett didn't care who or what was promised. He wasn't leaving Scarlett alone in the dorms. He wasn't going to leave her alone period.

A brand new SUV pulled into the parking lot, Scarlett's siblings pouring out from the doors. Her brother Andy looked both bored and sleep-deprived, his eyes underlined with dark circles. Her father, Lucas, wrapped an arm around Scarlett. Even from behind the brush, Everett could see her flinch. Everett waited for them to enter the dorm. He'd slip off to his car for a few minutes, knowing they'd need time to set her up. At least he knew she was here. And safe.

He turned and heard the front door of the dorm open again. Her family—except Scarlett—jumped back in the car. Everett froze, wondering what this turn of events meant. Her father threw the car in reverse while her brother sat in the passenger seat, cranking up the music. And then left. The entire family left. Everett stared after them. They didn't set up her room. They didn't say good bye—at least, not from what he could tell. He rushed around the building to the front door. The weather stripping had caught the bottom edge of the door, leaving it ajar. He threw it open and ran inside. Light spilled from a door down the hall.

Everett ran, pausing at her doorway to force a calm expression. Scarlett stood with her hand on the window, her gaze on the empty parking lot. A single box and duffle bag lay on the empty bed. Her profile was to him; the same profile he once thought was plain and forgettable now stole his breath. He stepped in the room and pulled the small gift-wrapped box from his pocket.

"Scarlett?"

Startled, she turned with wide eyes. In one graceful step, Everett tossed the small box to her bed and cupped her head in his hands. She bit her trembling lip.

He kissed her forehead and cradled her against him. "You're not staying here."

"They just left. They dropped off my stuff and l-l-left ..." Her voice caught on the last syllable. "I wasn't trying to be difficult."

Everett tipped her chin, drinking in the sight of her pain. "I'm so sorry. This is all my fault. I wanted you to be free, not alone."

She gave a pitiful smile. "It's okay."

"It's not okay." He brought his forehead against hers. "I swear I'll make it up to you. I'm so, so sorry."

Scarlett laughed, a mixture of nerves and caution. "It's fine. I'm fine."

Everett scowled and was rewarded with her true smile. He grabbed the thin box. "Happy birthday, Scarlett."

Her mouth fell open, tears falling. "You remembered."

And then Everett felt the heaviness. "They forgot?"

She bit her lip and looked down at her feet. He pulled her hand to him, placing the box in her palm. They'd dumped her at the school and forgot her birthday—and Jennifer Delfin thought Everett came from a messed up family. Scarlett glanced up, her eyes unsure. Everett smiled and hoped the anger didn't show.

With a fingernail, she lifted a corner of the wrapping and carefully unveiled the plain brown box. She eyed Everett, lifting the lid. She gasped and held up a silver car key.

"I promised freedom." Everett held her other hand, his thumb rubbing her soft skin. "Let's go, Scarlett."

"Wait, what you do mean, let's go?"

"I'm not leaving you here." Everett smirked. "Besides, you're my ride home."

He hitched her duffle bag to his shoulder and grabbed her other box. She hesitated a moment before following him out to the parking lot. Depositing her things in the trunk of the sedan, he held out his arms. "What do you think?"

Scarlett shook her head and said softly, "I can't accept this."

Everett's heart sank. He'd gone over and over consumer reports for the most dependable car, especially since she'd be commuting from Gainesfield. With every form signed, her parents couldn't renege on her admission. They couldn't do a thing, unless by some miracle Scarlett lost her emancipation bid. According to Marjorie's friend, that wasn't going to happen. All Scarlett needed now was reliable transportation, but with the look in her eye, Everett second guessed his gift.

"It's a car, Everett. A brand new car." She hugged herself.

"It's not *that* nice." Everett smiled and opened the driver's side door. "I got the basic model."

"How did you—but *you* don't even drive a new car."

"I don't need a car. I have one."

Instead of getting in the car, Scarlett walked to the trunk, the key in her palm. "You got me a car."

"It's not a Cadillac, but it'll do for the next four years. After that, we can get something else."

She spun around, whispering, "We?"

Everett caught the plea in her voice, the hunger in her eyes. Slowly, he walked to her, an electric pulse snapping alive between them. He picked her up by waist and set her on the trunk. She didn't flinch. She didn't blink.

He lifted her chin and leaned in. "We."

Her lips quirked to a flirtatious grin. "Is that a fact?"

Everett leaned closer, nearly brushing his lips with hers. "It's a promise."

She closed her eyes and whispered, "Kiss me."

"Marry me." He wrapped an arm around her waist.

She giggled and opened her eyes. "I'm sixteen."

Everett gently pulled the hair elastic from her hair, relishing the sight of her wild, untamed hair. "I'm serious."

She rolled her eyes and grabbed his shirt, pulling him closer. "I'll think about it."

"I won't stop thinking about it." He kissed her forehead, then her nose. She held her breath. With his thumbs on her jaw, he lightly brushed his lips against hers.

For a moment, Scarlett let down her walls, revealing the fear, the loneliness—and desire. So softly Everett wondered if he heard her at all, she said, "Promise you'll never leave me."

He pressed his lips against hers, pouring his promise into her. She kissed back, her hands clenching his jacket in tight fists. He pulled her against him. She was in his arms. She was safe. She was his.

Everett left soft kisses on her jaw, her neck, and nibbled on her ear. He tightened his grip when she sighed. He needed to feel her next to him, to know she was okay. He needed this mess of hair and emotions. Everett couldn't be Superman without Scarlett.

❧ 37 ❧

SCARLETT ASHLEY
PRESENT DAY

Both Missy and Everett paced the facility's hallway, neither of them able to deal with Marjorie's labored breathing, growing worse with each passing minute. Sitting next to Marjorie, I flattened her fingers against the mattress and reapplied lip balm. She'd not been lucid since the last video chat, but she'd said all she needed to say before Everett and I married all those years ago.

The nurses came and went, adjusting medications and checking vitals. The end was near. Her color became sallow and her ears began to flatten. She looked more and more like my own grandmother. Marjorie had stated she didn't want a funeral. In fact, she didn't even want a casket. She wanted to be cremated with her ashes spread along the Ashley Almond farm, exactly like her late husband.

Leaning in close, I whispered, "Thank you. For everything." My tongue felt thick. Grief threatened to steal my words. "It's going to be okay. We're going to be okay, Everett and me. It's time."

She didn't respond. The hum of the machines kept going, but I felt the draft, the whisper of a soul leaving. The warmth she'd given me for the too few years I'd known her was gone.

In what felt like hours, Everett and Missy were on either side of me. In a way, we were left orphans with her passing. Like drowning children, our hands grasped each other's, holding tight. We stood like that while the flurry of medical staff whirled around us.

Three days later, we stood in the exact same pose and watched the hired driver spread ashes along the property. We watched, without a tear or word. The following days consisted of Missy and Everett settling Marjorie's estate, leaving me to search the journals more carefully. I wasn't brave enough to read the files Everett had collected. The hint of betrayal was still too present. It wasn't his fault, but it hurt all the same.

My timeline grew from one page to ten, then twenty. But I still couldn't quit the nagging fear—if I couldn't remember, did the unthinkable really happen? And if it did, does it even count? Am I a victim if I don't have the memory?

Sitting at my desk, I typed out a letter to Marjorie, wishing I could talk to her about all that had happened. The journal. Everything, the feelings and missing memory—including the admission of not really knowing. Printing a copy, I taped it to the back page of my journal and wished she was still here, really here, alive and well. I felt untethered now, not having a maternal anchor.

I drove to Cal State Gainesfield where my old high school teacher had started working several years before. Peering into the classroom window, I watched him struggle with a laser pointer. Despite his hunger for technology, it'd never returned the affection.

Backpacks slung over their shoulders, the students filed out of the room. I snuck in during a gap and waited by the door. A student with a long braid down her back talked to Mr. Munoz, her hands moving wildly and her expression near panic. Mr. Munoz revealed nothing, his expression stoic and constant. Not much had changed in the last decade.

He handed her a paper and she left with her head down. I opened the door for her, the desperation falling like rain in her wake.

"What brings you in?"

I smiled. Of course he'd seen me enter. "Nothing."

"That's believable," Mr. Munoz said dryly. He slid stacks of papers into his shoulder bag. "What happened?"

The words hit me in the gut. I wanted to visit him, not confess.

"I can see it in your face, Scarlett." He zipped up his bag and held out his arm, indicating a chair for me. "I've known you too long."

"True," I whispered. He was pivotal in getting me to Gainesfield and maybe that's why I'd come. I sat on the chair and took a deep breath. "Why did you help me? All those years ago, why?"

Mr. Munoz leaned against the white board. "It was the right thing to do."

"But, why?" *How did you know* was the real question.

He raised his eyebrows. "You were drowning, Scarlett. Anyone with eyes could see."

Ducking my head, I twisted the hem of my shirt in my hands. "Not everyone."

"What's really bothering you?"

Closing my eyes, I told him everything I'd just written in my letter to Marjorie. I couldn't watch his reaction, even though I knew Mr. Munoz would conceal all emotion. Silence filled the room. Opening my eyes, I said, "Please say something."

His expression was anything but neutral. Mr. Munoz had taken a step toward me, his eyes soft and lips downturned in sorrow. "This won't be enough but I'm going to say it anyway. I am sorry."

"What now? Where do I go now?"

He shifted and rubbed the back of his head. "That's up to you."

"What would you do, if you were me, I mean?" I tucked my knees under my arms. "With Marjorie gone, there's nothing left. Not for me. Or Everett."

"I'm a guy, Scarlett. I, literally, can't imagine what it's like to go through what you did—what you are. I don't have your ghosts." He sighed and glanced around the room as if searching for the answers. "From an outside perspective, I'd say get the hell out of Dodge. Heal where ghosts can't reach, if that's possible."

"I have nowhere to go." At least, I'd never even considered going anywhere else. Gainesfield was as far as I'd ever gone.

"I think Everett's right, about leaving. He's wanted to take you far away from here." He smirked. "That idiot, he always loved you, even back then."

Like a school girl, my face flushed. "Without Marjorie, he'll probably go back to London."

"Go with him." Mr. Munoz shrugged. "But I do think you should write a column. Then leave to London. Your parents can't nag you if you have a different number."

"My house isn't even remotely finished." But what if Everett didn't want me in London? We'd never talked about it, not when he left and not now. "And isn't that the coward's way out? Write something and not stay to defend it."

"Because assaulting you is the brave thing to do?" Mr. Munoz folded his arms.

Assaulting you. The words sank into me, feeling too hard. "I don't know that for sure."

"What about all the people in the same boat as you?"

A chill ran through me. "What about all the people who get falsely accused?"

"I don't know, Scarlett. I don't know." He shook his head and clucked his tongue. "It's hard watching people get away with murder. Or in this case, rape."

I flinched. *Rape.* Even thinking the word made me wince. "That's harsh."

"The truth usually is."

"Mom and Dad would take it badly. It's not like they're having the best of luck right now." Standing, I glanced at the door. There was a time when all I could think about was escaping, school or the house. It consumed every thought.

"Yeah, it's kind of big news in Tule."

"Oh." Another wince.

"They've done a lot of good in the community, but that doesn't exonerate everything else they've done." Mr. Munoz grabbed his bag and slung it over one shoulder. "I don't know if they will ever fully understand what they did or the harm they caused. Even if nothing happened, they're guilty of hindering an investigation. They didn't want questions. What they wanted was more important to them than your welfare."

"You believe it?" The strength came back. The cool strength seeped into my bones and straightened my stance.

"I always believed you." He smiled sadly. "Even when you weren't speaking."

Neither of us were huggers, so we nodded at each other, the connection just as intimate. "Thank you, by the way."

He cocked his head to the side. "How's Will doing? I heard Gaines-Print merged with another media house."

"Hopefully, he'll be able to stay on. I'm not sure how all that works, but I know a position opened up in New York." I'd replied to Lincoln's email, declining the offer and encouraging him to hire Will. There were a few good things that came from my childhood. One of them was belonging to this small Tule community, Mr. Munoz, the Davenports, and Will Nations. We might have migrated, but there was still a thread connecting us.

"Scarlett?" Mr. Munoz opened the door for me, his arm holding it. "Don't be afraid to speak. You'll be condemned and attacked, but you won't be alone."

38

EVERETT ASHLEY
THIRTEEN YEARS AGO

Everett glanced at his grandmother's house and swore. He wiped his tired eyes and turned off the car. Driving back and forth from Tule to Gainesfield three times a week was becoming harder. It didn't help that tonight he knew Scarlett needed him, and he was exhausted. For the second year in a row, her parents had forgotten her birthday. He blamed himself. They were furious when they realized Scarlett had moved out of the dorms to Marjorie's house until they pocketed the housing reimbursement the university sent them. She was fully emancipated but that hadn't stopped her parents from inserting themselves as the beneficiary in Scarlett's life.

Scarlett didn't correct them when her parents assumed Everett lived in Gainesfield. She had blossomed under Marjorie's tender care, but last night something had changed. He and Marjorie had decorated her car, trying to celebrate Scarlett's eighteenth birthday, but Scarlett's smile didn't reach her eyes. It'd been years since he'd seen her facade. She was given the freedom he'd promised, but something was wrong and he hadn't been able to reach her.

He climbed the porch steps, not yet ready to face the heaviness. Marjorie's dog lay snoring, a paw on a discarded cushion. Only a living room lamp was on which meant everyone was in bed. He dropped off his backpack in his room and made his way to Scarlett's. He'd asked every year on her birthday to marry him; every year she sidestepped him. He'd been careful to never push too far, knowing the pain in her past. But last night, her distrust of men felt more personal. He felt her slipping through his fingers, and if he were being honest, he wondered if Scarlett was going to leave him. Everett's mother was unhappy for years before she went to the store and never came home.

The light was on in Scarlett's room, spilling into the hallway. He knocked softly and pushed the door open. She was asleep and curled into her chair, her notebook on the floor by the foot of the chair. Her neck looked uncomfortable and kinked. Everett picked up the open notebook and paused, the last couple lines underlined several times. *Help me say yes. Help me keep him.*

Everett glanced at her sleeping face and flushed with guilt; he shouldn't have read anything. Scarlett kept her feelings close. He should confess what he read, but hope began to spark. He wasn't rejected. She *did* want him. He closed the book and placed it on her desk. He leaned over and kissed her cheek. Scarlett stirred but not enough to wake. With a grin, he picked her up and carried her to the bed.

Startled, she grimaced. "What?"

He tugged on a strand, playfully rolling the end around his finger. "Hey, you."

"How late is it?" She blinked and rubbed her eyes.

"Past late. We're now into early morning. There was an accident on the ninety-nine." The drive was becoming unbearable. He was a TA for a couple English classes and still had meetings on campus despite the break. He leaned across her bed, his long legs stretched out. "What were you doing up? Before you fell asleep."

Scarlett threaded her hand through his. "I was thinking ..."

"Yes."

She rolled her eyes and laughed, her face transforming to the beautiful woman he loved. "I didn't ask for anything."

Everett kissed her hand. "Have I ever told you no?"

"What if we ..." She gave a little shrug that belied her seriousness. She was risking. "What if we moved to Gainesfield? I mean, we've been saving, so it's not like it's completely irresponsible. And now that I'm eighteen, financial aid will go through the university to me instead of my parents."

He squeezed her hand. "They'll still find a way to get the money. They knew you were emancipated and still—"

"You're right." She pulled her hand from his.

"Hey, wait." Everett tugged her hand back. "I wasn't saying no. I was saying we can't count on the money. But, yes, let's do it."

She nodded, her eyes dimming. "What about Marjorie?"

"She has the dog." He smiled but he'd worried about leaving Marjorie when the idea of getting Scarlett out of Tule began. He knew one day they would leave. Marjorie encouraged him to apply for post-graduate programs. With nothing close by, moving was in his future.

"I want to do something before we move." Her voice caught on *something*. "That way she's still a part of us."

"Yes." Everett grinned. She rarely asked for anything, and he'd give anything to grant her wish.

"I want to ..." Her cheeks blushed to a golden pink. "If you were okay with it, though ... I was wondering if, maybe, we could, I don't know. We don't have to."

"Never took you for a coward, Scarlett."

She narrowed her eyes, the spark alive again. "I'm not a coward."

He shrugged. "Just sayin'."

"Get married." She jutted her chin. "I want to get married. Nothing fancy, just ... just the courthouse or something."

Everett froze, scared he'd break the spell. She stared at him with her chocolate eyes. He released the breath he didn't realize he was holding. "Are you serious?"

Scarlett nodded, her blush deepening to a crimson red.

He laughed into his fist. "Let's do it."

"Everett?" Her voice was soft, almost childlike. "Are you sure? I mean, we've never really talked about what we are. Or what this is."

"If it isn't obvious, then I must be doing something wrong." The morning sun began to peek through her window, but suddenly Everett wasn't thinking of sleeping. "Get dressed."

"You just got home."

"I need to marry you before you change your mind." He pulled her to a stand. "You'll have the big wedding one day, mark my words, but I need to get you to the courthouse."

Scarlett folded her arms. "Why would I change my mind?"

"You scare easily and you know it."

"What about Marjorie?" She grabbed her shoes and fished out a pair of socks from her drawer.

"I'll wake her. You just get in the car." He felt lighter than he had in days and gently woke his grandmother.

His giddiness was obvious. Marjorie gave a loving pat to his cheek and began wiping the happy tears. A quick breakfast in downtown Tule and Everett decided to make one last pit stop with everyone in tow. He pulled into the familiar strip mall, a few parking stalls down from the Delfin's jewelry store.

"What are you doing?" Scarlett hunched in the passenger seat.

"Stay here." He grabbed her hand and gave a quick squeeze. "Trust me. It'll be fine."

Everett jogged to the store front and knocked on the window. With a hand shading the morning glare, he peered in, but instead of Lucas Delfin, Everett saw the frustrated face of Scarlett's older brother, Andy. Everett knocked again.

Andy froze but quickly recovered. He grabbed a key ring and circled the glass counters. He unlocked the accordion security gate and slid it open. "What brings you here, Ashley?"

"A favor."

"I'm in short supply." Andy backed up, allowing Everett inside.

Everett smirked. He'd caught the fear in Andy's eyes. Everett had that effect on boys still pretending to be men. "I need a ring but was hoping I could talk to your dad."

Andy's mouth hung open. "You can't be serious."

"I don't joke."

"Fair point." Andy pocketed the key ring. "We're not even set up."

"When will he be in?" Everett noticed the glass cases weren't completely empty. Only the jewelry in the line of sight from the front window were taken out. "Isn't it dangerous to keep the jewelry in the case?"

Andy scratched his head. "I guess."

"When did you start working here?" Everett had thought Scarlett was the only one Lucas trusted, and she'd left two years before.

"When someone decided to skip town." Andy flinched before adding, "In a good way, though. Good for her."

"Right."

A door alarm chimed. Everett straightened to his full height as Lucas rounded the corner from the back of the store.

"Andy, the back door was unlocked. You can't—" Lucas stopped mid-sentence.

"Good morning, Mr. Delfin." Everett stepped forward and extended a hand over the glass counter.

Lucas glanced at the offered hand but said nothing.

"He's a customer, Dad," Andy said before relocking the front door.

Everett didn't know if being a customer was for Andy's benefit or for Everett's. "I'd like to buy a ring, Mr. Delfin."

"The answer's no." Lucas ran a hand through his thinning black hair. He was the spitting image of his son. "You're not marrying my daughter."

"With all due respect, I am buying a ring, not asking for permission."

"No to both." Lucas made a display of pulling a gun from his back pocket and placing it next to the cash register. "You've done enough damage to our family."

"We are getting married." Everett squared his shoulders and tried to soften his voice. "It'd be great to have your blessing but it won't stop it."

"She won't marry you." Lucas pulled another key ring from his pocket, setting it beside the gun. "That I can guarantee."

Everett swallowed the rising doubt. "Then why did she ask me?"

"Why does she do a number of things?" Lucas wouldn't meet

Everett's gaze. He turned to the safe and pulled out a plastic tub with jewelry in it. He acted entirely unaffected, but Everett caught the tremor in Lucas's hand and the hesitation when he turned his back on Everett. "She makes promises she can't keep all the time."

"She's kept every promise to me." Everett's voice rose. He hated the defensiveness in his tone.

"For now." Lucas set the plastic tub on the glass counter. He slammed a display next to it. "I'm her father. I love her, but I know her."

"If you'd like to see your daughter get married—"

"I would." Lucas slammed another display on the counter. "But not to you."

Everett turned to leave. "I'll be—"

"Nowhere near my daughter," Lucas snapped. "I know where she's been living, and I know what we could charge you with."

Andy looked at the swords hung on the walls and then at the ground. Then back at the wall.

"Charge me with what?" In one step, Everett was towering over Lucas and the counters. "Tell me what crime I've committed. I'd love to hear what a man like you has to say about the law."

"What is that supposed to mean?" Lucas nearly spat out the words. "I'm her father—"

"Then act like it." Everett's hands pumped at his sides, clench and release, clench and release. "Because we both know what you've done."

"Enlighten me." Lucas's eyes took on a maniacal glare. "Tell me what I've supposedly done. What lie has she spun now?"

"She wasn't the one who told." Everett smirked at the fear growing in Lucas's eye.

"Get out," Lucas growled. "Stay away from my family, or I—and this is a promise—I *will* have you thrown in jail for statutory rape."

Everett held out his hands. "Cuff me."

"A guy with your past, it'll be the easiest conviction. A father's word against yours. You don't stand a chance." Lucas's face turned red, his anger radiating off him. "Andy, get me the phone."

"I'd love nothing more than a moment with the police." Everett leaned over the counter. "So much to talk about."

"Ash—Everett, come on, man." Andy patted Everett's back. "Another time. Come back another time."

Everett brushed off his hand, retreating while facing Scarlett's father. Only Lucas Delfin would be arrogant enough to think his word would be obeyed. "I'm not going away, Lucas. Marriage or not, I'm in Scarlett's life for good."

❧ 39 ❧

SCARLETT ASHLEY
PRESENT DAY

I 'd spent the morning directing construction workers. Everett had given up on handling the remodel, his focus on Marjorie's estate. We hadn't talked about London. We hadn't talked about much, period. There was a growing rift, or maybe the elephant of our future had settled in the middle of everything.

To be honest, my mind was reeling since my visit with Dr. Munoz. His words had encouraged me to reevaluate my old project—and reevaluate everything as well. *Assaulting you* had echoed in my head for days. David had called and texted, leaving messages daily. He vacillated between sickeningly sweet to false worry from my lack of response.

With my laptop tucked under my arm, I closed the bedroom door and logged onto the video conference call with Lincoln. On my computer screen, Lincoln stared at me, his expression uncertain. He was on the other side of the country and nowhere near me, but the slight tremor in my hands wouldn't believe it. The years had softened his voice and features, or maybe my memory was just as shoddy today as it was then.

Lincoln was heavy handed, not necessarily handsy. At least, that's what I told myself.

Behind Lincoln was an impressive view of a New York skyline. In all honesty, he deserved the big office and all that came with it. Working hard was never his problem. Aside from the haggard look on his face, New York had been kind to him. Or at least his career.

"You're resurrecting the producer project?" He arched an eyebrow. "The bit on producers taking advantage of interns. That same piece, *now* you want to run it?"

Pivoting my computer monitor toward me, I turned up the volume. "But I'd like to include an opinion piece with it. A column." It sounded lame now that I said it out loud.

"Why now?" Lincoln frowned with a swift shake of the head. "We've been down this road."

"I was wrong." The words were bitter. I could've gone ahead with the project but I was too scared. Missy and seven other women had actual, physical evidence—unlike me. Admitting a misstep wasn't something I did often, and for a moment, I regretted setting up the meeting. As terrifying as it was, this still felt right. All of it. "I shouldn't have buried the report."

"You didn't just bury it. You lit the damn thing on fire and *then* buried it." He wasn't unkind but he wasn't exactly mincing words.

There was a bit of comfort in that. He wasn't pitying me. He wasn't treating me like a fragile doll either. I'd forgotten what it was like to be taken seriously.

"And yet ..." He sighed again. "I don't blame you."

"I do."

He wasn't supposed to be this quick to forgive. "I mean, I did. For a long time I blamed you." He stood and threw his hands in his pockets. His office must be enormous if he could take that many steps back and still have room. "I couldn't blame you after—after I talked to my dad."

"This isn't about that." My pulse pounded in my ears. My hands were sweaty in an instant. Detective Davenport promised me he'd never tell. He promised. "This is about producers taking advantage. And my source finally feeling brave. Finally trusting me."

"I felt like a shmuck, Scarlett." His voice had taken on an apologetic tone. He leaned against a short bookshelf behind him, tapping his ankle against the edge. "The pieces. They all fell together after we talked."

"No." My hands shook. Nervously, I rearranged the pens on my desk. The shaking wasn't as bad when they were busy. "Stopping the report had nothing to do with me. Or you."

"I'm sorry, Scar." He finally looked straight at me. "I'm so sorry."

"Listen, are you interested?" This was supposed to be quick, concise, and help both of us. I pictured him being distant, even angry but not this. Not remorseful. "I don't want to pursue it without help."

"I thought I was different."

"Lincoln, stop."

"No, I have to say this." He cleared his throat and sat with his hands folded in front of him. "We were on the brink of uncovering the worst of men. These powerful men who preyed on women, tossing them aside as soon as they were done—"

"You don't owe—"

"And there I was, blaming you for me being an idiot. It wasn't your fault." His voice wavered. He swallowed hard before continuing, "I was no better. I was just like *them.*"

"I never said you were like them."

"You didn't have to." He gave a slight shake. "Everett was right."

"Lincoln, I didn't call to talk about Everett. Or me. I called because I need your help." *And that's all.* I almost added the lie. But deep down, it wasn't. His words echoed in my head. Something inside of me had begun to wake up. My parents had called, but I'd sent them to voicemail like I had David. There was a growing cavern between us. I was still scared—terrified actually. My life was what I knew, and changing course was swapping the devil I knew for a devil I didn't.

"I was so proud." He scratched his forehead with his thumb. "Everett twisted my own words. The blame I gave you, he threw back at me. And damn it, he was right."

"You're not the one who raped me so just stop." I covered my mouth. Mr. Munoz had been the first to say the words. Somehow they'd escaped me. *Raped.* My pulse pounded in my head. *Raped.*

Lincoln's head shot up, his eyes wide.

I looked at him. He looked at me.

The world stopped. *You're not the one who raped me*, echoed over and over again in my mind. Heaviness fell on my shoulders. I'd never said the word, let alone thought it. It made it too real. Or maybe it made me a liar. Without proof, nothing was certain.

"Scarlett?" Lincoln finally asked, his face drowning in shock.

"I ... I don't know why I said that." Tucking my chin, I whispered, "I never ... I don't know why I said that."

"I think you do," he added gently.

I looked at the camera, my reflection foreign. I was still Scarlett—and yet I wasn't. Flexing my hands, I stared at them, the rings shining brightly on my fingers, one from Marjorie. One from Everett. *Raped.* Such an ugly word, and yet, in a way, the sorrow had pointed me toward the Ashely family.

I cleared my throat. "Is that a yes?"

Lincoln opened his mouth and then closed it. He shifted in his chair. I wasn't sure if he was uncomfortable with my switch in topics or my outburst. Either way, I needed to get this over with as soon as possible. I needed to talk to Everett, to figure out a way to explain the change. Lincoln held up his phone, appearing to text someone.

He looked up and said, "Alright, Scarlett."

"Yes?" Shame crept in. He was doing this as penance. "I don't want you to feel obligated, Lincoln. It's a good piece. It's a solid piece."

"On one condition." He held up a finger. "I want your story, Scarlett. The full story. Not just an article."

It took a moment to register his words, the true meaning. My father. My brother. I glanced back at the computer. Lincoln shot me a knowing look. "Not just back in high school. The whole story."

"How do you know about my story?" It was barely above a whisper.

"I didn't." A confident grin appeared on Lincoln, and just like that, I was transported back to the naivety of learning about powerful men and their dark history. The memories that were triggered sent me to a counselor. Bits and pieces were all that was ever recovered before giving up a few weeks ago. Skeletons were the remains of something warm and beautiful, leaving only the cold and unkind secrets no one wanted to see.

"I don't know, Lincoln." There was a knock at the front door.

He leaned forward. "I won't force you, but I think there are a lot of people that need to hear it."

"That's the whole point of my piece." The doorbell rang. Whoever was there wasn't patient.

Lincoln must've heard it because he hurried. "Those are abstract women with powerful men. We need to hear the humanity. We need to hear your perspective. We need to hear about the daughter, the sister, the woman in front of us."

"I have to go, Lincoln."

"Think about it," he said a second before he signed off.

Opening the front door, a courier had his hand mid-air ready to knock again. He held out a signature pad and left me with a hard envelope. Turning it over, Everett's name was front and center with the sender's address in London. The time had come. England was calling.

As if on cue, Everett sent a picture of a truck and texted, *Get ready for a joy ride.*

He'd swapped the sedan for a rental truck. It looked similar to the one he used to drive. I threw on a jacket and my shoes. By the time I reached the garage, Everett was pulling into the drive.

With the engine still on, he beamed and climbed down. "Let's go."

"Where?" My phone beeped in my back pocket. Everett grabbed my hand before I could check the text. "Wait, the front door's unlocked."

He gave me a gentle push toward the truck and ran to the front door. With his long legs he still reached the truck before I did. There was so much I wanted to say, but the heaviness that had been on my shoulders had dissipated. The more I reflected, the more I realized the spark. The turning point wasn't just Lincoln and Munoz. It was when Everett returned.

Everett opened the car door, his excitement contagious—wheels turned even the surliest men into giddy boys. Everett shut my car door and all but skipped to the driver's side.

If anyone deserved to play, it was him. "Where to 'O Captain! My Captain?'"

"Wait and see." His eyes took a mischievous glint.

"You said a joy ride not a road trip."

"Semantics."

Playfully punching his shoulder, I rolled my eyes and wished this moment would stay forever. This was us, Everett and Scarlett—either really, really good or really bad. There was only laughter and sadness, never neutral. For once, that was fine by me.

He turned the heat up for me and rolled his window down, his palm out, feeling the wind. Five minutes later, we were down the backroads of the outer country of Gainesfield, my gaze on him, his view on the horizon, his fingers twitching a future sketch. Silence stretched between us, calm and soothing. Turning down a long, dirt driveway, Everett cast a sidelong glance, beaming once more.

"I wasn't staring," I lied.

"That's not why I'm smiling." He reached for my hand and squeezed it.

"I have a pretty good idea on why you're smiling." I twirled my index finger in a circle, encompassing his new truck. "Pretty obvious."

"Wrong again."

"Liar."

He shrugged or at least tried to. He was none too subtle and way too eager. He nodded at the road. "How much are you willing to bet I'm lying?"

Nothing. I'd learned to never bet against Everett. "Whose house is this?"

"Wait and see, Sherlock." The idiot was grinning and entirely too proud of himself. Rolling up the window, Everett slowed the truck to a crawl, the dust billowing around us.

We didn't know anyone in the country. At least, I didn't, and Everett dealt with politics and tariffs, not farmers. I wondered for the hundredth time if he'd ever be satisfied in Gainesfield. For California, the city might be a booming metropolis, but for Everett, would it be a bore? Gainesfield was where he cut his teeth on oil contracts and where he considered home, but he never stayed for long. Los Angeles, Houston, and New York enticed him for days, sometimes weeks at a time, until London courted him.

Three other trucks were parked in front of the house, a plain ranch-style home that was more practical than pretty.

"So it wasn't one truck that made you all giddy. It was three?" I teased.

"Your deductive skills are astounding." He turned off the car and hooked an arm around my waist, pulling me to his side across the bench seat. "Come on. Let's see just how right you are."

Opening the door, he helped me down and held out his arm. "After you."

"Oh, no you don't. You're leading the way."

Everett wrapped an arm around my shoulder. "Pretend you're submissive. And obedient."

I tried elbowing his side.

He cupped my elbow and moved me closer against him. "Nice try."

The sound of children talking stopped me dead in my tracks. I looked around and saw no one. Everett nearly tripped on my sudden stop. His puzzled look didn't help.

"Kids," I managed to say. He'd mentioned it the other day in the kitchen. Kids meant family. And intimacy. Or adoption. Three of my biggest fears.

"What are you talking about?" He scanned my face and then the area.

"Why are we here?" I folded my arms and ducked out from under his arm.

He held out his palms but kept his eager smile in place. "Come on, it's not what you think."

"You don't know what I'm thinking."

"Right." He rolled his eyes and tugged on my hand. "I promise they bite."

Retreating, I pulled my hand free. He laughed. I scowled, mostly because his stupid laugh put me at ease. Ignoring his outstretched hand, I followed him to the side gate, the sound of children giggling growing louder. Everett reached over the fence and unlatched the gate. Being freakishly tall had advantages.

"I'm not going in there." Folding my arms, I dared him to make me.

"Oh, I think you are." He leaned over, and with dramatic flourish, swung open the gate.

A couple hundred yards away were clumps of kids and adults

surrounding white, fluffy Great Pyrenees puppies, each already the size of a medium dog. A boy, roughly eight or nine years old, struggled to pull a sleepy puppy into his arms. With a squawk, the dog yawned and licked the boy's chin.

A little off to the side stood the puppies' mother, her head coming to the hip of most of the men. She nudged her enormous head in between people, sniffing.

Nodding to the mother, I asked, "You know puppies grow up to be dogs?"

"I wasn't getting a puppy." Everett leaned his back against the fence, thoroughly pleased with himself. He wore a confident grin, and his relaxed jaw was on the verge of needing another shave. For a moment, I wished we were alone. His grin grew into a knowing smile. "The mother showed up one day, pregnant and sick. Our neighbor's secretary heard about it. She said this family fostered the mother until her puppies were weaned but they all need to go."

"You don't like dogs."

"Neither do you."

"I like dogs." I shot him a look. "Okay, maybe just one dog."

"Who looked an awful lot like her." Everett held my gaze and pulled me into an easy hug, the fence supporting us both.

"Marjorie. She was more than just your grandmother." Even with his arms around me, London was on my mind.

"She was just as much your family as mine. Same with her dog."

"The dog's huge." On cue, she raised her head and swished her gigantic, feathery tail. The dog kept her gaze on me and ambled forward, just as slow and deliberate as Marjorie's old stray. "She's beautiful."

"She's yours." Everett held out his hand for a greeting. The dog nudged it out of the way and tossed her enormous body to the ground in a graceless huff. Covering my feet completely, she sighed and pawed at my shin.

"I don't know." Kneeling, I reached out to pet her. Instantly, she stopped pawing. I stood; she pawed again. "She's a needy girl." *And what about London,* I almost asked.

"Aren't they all?" Everett scowled but his eyes twinkled.

"Dogs or girls?"

"No comment."

"Smartest thing you've said all day." The families began shuffling past us to their cars. "I don't know, Everett. It's a big dog."

"We have a big lot."

"Why are you wanting a dog? Why now?"

Everett shrugged and nodded to a middle aged woman carrying a leash and a smile.

"Kind of need more of an answer." We hadn't really discussed our future. Adding a dog wasn't going to help.

"Are you saying you *don't* want the dog?" He arched an eyebrow. He had me.

"I didn't say that." Shoving my hands in my pockets, I forced myself to ask, "What about London?"

"What about it?" Everett kicked the grass with his toe.

"Are you going back?"

He stopped and cocked his head to the side. "Not without you."

"I signed for an envelope. Came from England." A breeze played with my hair, carrying the chill of winter with it. "Seemed like a big deal."

He rubbed the scruff on his jaw. "It's an offer."

"What about the leave of absence?" The little crowd of kids was thinning, making our conversation more awkward with families leaving around us.

"I was offered before I took the leave of absence. They knew about Marjorie." Everett nodded to a boy holding a puppy. "I have time. They're not expecting an immediate answer."

"But they are expecting an answer." I glanced again at the mother, her soft fur and oversized body. "What do you want to tell them—be honest."

"I can't ask you to come. I can't ask that of you." He followed my line of sight. "Especially if it's only for a few years. I can't have you uproot your life to follow me around the world."

I can't ask you to come. Blinking, I let the words fall over me, rinsing me from the doubts. "You want me to come?"

"Why wouldn't I?" Everett scoffed, his scowl reappearing—and in that moment, it was us, Scarlett and Everett.

"What about the house?" Motioning to the enormous dog, I added, "And the dog?"

His scowl changed to a lopsided grin. "Are you considering it?"

"Maybe." Shrugging, I tried to seem nonchalant.

"Alright then."

"Wait." I grabbed his arm. "You didn't answer me. We have a house that's not finished and now a dog to figure out."

"I don't care." Everett beamed. "You said *we*. And guess what, *we* will figure it out." He left me with 150 pounds of fur and greeted the woman. She seemed to thank him and after mouthing *thank you* to me, handed the leash over.

The dog stood just as Everett arrived and, without a glance to him, trotted to the truck, her tail swishing.

"I don't think she's going to take direction from you."

He smirked. "Great, now there's two of you."

Curling an arm around his, I whispered, "Thank you, Everett."

I felt, rather than saw, his gaze. He didn't say anything. He didn't have to. He didn't like dogs or any animals. He barely tolerated Marjorie's, and even then, it was out of love for his grandmother. But this, this was for me. He'd given me something I didn't know I wanted —like he'd done for the last fifteen years.

❦ 40 ❦

EVERETT ASHLEY

THIRTEEN YEARS AGO

E verett opened the wooden door of the courthouse, the marriage application in hand. He waited for Marjorie and Scarlett to walk through before letting the door close. His argument with Scarlett's father kept replaying in his mind. Everett knew her family wouldn't approve, but he'd at least hoped to give her a ring, preferably one made by her father.

He'd dreamed of giving her the lavish wedding and an expensive diamond. He wanted her to have the white dress and the big reception. But funds were tight. His newspaper cartoons weren't doing as well as they once had. He'd also cut back on submissions, dedicating more time to school. His tuition was paid through a family education fund meant for his father. Richard's disgust for any and all education left a hefty amount for Everett's schooling—not a marriage.

Regret filled him. Maybe he was just as selfish as his father. Richard took what he wanted, Everett's mother. Hadn't Everett done the same? The more Scarlett's parents rejected him, the more protective he became. That was the truth. And it sank like a cold, wet stone in the pit of his stomach. Was Everett marrying Scarlett out of spite? *No.* The answer shook the thought. He loved her.

Dressed in jeans and sneakers, neither Everett nor Scarlett looked ready for matrimony. Marjorie didn't seem to care; she hadn't stopped grinning since breakfast. She patted Everett's hand and glanced at the packed courtroom. "Looks like we're going to be a while. I'm going to visit the lady's room."

The moment she left, Everett pulled Scarlett aside. She gave a hesitant smile before slamming down her facade.

"Don't do that. Don't shut me out," he pleaded.

In an instant, Scarlett returned, a half smile on her lips. "Have I ever shut you out?"

"All the time." He grinned, hoping he looked lighter than he felt. "Seriously though, we don't have to do this."

Her hands were wringing in her lap.

"I don't have a ring. You don't have a dress." Everett pulled one of her hands into his lap and waited for her to look at him. He scanned her face. He needed to know if this wedding was what Scarlett wanted, or if it was just another moment of her giving in. She'd spent her childhood helping her father. Everett wanted her to love him, not feel obligated to please him. "You aren't okay with this, are you?"

"You don't have to marry me." And there it was again, her muted expression and stoic eyes. "It's fine."

"Whoa, whoa, that's not what I said." Everett ducked down to meet her lowering gaze. "I've been waiting for this day. I've wanted you as my wife since day one. But are *you* okay?"

"Yeah." Scarlett didn't look up. She'd retreated into herself. "I'm fine. You're the one I'm worried about."

Everett felt the rising panic. If he married her, she'd think it was out of duty. If he didn't marry her, she'd assume rejection. "What can I do to make this right?"

"Oh my gosh, Everett. I said it's fine."

"You don't sound fine." Everett hooked a finger under her chin, turning her face back to him. "I'm not going anywhere. We—you and I —we're not going anywhere. If you want to wait, I'll wait forever." Scarlett opened her mouth, but Everett shook his head. She started again, but he blurted, "No, don't think this is me trying to back out. Because it's not."

"That's exactly what it sounds like." Her voice held an edge. She was close enough to touch, yet felt out of reach. "You keep asking me to marry you. I finally ask you but *now* you're freaking out? Did you even mean it?"

"Yes." Everett leaned in, his forehead resting against hers. This was all wrong. There was only one way out. "Marry me, Scarlett."

"You don't—"

Everett brushed his lips against hers. He didn't know what else to do. He loved her. He loved all of her, even the hesitant, frightened part of her. Scarlett was home and even if this was wrong, losing her wasn't an option.

She froze but didn't retreat. He kissed her again, cupping the back of her neck with his hands. Slowly, she relaxed.

"Oh, my loves." Marjorie chirped behind them.

They broke apart, Scarlett's face turning crimson. Everett pulled her against his chest so she could hide.

"Don't be embarrassed, Letty." Marjorie patted Everett's shoulders, a faraway look in her eye. "If only your grandfather were here. He'd have loved this."

Scarlett's head popped up. "A courthouse wedding?"

A suspicious pink blossomed on Marjorie's cheeks.

"Wait a minute ..." Everett didn't miss a thing.

Marjorie pulled on the cuffs of her cardigan. "We were in a bit of a rush, if you must know. The town was a lot more traditional back then. We needed to be married. Quickly."

Scarlett covered her mouth but not quickly enough. She burst into laughter, transforming her to the brilliant woman Everett loved. Her eyes were lit and the smile wide.

Marjorie's blush grew, and for once, Everett felt the beginnings of peace. Behind the wooden pew, hidden from Scarlett's laughing profile, he reached for Marjorie's hand. She squeezed it back in return. He'd never loved his grandmother more.

The bailiff called them forward, and Everett helped both Scarlett and Marjorie to their feet. All three stood in queue behind two other couples underneath the clock. Every tick added weight to Everett's already heavy heart. This was a moment he'd wished for, yearned for more than anything else. and yet nothing felt right. Naive, he'd pictured her parents in attendance and Scarlett with tears of joy. The *happily ever after* he believed in wasn't coming. Everett's fingers twitched. He was too far down this road to back out now. They would marry—and he hoped there was a silver lining to it all.

The judge's thick accent made it even harder to hear. Everett didn't dare look at Scarlett or Marjorie. He couldn't bear to see sadness or worse, Scarlett's blank stare. And then they stood, hands clasped while the judge spoke to them. They raised their hands, nodded, and spoke when prompted.

Marjorie dabbed her eyes and prattled the entire way back to the house, leaving Everett to his thoughts and Scarlett in silence.

Marjorie scrambled up the porch steps, moving faster than Everett had seen her move in years. She tossed over her shoulder, "Let's get you packed."

Scarlett's face was awash in confusion. "Packed?"

Everett shrugged and helped her from the car. He turned to close the door and heard Marjorie say to his new wife, "You can't stay here on your wedding night."

Everett closed his eyes and waited for Scarlett's response.

There was nothing but silence.

He finally turned to see Marjorie's dog staring at him, its face pivoting from the open front door and back to Everett. He climbed the steps toward the fluffy animal, feeling the lack of sleep with each step. The dog sniffed, disgruntled at Everett's shoes, and pranced inside. Everett couldn't blame the animal. Everett didn't like himself very much at the moment either. He'd taken the coward's way out. He should have stopped the wedding or done something, anything, to make Scarlett feel better. Not worse.

Before he could close the front door, Marjorie shooed Everett and a pale Scarlett back to the car, suitcases in hand.

"Bless my soul, what a beautiful day." Marjorie clutched a tissue in her hand and stood on the porch, waving until Everett realized he had to drive away. He had to take Scarlett to a hotel. His stomach tightened. He was taking her to a hotel, and Scarlett's pale face underlined what that meant. She feared the intimacy. Her anxiety stood like a stranger between them, a constant and disruptive companion.

Everett drove to the old Anniversary Inn on the east side of Tule, a hotel teetering on the edges of the rolling Tule River. He'd never hated himself more. Turning off the car, he felt the full weight of the decision, coupled with sleep deprivation.

"She tried to give me her wedding ring," Scarlett whispered. "But my hands were too small."

Everett reached for her petite left hand, wishing he'd figured out a ring, something tangible to show his devotion. Words were never his strength. "You should've had one."

"Everett?" Her voice was small, weak. Terrified.

"I will never hurt you." He tapped the steering wheel, his hands empty and awkward. "I expect nothing."

"But—"

"Nothing, Scarlett." He saw a flicker of something in her eyes, an emotion he'd not seen before. He felt her shiver, and he doubted it was from the winter air. In one fell swoop, he'd married and lost Scarlett. The worst part was not knowing how or why. "We're okay, Scarlett."

"Okay." Her lips moved but the voice wasn't hers.

"I promise you, I will protect you—"

Scarlett pulled her hand from his. "I wanted to be loved."

Shocked, Everett shouted, "I *do* love you."

"You love saving me." Scarlett turned her head to the window.

"That's not true," he lied. Being her hero had given him purpose, had focused him in a way nothing else had. He needed to do well in school to provide for her. Everett owed her everything. He wanted to give her everything. He would study law in case her father ever cashed in on his threat. Knowing Lucas, he'd throw Everett in jail with trumped-up charges the second he found out about the marriage.

Scarlett spun around, a question in her eyes. "Tell that to your face."

"Screw my face. I'm telling you." His voice rose but he couldn't stop it. How had this gone so wrong? He sat next to Scarlett, but she was a million miles away. "What do I have to do? It's you. It's always been you. I love *you*."

In a voice that broke his heart, Scarlett lowered her gaze and said, "And I will always love you."

❧ 41 ❦

SCARLETT ASHLEY

PRESENT DAY

Aside from the kitchen cabinets, which hadn't arrived, everything was finished on the main floor. The second floor was now consumed with construction workers, effectively kicking me out of my office. Everett had once vowed to never pay someone else to do what his own two hands were capable of, but the offer from London and my semi-commitment had given him a completely new perspective.

In our bedroom, I read through my files, filling in my outline. It'd grown to just under fifty pages. Will had texted, asking if I had the opinion piece—I hadn't told Will about it, but I had no doubt Lincoln put the idea in his head. What Lincoln really wanted was the full story, not just a small, local column. He hadn't stopped emailing, each a gentle reminder that both women and men needed to know my story. That's where I wasn't sold. I wasn't sure I had a story. Not yet.

David and my parents appeared to have given up. Instead of suspicion, I felt relief.

Everett's hoodie was still in the box, but I'd gone through my mother's journal he'd snuck out. I didn't know if or how I'd return it to her. There were still a dozen blank pages left. I ran a finger down the spine of her journal. Authoring the column or a larger piece, I wondered if I could survive the backlash, here or in London.

The *what ifs* began circling in my head. If my parents found out, if David knew ... and then Everett's words, *there's a lot of people that need to know they're not alone.* There were so many holes in his line of thinking. Reading a story didn't change lives. Knowing the characters were real people that influenced others, inspired people to be brave—at least according to Lincoln.

That was the part that scared me. I didn't want anyone to know that it was real, that I was *that girl.* The girl who'd never had a drop of alcohol but had pictures plastered on her locker with her dress ripped and eyes closed. The girl who flinched every time her dad wrapped his arm around her and still couldn't take a bath without the door locked and drawers pulled out in case someone opened the door. That girl. The one still running from irrational fears. The one who desperately wanted to be intimate with the one man who meant everything—my chest tightened. Even the thought haunted me.

"Hello?" My mother's voice echoed down the hall. The door must have been left open.

Tossing the journal to the floor, I ran to the entryway. She took in the floors and the vaulted ceilings, wincing when a worker swore loudly upstairs.

"Hi." It was the only thing I could think of. We hadn't spoken since the confrontation on my front lawn, her voice shaking in anger that I was already married. Mom was on a mission, and Everett wasn't home.

She lifted her chin. "Are you going to invite me in, or have I been reduced to standing on your doorstep?"

You already let yourself in. I bit back the retort and said, "Come in."

Over her arm, she'd draped dry cleaner bags, the hem of several prom dresses sticking out. "I can't get a hold of Avrie, and Elaine doesn't want these."

With a sigh, she walked around me and laid them on the empty refrigerator box. A good daughter would offer her to sit, but I wasn't there. Not yet. My childhood had taught me to give her a wide berth. Like a rabid dog, Mom might need help, but if I wasn't careful, she'd bite.

Mom pulled a framed picture of my dad and me from her purse, setting it on top of the bags. Without thinking, I grabbed the frame, my finger tracing the letters *Daddy's Girl*. I was about eight, just before Kelly came to live with us. My smile was bright. I held up the ring I'd made. The edges were rough and the cast wasn't done properly, but I remembered feeling like a master goldsmith that day. It was around tax season when no one bought jewelry. He'd let me take over the back of the store where his tools were neglected and unused. It was before, before I made the mistake of talking about things. Breaching the unspoken trust of secrets had fractured our family.

Mom's voice pierced the moment. "If there's something you're missing, I'm sure it'll turn up in another room."

I gently put the picture back on the dresses, just in case my mother changed her mind and took everything. Heavy bricks of tension stacked up between us. "Is there a reason you're doing this?"

For a half second, Mom looked ashamed. "We're selling the house."

"Oh ..." Her admission didn't sit well. There was more going on than her sudden announcement.

She pursed her lips. "It's time to downsize."

"Right now?" Elaine had just broken off her engagement, and my father was fighting for his freedom. I'd yet to be served papers regarding the title on their home but *now* seemed to be the worst time for them to sell.

"Yes, now." Mom shuffled the keys in her hand and shifted her purse from one arm to the other. "Your father's case was thrown out. Now is as good a time as ever."

"So, that's good news, right?"

"The criminal case was thrown out." She examined her nailbeds. "Only to be slapped with a civil case on the way to our car. So, no. Not good news."

"But he's not going to prison." There had to be something good.

"Just because your father is not going to prison does not mean all is well, Scarlett. Far from it." Mom's eyes flicked from her hands to me, her fear piercing. "The lawsuit isn't just for the stolen jewelry but the pain and suffering of the victims." Mom's face darkened at *victims*.

"The victims?"

"Their lawyer thinks I conned them out of the home."

You did, I almost said. "Mom, the house is an asset. Anything of value—"

"That's what they're after." She waved her hand around, as if my house was part of the problem. "Money. Apparently, it's okay to be traumatized by missing jewelry, but *we* aren't allowed to complain when sued for a crime we didn't commit. Your father bought stolen jewelry, but you'd think he robbed them at gunpoint."

"But why sell now?" I sat in the stiff armchair close to the dresses she brought. This would be the time I would have offered Marjorie some food or a drink. But Mom wasn't Marjorie. She never would be— and I would never be the devoted daughter my mother needed. Everett tried to buffer me from my family but I hadn't checked in on my parents in their time of need. No text, no call. Nothing.

"I refuse to just roll over and surrender. Why should I lose my home over this?" Mom's hands gripped her keys, knuckles turning white. "He's a doctor. He doesn't need the money."

"Wait, what?" Immediately, guilt fell heavy on my shoulders. I rubbed my hands together.

"The so-called victim, Scarlett." Mom clenched her jaw, clearly irritated that I wasn't keeping up on her financial issues. "The stolen jewelry came from a doctor. Or his wife. Whoever it was, they have money and can sue whoever, whenever. They sued the alarm company and won. They sued the safe company and won. Now they're suing us, and because I happened to file the title paperwork wrong, they think I purposely tried to hide assets."

"What does the house have to do with the stolen jewelry?" It didn't matter that I spoke softly. I could tell by the tightening of her hands that she heard the true accusation.

"I just told you." She glanced around the room, searching for Everett I assumed. "Because the title was transferred to your name after—"

"Right there." I tapped the armrest and stood. "That's all I needed to know, Mom. You just told me you were slapped with a civil lawsuit after the criminal case, but you knew the other lawsuit was coming, otherwise you wouldn't have forged my signature. You knew—"

"Give me a break, Scarlett. Don't make this more complicated than it is. It isn't forgery if you knew what we were doing."

Taking a deep breath, I forced the words to come. "I told you. I won't lie for you."

Mom glanced at the counter before returning her focus on me, her frown severe. "We're being sued for a million dollars. A million dollars. Who came up with *that* number? How much pain and suffering equates to *one million dollars?*"

"One million ..." I couldn't finish. There was a time when I worked to near exhaustion every weekend and every holiday to help my parents break the million-dollar threshold. It was the same year my parents bought the new house and two new cars—and the same year we spent Christmas without heat because neither parent paid the gas bill. The moment I left for college was the last time my father made a profit. Mom had been paying the store's rent every month since. They didn't have a million dollars. Maybe in inventory that hadn't sold and wouldn't sell—but not in cash. Or in sales.

"That doesn't include the separate suit about the house." Mom scoffed. "Regardless of what you think, I didn't purposely do a bait and switch. I mean, come on."

"Whether you meant to or not, that's exactly what it looks like," I said, more to myself than her. She hadn't really responded to me saying I wouldn't lie for her. Which meant she wasn't done. She'd try again. And again. This was never going to stop. Not if I lived here.

"We don't get appointed an attorney for civil cases. We have to pay that out of pocket. Do you have any idea how much we've paid? We haven't even gone to trial." She squeezed the keys in her hand and shook her fist in the air. It should've scared me, but her losing—or starting to lose—control somehow handed me the reins.

"I haven't been served yet, if that helps. But either way, I won't—"

"No, it doesn't help." But the softening of Mom's voice said otherwise. "Look, we're selling the house. Our attorney said our retainer would double if we file bankruptcy before the trial. The bottom line is this, we're getting screwed. That's our lot in life. The Delfins get screwed. We could have our own reality show for crying out loud."

She had me. Guilt wrapped a noose around my neck. "Are you

allowed to sell the house? Did you ask your attorney if that's even possible during a lawsuit?"

"It's my house, Scarlett. Of course I can." She gave a dismissive wave to the dresses. "We're clearing everything out."

"I guess I didn't leave much." My journal was the most important thing, and yet I doubted my mother would have handed that over.

"It's not like you ever really lived at home." Mom sniffed, her feelings still hurt; I assumed, about the wedding she missed. "None of my kids stick around."

"Everyone lives in California, Mom." That wasn't what she meant and I knew it. But none of my siblings were close. We weren't at each other's throats, but we weren't exactly friends. "We're just not in your backyard."

"Or anywhere near our home." She gave a one shoulder shrug. "Except for Elaine."

Glancing at my watch, I stood. "Thanks for bringing this by." Everett was supposed to bring our yet-to-be-named dog home from the vet. "But I need to get going."

Mom nodded but didn't move. "It's not too late, you know."

"For what?"

"You could get it annulled." She waved her hand in a circle, indicating the house. "You could even get this house, I bet."

Taking a deep breath, I closed my eyes for a second. Annulled. The thought of being permanently separated caused my heart to slow and my mind to race. Everett was everything. He was safety and danger, love and fear. He was who I needed. He was the family I wanted. I just had to be brave enough to accept him. Brave. I needed to be brave. "Mom, it's been years."

"What's that supposed to mean?" Her voice held a warning.

"I've been married for years."

Mom gasped, covering her mouth. She shook her head, and her eyes narrowed.

"Before Everett left to London. Before I even graduated college." Each word came faster than the next.

"You *lied* to me?" Mom marched to the door. "How could you do this?"

"I didn't lie to you." Shoving my hands in my pockets, I admitted, "I wasn't exactly forthcoming, but I didn't lie to you."

"You weren't honest, Scarlett, and I raised you better than this." She turned the handle and threw open the door. "You've made your bed. Let's see how well you lie in it."

"Why do you hate him?" It took me a moment to realize I'd said it out loud.

Mom slowly spun around, her mouth open and her eyes wide in surprise, as if she'd never thought about the reason. "Because ... of who he is. What he's done. He's just like his father, Scarlett. Men like that are no good. They never change—"

Nodding, I said, "Everett doesn't change. He's never wavered. That I know."

"That's not what I meant and you know it." Mom pursed her lips and said slowly, "He's manipulated you for years. Ever since he walked into your life he's done nothing but divide you and me."

I took a step toward her, a lump in my throat. "We were divided before Everett came."

"That's not true."

And there I was, catapulted back to my eight-year-old self with sweaty hands and ragged, panicked breath. My mother had ushered Kelly to sit next to my brother, two people down from me. Kelly did his usual nervous smile while I pretended to ignore him and stare straight ahead. His dirty blond hair and squeaky voice had me digging my nails into my thighs.

A whimper escaped. It was mine. "Secrets divided our family. The men in our family did a number on us." I'd said it. The truth was in the air between us. "You can't blame Everett. Or me. You could maybe blame yourself for insisting on Kelly sharing the same row at church week after week. Keeping up appearances was more important than my fear."

"He was a lost boy who needed some guidance. Whether he still lived with us or not, it was the right thing to do. The Christian thing to do, Scarlett." Mom's shrill voice burst through my memory, shattering the moment.

"You made a choice, Mom." Swallowing the dread—stupid, stupid fear—I motioned to the door. "But don't blame Everett for what you chose."

"Scarlett Deflin—"

"Ashley." Rubbing the hem of my sleeve, I whispered, "My name is Scarlett Ashley."

❧ 42 ❧

EVERETT ASHLEY
ONE YEAR AGO

T ucked away in the corner of the garage, Everett stretched his cramping hand on the poor excuse of a tool tabletop. He'd written dozens of calligraphy wedding invitations, leaving the date blank. The hours spent on the invitations stole the much needed time on the house he'd purchased. He had hoped to already have the ground floor livable before now. He pulled out the ring from his suit pocket once more. He'd been carrying it around for days. He slid the sparkler on his pinky and smiled.

Years before, Everett had overheard Andy asking Scarlett about rings. Her brother was working up the nerve to ask his girlfriend to marry him and wanted to make sure he had the perfect ring. Andy had wrongly anticipated that he had a choice. He was limited to what Lucas Delfin allowed.

Everett had written down every detail about the ring, down to the micro pave band and the enormous center stone. Scarlett rarely wore make up or expensive clothes but she'd dreamed of this ring—and that's what she was going to receive. Her brother had kept interrupting her and scoffing until she stopped talking altogether. It'd taken every ounce of control for Everett to stay quiet in the hallway.

But today, today would be different. The ring gave Everett hope.

Since their impromptu marriage, a gulf had grown between them but they'd become closer of late. Although it was bittersweet. News of Marjorie's severe osteoporosis had instantly bridged the gap between them. His grandmother had been his answer to prayer for most of his life. She'd been given a harsh sentence by the doctor, but without skipping a beat, she'd brought their hands together in hers. It's as if Marjorie knew the power she held.

Everett needed Scarlet to believe that he was her husband, that he *wanted* to be her husband. He wanted Scarlett as his wife and for her to believe in them as a union. He'd just turned in a deferment for the London position, asking for more time due to Marjorie's failing health.

The click of the garage door opener springing to life startled Everett. He shoved the invitations into his toolbox and slipped the ring back in his suit jacket. He'd look like he'd just come from work. His back ached like he'd been poring over legal documents instead of squeezing his giant frame into the garage corner. He rushed to the front of his coupe just as the garage door lifted.

Scarlett's brakes squeaked something fierce as she pulled in. The car sighed when she killed the engine. It was the same vehicle he'd bought her ten years before. Everett had tried to trade it in a few times, but she'd come up with weak excuses. He didn't understand her resistance. The only thing she'd accept as gifts were new computers. For some reason, her strange guilt allowed her to accept technology—for work, not play. The more Everett pushed, the more she resisted.

In the car, Scarlett seemed to hesitate while Everett failed at containing his excitement. He wanted nothing more than to pounce and spill the surprise, propose and start planning. If everything worked out, they could set a date tonight and send invitations in the morning. He'd stayed up all night writing in a date if that's what it took.

Scarlett opened the car door, a strange look in her eyes. "You okay?"

"Yeah, yeah. I'm good. I'm okay," he said quickly, then swore too loudly.

Her face broke out into a true smile. His surliness somehow kept her facade at bay. It was just another fact he'd filed away as reasons for loving her.

"Right." She hitched her workbag to her shoulder and closed the door. "And the reason you're *so* good and *so* okay is?"

"Nothing." He knew he looked guilty. He was a terrible liar.

"Do I need to get a shovel?" She bit her lip, failing at keeping a straight face.

"Why would I need a shovel?" Everett scowled, irritated with himself.

Scarlett shrugged. "To bury the body."

He froze in confusion. She burst out laughing. He ran a hand through his hair and smiled. "Damn it, woman. Get over here."

She came to him, and he wasted no time in wrapping his arms around her. Everett closed his eyes and relished the moment. This would hopefully be the last time she'd come home as simply Scarlett Delfin. Tomorrow she'd come home as his fiancée and soon after, as Scarlett Ashley. This time, for real.

She tightened her hold and sighed. "Did you know you have a smell?"

"You're asking if I know I smell?"

"No not smell, smell. I mean you have a scent." She glanced up, emptiness filling her face.

"What happened?" Everett's heart sank. He'd been too preoccupied to notice her ticks.

Scarlett shook her head and let her arms drop. "The project. It's over." She gripped the straps of her purse. "It blew up. No, it didn't blow up. That would imply something happened. It imploded, disappeared. Poof. Gone. Destroyed. Never happened."

"What does that mean?" He'd never known the details, and honestly, he didn't want to pry. She never whined about not knowing his caseload. Most of his colleagues flirted with breaking confidentiality to appease their spouses. But Scarlett had understood and now he'd wished they hadn't been so honorable. "You've lost projects before."

"This one was different."

"Personal." It wasn't a question. Everett felt the difference. She'd born this project like a pregnancy. This report or column—or whatever it was that she didn't get to show the world, had touched her personally.

"Sure." She shrugged, her eyes sad and forlorn. "It's been a big, fat waste. Not just time. I just invested so much." She hugged herself, keeping just out of Everett's reach. "I look like an idiot to Lincoln."

"Does he know?" Everett couldn't hide the jealousy. He folded his arms and puffed out his chest, knowing he looked ridiculous. His frame was enormous. There was no reason for him to enlarge his stature.

"Know what?" Her eyes begged for answers, but Everett doubted she would voice her real question.

"That we're married." He held up his left hand. He'd purchased the silver band a few years ago, hoping it'd prove to Scarlett how serious he took their marriage. Consummated or not, he was hers.

"Are we?" Pleading gave way to frustration. She blinked and turned her head.

"Yeah. We are."

With a finger pointed at him, she faced him, her voice shaking. "To you, maybe. To the rest of the world, no."

"Screw the world." He dismissed the idea with a wave. "They don't matter. You matter. We matter."

Scarlett backed into her car, her arms hugging herself once more. "This isn't a marriage, Everett."

"Don't do this." He paused and focused on keeping his frustration reined. "We've been over this."

"I'm aware." Her dark eyes looked at him, her lips quivering and her hands clasping together in front of her. "I need you to be honest with me."

"I've never been anything but—"

"Have you talked to Marjorie about everything?" She shoved her hands in her pockets, more than likely to hide the shaking.

He swallowed hard. Scarlett had taken over and derailed the night he'd hoped for. This was supposed to be a happy occasion, a moment to remember. "I was there at the doctor—"

"Have you spoken to her about long term care?" Her lips were drawn to a severe frown.

"What does this have to do with—"

"I'll take that as a no." She nodded once. "It's bad, Everett. Her fall, the risk of infection. Her bones have been bad for a long time. The mortality rate—it's awful. Do you understand how bad this is?"

He stepped back. The news sent him reeling. He braced himself on the hood of the coupe.

"She didn't say it, but I know she thinks she's a burden." Scarlett's voice sounded foreign.

"She's not a burden," Everett barked. "She's growing old."

"She's lonely."

Everett's head snapped up, leveling Scarlett with a glare. There was much more being said than the words being aired. "What are you saying?"

"That I should move in with her." She pulled on the sleeves of her jacket.

"You're leaving me?"

"To take care of your grandmother." Scarlett kept her chin down, her focus on the ground.

"Then look at me." He banged the hood of the car when she didn't move. "Look at me!"

With a murderous stare, she lifted her gaze. Her cheeks were blushed with anger, and her eyes narrowed in fury. "I'm open to suggestions. Do you have a better idea?"

"Hundreds." Everett felt his pulse race. She was baiting him. There was something else going on. Holding out his arm, he snapped, "She could move in here, for one."

"Into a construction zone? With only one room completed?"

"We buy a condo here in town." Both arms were out now.

She placed a hand on her hip and leaned forward. "She would still be alone. What if she falls? How will she cope in the coming weeks? Days?"

"Spit it out, Scarlett," he growled. "Tell me what you're really talking about."

"For someone so eager to call us a family, you haven't thought at all about what that means." Her eyes widened. She covered her mouth, the realization of what she'd said written on her face.

Everett couldn't speak. Couldn't breathe. He felt the weight of the ring in his suit jacket. He'd thought they were growing closer, not further apart. No matter what he did, nothing changed. Scarlett would always be out of reach.

"You're a good man, Everett." Scarlett folded her arms tightly against her, her voice small again. "But you can't just hope it'll all work out. Some things you just have to face."

It's over was all Everett heard.

✿ 43 ✿

SCARLETT ASHLEY
PRESENT DAY

With fury in her eyes, my mother slammed the door and drove away. I waited but the tears didn't fall and guilt didn't consume me. Nothing was what I felt. Grabbing the dresses she brought, I went back to my bedroom, tripping on Mom's journal. The dresses fell. I stepped on the bag, pulling three dresses from their hangers.

The garage door closed, followed by the sound of Everett coming in. "Scarlett?"

"In here."

I picked up the journal and tossed it toward the box. Dress and plastic pooled around me. A hot pink dress with a mountain of tulle must have been Avrie's. I rolled it in a ball and threw it over my shoulder—it was hideous and headed to the thrift store. Turning back to the pile, I pulled the plastic off the next dress and froze.

It was familiar.

And black.

The same dress I wore *that night* in high school. It'd haunted me for over a decade. Slowly, as if it'd bite, I circled the dress, sinking down next to it. With a pen, I lifted the fabric, the jagged edge of the rip cooling the room. And my heart.

"Our newest member of the family is officially spayed." Everett's voice carried down the hall and into the room. "Scar—" He cut himself off, his eyes on the dress.

I opened my mouth but the words wouldn't come. Everett being here made it more real.

Everett stepped slow and steady toward me, squatting lower as he approached. "Hey ... hey, it's okay."

I reached for him—instantly I was against him, his arms crushing me to his chest. He cooed in my ear and rocked me in his lap. There were no tears. Closing my eyes, I breathed in his scent and kept a hand on his chest, his heart steady.

After what felt like hours, I whispered, "Mom came. Dropped off the dresses."

"I ... was wondering ..." Careful and sure, he chose his words. Thankfully, he didn't mention the dress.

I had to think of something, anything other than the black mess of silk.

"She said it wasn't too late." I rubbed the collar of his favorite *Ashley Almonds* shirt, the hem starting to unravel. "That I could still get an annulment."

Everett stiffened but said nothing.

"I told her ..." Gripping his shirt, I prayed for courage. "I told her I'd been married for years. And then I might have corrected her when she called me Scarlett Delfin."

"Did you now?" He relaxed and kissed the top of my head.

"It was real, wasn't it?" I risked a glance at him. Warmth and kindness stared back at me.

He tucked a strand of hair behind my ear. "Which part?"

"David. The dance." I broke our gaze. Everett didn't need to see the hurt I knew was in my face. "All of it."

"Yes." He cleared his throat. "Marjorie knew the truth and took it to her grave. It hurt too much for her to talk about it. I can't blame her. We don't know everything that happened that night. We don't know if it was David. It could have been your brother. It could have been anyone. But if I could have taken that night, if I could have stopped it—"

"I know."

His eyes widened as if unsure what I meant.

The electric hum was back, this time deeper. Peace came over me. "Everett ... I kind of love you."

Everett gave a wicked grin and read me.

"Scarlett. Scarlett *Ashley*," he corrected himself and leaned forward, our faces nearly touching.

"Yes, Everett Ash—"

"Marry me." His breath tickled my lips.

"I already answered that question."

Everett smiled, his lips moving against mine. "I'm sorry, Letty. For everything."

The dog barked from what sounded like the kitchen. The poor animal sounded groggy but not in pain from being spayed.

"Don't go anywhere." Everett gave a quick peck and untangled himself from me. "Let me check on her, and I'll be back."

I caught sight of the dress. "Wait, I'll go with you."

Everett pulled me to a stand. "You okay?"

"I'm going with you. To London." Hope filled me. And then the light, fluttering feeling of freedom.

Everett hesitated. "Are you sure?"

"And I'm burning that dress." The dress. A wave of nothing, of overwhelming numbness crashed over me. I bit my lip to feel pain, to feel something. This nothingness felt wrong.

"Scarlett—"

"Let me burn something."

"There's an ugly pink dress in the hallway, let's burn that."

"You see the dress, right?" I gripped his arms, needing to feel his strength, the taut muscles that had comforted me for years. The dress was real—were the other memories as well? A vague memory of my father looking at me in the bathtub. Then my brother judging me as I stood in only a bra and underwear. My lungs froze. The room spun. A lump formed in my throat. Air. Heavy.

"It's real, Scarlett."

Nodding, I dug my hands into his arms. My chest tightened. And then tightened more. My nails dug deeper. He didn't flinch. He didn't move. He waited, his eyes on me. "Breathe. Scarlett."

And I did.

"That's my girl." He stared—his eyes bearing into mine. "Breathe."

I did.

And again.

A warmth spread from his arms to my chest, freeing the heaviness. I coughed. And gasped. Everett kept his arms around me, whispering my name in my ear.

The dog barked again. Everett stiffened.

"It's okay," I lied.

He squatted, keeping eye contact. Motioning to the dress, he said, "I'm putting that thing in a container. I'll be right back. I'm not leaving you."

I'm not leaving you. The words calmed me, rooting me in place until he reappeared.

"Just gave our girl more medicine. She's fine." Everett held out a hand. On both forearms, nail marks littered his skin.

"I'm so sorry." I turned from him. Hurt. I'd caused him pain. This was wrong. So, so wrong.

"I'm not." His voice was sure and bold. "I'm good, Scarlett. You trusted me."

"I do."

He circled me and sat on the bed, his feet on either side of mine, our hands intertwined. "I told you, I don't care if we're ninety—"

I leaned forward and traced his scar. In a moment, I was brought back in time. It seemed natural so many years ago to touch the broken boy. He was the new kid. A stranger. And yet, in a way, I'd always known him.

"I'm going to do it. I'm going to write it out and include the dress. Give it all to Lincoln." The anger—or what I thought was cool anger—filled me. "It's going to be awful. It could ruin David or Andy. But I don't know. I can't be the only girl, right? And the timing. It couldn't be worse. I mean Dad and Mom are in the middle of—"

"It's never going to be the perfect timing." Everett covered my hand with his. "Whatever you decide, I'm here. No matter what."

"I know." And I did.

Hours later, in the dead of night, I snuck out from under his arms. Dragging the other dresses Mom had brought, I threw them in the small metal trashcan that was left behind from the previous owners. Lighting a match, I tossed it in the trashcan and watched the fire burn.

I stood on the back porch, my dog following me with a yawn. Everett's toolbox was dangerously close to the trashcan. With a broom, I pushed it away before sitting down for my private bonfire.

There was hope in this small act of rebellion. As if burning something my mother brought liberated me. It wasn't true but it felt good all the same. The light of the fire spilled over, bringing warmth I didn't know I needed.

A foot away from the small fire, I sat next to Everett's toolbox, shadows dancing on the cement. Pulling his toolbox closer, the lid flapped open. A breeze ruffled papers inside.

Holding the lid, I pulled out a sketch, settled on top of what looked like invitations. On the left side of the paper, Everett had drawn me looking in a mirror. In the glass were three images, one of me laying on the grass with a ripped dress, one cowering beside lockers, and one hiding behind a couch with parents on the other side. The right side of the paper was Everett staring at me with the mirror, a thought bubble above his head. In the bubble were three other images of me, completely different than the mirror's. One glanced lovingly at a baby in her arms; one held out a quill toward a group of people like a sword, and one was putting stitches on the forehead of Superman, Superman looking suspiciously similar to Everett.

Cradling the sketch in my lap, I stared at the fire, the warmth of Everett's love settling nicely around me. Everett had protected me and cared for me like the superhero I'd named him after. It was the reason I loved him—and the reason I kept him at bay. But the drawing in my lap showed something else. His view of me was vastly different than what I thought. He viewed me as a possible mother, a defender of some sort with a pen, but more importantly, as *his* healer—as someone who stitched Superman's wounds.

The fire sputtered to a smoky death, and the dog yawned again.

This was the ending of what my life had been. And the beginning of what it could be.

❧ 44 ❧

EVERETT ASHLEY

A FEW WEEKS BEFORE

U sing his teeth, Everett pulled the Velcro of his boxing gloves and tossed them in his gym bag. He wiped the sweat from his forehead and took the elevator upstairs to his hotel room. He'd just been offered a full contract, allowing him to rent a flat. Something large enough for Scarlett. The thought set him back. She wasn't coming to London. Not that he'd invited her. In a joke or teasing, yes. But not officially. He wasn't brave enough to ask.

He put the gym bag on the tiny kitchen table and showered. It'd been nearly a year since Marjorie had fallen and the fear hadn't dulled. The woman was everything—father and mother to him. Her love, her warmth. Because of Marjorie, he had Scarlett.

At least, he wanted to believe she was his.

Detective Davenport had warned Everett years ago that his presence would be a constant reminder of Scarlett's pain. He felt her hesitance whenever he'd kissed her or held her too long. He loved her, even when it hurt. And yet, not enough to stay when she and Marjorie needed him most. He dragged the guilt with him every morning and lay with it every night.

Here in London, he felt untethered, flapping about as he waited for

Marjorie's impending decline. He was still too stubborn to admit he was wrong in coming. Not just because of Marjorie but Scarlett as well. Even thousands of miles away, she still held his heart. And decorated his walls. Sketch after sketch didn't make it easier, although the images of Scarlett brightened the dim hotel room.

Everett's phone pinged. Half dressed, he ran across the room to answer. It was the video chat app. Scarlett was calling with Marjorie.

He sat on the edge of the bed, his phone in his hand. Like a kid waiting for Christmas, he loved these moments. He ignored the clock, another night of little to no sleep.

Scarlett gave an apologetic smile. "Hey, I know it's late—"

"I was up, I promise." Everett would have taken the call no matter the time. He loved his grandmother but the real reason was Scarlett. He needed to hear her voice and see her face. London had been a respite. No one knew where he'd come from, nor did they care. Even in New York he'd see *Ashley Almonds* on grocery store shelves. The company was sold long before his time, but the reminder that he was an Ashley didn't bring comfort, it underlined that he was Richard Ashley's son. England had never heard of the family or the farm.

Scarlett wrinkled her nose, pretending to sniff at the screen. "You've been working out and need a shower."

"See, I told you I was up."

"Tell him to go to sleep." Marjorie's shaky voice came over the speaker. "We can ... call later."

The view flipped from Scarlett's face to Marjorie's, her skin pale. The sight of her, the long blinks and labored breathing, clenched Everett's heart. The grandmother he knew was strong and stubborn. The woman in the bed looked frail, terribly, terribly frail.

"You look good," Everett lied with a smirk.

"London has made you blind." She smiled, her lips quivering with the movement. She touched the screen, appearing to trace Everett's face. "You were always good."

There was a farewell in her words. Everett shook his head and tried to scowl—he would not cry. "Don't think you can just slip away now."

Marjorie shrugged, or tried to shrug. "Maybe I'll wait for you. If I feel like it."

Scarlett chuckled behind the camera. "Maybe?"

"You've got plenty of time, Marjorie." Everett waited for them to agree, to reassure him.

Marjorie smiled again, her eyes blinking slowly. "I ... love you ... Everett."

The view switched to Scarlett's profile, her gaze on Marjorie, Everett assumed. Scarlett moved and the lights dimmed. Whispering, she said, "She's sleeping."

"She barely said anything."

Scarlett faced the camera. "She's sleeping more and more."

Everett gripped his phone. "But she's okay, right?"

"It's time." Scarlett softened, her eyes downcast. "She's tired, Everett. She's had two infections in the last few weeks. It's hard on her body. And she's really only with it when we're on the phone. If you want, I can have the doctor call—"

"No," Everett blurted. "I'll book a flight tonight."

Nodding, Scarlett asked, "When do you think you can get in?"

"When do you want me?" The question was loaded and probably not fair, but Everett asked anyway.

Scarlett turned, her profile to the camera. In a voice so soft Everett thought he'd imagined it, she said, "As soon as possible."

"I'm on my way." Everett got off the phone and began searching for flights. Scarlett's cousin was getting married on Saturday. She could use reinforcements. He paused. Would he still be considered an ally after everything? He'd left his grandmother in her care and disappeared.

Everett stared out the hotel window, placing a hand on the cold, drafty glass. A year ago, Scarlett pulled into the driveway, ready to pick a fight, making up for a battle she'd just lost. The project, the big break that was going to catapult Scarlett into the journalism world, had imploded. And his aunt Missy was at the center. Scarlett wouldn't get angry, that wasn't her style. If she couldn't blame her parents or force them to own up to anything, she certainly wouldn't blame his aunt. It's what drove Everett crazy—and what he admired most, her inability to hate.

He could still see Scarlett's face and the words that continued to haunt him, *For someone so eager to call us a family, you haven't thought at all about what that means.*

Everett opened the top drawer of his dresser and pulled out the ring he'd purchased last year. *It's time* repeated in his mind. He booked the flight and emailed his human resource contact, submitting his official leave of absence.

He arrived in Gainesfield with the few belongings he'd taken. Slipping through the side door of the garage, he saw the coupe his grandfather had given him before passing away. He had been a better man than Everett; he'd never abandoned Marjorie. He'd loved her and provided for her—and his grandson.

Everett tapped the hood and prayed it wasn't too late for his marriage. He cracked open his old toolbox, pulling out the invitations he'd handwritten years before, the date still blank. He turned to the empty space where her car should be. She'd already be in Tule. Alone.

Everett dressed and jumped into the rental car, jet lag settling in his bones. The music was blaring as he pulled into the parking lot. He slipped inside through a side door. Scanning the dance hall, he saw her, his throat immediately dry. His heart pounded. She wore a deep purple dress and pulled the elastic from her ponytail. She ran her hands through the ends of her hair. Everett's hands twitched, wishing he could capture her. David wrapped an arm around her, and she winced, recovering a second too late. Everett clenched his hands. He pulled the note from his pocket, flagging down a caterer.

"See that girl." Everett pointed to Scarlett. "Give this to her."

The girl's eyes were wide. She took the note, shrinking from Everett. A moment later, he gripped the doorframe, just out of sight. Jennifer and Elaine crossed the room, marching toward Scarlett. Without thinking, Everett stepped into the dance hall, ready to intervene. If Jennifer saw him, she'd switch tactics, attack him instead of her daughter. David put his hand on the small of Scarlett's back. Everett nearly choked on his anger.

Scarlett stepped from David's touch, the caterer angling herself between them. She handed Scarlett the note. Scarlett's hands shook while David tried to read over her shoulder. Everett couldn't see her face, couldn't gauge her reaction.

Jennifer's face darkened. Scarlett stepped from their circle and turned. Her eyes met Everett's. With one look, she pierced him. Her hair, wild and free, framed her face. Her dress gave a soft silhouette. Her lips were parted, unsure if they should smile or speak.

One thought rang through his head, *I will never leave you. Never. Never again.*

✥ 45 ✥

SCARLETT ASHLEY
PRESENT DAY

verett's arms were wrapped around me, and my face was pressed against another of his faded *Ashley Almonds* shirts. Rubbing the sleep from my eyes, I spotted my dog leaning against the doorframe, her white tail wagging. "We need to name her."

She answered with a low, guttural bark, almost a growl.

Everett stretched next to me. "How about Grumpy?"

Poking him in the ribs, I said, "You two are one and the same. She's perma-bark and you're perma-scowl." Everett and me, we were dysfunctional and ridiculous but this was home. He was home to me before I knew I was homeless.

Everett yawned like he hadn't slept in years. "Good morning to you, too."

"Right." Propping myself on my elbow, I twisted the bottom hem of his shirt. He'd slept next to me with constant contact off and on for weeks. Before he'd left to London, we'd hug, even kiss, but not like this. He'd not wrap an arm around me in the middle of the night. He was a man that, for some reason, hadn't crossed the line. He didn't pout like my father did or broadcast to anyone within earshot of his *empty tank* as my family called it. As a husband, he didn't grope me in front of people—or like my brother and father, in front of kids. He hadn't burst into the bathroom when I showered. He'd done none of it. He was safe. And he was hope.

Everett wrapped a warm hand over mine. "What color is your sky?"

Not brave enough to look at him, I stared at our entwined hands. "I do want to, you know. I do want to be that with you."

"We'll get there." He pulled me close. "Look how far we've come."

"Should I warn my parents, tell them what I'm doing?" The thought had become like a loose tooth that I couldn't stop wiggling. "It feels like betrayal."

"Hey, listen. You can do whatever or not do whatever you want. But I need you to do it for you, not me. It doesn't matter what I think. Or what they think." He started to say something, then stopped. He sighed and finally added, "I can't make you do this. It's going to be hard on you. It hasn't really begun yet. Once the story is out people are going to start attacking you. They're going to attack why you waited so long. They're going to question your character and bring everything else into question. They—meaning journalists like Will or Lincoln—will search for truth. That might mean digging into confidential files. David's a politician and people tend to use different rules, not always legal when it comes to protecting their own. Even if it wasn't him, he was there. An event like that could cast a long shadow on his career, because whether he admits it or not, he knew something that night."

"I know." And it'd been just one of many reasons I'd stayed silent. "Not having evidence is what kept me wondering. What if it didn't happen? I mean the memories aren't exactly consistent. But now there's proof, kind of. As much proof as a ripped piece of fabric could be."

"Just promise me you're doing it for you."

I shook my head. "I'm not doing it for me. Or you."

Everett arched an eyebrow but before he could argue, I blurted, "I'm doing it for Elaine. And maybe, whether she ever admits it or not, my mom."

He kissed the top of my head. "You're a good person, Scarlett. Just remember that when it all comes crashing down. You're the good in all of this."

Sneaking a peek at Everett, I wondered how tired he was. It'd been a rough week, and I wouldn't blame him. By the time January 2 came, most people were tired of celebrating. That was the excuse I'd allow my mother for habitually sending a *Happy Belated Birthday* card. But today wasn't about me. It was about him, about *us*. Not all secrets were bad.

"Get up. Let's go." Everett pulled out four of his work suits, laying them on the bed. He'd wanted to celebrate my birthday with a fancy lunch in downtown Los Angeles. He put two suits back and went to the closet, tossing different ties on the bed.

I sat back on the bed, rolling the end of a plum colored tie over my hand. "This was the color of my dress when you came home."

He smirked—sort of. It was an Everett smirk which had a slight frown to it. He was the most beautiful, consistent, and grumpy person I'd ever known. "Plum looks good on you."

He tugged the edge of the tie. His thumb and forefinger were stained black like he'd been drawing. Other than walking the dog, we'd been together almost every day for the last week. When he'd been on the computer finalizing details for our London move and the renting of this house, I'd rushed to the post office and mailed invitations.

Everett kneeled on the bed. Leaning over, he said, "Happy Birthday, Letty."

"I miss her."

"She's with us today." He nodded his head toward the bathroom. "Get in the shower. We're celebrating."

With a playful shove, I pulled a dress out of the closet, hidden in a plastic dress cover. The steam from my shower made both the mirror and my hair uncooperative. I moved to open the door and froze. I hadn't locked the door. For the first time in my life, I hadn't checked or triple checked the bathroom lock. Maybe, just maybe, I wasn't beyond hope.

I opened the bathroom door. Everett stood in a black suit with the plum tie. Like the night of my cousin's wedding, I smiled, feeling something both delicious and dangerous inside me. This was the moment, the one surprise I could give him.

He offered a wicked grin—and froze. I felt the weight of his stare.

The wedding dress I'd picked was a fitted bodice with plum colored accents trailing in swirls along the flowing skirt. Missy had done the impossible, securing and hiding the dress for me.

The realization slowly crossed Everett's face. He blinked and stepped forward and then back. The doorbell rang and the dog barked, breaking the spell. He smiled hesitantly, as if unsure what to do.

"Answer the door, Everett."

He didn't move.

I grabbed his hand and together we walked to the front door. Everett kept his gaze on me as I opened the door. On our front lawn were our closest friends, each carrying a white chair. Before he could say a word, I handed him an invitation. He cleared his throat and opened it. His beautifully written letters decorated the inside, all except for my poor calligraphy attempt with today's date, *January 2*.

Within minutes, a few dozen white chairs and a white podium stood in the center of my living room. A framed photo of Marjorie was wrapped with white lace on a chair in the front row. To the side of the podium, completely in the way, lay my dog. Mr. Munoz, our old high school teacher, ushered his youngest child around the dog. Detective Davenport and Lincoln exchanged smiles in the back row. Will and his wife, each holding a child, hugged another one of my high school teachers. Elaine stepped back from an embrace, revealing Missy. They'd connected, and Elaine—if she could hold onto her courage— was moving in with Missy.

Everyone who ever mattered to me was here. I searched the room once more and waited for the guilt to come. I hadn't invited my parents. Or my brothers. The guilt didn't come. Nor did the shame.

Everett kissed my temple and whispered, "How in the world did you pull this off?"

"Sometimes Superman needs a little help." I threw my arms around his waist.

Everett guided me to the podium where Detective Davenport stood in a white tux. The man winked at me and began. Words ran together, along with my tears. Only when Everett turned to kiss me did I realize it was real. The marriage. All of it.

Chairs were moved to the periphery, and our small wedding party circled us while Everett and I slow danced. Between Everett and me, we could count the number of family members who came on one hand. And like the house, both of us were still under construction but right here, in this moment—everything was beautiful and perfect.

✻ 46 ✻

EPILOGUE

THREE YEARS LATER

Through the window of the operating room, Everett watched the flurry of medical staff surround Scarlett. A childhood of hospital stays gave Everett a sense of dread, a feeling so deep his bones ached at the mere mention. But today—no, today the facility promised to bring life, after a lifetime of offering pain. Marjorie's passing marked the last time Everett visited a hospital.

The familiar scent of antiseptic and anxiety hung in the air. Facing the operating room, Everett tried to keep the scowl off his face. The doctor hummed a cheerful tune, the sound muted by the window. The nurse monitored Scarlett's vitals, and Everett stared at the orchestrated chaos, fear rooting him to where he stood.

Both Everett's and Scarlett's lives had shifted, pivoting completely in just a few short years. It'd taken a while, but gently, ever so softly, they tiptoed through the delicate minefield of intimacy. Everett was transferred from London to Texas seven months ago, just a week before Scarlett surprised him, sharing her pregnancy test. Everett attended every doctor's appointment, holding Scarlett's trembling hand. Scarlett never felt comfortable with anyone touching her—doctor or not. Everett was the one and only exception. He'd earned the right to be at her side.

They'd sold the Gainesfield house when they moved to London. Scarlett's exposé caused a hurricane of press, dividing the Central Valley in half. Tule refused to believe anything negative about their golden boy, David, even after he became embroiled in civil suits from other women. He was never arrested and touted that fact, fueling his political success.

The Delfins were still beloved by the small town. Their innocence was shouted from the rooftops by the young men and women the family had helped through the years. Andy stood by his parents, offering an impassioned plea to his wayward sister to get help and return to the fold of the Delfin family. As predicted, the valley turned on Scarlett, painting her the villain while Los Angeles, New York, and even London came courting, eager to hear her story.

In the Delfin's civil suit over their property title, Everett and Scarlett gave a damning deposition. The Delfins lost and filed bankruptcy to avoid paying restitution—a move anticipated by opposing council. Their bankruptcy protection was contested. For the first time in their lives, the Delfins had to pay the piper.

They were angry and blamed their misfortune on Scarlett. The more desperate they became, the easier it was for Scarlett to let go. Everett would hold her a little tighter on every holiday, especially her birthday. But today, this was a birthday neither of them would ever forget.

Scarlett's water had broken a few hours ago, but the baby was in the wrong position, one foot down and one foot jammed into the pelvic area. When the emergency C-section was announced, Everett didn't know who was closer to fainting—Scarlett or him. A nurse whisked her away to the operating room, Everett running after them. It took two nurses to calm him, one on each arm, to explain Everett could join Scarlett *after* he changed into hospital scrubs.

Everett glanced down at the borrowed scrubs. He mouthed, *I wish you were here,* to the empty hallway, praying his grandmother could have witnessed her great-grandchild's birth. Scarlett lay on the operating table. Her gaze flicked to the window where Everett stood. Her gaze shifted to his left. He followed her line of vision, and for a second, the stooped image of Marjorie was next to him. He reached for her—she disappeared, her presence like a whisper.

A crack of lightning lit in his mind. A forgotten memory came over him—the first time he was dumped at Marjorie's, his face bloodied and his back burned. The thought dissipated, replaced with a picture of Scarlett in the high school office, her profile turned to Everett. His heart was pricked—these weren't his memories. They were Marjorie's. His pulse calmed. He wasn't a lost little boy, and Marjorie hadn't abandoned him. Everett was Superman, and he was needed in the operating room. With his heart in his throat, he turned his focus on the woman who'd sewn his broken soul together, one touch at time. Everett came to Scarlett, clasping her trembling hand in his. If he could switch her places and take the pain and fear of childbirth, he would.

Her quivering lip turned to a smile. "I heard you gave some nurses a run for their money."

"Maybe." He squeezed her hand. All was right in the world.

Scarlett's face softened, peace filling her eyes. The world around him faded. Scarlett was the only one who mattered. He kept her gaze on him—a trick he'd learned from their years together. If she focused on him, her anxiety would lay back down. They blocked out the murmur of the staff. Like a crack from a whip, the cry of a baby rang out—shattering their bubble.

"A beautiful baby girl." The nurse cooed, handing the screaming child to Everett.

He froze, the wriggling human so tiny, so fragile. The baby wrapped her petite hand around Everett's finger. Her eyes, dark and searching, captured Everett's heart. He caressed her cheek. She spun her head, sucking on the tip of his finger.

Everett smiled and leaned over, allowing Scarlett to see their creation. "She's perfect."

Scarlett's eyes filled with tears. "Marjorie Mae."

Everett swallowed the rising emotion. *Marjorie Mae.* Like a whisper, he felt the presence of his grandmother once more. Peace settled on his shoulders. Scarlett might have felt crippled, but Everett was the one who needed saving, and Scarlett was the only one up for the task. Stitch by stich, she'd healed him, molding him into the man he needed to become. She was the reason he graduated high school and eventually law school. Scarlett was the center of everything—and now she'd made him a father. He blinked, fighting the tears.

"It's okay, Everett," Scarlett whispered, a glint of mischief in her eyes. "Even Superman cries sometimes."

"Thank you." His voice caught. The humor fell from her eyes, replaced with worry. "For giving me a family."

Her eyes welled with moisture. And with love. Everett threaded his free hand with Scarlett's. They were no longer broken teenagers. He'd found the missing pieces of his soul in Scarlett. With a little guidance from his grandmother, they'd mended each other.

Everett kissed his baby on the forehead. "Marjorie Mae, welcome to the Ashley home."

ALSO BY CLARISSA KAE

Prince of Death

Reign of Mercy

Reign of Chaos (Winter 2026)

Time Slip Novels

Of Ink And Sea

Women's Fiction

Pieces To Mend

Once And Future Wife Series

Once And Future Wife

Victorian Retellings

A Dark Beauty, Beauty & the Beast

Cinders Like Glass , Cinderella

A Stolen Heart, Robin Hood

Taming Christmas, Taming of the Shrew (standalone)

A Light So Fleeting, Rapunzel (novella)

The Wolf of Heathclove Manor (novella)

ABOUT THE AUTHOR

Clarissa Kae is a preeminent voice whose professional career began as a freelance editor in 2007. She's the former president of her local California Writers Club after spending several years as the Critique Director.

Since her first novel, she's explored different writing genres and created a loyal group of fans who eagerly await her upcoming release. With numerous awards to her name, Clarissa continues to honor the role of storyteller.

Aside from the writing community, she and her daughters founded Kind Girls Make Strong Women to help undervalued nonprofit organizations—from reuniting children with families to giving Junior Olympic athletes their shot at success.

She lives in the agricultural belly of California with her family and farm of horses, chickens, dogs and kittens aplenty.

Discover more...
    www.clarissakae.com
    Insta (@clarissa__kae)
    Facebook (@authorclarissakae)